SMART HOUSEKEEPING

For The Woman Of Today

Rupa Chatterjee

V&S PUBLISHERS

Published by:

V&S PUBLISHERS

F-2/16, Ansari Road, Daryaganj, New Delhi-110002
☎ 011-23240026, 011-23240027 • *Fax:* 011-23240028
Email: info@vspublishers.com • *Website:* www.vspublishers.com

Branch : Hyderabad
5-1-707/1, Brij Bhawan (Beside Central Bank of India Lane)
Bank Street, Koti, Hyderabad - 500 095
☎ 040-24737290
E-mail: vspublishershyd@gmail.com

Follow us on: 🇹 🇫 in

For any assistance sms **VSPUB** to **56161**

All books available at **www.vspublishers.com**

© **Copyright:** *V&S PUBLISHERS*
ISBN 978-93-813846-5-7
Edition 2014

The Copyright of this book, as well as all matter contained herein (including illustrations) rests with the Publishers. No person shall copy the name of the book, its title design, matter and illustrations in any form and in any language, totally or partially or in any distorted form. Anybody doing so shall face legal action and will be responsible for damages.

Printed at : Param Offseters, Okhla, New Delhi-110020

Contents

Preface 7

**10. Home Management
—A Necessity** 9-17
   Organising the Household 9
   Types of Houses 10
   What Our Home Says About Us 10
   Time Management 14
   Organising Household Chores 15
   Chores for the Day 15
   Weekly Chores 16
   Monthly Chores 16
   Maintaining the Household Records 16

**2. Cleaning the House and
its Security** 18-36
   Self Help 18
   Domestic Help 19
   Types of Cleaning Tools 19
   Maintaining the Walls 20
   Maintaining the Floors 21
   Maintaining Tiles 21
   Cleaning Carpets 21
   Removing Spots from Rugs 22
   Cleaning Curtains/Blinds 22
   Maintaining Upholstery 23
   Polishing Silver 23
   Furniture 23
   Appliances 25
   Cleaning Light Fixtures 26
   Handling Domestic Garbage 27
   Household Hints 27
   Problem of Household Pests 28
   Using Pesticides 30
   Security 31
   Personal Safety and Security Measures 31
   Making Doors and Windows Foolproof 32

   Types of Alarms 32
   Safety Lock 32
   The Use of Manpower 32
   Security Check of Domestic Help 33
   Safety Guidelines 33
   Safeguard Against Purse Snatching 34

3. Maintaining the House 37-52
   The Exterior 37
   The Interior 38
   Care for Your Appliances 43
   The Kitchen 47
   The Bathroom 52

**4. How to Wash, Iron
and Maintain Clothes** 53-66
   Handwashing 53
   Washing in the Machine 56
   Starching 57
   Types of Materials and Their
      Requirements 57
   Stain Removal—A Guideline 58
   How to Keep or Store Your Garments 60
   Ironing 61
   Home Crafts 63
   Embroidery Threads 63

5. The Household Budget 67-79
   Tracking One's Money 68
   Living Within the Budget 68
   Organisational Aids 68
   The Value of Making Lists .... 6.
   Simple Hints to Economical B........... 70
   Shopping for Foods .... ct Quality? .. 70
   How can the 71
   that ? 72

How to Select Fruits 73
Storing Vegetables and Fruits 73
Shopping for Electrical Appliances 73
Save Energy to Better Your Budget 75
Tips on Energy Conservation 75
How to Buy a Mattress 77
How to Buy a Carpet 77
Setting up and Maintaining Bank Accounts . 77
Procedure for Opening a Bank Account ... 77
Types of Cheques 78
Some Banking Tips 78
Credit Cards 78
Safe Deposit Lockers 79
Nomination 79
Wills 79

6. A Guide to Home Decor 80-98
Some Tips About Vaastu 80
What Decoration Achieves! 86
The Importance of Having a Neat Entrance . 87
The Drawing Room or Living Room 88
The Dining Room or Dining Area 91
The Bed Room 92
The Children's Room 94
The Guest Room 94
The Study 95
The Utility Room or Store Room 95
Storage Ideas 96

7. Etiquette for All Occasions 99-115
Marriage Festivities 99
Paying Condolence 99
Anniversaries 100
Correct Telephone Manners 101
Entertaining Successfully 101
Giving a Party 101
Plan Invitations 102
Table Settings 102
Laying the Table 103
.... 103

Buffet Settings 103
Table Service 104
Etiquette at the Table 105
Different Kinds of Parties 107
Picnics 108
Proper Social Attitudes 109
Etiquette for Children 110
Miscellaneous Hints 112
20 Things You Must not Do! 114

8. Health & Nutrition 116-140
The Weather and Health 118
Food, Dieting, Anorexia and Bulimia ... 120
Exercise and Good Health 120
Health Check-Ups 123
Investigations 125
Good Health and Water 126
Constipation 128
How Yoga Fights Stress 129
Breathing Correctly 130
Sleep and Sleeping Disorders 130
Sleep Well-Hazards to Our Health 131
Hazards to Our Health from Pollution ... 132
Health Effects 135
Food and Nutrition 136
Storing Food 136
How to Buy Medicines Over the Counter .. 138
Menu Making for Daily Meals 138
Menu Making for a Party/ Party Cooking .. 139
Health Watch 139

9. First Aid 141-161
Work, Emotions and Mental Health 141
Caring for the Sick 142
Alternative Therapy 143
Home Remedies 144
First Aid 150
Shock 151
Asphyxia 152
Colour Therapy 158

Food Poisoning 158
Foods that Will Fight Cancer 159
Water 160

10. Making a Home Happy! 162-183
Be Happy, Be Positive 162
Tips on Positive Thinking 163
Laughter Banishes the Blues 164
Adjustment is Necessary 165
Patience is a Virtue 165
Tidiness is a Must 166
Anger—A Volatile Emotion 166
The Power of Love 168
The Power of Communication 169
The Theory of 'Instant' 170
Curbing Materialistic Values 172
Don't Neglect the Children 173
Doing one's Duty-Caring for the Aged 176
How to Make Friends 179
Home and Family as the
  Basic Unit of Society 180
What About the Position of Women? 182
Be a Good Member of Society 183

11. Travel and Transfers 184-194
Choosing A Destination 184
Advance Planning and Its Benefits 185
Travelling by Car 185
Packing Correctly 186
Emergency Travel Kit 187
Arrangements to be Made Before
  Leaving for a Holiday 188
Tips About Foreign Travel 188
What Happens When You're Jet-lagged? 190
Coping with Transfers 191
Packing Materials 193
Transporting Luggage 193

12. Personal Grooming 195-226
Exercise 195
Calories 195
Massage 198
Good Posture 199
Skin Care 200
Facial 201
Hair 204
Make-up 208
Clothes and Jewellery 213
Know Your Body Type 214
Fashion and You 216
Colour Aesthetics and You 218
Men 218
Summer Clothes 219
Chiffon 222
Jewellery 224

13. Gardening 227-247
The Soil 227
Planting Trees 227
Maintenance of Your Lawns 228
Fruit Garden 228
Growing Vegetables 230
Flowers 230
Chrysanthemum 231
Different Types of Pots 234
Manures 235
Calendar for Monthwise Gardening 239

14. Home Crafts 248-259
Knitting 248
Macrame 258

15. Flowers in the Home 260-267
Vases 261
Japanese Flower Arrangement
  its Requirements

Utensils 261
Indoor Plants 264
What Flowers Say... 266

16. Interpersonal Relationships . 268-294
Pleasing One's Spouse 270
Helpline for Students 283
For Parents 283
Handling Teenagers 284
Handy Tips 285
Avoid being... 286
Coping with Mother-in-Law 287
Handy Tips 288
Coping with Daughters-in-Law 289
Handy Tips 289
Coping with Sons-in-Law 290
Son-in-law should... 291
Parents-in-law 291
Bonding with Grandchildren 291
The Pitfalls of Being Grandparents 292
Grandchildren—do's and don'ts 292
Relations with Neighbours 293

Home Management — A Necessity

If management is the key to modern life, why should the home and household be left behind? As modern life hurtles along at an unrelenting pace, people find that they have endless chores to be done, but hardly any time to do them. Moreover, there is no longer a clear division between men and women into breadwinners and homemakers.

There are many types of households today—there may be a traditional household, a double income household, a nuclear household, a modern joint family, a traditional joint family, a single person household or a single parent household. However, the bottom line in all these set-ups remains the same—the house or household has to be managed and all activities have to be organised in a systematic way if the members are to lead happy and efficient lives. Household work is of an unending nature—meals have to be prepared, clothes and dishes have to be washed, shopping done, milk, water have to be boiled and beds made. Once the chores are done, the cycle starts again, with the chores being done once or even several times a day. In those households where there are servants, things may function more effortlessly, but it nevertheless devolves on the housewife to streamline all activities into an efficient system so that all members of the household function effectively. How can one go to office or school without meals being cooked and eaten, clothes washed and ironed, beds made and adequate rest taken in congenial environment? Some one, therefore, has to manage the home, whether it is in a remote village, a small town, a metropolis or amidst palatial surroundings. Budgets and needs may vary, food habits may differ but the necessity for home management cannot be denied. In an increasingly systems-oriented world, there is today a need to understand and appreciate the value of home management. What is unique about household management is that all chores have to be done so routinely and repetitively, that there is little appreciation for all the planning and hard work that has preceded the smooth functioning. Only when there are no meals, no clean clothes, and no well-maintained household that one realises the chaos that results from a disorganised home. Hence, home management is essential to ensure a smooth and well run household in which all members are able to function efficiently outside the home.

Organising the Household

Having pervaded every sphere of modern life, the home cannot get exempted from the purview of management. Every housewife is a manager in an unpaid, unofficial capacity and irrespective of whether the setting is rural or urban, it is evident that every household has a domestic management routine. For example, a housewife in rural India would count getting water from the well, milking the cows and lighting the "chullah" as part of her early morning chores. The urban housewife on the other hand, may just have to press a switch to start the water pump and turn a knob to light the gas to start cooking. While the chores may differ, it is nevertheless necessary for the home maker to organise the household into a certain routine in which the essential chores fall into a systematic pattern.

Organising the household entails not only systematising different chores but also ensuring the cooperation of all family members and the domestic help, if any. By seeking the participation of the whole family there would be a joint effort towards the common goal of having a happy home in which all members find contentment and peace of mind.

The household should be organised in a flexible way so that all exigencies are taken care of. For example, a fixed cleaning schedule should not be placed above the needs of a family member who may be unwell and hence in need of extra sleep to make up for a disturbed night. Organisation should not be equated with rigidity and inflexibility.

Management of the household depends upon the type of house you own, the time you have and the will to carry out the affairs efficiently.

Types of Houses

Ever since civilization began, human beings have tried to live in a sheltered abode. From the ancient to the modern times man has striven to make his abode into a place of shelter, comfort and beauty. Starting from the cave paintings of Ajanta-Ellora to the fabulous gem studded palaces of royalty, there has been a constant endeavour for man to live amidst beautiful surroundings. Even villagers living in mud-huts decorate their walls with paintings so that they look attractive.

Today one lives either in a bungalow or increasingly, in a flat or apartment in a high rise building. Fortune smiles only on a few lucky ones who live in farm houses, independent houses, castles and palaces. For the general public one can at best aspire to own an apartment, hopefully a spacious one.

The type of house required differs from person to person and on one's circumstances as well as one's economic status. A family which is growing requires more space, whereas a single person or an elderly couple would find it burdensome to maintain a huge apartment or even a bungalow.

Therefore, in choosing a house or flat, individual's requirements, budget constraints, and the place or city in which one is living, plays a critical role in the selection of a flat or apartment.

What Our Home Says About Us

Interiors—we make them, and they make us. They shape our spirit, pushing us towards comfort or austerity.

Anyone who's ever trailed from door to door in the most anonymous block of flats will have noted the very individual smell that comes from each human burrow.

A home doesn't invariably reveal someone's job, though actors and artists often have rather self-conscious interiors (sometimes self-consciously conventional) as if they're on display, even to themselves; and pop and football stars' homes are instantly recognisable—awards glinting in gilt-encrusted settings which display money earned beyond their owners' wildest dreams.

Our interiors say a lot about the way we see the world. Researchers believe people are oriented in one of three ways: visually, audially, or kinetically (which means feelingly).

A "visual" focuses his or her room very clearly round an object, the fire-place, perhaps, or the TV; an "audial" has radios or hi-fi in most rooms, displays objects as "talking points" and creates areas for easy communication. "Kinetics", on the other hand, spread themselves and their belongings over comfortable sofas and soft carpets.

Home, as the saying goes, is where the heart is. And it's certainly where most of our treasures are kept—and most of our dreams, too. For, in the creation of our modest palaces, most of us are in a way, trying to fulfil a dream. Most of us tread softly when first we enter a home, exclaiming pleasantly over this light or that mirror, however banal or ugly it may seem in truth. We do this because we know how vulnerable the owner is—how their house is a subtle blend of what they are and what they hope to be, and they are offering this to us if only we have eyes to see.

Utilising space effectively

In modern life two things are at premium—time and space, hence both must be used effectively so that there is no wastage. The best way to utilise space effectively is to follow the motto—"a place for everything and everything in its place". In some duplex flats or double-storeyed houses, the space below the stairs can be effectively utilised for storage. The top of cupboards can be used for storing empty suitcases, while beds could have drawers in which linen or mattresses can be placed. In a small flat it is best to keep things to a minimum so that there is no clutter. Storage units and cupboards should be neatly lined with newspaper, brown paper or coloured paper and crockery, clothing, books arranged neatly so that essentials are within one's reach.

If the house is a shelter consisting of walls, floors, doors, windows and a roof under which human beings live, a home is a house in which a family or even an individual enjoys happiness, privacy, good health, ease and comfort. It is also a place where one entertains, has social interaction and indulges in one's hobbies. A home is one's sanctum sanctorum where one can relax, meditate and pray. If one builds one's own house then that becomes, in our country, a life time investment unlike in the west where people buy and sell houses frequently. Those who purchase their own apartment or buy a readymade house have to accept, for the greater part, the built-in infrastructure. Those who build their own house or those who acquire flats/houses in a modular state can put in fittings according to their taste and requirement such as the bathroom and kitchen tiling, the placement of storage cupboards and lofts, electrical fittings and so on. If one is fortunate enough to build one's own house, then with the help of an architect it could be designed to suit the needs of the family as well as to take full advantage of Nature in the sense that the sun, the wind, the aspect and the view are taken into consideration during construction. If it is bright, cheerful and airy, it would certainly guarantee that the owners would enjoy living in it. Perhaps the single most important element in the design of a small compact house or an apartment is the feeling of openness and space and the efficient use of this space. Proper orientation or the setting or facing of the plan of a building ensures that the inhabitants enjoy to the utmost whatever is good and avoid whatever is bad in respect of comfort and the normal elements such as the sun, wind, rain, topography and outlook and at the same time it provides a convenient access to both street and backyard.

While in most western countries, an aspect which gives the maximum sunshine is preferred as in these latitudes the sun never goes overhead, being always to the south of the zenith. The requirement in India and other tropical countries is exactly the opposite. The sun's heat in tropical countries must be kept to a minimum, particularly in summer when its rays are vertically overhead. The purpose of proper orientation is that the house or flat must be protected from the sun's direct rays during the day and from indirect heat during the night. The sun's action in causing heat is mostly direct by day but by night it is entirely indirect since the stone, brick or tiles of which the walls are made, absorb the sun's heat by day and radiate this heat at night. While doing so, the air in contact with them is heated, which is the real cause of discomfort during night. Thus, proper orientation must ensure that the house is protected both from the sun's direct heat by day and the indirect one at night.

The total heat absorbed depends on two factors, namely the intensity of the heat and its duration. The main aim of proper orientation is to admit the required amount of sunshine into the house in the morning when it is very pleasant and the intensity of its heat is less, and to minimise its duration in the afternoon and evening when its rays are again likely to enter the house. While the sun's rays are potent enough to kill germs, severe heat is not necessary for this purpose. The morning sun is satisfactory for this purpose so it is necessary that a certain amount of sun enters the house but it should be "shut out" when it becomes warmer. Merely closing down the windows for this purpose is not practical because the walls will still become heated and then radiation will make the rooms on that side quite uncomfortable. Hence, the building must be faced in such a way that the sun's rays will be effectively excluded without closing the windows in the late hours of the morning, especially in summer. If a certain amount of sunlight is allowed to penetrate into the house in the early morning, it is bound to do so also for a few hours in the late evening on the opposite side as well. Deep verandahs or sunshades in the south and the west would effectually exclude these strong evening rays.

The direction of the prevailing wind, especially in summer is between the west and the south but the exact angle depends on a number of local influences. Therefore, bedrooms, for example which are occupied at night must be located in its direction.

While a number of varying factors affect the consideration of planning a domestic building, no hard and fast rules can be laid down as no two sites would have identical conditions nor would individual requirements and idiosyncrasies be the same. Nevertheless

Preface

Management has become a key element of modern life. Whether in office or factories, commercial businesses or the hotel industry, systems have been developed to ensure the smooth and efficient functioning of any organization. Since this is so, why should the home which is the first and primary unit of organization be left behind? There is a need to organize the home front so that we are able to function efficiently when we step outside its doors.

Why should the home, which is the primary and most important unit of society be left outside its purview? If men, women and children are to reach their work place and schools or colleges on time, they need to be properly clothed, fed and rested in order to perform effectively. Since modern life proceeds at an unrelenting pace and time is a precious commodity, there is a need to systematize our activities.

For centuries, the role played by the homemaker—wife, mother and housewife has not been adequately appreciated. This job receives no monetary remuneration, there are no prescribed working hours and often the housewife downplays her role by saying, "I am just a housewife". This is a sad spillover from the success-driven, money chasing Western norms that are invading our society. In keeping society healthy, happy, well-nourished and balanced, the home manager and home management plays a pivotal role, since she is called upon to be a chef, a financial wizard, an interior decorator, a doctor, a nurse, a psychologist, a wife, mother, daughter-in-law, friend and social worker—all rolled into one!

I strongly believe that the homemaker/housewife plays an invaluable role. For example, the child or teenager who is given nutritious and lovingly prepared food at home, will not be forced to live on a diet of fast food which leads to obesity and also malnutrition on account of the empty calories present in the food. In fact, Dr. Jyoti Sharma in an article entitled "Straight To His Stomach" published in the September 2000 issue of *"Woman's Era"* magazine goes so far as to say, "What ails Western society is lack of cooking skills" as she noticed that in Frankfurt, Germany, ..."women do not cook there. They survive on canned food, or they buy fast food."

There is much more to home management than cooking although this is undoubtedly an important ingredient in building up a happy home. I have tried to touch upon all aspects that contribute towards the running of a household, which unlike an office is a twenty-four hour, endless assignment. The cycle of cooking-cleaning-washing clothes-washing dishes-ironing clothes-putting them away is never ending. In order to eliminate the twin phrases of 'harried' and 'harum scarum' housewife, I have tried to introduce systems into every sphere of housekeeping so that the house runs efficiently.

I hope this book will be of practical use to both young girls who are expecting to set up house, as well as to experienced homemakers who may also find some of the information innovative. I also hope that this volume will bring a greater understanding and respect for the many hours of continuous hard work that goes into the running of a well-managed household.

—*Rupa Chatterjee*
July 1, 2001

certain features are common in the planning of buildings of all categories intended for use as residential accommodation. Among these are the above mentioned—aspect, privacy, grouping, spaciousness, sanitation, flexibility, circulation, practical considerations and furniture requirements. The shape of the plan is governed by the configuration of the building plot and its nature whether compact and closed or extended and open, and influenced by the local climatic factors. Where the climate is very cold, such as in Shimla, the plan should be closed and compact. Similarly, in the plains where it is very hot such as in Allahabad, the extreme heat in summer makes it mandatory to design a house with one or two central lofty apartments, ventilated and lighted by means of skylights below the ceiling. On the sea coast such as Bombay or Madras, moisture rather than heat affects comfort. The object here is to expose as much of the area of the house to outside air so that a lot of breeze is able to come into the rooms. Hence, an open extended plan shaped like the letters L, E, U or H with large windows on the outside walls is appropriate for the climate.

Aspect refers to the arrangement of the doors and windows on the outside walls of the dwelling so that the gifts of Nature in terms of the sun, air, and view are incorporated in the planning. Aspect not only provides comfort but is necessary from the hygienic point of view as well. The value of the sun's rays in destroying germs and comfort cannot be overemphasized. By careful positioning of the windows it is possible to admit the sun's rays into any room as desired. A kitchen should have an eastern aspect so that the morning sun streams in and that it would be cool in the latter part of the day. The bedrooms should have a south-east or south-west aspect, while the drawing room a north-east or south-east one.

Privacy is essential in a house and is of two types:
1. Screening of the interior of any one room from the other rooms in the house and also from the main entrance.
2. The privacy of the whole house from the street.

Privacy is of great importance and is especially important for bedrooms, bathrooms and the kitchen. As far as possible, every room except perhaps the drawing room shall have an independent access to it. The skill of the architect is called for while planning these aspects of any house or flat.

Grouping refers to the placement of rooms in relation to each other. For example, the kitchen should be close to the dining room but away from the main living room so that the smoke and smells from the kitchen do not bother those in the living area. Similarly the toilets should be accessible from the bedrooms.

Spaciousness refers to the effect produced by making the best of small proportions of rooms, by deriving the maximum benefit from the minimum dimensions of the room. Alternately maximum benefit should be derived from the minimum dimension of a room to give it a feeling of being roomy. This again requires a great deal of skill on the part of the architect as a room whose walls are disproportionately high, looks much smaller than what it actually is. Similarly, if the length of a room exceeds its width, it looks cramped. A square room looks smaller than an oblong one and in terms of utility this is also true. Space should be well utilised for cupboards, such as under the staircase, below the windows and so on.

Furniture requirements for different rooms must be kept in mind. For example, the positioning of the bed is very important in a bedroom and provision must be made for it. It is necessary to exercise forethought and imagination so that there is provision in every room for the placement of essential furniture.

Sanitation is of primary importance in a dwelling for the health of its inhabitants. The importance of light and suitable sanitation arrangements must be built into the plan. Dust is another great enemy of human health as it causes the spread of many diseases. No mouldings or even skirtings and cornices should be allowed in the inner surfaces of walls as dirt and dust accumulate in them. Ledges, nooks, crevices and all other spaces in which dust can settle should be avoided. All edges and corners and angles made by junctions of walls with floors and ceilings should be rounded.

Ventilation is a prerequisite for any room as it means that the stale air will exit from the rooms and also the maintenance of a movement of air within the house. Movement or the lack of movement of air in a house or the lack of it can lead to a feeling of well-being or discomfort. Lack of movement of air, especially in a tropical country leads to the increase in temperature and humidity which in turn leads to lack of evaporation from the body surface and the subsequent accumulation of heat. For cross ventilation, one window situated in the centre of an outer wall is insufficient. It is, therefore, necessary to have another window or windows in the opposite wall. The so-called "stuffiness" in a crowded room is caused not only by the partial exhaustion of oxygen and the presence of an undue amount of carbonic gas in it, but more by the fact that there are human exhalations in it which are warm, and contain water vapour. Also germs and odours emanating from these exhalations add to the stuffiness in the atmosphere. The purpose of ventilation, therefore, is:

a) to give a sensation of comfortable coolness to the body
b) freedom from bad odours
c) reduction of humidity, and
d) proper supply of oxygen.

A house is arranged into various rooms for the comfort of its inhabitants and each room is required for a different purpose. The size of a house, apartment or duplex apartment may vary but if possible there should be different rooms so that family members and guests can come together and stay in comfort.

Time Management

For a household to function smoothly, time management is as valuable at home as it is in an office. Effective time management ensures that there is no pressure to hurry and perform tasks at breakneck speed, as in household chores the old adage, "haste makes waste" is true. If one tries to cook too fast, put the milk to boil on high heat or if one washes or takes out dishes in a hurry, there is a danger of spilling or breaking things. Hence, allowing reasonable amount of time for different chores, one can always work backwards. For example, if it takes an hour to get the children ready for school with their breakfast and lunch boxes, and if they have to leave the house at 7 a.m., it is best to start at 6 a.m. so that unnecessary hurry is avoided. Working against the pressure of time increases anxiety and gives rise to tension.

The full-time housewife is the mistress of her time, but for those who are working, the time would have to be divided into pre-office and post-office segments, with household chores being divided accordingly. The full-time housewife would divide her day with different chores being performed at different times. For example, early morning chores such as giving the children their breakfast and tiffin and sending them to school, organising her husband's breakfast and packed lunch and supervising the work of the domestic help.

The latter part of the day would include cooking lunch, daily shopping and arranging social calls. Once the children return from school, they would have their lunch, and then study. The evening would revolve around the preparation of dinner, the return of the husband from office and of older children from college. The arrival of guests would necessitate extra preparations according to the situation.

The housewife has the innate advantage of being able to organise her schedule according to her needs, thus giving her great flexibility of movement. In the afternoon a visit to the beauty parlour, a hobby lesson or a visit to the market are all within her ambit.

Having chalked out her schedule for the day, there is still a lot that can be done when there are a few minutes to spare.

The following can be done in 5 minutes:

a) an appointment made with a doctor, lawyer or dentist
b) a list of guests can be made for a party
c) indoor plants can be watered
d) a button can be sewed
e) nails can be filed.

The following can be done in 10 minutes:

a) some exercises
b) washing a few clothes or dishes
c) tidying the top of the desk
d) dusting
e) writing out short notes, letters or birthday cards.

One can do the following in 30 minutes:

a) one can go through the newspaper or magazines
b) polish silver or brass
c) do some ironing
d) make phone calls
e) work on some craft project or arrange flowers.

Organising Household Chores

Household chores are of three or four types and can be divided into those that are compulsory and those that are optional, those that must be done daily and others which are weekly or monthly.

Chores for the Day

These include cleaning the house, dusting, bed making, clothes washing, dish washing and cooking.

In western countries where houses are thermetically sealed to keep out the cold, there is less dust, fewer guests and frequently no children. Hence, it is possible to vacuum the house once a week and cook in bulk once every second or third day. However, if a similar schedule were to be adopted in India, the end result would be disastrous! Due to the heat and frequent electricity failure, eating food that has been cooked and kept for two or three days in the 'fridge' is fraught with risk. Moreover, the houses are open hence there is a considerable amount of dust and dirt which comes as children, guests and domestic help come in and out of the house. Hence, in India it is essential to cook and clean on a daily basis.

Most Indian families have four meals per day, in addition to the tiffin for school children and office goers. Apart from this, snacks must be offered along with a beverage to visitors who drop in. Thus, cooking, cleaning and dishwashing have to be done on a daily basis, if not several times a day.

The heat and humidity make the stacking of clothes, so that they can be washed in one lot in the washing machine, an unhygienic proposition in the Indian climate. Hence, clothes washing is, also, necessarily a daily chore irrespective of whether one washes by hand or in a machine. Thus, there is really no short-cut to the drudgery of performing certain chores on a daily basis. If one looks upon these tasks in a positive way it becomes easier as it is indeed a pleasure to live in a clean house, wear freshly washed clothes and eat well-cooked meals on sparkling dishes.

Some amount of shopping as for milk, bread and fresh vegetables and fruit is also a daily feature of an Indian household.

Weekly Chores

Certain household chores can be done on a weekly basis such as shopping for meat, fish, eggs, chicken as well as fruits and vegetables. Fruits and vegetables must be stored carefully in the 'fridge' as they are perishable products. For example, bananas turn black if kept in the 'fridge'.

The bed linen and table linen must be changed once a week, along with hand towels and bath towels. In case there are house guests, they must be given fresh sheets and towels.

Bedspreads can be changed once in two weeks.

Monthly Chores

These would include grocery shopping and "rations" such as rice, wheat, dals or pulses, flour, tea, sugar and edible oil as well as spices and detergents. Every housewife would have a rough idea of the family's monthly consumption and would purchase according to the requirement with a little extra for guests and visitors.

Another important monthly chore is the payment of bills and payment to the domestic help. Bills and salaries should be paid promptly and one can have a diary or account book in which accounts are maintained on a daily, weekly and monthly basis.

Some cleaning chores can be done on a monthly basis, such as the cleaning of doors and windows. The mattresses and pillows can also be put in the sun once a month.

Maintaining the Household Records

While people in other parts of the world may be moving towards a paperless society, we in India cannot afford to adopt a casual attitude towards paper as we live in a "paper raj". Electricity, water and telephone bills along with their receipts, house tax, municipal tax, income tax and children's school fee receipts must be kept with the utmost care. There are so many instances of double billing and claims of "non-receipt of payment", that it is vitally important for all bills and their receipts to be kept carefully for many years as a measure of both caution and necessity.

Photocopies of important documents can be made and kept in another place such as in a safe deposit vault or in the work place so that they are not destroyed in the event of a fire or flood.

Bills, taxes, insurance policies, children's school records and a separate medical file for each member of the family should be kept in well marked and easily accessible plastic folders.

A list should be made of the last date for the payment of telephone, electricity, water, credit card and club bills and payment should be made before the last date so that one can avail of the possible rebate given for early payment.

Household insurance and car insurance policies should be kept in separate files so that payment for renewal can be made prior to the expiry date.

Important papers can be thrown away only after a suitable period has elapsed and when one is sure that they are no longer relevant. All important papers have to be scanned periodically so that unnecessary clutter is not created.

■■

Cleaning the House and its Security

Cleaning the house is a daily chore and due to the high levels of dust, dirt and pollution in our environment it is compulsory to conduct at least once a day, some 'mopping up' operation. Unlike in the western countries where houses are thermatically sealed to keep out the cold, houses in India are open to cope with the vagaries of nature. Therefore, it is not enough to vacuum the house once or twice a week as is common in the west. Also, homes in India have much more traffic in terms of visitors, family members, domestic help, and others who come in and out of the house. Thus cleaning the house is a daily essential and all members of the house must contribute towards this end. Every homemaker has a standard of cleanliness for the home and if these standards are not adhered to and if the house is disordered or dirty, the housewife feels uncomfortable.

Self Help

The pressure of cooking meals, washing clothes, caring for the children, working at home or outside makes it difficult for the housewife to keep the house clean on her own. Frequent light cleaning is the most economical. The homemaker with a schedule and sound methods is better equipped, not only to do the task at hand, but also to teach and guide her assistants whether they are members of the family or paid employees. The main object is to make the job easier and less tiresome by taking a few practical steps.

a) Daily cleaning consists chiefly of sweeping, swabbing and dusting the rooms. In the bedroom, beds must be made and covered with a bed cover.

b) Rooms should be dusted after sweeping but before swabbing so that the consequent dust is mopped up by a wet cloth and is not allowed to circulate and pollute the air.

c) Rugs should be brushed with a carpet brush and so should the upholstery.

d) Weekly cleaning follows the same general procedure but must be done thoroughly. Pictures, mirrors, light bulbs and light fixtures, closet floors, backs of furniture and window shades are dusted.

e) Wherever there is too much dust it is advisable to wipe with a damp cloth.

f) Every other week upholstered furniture may be cleaned with a vacuum cleaner.

g) Mattresses may be put in the sun and turned side for side one week and end to end the next.

h) Light bulbs, enclosing globes and shades in a few rooms should be cleaned each week so that all are included once a month.

i) Draperies and curtains may be washed or dry-cleaned as and when required.

j) Furniture should be polished from time to time.

k) Rugs and carpets have to be rolled so that the floor beneath can be wiped.

l) In case one has a lawn, sunning a carpet and then pulling it along the grass effectively removes a lot of dust and dirt and prevents the carpet from getting damaged as it may through improper vacuuming and dry cleaning.

Domestic Help

India is perhaps one of the few countries in the world where the housewife has the option of keeping servants. Domestic help makes the task of the homemaker easier. However, one should keep the following points in mind:

a) Assign specified tasks to your domestic help, e.g. sweeping, washing.

b) Explain to him/her where you help your clearing utensils.

c) Specify the days of the week when special cleaning needs to be done, e.g. cleaning the carpets, sunning the mattress, etc.

d) If you have more than one servant, assign separate tasks to each of them to avoid confusion and ensure efficiency.

e) You can also explain to them your cleaning schedule.

The situation of servants, however, varies throughout the country, e.g. in Bombay part-time help is more common. Whereas in Delhi, you have the option of both. Hence, depending on the situation, you can decide whether you would like to have all full-time servants or a combination of full-time and part-time or only part-time servants. Many newly married couples, where both the spouses are working, prefer the option of part-time servants as this enables them to lock the house before going off to work.

Types of Cleaning Tools

Brooms

A good broom is essential for cleaning the house. It may be made of vegetable fibres or a harder broom with sticks can be used for washing verandahs, kitchen and the extended portion of the house.

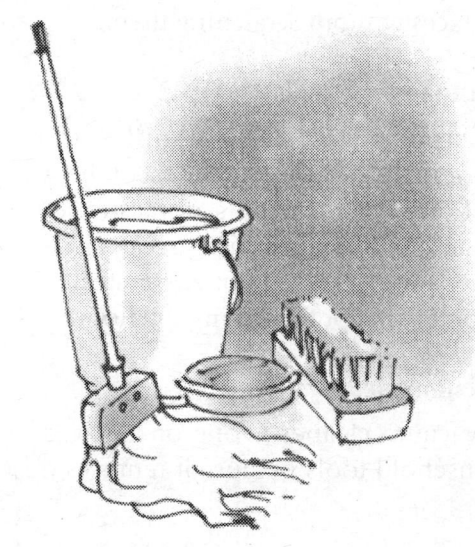

Brushes

There are many types of domestic brushes ranging from a hard bristled carpet brush to a bottle brush, toilet brush, shoe brush, clothes brush, bath tub brush.

Mops

Mops should be washed in suds as often as necessary to keep them clean and then rinsed and dried in the sun. Dry mops also require washing but they are not so frequently used in India as wooden parquet floors are rarely used.

Duster clothes and sponges

Dusters may be made from old clothing, towels or household fabrics. Pieces of fine, soft wool make the most satisfactory dusting cloth or linen. Chamois is excellent for washing windows because it cleans and polishes at the same time. It is made of sheep skin and is oil tanned. The quality of a chamois can be judged by its elasticity. Sponges are better than cloth for washing walls, tiles and stone surfaces. Sponges and steel wool sponges are often used for cleaning utensils. Damp and crushed newspapers are a good way of cleaning glass surfaces without scratching them.

Dustpans and pails

Dustpans with long handles eliminate stooping. However, since most of the sweeping in houses is done by a domestic servant by squatting, a smaller dustpan can also be used. A separate pail made of either steel or plastic should be kept for wiping the floors.

Vacuum cleaners

A vacuum cleaner is one of the most useful household tools because it removes dust and litter effectively. Suction sweeping and agitation are employed in the different types of vacuum cleaners to remove dust. Vacuum cleaners are particularly useful on areas which are carpeted.

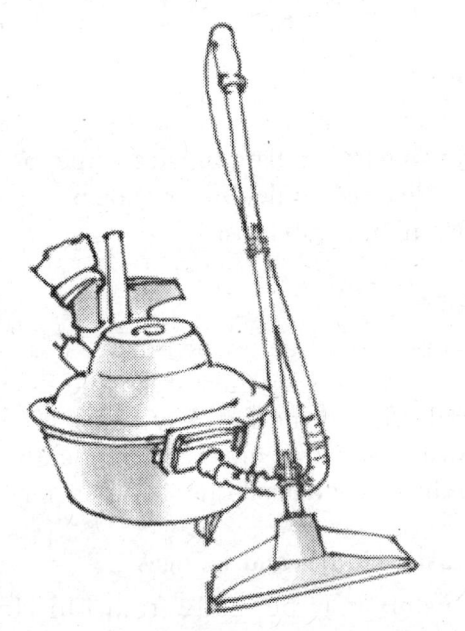

Cleaning supplies

Water, particularly warm water is a good cleaning agent. Although it loosens dirt, it should be used sparingly and wiped off quickly. It should never be allowed to stand on wall, floor or furniture, nor should it be allowed to soak into seams and cracks.

Detergents

Some synthetic detergents are superior to soap for washing dishes and clothes.

Polishes

Waxes and metal polishes protect the floor, furniture and metals respectively. They not only give a shine but also offer protection against insects. Since wooden floors cannot be swabbed with soap and water, it must be waxed. Light scratches on wooden furniture and wooden floor can also be eliminated by waxing and polishing.

Maintaining the Walls

Get your house painted at least once in two years.

Sometimes washing walls is also a feasible option. You will need:

a) Sturdy ladder
b) Detergent mix
c) Clean water
d) 2 buckets.

Always remember to start at the top as this avoids permanent staining due to the detergent. First wipe the wall with a washing sponge, then rinse out the dirt into an empty bucket. Now restart the process by dipping your sponge into the cleaning solution. Avoid using coloured sponges as this may leave stains. Now wipe the walls dry with terry cloth towels.

However, weekly cleaning of ceiling is also a must. Always start high up. You will need a duster and a stepladder.

Another handy hint is to apply a thin coat of laundry starch after washing the walls. This will make your task easier the next time around.

Maintaining the Floors

a) Never scrub wooden floors with water. Dry mopping and sweeping is sufficient for a routine cleaning.

b) Never use an oiled dust mop on a waxed floor.

c) Clean varnished floors with a long handled brush and a dust mop.

d) Waxed floors—to remove excess polish, use a special floor cleaner and a scotch brite pad. Don't forget to wear gloves. For a regular cleaning, use cheesecloth and one can renew finish with liquid wax.

e) Ordinary mosaic flooring or tiled flooring is cleaned most effectively with a sweeping mop and a floor cleaner e.g. Domex, Phenyl, etc.

f) To avoid scratching your flooring while shifting furniture, either lift the furniture or slip old socks over the legs of the table before sliding it.

Maintaining Tiles

a) Tiles in the bathroom should be washed at least once in two days with a sponge and detergent soap.

b) Ceramic tiles on walls or floors should also be cleaned with the help of a household cleaner and a sponge/mop.

c) To make ceramic tiles look fresh, brush white shoe polish into the cracks around the tiles (using an old toothbrush). Wipe off the polish streaks with a damp cloth.

Cleaning Carpets

Use a carpet sweeper to remove dirt daily.

Do not attempt to shake your carpets violently.

Do not varnish the floor under the carpets as the dirt that seeps through ruins the varnish.

To make your sweeping more efficient drop some moist newspaper strips before sweeping.

While vacuuming your carpet remember to move your vacuum in the direction of the pile. Work in overlapping parallel strokes paying special attention to areas in front of furniture pieces.

For shampooing carpets, you will need an aerosol spray foam. First vacuum your carpet thoroughly then apply an even layer of foam over the surface of the carpet. Now let the foam dry thoroughly then vacuum the carpet at top suction. Or alternatively, you could also use any detergent that you use for washing woollen clothes. To drain out the water from the carpet, use a long wooden stick with rubber attachment. Allow the carpet to dry thoroughly before placing back in the room.

To store away carpets, first sun them for at least two-three days, clean them thoroughly. Spread dried *neem* leaves all along the surface. Roll tightly and wrap in brown paper.

Lay carpets only on level surfaces.

Spray the underlay with insecticide at regular intervals.

Turn the carpets around at frequent intervals to distribute the weight of the furniture.

Do not use hard brushes on carpets as the pile gets disturbed.

Do not drag heavy furniture over carpets. Also move heavy furniture around frequently to avoid crushing a carpet.

Protect carpets from strong sunlight.

Another effective way of shampooing your carpet is to use the foam collected from reetha nuts. Apply the foam and start cleaning the carpet from one end. Rub the lather in a circular motion.

You could add 1 teaspoonful of vinegar to the shampoo to yield better results.

Tips for removing carpet stains:

a) Always work inwards from the edge of the stain.
b) Apply only small amounts of cleaning agent at a time.
c) Never overwet the pile carpet.
d) Rinse the treated area with clean water.

Removing Spots from Rugs

Food Stains: Use ordinary washing methods. For radical procedure, add 3 tablespoonfuls ammonia to 2 gallons of suds.

Oil Stains: (from fibre rugs). Apply cleaning fluid periodically until stain is removed from rug permanently.

Ink Stains: Flush out stain with water, blot with soft, dry cloth. Or apply fresh milk as quickly after the accident as possible. Cover with cornstarch and remove, and then apply solution of mild soap and water. If stain persists, apply paste of milk and cornmeal and allow to remain overnight. If stain still persists, loosen with ink eradicator No.1 solution, then sponge with oxalic acid, and wash with water to which 3 drops of ammonia have been added, wash with clear water.

Paint: Apply turpentine, soap and water. If paint has hardened, soften with paint remover, scrape, and then apply turpentine. Don't use liquid paint remover if stain is wet.

Argyrol: Dissolve 2 tablets dichloride of mercury in 1 ounce water. Apply with dropper till stain disappears. Remove solution. Rinse dry.

Iodine: 1 ounce hyposulphite in 3 ounces water. Add 1/2 ounce ammonia; apply with dropper till stain disappears.

Rust Stains: Apply a mild solution of oxalic acid and rinse immediately.

Shoe Polish: Use dry-cleaning fluid, then wash with solution of ammonia, soap and water.

Cleaning Curtains/Blinds

Curtains

You can dry-clean your curtains once in 6 months.

However, you can wash the lighter curtains at home once in 2 months either in a washing machine or with the help of a detergent.

Remember to wax the curtain rods every time you wash your curtains.

If a freshly washed curtain does not hang well, send it for a steam press to the drycleaner.

Blinds

a) Venetian blinds - to clean use a feather duster. However, for a special clean up take them down and wash in a detergent.

b) Holland blinds - use the dusting attachment for your vacuum cleaner or take down and scrub with detergent.

c) Plastic blinds - should be washed in detergent and hung to drip dry.

Maintaining Upholstery

Fine fabrics and pale coloured upholstery should be given to the dry cleaner.

If cleaning at home make sure you use the upholstery shampoo according to the instructions.

Brush upholstery once a week with a carpet brush.

Polishing Silver

Maintaining silver articles around the house is a demanding task as sulphur compounds in the air cause it to tarnish easily. To keep your silverware shining:

Electrolysis: This process is an effective way to remove tarnish. Fill an aluminium vessel with hot water (before using the vessel boil it in a weak vinegar solution). To the hot water, add 1 tsp. of salt, and 1 tsp. of baking powder for each quart of water. Bring the water to boil and drop in the pieces of silver. In a few seconds, the silver will be bright. Now wash in soap water. Rinse and wipe dry with a soft cloth.

Silver polishes are equally efficient. Remember to follow the instructions on the bottle.

While washing silverware, separate cutlery and tableware to avoid scratches. Soak in warm soapy water. Rub well and rinse with hot water. Now lay them on a clean towel to dry.

To remove egg stains from your silverware, sprinkle salt on it and then rub with a wet cloth.

Lacquer your ornamental silver to prevent tarnishing.

Wash oxidised silver in lukewarm water and soap at frequent intervals.

Furniture

Marks on furniture
Scratch marks

Fine scratches can be disguised by rubbing with half a Brazil nut kernel. The oil from the nut will darken the scratch so it tones with the surrounding surface.

Alternatively, dip a piece of flannel in linseed oil, then lay it over the scratch and press it down firmly. Leave it for three hours, remove the cloth and rub in a good wax polish, again leaving it for a few hours before dusting off.

Deep scratches can be filled with plastic wood or wood stopping in a suitable colour, applied with an orange stick.

Spilled perfume, hair spray or nail varnish

Don't try to wipe off the spilled liquid, because this simply makes the mark worse. Leave it to dry before tackling the problem.

If the damage is slight and only the top layer of polish has been affected, try rubbing it lightly with 9/0 grade (very fine) sand paper. Rub uniformly over the entire surface, working in the direction of the grain. This will gradually remove a thin film of polish together with the marks.

Once the marks have disappeared you can rub the surface with metal polish applied with a damp cloth, to revive the gloss. Then buff up with a clean duster.

Heat marks and water marks

On a varnished surface you may find that the marks will disappear if you rub them with metal polish. Follow this up with brown shoe polish applied sparingly with a soft cloth, and buff up well.

On polished furniture you can rub the marks with a cloth which has been moistened with a mixture of linseed oil and turpentine. You can make this yourself by adding 1/4 pint of turpentine to 1 pint of linseed oil (the boiled variety). Mix well, rub the mixture into the affected areas, leave overnight then polish. Keep the mixture in a bottle for future use.

Cleaning up teak

To cure marks from sticky fingers, hot dishes and cosmetics, apply white spirit (turps substitute) on a lint-free cloth, then rub with a very fine grade (000) wire wool, rubbing along the direction of the grain only (if you go across the grain you will scratch the surface). After this wipe over the surface with a cloth moistened with white spirit, then dry off with a dry cloth. Finish off by applying teak oil in the normal way.

Upholstered furniture

Non-grease marks should be sponged with a soft cloth wrung out in cool water. Remove grease marks with a spirit dry-cleaning solvent such as carbon tetrachloride, applied with a soft clean cloth.

Alternatively, the odd grease marks can be treated with French chalk or fuller's earth. Leave overnight to absorb the grease and then brush off the following morning. If this hasn't removed the mark, repeat the process several times. If the mark is on the back of the furniture and the powder does not stay put, mix it with a little carbon tetrachloride to form a thick paste and spread this over the stain.

On wool, tapestry and velveteen to remove light surface dirt, first vacuum the furniture thoroughly with a shaped cleaning nozzle. Then use a soft, clean cloth moistened with cleaning fluid, such as carbon tetrachloride, and rub lightly over the upholstery. Alternatively, wring out a cloth tightly in mild detergent suds and rub over the surface. Dry foam shampoo cleaners applied with a large-pored sponge are also suitable for these materials—and for Dralon flat-woven and Dralon velvet upholstery. Velvet, brocatelle, silk and non-fast coloured fabrics should be professionally cleaned. Vinyl upholstery should be washed with a cloth wrung out in mild soapless detergent or soapflakes. Scrub heavy vinyl but never use chemicals, soda, strong soap powders or abrasives. To remove ballpoint ink stains, sponge with a cloth moistened with methylated spirit and then rinse well. Another method is to rub the stain with a cloth dipped in neat liquid detergent.

Hide furniture needs dusting and occasionally a rub with liquid silicone polish. To treat soiled hide, clean it with a cloth dipped in a solution of half vinegar and half-warm water. Leave to dry then rub with linseed oil. Leave for twenty-four hours then rub off any remaining oil and polish with white silicone cream.

Wooden furniture is usually finished with varnish lacquer or shellac and rubbed to a high polish. To dust, use a clean dry hemmed duster and give each piece an extra rub to keep it shining. Always use coasters when serving drinks or heat-resistant pads to take your dishes. Wipe up spills immediately and then rub with the palm of your hand or a cloth moistened with oil polish.

For old stains, use powdered pumice mixed to a paste with linseed oil. Rub lightly in the direction of the grain. Wipe with a cloth soaked in plain linseed oil.

Deep-seated stains should be treated professionally.

Candlewax must be scraped off with a stiff card or your fingernail. Wash with warm soapsuds.

Grease spots should be wiped with a cloth moistened with cleaning fluid and then polished. For ink spills, blot it up quickly and apply a damp cloth to the spot, pressing firmly. Continue blotting with a dampened cloth using a clean portion every time. Don't rub the ink in.

Wipe off fresh paint blotches with a cloth dipped in turpentine polish.

Soften old spots with linseed oil. Soak for a while. Scrape away softened paint and use pumice stone treatment for remaining traces of polish.

A well-waxed surface is a safeguard against watermarks.

Bamboo or cane furniture should be dusted with a damp cloth to prevent the drying out or splitting of this type of furniture.

Leather upholstered furniture should be dry dusted. To prevent leather from cracking, rub it occasionally with castor oil on dark surfaces and white Vaseline on light surfaces. Wipe out all traces of oil thoroughly. Upholstered furniture should be kept clean with a good stiff brush.

Appliances

Wash your pressure cooker after each use, but do not immerse the cover in water to avoid clogging the vents. Wipe the cover with a soapy cloth, and rinse with a damp one. Clean openings and draw a string through them. Carefully wash the gasket. Reversing the gasket sometimes helps if steam tends to escape from the cooker.

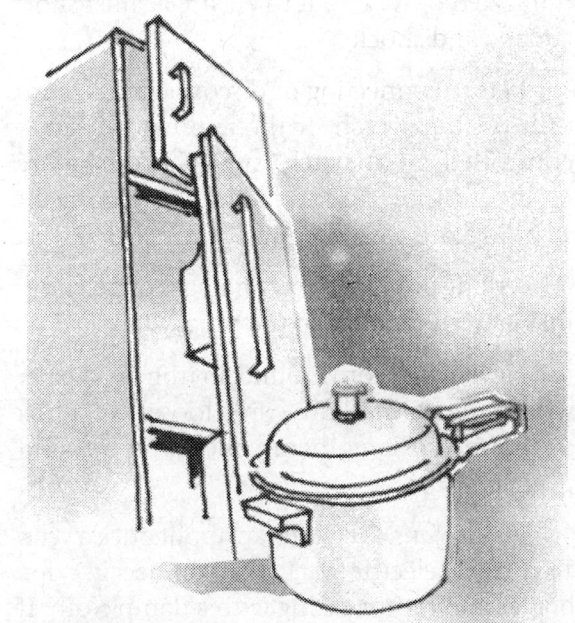

Refrigerators should be defrosted before the frost is more than an inch thick. Clean out the interior. Remove all the food from the shelves.

Clean and wipe all surfaces. Clean gasket and accessories with soap and water. Rinse and wipe dry. Clean the outside of a refrigerator at least once a month.

Let hot dishes partially cool before refrigerating them.

Keep the refrigerator full. A half-empty appliance uses more energy because air is harder to keep cold than chilled food.

Cover dishes with moisture and vapour proof wraps to prevent frost from forming and liquid from evaporating. This will help retain flavour too.

Electric bulbs should be dusted regularly and washed once a month to get full lighting value. Shades and glass fixtures should be given the same treatment.

Electric wires should be replaced or repaired if frazzled or worn out to ensure against short circuits and shock.

Before connecting or disconnecting a cord turn off the switch. If the appliance itself is controlled by a switch, switch it off before connecting or disconnecting it to prevent sparking and wearing away of contacts.

Jerking plugs out may damage copper wires inside or the prongs of the plug.

Never wrap cord around an iron or a heater while still warm. Store cords loosely in a box or drawer or hang them coiled over a round peg.

Electric fans. Oil your fan about once a year. To clean an electric fan, first disconnect it. Wipe blades and motor casing with a damp cloth. If the casing is very dirty, use a cloth wrung out of soap suds taking care not to let any moisture permeate the casing. Rinse and dry. When storing your fan, cover it completely with paper or a cloth.

Electric iron. Always disconnect the iron as soon as you've finished your work and allow it to cool. If the bottom has become stained with starch, wipe it with a cloth wrung out of hot soap suds. Never scrape with a knife. Avoid using the iron over zippers, hooks or buttons as it might scratch the plating. About once a month, rub the bottom with paraffin or beeswax, carefully wiping out surplus with a piece of cloth or paper. This keeps the iron slick and prevents starch stains. Replace worn cords promptly. When ironing don't press too hard.

Stoves. Wipe food spills immediately, while the stove is still warm.

Cleaning Light Fixtures

a) Wipe light fixtures with a damp cloth at least once a month. However, make sure you shut the mains off.

b) To clean chandeliers spray with glass cleaner till the dirt starts dripping. Now wipe off with a soft cloth. However, switch off the mains.

c) Always remove bulbs from the fixtures before cleaning.
d) To clean tubelights use a cloth dipped in detergent. Then wipe off with a soft dry cloth.

Handling Domestic Garbage

Provide waste paper baskets in every room to take care of everyday garbage.

These waste paper baskets should be cleaned out everyday.

Wash these baskets once a week to keep them clean.

One big bin should be provided where the garbage of the house should be thrown. Line this bin with special garbage bags to facilitate cleaning. This bin should also be cleaned everyday, and washed with Dettol once a month.

On old stains try vinegar and rinse carefully with water. Yellow stains that remain after treatment with detergent may require the use of bleach.

Should perspiration odour cling to washable materials after they have been laundered, soak them for an hour or more in warm water - 3 or 4 tbsp. of salt to a quart of water.

Always remove perspiration stains before ironing, as ironing a stain weakens the fabric.

Household Hints

Clear nail polish can often be substituted for glue. If a stamp or envelope won't stick, dab some on.

To catch drips from a tea or coffee pot, slit the centre of a paper coaster and slip it over the spout of a pot.

If hems of shirt or dress come undone, and you need to reattach them in a hurry, use cellophane tape.

To clean silver, try fine-pored, very soft sponges instead of cloth. They penetrate hard-to-reach crevices and rinse quickly.

To clean louvers on shutters and doors easily, use ice cream bar sticks wrapped in detergent saturated cloths.

Apply a little furniture wax to the insides of metal ashtrays. Ash won't cake on the bottoms and cleaning is much easier.

To wipe paint off hands, arms and face, try using cooking oil instead of the regular paint remover that often burns the skin.

Wash ice cube trays in hot, soapy water. This prevents them from sticking to the freezer compartment. Or, after defrosting the refrigerator and cleaning out the freezing compartment, place the trays on aluminium foil.

If a raw egg spills on the floor, avoid messy cleaning by covering it thickly with salt. Let it dry and sweep up.

To remove stubborn stains from stainless steel, use a scouring pad dipped in a mild solution of ammonia and water.

To brighten aluminium or other utensils, rub them with lemon peel, and then rinse with warm water.

Add a few drops of ammonia to finally rinse for sparkling glassware.

If pans get burnt, fill them with soapy water and boil the water for 10 minutes.

Cotton socks make a good applicator when you have to stain intricately carved pieces. First don a rubber glove, then pull on the socks. Dip your fingers in the stain, then rub it on the work.

A clean cotton sock is also a handy dusting tool that works well on venetian blinds. Wear the socks on your hand and wipe the slats between the thumb and fingers. White tapes on the blinds that are slightly soiled or discoloured can be touched up with white liquid shoe polish.

Dust behind radiators or under appliances. You can easily make a dusting tool by slipping heavy cotton socks on a stick. Secure the socks with a rubber band, then spray it lightly with a dusting spray.

A stick can also become a handy tool for retrieving small parts that roll under the sofa or behind a cabinet.

Sealing a can of paint seems simple enough, but it can be difficult when paint collects in the rim groove. Use a thin nail to punch holes in the groove. The holes will allow the paint to drain back into the can and keep the groove clean.

When sealing the can, put a mark on the lid and a corresponding mark on the rim of the can. Always align these marks when resealing the can.

Finally, after pounding the lid in place, turn the can over and hold it upside down for a few seconds—be sure to support the lid with your hand. This upside-down posture will allow the paint to flow around the lid and form an airtight seal.

Keeping the garage floor clean: Sand is handy even if you don't have a pet—for whom a sand box can be useful before it learns toilet training. There is a better way to take care of nagging oil spills. Take a large metal lid or use an unused shallow pan. Put some sand in it and place it under the leaking engine. The sand will absorb the oil and can be changed anytime.

Problem of Household Pests

The problem of household pests such as ants, flies, silver fish, spiders, cockroaches and rats are particularly acute in a hot humid and crowded country like ours. Unless kept under control these pests cause a great deal of damage in the house. There are many professional pest control companies which come in and fumigate the house from time to time. However, many of these pests, particularly cockroaches have increasingly become resistant to these sprays. The key to keeping the pests away is to deny them food, water and a place in which they could find shelter. Food should be stored in tightly sealed glass or plastic containers (airtight). Crumbs and spills should be cleaned up immediately and counters and cabinets should be kept spotlessly clean. The sink area should be kept dry and garbage can should be cleaned out regularly and covered with a secure lid. Cracks and crevices in the walls should be filled in immediately. Electric bug zappers are not effective for bees, wasps and mosquitoes, however they do keep other flying insects away.

Black Ants: A black ant nests mostly on moist or decaying wood and can cause severe structural damage. The nest area has to be treated with a household formulation of chloropyrifos, diazinon, malathion or proposur.

Small ant or household ant: is attracted by sweet or greasy food. It can be traced by following the ants' path from the food supply to the nest. Apply dust or spray at points of entry into the house, beneath the refrigerator, cabinets, sinks and around table legs.

Termites or white ants: Call for professional treatment. To safeguard your precious books, spray with insecticide till eliminated.

Bed bugs: Spray every possible hiding space in an infested room. Bed bugs are commonly found in mattresses, box sprungs, floor and wall cracks, furniture and wall paper. They feed on human blood and appear flat and brown when empty and round and red when full. It is a nocturnal pest. Spray over the entire mattress paying particular attention to tufts, folds and seams. Let the bed remain unmade for one or two hours before sleeping in it. In treating cracks and crevices, spray until the liquid begins to run off. Spray walls upto several feet from the floor. A thoroughly administered single spray usually kills all insects present and leaves a film that protects for several months. If seen again after two weeks, the treatment must be repeated. Professional pest exterminators must be called in for badly infested houses.

Cockroaches: It is said that cockroaches will survive a nuclear holocaust. It is difficult to keep them away especially in multi-storeyed apartments as they creep in from flat to flat. They hide in moist, warm and dark areas and feed on food and garbage at night. Sprays and powder should be put around the stove and kitchen sink or underneath cupboards, behind refrigerators and in other hard to reach areas. Keeping *neem* leaves in the store cabinets and drawers is another method of keeping them at bay. Lining kitchen cabinets with newspaper or brown paper also reduces cockroaches.

Flour Moths: These flourish in flour, grain bud seed and pet food. Throw away all infested foods and store fresh supplies in tightly closed plastic or metal containers.

Silver Fish: These are found in cool, damp areas such as basements or cupboards. They feed on starches including glue and paste. They are nocturnal. Silverfish also attack clothes e.g., woollen sweaters, silk sarees, etc. One should treat cracks and openings around wall paper with a household formulation of diazinon, malathion or proposur. Another treatment is to remove all clothes and spray walls, doors and ceiling with 5 per cent DDT in oil or aerosol bombs containing pyrethium extract. In extreme cases professional help may be sought. To prevent damage by the silver fish, thorough cleaning and packing clothes in sealed packages containing flake naphthalene or para dichlorobenzene cedar lined chests may be dependable but not cedar lines closets. Rugs and upholstery should be brushed frequently in heat or cold. Seal off all cracks and openings. One could also hang in a muslin bag 1 lb of flake naphthalene or para dichlorobenzene to each 100 cubic feet.

Spiders: Spiders feed on insects. They are generally harmless except for the black widow and the brown recluse varieties. Spiders spin webs in corners and crevices that are unsightly and unsafe as spiders can cause skin allergies. Remove webs with dusting brush attachment. One could effectively keep them away by spraying kerosene, pyrethiun, and crushed white eggs.

Mosquitoes: The most common habitat for mosquitoes is stagnant water. Adult females feed on human and animal blood. Many of them transmit debilitating diseases, e.g., malaria, filaria, dengue fever, yellow fever and encephalitis. The most effective way of keeping them out is to have mosquito meshing on doors and windows. Alternatively mosquito sprays, repellants and electronic mosquito repellants can be used to prevent harmful mosquito bites.

Wasps or Hornets: These are found in attics, porch ceilings, roof-tops, trees and so on. There are many people who are allergic to their sting. Their outdoor nests should be treated with a commercial wasp and hornet spray. Mosquito meshing on doors and windows prevents their entry into the houses.

Houseflies: They thrive on food garbage and decaying organic matter such as manure or cut grass. Many diseases such as typhoid, jaundice can spread when flies settle on food. Therefore, food must be kept covered at all times. Spraying should kill them. Screen doors and windows can prevent their entry into the house. Fly swatter is another useful mechanism.

Crows: These are a nuisance and also spread germs if windows do not have a wire meshing. They do not hesitate to enter the house and feed on any food, which may have inadvertently, be kept on e.g., dining table or kitchen counter. The best way to keep them away is to have screen mosquito meshing on doors and windows.

Rats and mice: They are carriers of diseases like plague, typhus, food poisoning, jaundice and rat bite fever. They destroy food, clothing, draperies, upholstery, shrubs and trees. They breed in all seasons—4-7 times a year with litters of 6-22 that reach maturity in 100-120 days. It is essential to control rodents by rat proofing the house and ensuring that there are no entry points through which they can sneak in. Traps and poisons can be used but the rodents often evade these. An energetic and well fed cat often serves to eliminate these destructive creatures.

Stray cats and dogs: While stray cats can enter a house if windows do not have a meshing or grill, stray dogs do not normally enter a house. However, both are a nuisance and can be carriers of rabies. The gates and fencing of the house should be such that stray dogs are not able to enter. Cats, however, are more difficult to keep out as they can scale heights. An effective way of keeping them out is to seal garbage cans and ensure that no food is left outside.

Using Pesticides

Do's

- Read and follow the instructions and warnings on the package carefully.
- Mix pesticides in a well-ventilated area.
- While handling pesticides it is advisable to use rubber gloves.
- Keep pesticides in their original packaging, which should be tightly sealed and clearly labelled to avoid accidents.
- Pesticides must be stored in a locked well-ventilated area away from heat and direct sunlight.
- Wrap empty containers in thick layers of newspaper before discarding them.
- Exhaust all gas from pressurised cans before disposing of.
- Remove food, utensils, pets and their dishes prior to spraying indoors.
- Darkening rooms before spraying is the most effective way of spraying cockroaches.

Don'ts

- Don't use pesticides near children or pets.
- Don't smoke, eat or drink or chew gum.
- Avoid strong pesticides near food.
- Don't dump pesticides in places where they could endanger fish or wild life or contaminate water.

- Don't re-enter a room for half an hour after it has been sprayed.
- Close doors and windows after spraying a room.

Security

Old timers say that doors and windows were never locked in earlier times and gates were always kept open. The incidence of petty thefts and burglary were apparently less in the earlier decades of the century in this country, probably because of a greater awe and fear of the law enforcing authorities. Today, although India is a relatively safer country than many of our counterparts in the western world, given the sheer numbers of our people and the disparities between the haves and the have-nots, the time has nevertheless come for us to be more alert to security in our domestic sphere.

While the police is expected to keep the law and order machinery in such a manner that crime is kept under control, it is nevertheless incumbent on the householder and apartments, societies to make provision for security. At the village level, there is very little protection as the houses are mainly mud-huts. Moreover, earlier on there was a system of village chowkidars and the entire village being protected by gates. The same system of gates has now been introduced in Delhi in an attempt to make the neighbourhood secure.

Personal Safety and Security Measures

The Delhi police have issued certain do's and don'ts to maintain personal safety and to have certain basic security measures.

Do's
a) Put effective barring mechanisms on doors and windows, such as iron grills.
b) Put a magic eye on the door.
c) If possible, keep a dog as a pet.
d) Keep fit and alert.
e) Always go out in a group for an evening or morning walk.
f) Connect your neighbour's house and your home with an alarm bell.
g) Keep vital telephone numbers for emergencies.
h) Inform your nearest PCR Van and neighbours if you are suspicious of someone.
i) Get your servant or attendant verified at the nearest police station.
j) Ensure that all doors, especially the main entrance of the house has grills and proper locks. An electronic alarm system will also be of help.
k) Neighbourhood watch scheme for more interaction with the neighbours.

Don'ts
a) Don't leave valuables lying around in the house.
b) Don't make an ostentatious display of cash and jewellery.
c) Don't trust strangers and open your doors to unidentified people.
d) Don't be a recluse, keep socialising and be in touch with neighbours.
e) Don't ignore any suspicious incident. Inform the police.
f) Don't let your servant have an access to your almirah, safe, bank passbooks, etc.
g) Don't talk about family secrets/property in front of strangers/servants.
h) If alone at home don't open the door, preferably talk through the grill door.

Murders have taken place in high rise buildings also, highlighting the fact that people living in apartments are like sitting ducks waiting to be attacked by the assailant. Apart from the failure of the police in providing security to those staying in residential apartments, the private security system also seems to fail frequently. The police wash their hands off the security aspect in apartments by stating that the residential associations should keep private security guards or agencies. The apparent disinterest of the police coupled with the failure of private security makes people living in apartments more vulnerable to attacks by robbers and murderers. With the extra onus being on private security guards, police patrolling is rare in the jungle of concrete apartments which have mushroomed in many of our cities. With the neighbourhood watch scheme system missing in the majority of residential colonies, a lone security guard stationed at the colony gates with a register and stick in his hands cannot be expected to provide security to the hundreds of residents living inside. Since nuclear families are the order of the day and as neighbours are not really interested in what is happening in the flat next door, each person in an apartment is left to fend for himself, interaction among residents being at the bare minimum.

Making Doors and Windows Foolproof

Doors and windows must be made foolproof so that intruders do not have easy access to a house or apartment. Usually apartments have two entry points, i.e. a front door and a back door. Hence these must be kept securely locked at all times. There should either be a magic eye or a safety chain (preferably both) so that one can ascertain the identity of the caller before opening the door. A double door in which there is a wooden door as well as a door with wire meshing on the inside helps greatly as it makes it possible to see and talk to visitors without opening the door. At night, doors and windows should be properly shut and secured with bolts. Grills on the windows are also deterrents to intruders. Independent houses have many doors which make them less secure. One should try to limit the number of entry and exit points to two, i.e. a back door and a front door to make the house safer.

Types of Alarms

Due to the increase in crimes like theft and break-ins many types of safety alarms are available in the market. Some of these are electronic while others operate on a battery system. Depending on one's needs, these are a worthwhile investment.

Safety Lock

Safety locks for doors and windows are available in the market. These are expensive but make access to the house more difficult for intruders, e.g. in foreign countries there is an electronic burglar alarm which the householder switches on before leaving the house. In some farm houses and in other residential accommodation, people often use an electrical fencing whereby any person attempting to scale the fence will get an electric shock.

The Use of Manpower

Security agencies employ personnel who are specially trained and also certified by the police to work as security guards. Normally they work on a shift system and are rotated so that they do not develop vested interest in any particular place. The presence of such guards often acts as a deterrent to intruders. Some people also employ their own chowkidars or watchmen who are armed with sticks and are expected to maintain vigil on the house, especially at night.

Security Check of Domestic Help

Although domestic servants are a part of our lives in India, unfortunately, it has been seen that this class is more often than not involved in cases of burglary, theft and even assault, particularly on elderly people. If the antecedents of the domestic servant are not properly verified, he or she may commit a theft and then vanish to their far-off villages. Therefore, the police insist that in the interest of employers, they should have these domestic help verified by them. This implies that their photograph, name of the village, address are registered with the police so that they can be traced easily in case of any untoward incident.

Safety Guidelines

For the home

1. Lock all the doors while going out and install slam-shut doors in preference to padlocks. Leave one light on in the house while going out.
2. When going out of town, lock each room in addition to the main door of the house and ask your neighbours to keep a watch.
3. Do not open the door without first ascertaining the identity of the caller through the magic eye and always keep the door-chain in place when accepting mail or parcels.
4. Keep the door bolted even during the day.
5. A safe neighbourhood ensures a safe home, be an alert neighbour and watch out for suspicious people.
6. Apart from magic eyes and door chains, install iron grills, burglar alarms and car alarms.
7. Do not open cupboards in front of servants or unknown visitors.
8. Do not hire masons, plumbers, white washers etc. without verification.
9. When going out of town inform the local police, beat constable or watchman of your area. Tell the newspaper vendor not to deliver papers.
10. Do not let strangers in, even for a glass of water.

For the car

A large number of vehicle thefts can be checked if the car owners take the following precaution:

1. The owner or authorised driver of the car should not leave the vehicle unattended without locking the ignition and removing the key. A significant number of automobiles are stolen because drivers fail to remove ignition keys.
2. All members of the family should know how to protect the car against theft. Licences, registration cards or other identification papers that a thief could misuse should never be left in the car. The documents can be used to sell the vehicle or to impersonate the owner if the thief is challenged by the police.
3. Keys should be carefully guarded. If the keys have punchout numbers, these should be removed and kept at home for reference in case of loss.
4. Park in a well-lighted area.
5. Close all windows, lock all doors.
6. Activate any theft deterrent device you may have.
7. Put packages or valuables out of sight. Tapes and cassette decks and other expensive items in full view invite theft.
8. If you have a garage, use it. Lock both the vehicle and the garage.
9. Install auto-theft security devices. In case the car alarm goes off, observe

behaviour around the car, inform the police. Do not take direct action, your safety is of primary concern.
10. Etch the vehicle registration number in several hard-to-find spots using an engraving tool. In case such a vehicle is stolen and recovered, identification is made easy even if licence plates are altered and the vehicle is repainted.
11. If your car gets stolen, report to the police. (Note: false reporting of vehicle theft is a punishable crime.)
12. Proper maintenance of vehicles prevent breakdowns thus avoiding vulnerable situations.

For handling cash

The following safety precautions should be taken while handling cash:
- All transactions should be kept secret.
- Avoid withdrawal/deposit from the bank at fixed time and date.
- Avoid particular fixed route while carrying out business with bank.
- Avoid carrying cash alone or on foot. There should be sufficient number of persons for safety of cash.
- Avoid hiring taxi/TSR for the transportation of large amount. Use own transport.
- Avoid carrying large amount on two-wheelers.
- Carry a licensed weapon while carrying out transaction with bank.
- The money should be kept in a proper cavity in the vehicle or camouflaged.
- In case of suspicion of being followed, seek police or public help.
- Mobile phone should be carried for seeking timely help.
- Do not converse with strangers while carrying out bank transactions.

- Remain alert and observant during bank transactions.
- Do not get tricked by cheats who may tell you about petty currency notes on the floor inside or outside the bank.
- Payment of huge amount should be taken in a safe/ secured room of the bank.
- Only a secure bag or briefcase should be used for carrying cash in public places.

Safeguard Against Purse Snatching

- Do not carry a bag that makes you a target. A bag that dangles from the shoulder can be easily yanked off. On the other hand, bags that act as handcuffs injure women, as they don't come off easily.
- Be aware of your surroundings and carry your bag close to the body, tucked in at the elbow bend.
- Carry minimum cash, credit cards. Divide the money between pockets of the bag.
- If you are a victim of purse snatch, do not fight to hold on to your bag, as the snatcher could be armed with a weapon.

For the elderly

These special guidelines for senior citizens can help in making them less vulnerable:
1. The beat constable should survey the residence and point out the vulnerable spots and help block loopholes.
2. To help in an emergency, senior citizens should consider installing a distress alarm or a panic button or even a hooter.

3. Residents should realise their social responsibility and neighbours should adopt the senior citizen in their locality.
4. Senior citizens should not keep too many valuables in the house and these should not be displayed in the open.
5. Ostentation is likely to attract the attention of unsavoury characters and should be avoided.

For women
1. When coming home late at night, avoid shortcuts that are not well travelled or well lit.
2. Know the proprietors of reputed neighbourhood stores which are open late in the night and if you feel you are being followed, go there.
3. When walking to your car or on your way home, keep your keys in your hand till you are safely inside.
4. If someone drops you home, ask them to wait till you are inside.
5. If a motorist bothers you while you are walking, turn around and walk in the opposite direction.
6. While driving alone keep your windows rolled up and doors locked.
7. If someone attempts to force you off the road, don't panic, blow your horn constantly to attract attention. If you are forced to stop, put the car in reverse and back away as soon as possible. Keep your hand on the horn and the car in motion.
8. If you are being followed, make a few turns down active streets if possible. If the vehicle continues to follow you, head for the nearest police station, fire house or open store. Don't try to make it to your own quiet residential area.
9. Park your car in a well-lit area.
10. Before getting into your car, look inside first to make sure that no one is hiding in it. Make sure your car is locked when you leave it.
11. If you are alone at home, have your key ready before you get to the front door.
12. If a stranger wants to use your phone for any kind of emergency, keep him out and make the call yourself.
13. If you arrive home and find your door open, do not go inside. Call the police from a payphone or a neighbour's house.

For children
Guard against these common hazards.

BUCKETS
Babies often hold buckets, look in and reach out for their reflection. If they topple, their head weight instantly makes them plummet down.

Prevention:
If you must store water in a bucket, lock the room. Never leave a child alone near a filled bucket. And keep empty buckets upside down.

DRUGS & POISONS
Prevention:
1. Never leave drugs or household poisons within reach of children.
2. Some pills are easily mistaken for sweets, and kerosene kept in colourless bottles looks just like water. Store kerosene in cans or dark bottles, and keep it well out of reach of children.

BURNS
Prevention:
1. Most accidents at home take place in the kitchen. Children should never be allowed to use the stove and if there's a toddler in the house, remember to keep all hot liquids safely out of reach.

2. Diwali is a time when the incidence of burns among children rises sharply. Small children should never be allowed to handle fireworks.
3. Keep an eye on older children too. They should never play with fireworks inside the house, or when wearing loose-flowing clothes. Fireworks that fizzle out or don't explode should be doused with water.

ELECTRIC SHOCKS

Prevention:

1. Ensure all your electrical appliances are in good condition. Immediately discard those that are worn out.
2. Place dummy plugs over all unused electrical sockets.
3. Have an electrician install residual current circuit breakers (RCCBs) in your home. An RCCB (also called ELCB, for earth leakage circuit breaker) instantaneously cuts off power when there is any leakage of current, as when somebody gets a shock. Although the Indian Electricity Rules make RCCBs mandatory only in places that consume five kilowatts or more of power, every home should have them.

Falls

Prevention:

1. If you live on an upper floor, check that your balcony railings and grills aren't of the kind that children can climb.
2. Windows should also be fitted with fixed grills so that there's no way children can fall out.
3. Do not keep chairs, tables or stools on balconies, kids are sure to climb on them.
4. And never stand at the edge of a balcony holding a baby.

UNSAFE TOYS

Prevention:

1. Small children should never be given flimsy toys with small parts that can come off.
2. Even peanuts, button cells, coins and balloons pose major risks.
3. Young children have little control over their swallowing.

SCHOOL BUSES

Prevention:

1. Teach your child to walk slowly and carefully into his bus and to wait well away from it (never behind it, where the driver can't see), until a teacher or helper asks him to board.
2. Sometimes neither teachers nor helpers take care, it's vital that children be made aware of the dangers.
3. Make children understand that getting a front or window seat isn't important.
4. And that rushing into a bus can be very risky.

KIDNAPPING AND CHILD ABUSE

1. Instruct your child never to go off with strangers even if they are offered sweets and toffees.
2. Never to go off with anyone who is saying that your father or mother has sent for you if the person is unknown.
3. Always try to raise an alarm.
4. Instruct your child, irrespective of whether it is a boy or girl against immoral advances towards them even if it is a relative, friend or servant.
5. Parents should make foolproof arrangements when children go to school and when they return.

■■

CHAPTER-3
Maintaining the House

The Exterior
The exterior of the house is subject to a great deal of weathering. It also forms the first impression of the house.

While, some houses have the exterior of stone, open brick or marble tiles, the most common in India is the one of cement plaster. Painting the exterior is highly expensive and therefore, the paint used should be such that it stays for at least 3 years, if not more.

Checking the roof
The roof of the house must be checked periodically to ensure that cracks do not develop as these cracks will result in leakages during the heavy monsoon rains in our country. One also has to check the roof to ensure that small plants have not taken root as these would cause cracks to develop. The roofs should have projecting pipes through which excess rain water drains out. One should check the roof particularly before the monsoons to ensure that these defects have not cropped up. The water storage tank on top of the house should have a bab-cock system and should be kept covered to guard against birds, insects, etc. from falling in. The bab-cock should function to ensure that water does not leak out as constant leakages would cause damage to the roof.

Repairing cracks
Today, many durable adhesive mixtures are available for repairing cracks on the roofs. One should not try to cut corners by using cheaper materials.

Plumbing
The plumbing systems in the house especially sewage lines need to be checked by a plumber and sanitation expert periodically.

The electrical outlets connecting the internal connections of the house to the electricity board lines should also be checked at regular intervals against wear and tear.

Telephone connections come into the house from an external pole. If this wire is loose, cut or damaged in any way the phone connection is affected. Therefore, the proper maintenance of this line is essential.

The Interior

How often should rooms be painted?

There is no strict rule on how often rooms should be painted. Some paint their rooms as often as once a year while others do not undertake this inconvenience for years together. In India paint rather than wall paper is the norm and due to our vast manpower, painting the house is entrusted to professionals rather than the self help method necessitated in the west. The cost of painting the room depends on the quality and category of paint used. While ordinary white wash is inexpensive but not long lasting, oil based washable paints are quite expensive. As getting the rooms painted while one is living in is a mammoth task, it may be done once in two-three years. Due to the high percentage of pollution in the air and dust and dirt particles in the house, it is advisable to paint the interiors within this time frame so that excessive scrapping is not necessitated. It is best to paint the interiors after the monsoons so that any damp patches which may have developed can be repaired and painted over. As far as possible it is best not to paint the house during the monsoons and winter in the northern part of India as the humidity and extreme cold make it difficult for the paint to dry quickly.

Why are paints used?

Our homes are made up of wood, metal, cement, bricks and many other materials and over a period of time the beauty and strength of these get decreased. Walls crack and chip, metals rust and corrode and wooden parts warp and scratch. Paints form a protective layer over these surfaces. They do not allow them to get weathered or affected by other external factors. In short, paints keep them looking as good as new.

WALLS

The kinds of paint available for walls are sold under many brand names but are of the following types:

Emulsions: These are water based paints. Acrylic Emulsions are extremely durable and give walls a matty, smooth finish. They are washable and are therefore easy to maintain.

Distempers: These are also water based paints. But their binders may be natural or synthetic. Distempers are economically priced and offer good value for money as they are very durable. Another type of distemper also available in the market is Synthetic Distemper. It is offered as the lower end product in distemper category and can last for one year.

EXTERIOR FINISHES

For exteriors, cement paint is most commonly used as it is economical. However, its resistance to fungus and algae is relatively low. The available alternatives are given below.

Texturised exterior finishes with sand finish.

100% Acrylic exterior emulsion paint.

For high performance and protection of exterior walls against fungus, algae and mould growth, one can go in for either Texturised exterior finishes or 100% Acrylic exterior emulsions depending on the budget.

SURFACES

The best coating for metals is provided by synthetic enamels. Also, available are paints that are specially developed for particular metals.

METALS

Synthetic enamels provide the best coating for metals. They are tough, durable and glossy in finish. Enamels protect metals from corrosion. Synthetic Enamels are also used for wooden surfaces like doors, windows, furniture, etc. since they give longer life to the wood. However, they do not retain the original beauty of the wood. Synthetic Enamels generally come in 3 grades: First, Second and Third quality.

WOOD

When painting wood, there is a choice between covering the surface with an opaque coating like enamel or bringing out the natural beauty of the wood grain with a clear transparent finish.

Transparent finishes for wood are of the following types:

Melamine based finishes: These are superior transparent finishes that enhance the natural beauty of wood. They are tough, scratch and stain resistant.

Primers: Other than actual paints, you will also need to purchase primer suitable for the surface to be painted. Primers are as important as paints as they provide the basis of a good paint job.

A few words of advice

- Rectify any existing surface problems such as dampness and crack before painting.
- Thinners, primers and undercoats should be of good quality. Though most painters would suggest the use of low quality ones, you must insist on buying these from major paint companies to get the full range of good quality. These provide the foundation of any beautifully finished surface.
- Make sure the surface is clean and free from dust, loose particles and grease before painting.
- Remove rust and scale from metals using a wire brush or sandpaper.
- Test the paint on a small area on the wall before buying the full quantity.
- Make sure you have enough paint for the job before starting work.
- Stir and strain paints thoroughly before application. Most paints settle to a certain extent in the can. The paint should also be thinned properly to ensure adequate application viscosity.
- Buy readymade shades as far as possible. Mixing and tinting of shades done by painters may give you different results from wall to wall. However, if you buy tinted shades through computerised colour dispensers, you can be sure of consistent shades as you would get in the case of readymade shades.
- Leftover paints can be used innovatively—paint a motif on the wall, paint a stool or a door.
- It is not advisable to paint in humid conditions. Avoid painting in the monsoons as the paint takes long time to dry and the film will not cure properly.
- The room to be painted should be well ventilated and free from dust.
- Always clean spilt or splashed paint with the recommended thinner while it is still wet.
- To guarantee a neat edge around window panes, protect the glass with paint shield or apply masking tape before painting. Remove it before the final coat is dry to avoid peeling a layer of paint off.
- Always allow the paint to overlap slightly on the glass to prevent moisture

from seeping to the joint between putty and glass.

- When spraying paint, mask other surfaces around the area with newspaper or plastic to protect them.
- Wear a mask while rubbing down paint surface.
- Do not breathe vapour/spray.
- Keep paint away from food, drink and animal feed. As far as possible, use water-based paints for your interiors to make the process of painting comfortable to the people living.
- Wear eye protection masks when painting. In case of contact with eye, rinse thoroughly with water and seek medical advice.

Some maintenance tips

Like painting once in 2-3 years gives a new look to the wall, maintaining the painted surfaces is also necessary to give a good look. Take some time at least once in a month for this activity.

- To remove stains and dust from a painted surface, use a clean white cloth or a sponge, dipped in a mild detergent solution. After cleaning, wash away all traces of detergent and wipe dry.
- Never use water for spot cleaning unless the wall is totally free from extraneous dust.
- For distempered walls, minimum pressure should by applied while cleaning.
- Enamel surfaces should be cleaned with a detergent solution and immediately wiped dry. Never use thinners to clean enamel painted surfaces.
- If paint on metal or steel furniture is damaged, have it touched up immediately with primer and paint to avoid rusting.
- The recommendations for wood given above are for clear wood finishes. If one wishes to have coloured finishes, synthetic enamels in third or second or first quality can be chosen depending on the budget.
- For metals to obtain silver coloured finishes, aluminium paints can be applied in first or second quality after thorough preparation by metal primers.
- With medium budget, one can also get walls done with lustre finish instead of plastic/ acrylic emulsion.

Coping with damp patches

Whenever damp patches develop they normally do so in the corner of the ceiling of the rooms, below windows or at any point where pipes are running through the wall, e.g. in the wall between a bedroom and bathroom. Adequate measures such as re-plastering should be done after ascertaining the cause for their occurrence so that they do not recur.

Ensuring electrical safety

Due to the threat of electrical short circuit and the danger of electrocution specially with children in the house, utmost priority must be given to electrical safety. No expense should be spared to ensure the best quality of electrical wiring, switches and safety devices, such as childproof switches. Low plug points should either be capped up or covered by a piece of furniture so that children are not attracted by the empty holes of the plug points into which they may be tempted to insert either their finger or any other pointed object.

For heavy equipment, such as air conditioners, refrigerators, geysers and room heaters, a suitable MCB switch should be installed. The proper earthing of wires and the safety of the fuse boxes should be ensured. If a fuse blows, the cause of the fault should be ascertained rather than putting in a heavier fuse so that the fuse does not blow out. It should be remembered that the fuse blowing is indicative of some fault in the line which should be attended to promptly by a reliable electrician. It is best to employ the services of one electrician who is familiar with the wiring of the house rather than getting help from different people whenever the need arises.

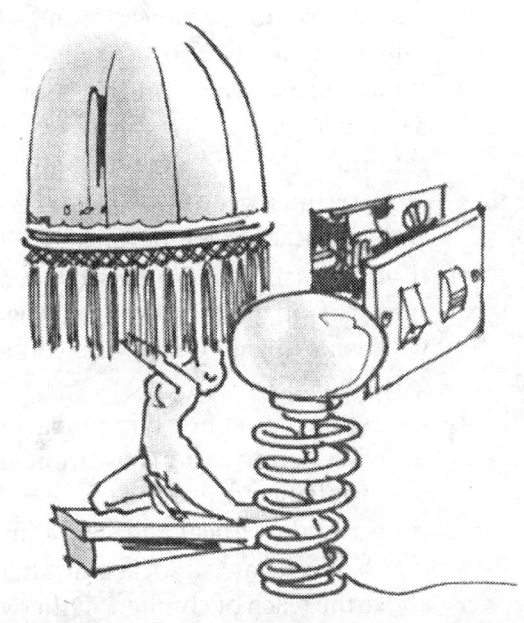

Nobody can afford to be complacent about the electrical safety of their home. Most defects are in plugs, flexes and fuses and can result in fire or serious electric shocks. Thus, 'weak line' which melts and cuts off the current if the circuit is overloaded is often replaced by tin wires too thick to melt. Many faulty socket outlets are broken, exposing live parts which could kill anybody who touches them. Wrongly connected or defective electrical appliances such as refrigerators, washing machines and immersion heaters are used in kitchens and bathrooms where water and damp floors increase the possibility of electrocution. Have a look at every plug in your own home. Does it bear the ISI stamp? Those without this government seal of reliability should be replaced. Don't use two-pin plugs. These lack an earth terminal and are forbidden under the Indian Electricity Rules. Now check that the plug's case is not cracked or broken. Unscrew the cover and check that the wires are connected correctly, the green wire to the earth terminal at the top, the live brown or red wire to the terminal on the right, the black or blue neutral wire to the terminal on the left. If the live and neutral wires are reversed, the appliance at the other end of the flex may be 'live' even when it is apparently switched 'off.' And if the 'live' and earth wires are reversed, and the fuse does not blow, any metal part in an appliance will be 'live.'

With a screwdriver, make sure that the terminals hold the wires firmly. Loose connections cause sparks and overheating. Cut away any stray wisps of wire and shake them out of the plug. Even a single strand could lead to tragedy.

Criminal Negligence: Make sure the cord grip holds the flex firmly. Otherwise a tug may drag the wire from its terminals. If that happens to the earth wire, the appliance will still work but it will be a potential killer.

Examine all socket outlets for fractures and replace those that are faulty. Ask an electrician to check that your sockets are properly earthed. It's not uncommon for unscrupulous electrical contractors to cut corners and not provide proper earthing. Using water pipes for earthing is dangerous, since in many modern buildings water pipes are not buried in the ground. In theory, government electricity inspectors are required to check and certify the safety of all new wiring. But unfortunately, in practice even such criminal negligence is often winked at – for a price.

The bathroom can be an efficient death chamber, as several murderers have proved by dropping live electrical appliances into baths containing their victims. Geysers, especially the instant types, should be permanently fixed (with outside or pull-cord ceiling switches). You should not use an electric *sigree*, hair-dryer or other portable appliances in a bathroom. The only advisable outlet is a shaver socket with a built-in transformer.

If you think your bathroom fittings are not safe, have them replaced or removed immediately. Tomorrow may be too late. Bathrooms and kitchens are potentially the most dangerous places in your homes, but there are hazards wherever there is electricity. Follow these points:

- If an electric iron or any other appliance has too much flex, resist the temptation to coil it. Shorten the flex so that it does not get damaged and overheated, perhaps causing a short circuit and fire.
- Never join two lengths of flex together with coloured adhesive insulation tape. It's not safe. Use flex of the correct length instead. Make sure all plugs fit snugly in the socket.
- If you hear a whirring or a crackling sound in the plug or the appliance, switch it off immediately. It means there is a fault somewhere. Often fires start from flashing, sparking and short circuits in wiring.
- Watch the flex feeding an electric iron or a table lamp. Constant rubbing on a table or ironing-board wears away the insulation and in time exposes the bare wires.
- Switch off appliances at the socket, and, just in case the socket switch is faulty, play doubly safe and take the plug out at night. Do this with all appliances when you go away on a holiday or switch off at the mains.
- Don't move an appliance around while it is connected to a socket.
- If the radiant electric fire does not have a guard angled so that the live element cannot be touched, get one made.
- Don't rig up makeshift electrical equipment, even temporarily.
- If you're using an immersion heater, switch it off before testing the water with your finger. Otherwise, you may get a shock.
- Unless the current carrying capacity of the wires permit it, don't use more than one appliance from one socket. The wires could overheat and start a fire.
- If possible, locate all sockets at a height above the reach of children. Otherwise, secure sockets with 3-pin plugs.

What about all the wires you can't see-- those buried behind plaster, under the floors and above your ceilings? If they are more than 25 years old, they may need replacing. The danger signs are fuses which frequently blow and sockets which become hot. During the rainy season, water may seep into the walls and damage the wiring inside. And once the insulating material is damaged, you can get a shock merely from touching a wet wall. Waterproof all walls exposed to heavy rain. In particular, terraces—where water often accumulates—should be waterproofed or at least given a tar coating before every monsoon.

A licensed electrical contractor will give your wiring a visual check and an estimate of the cost of putting things right. Get estimates from at least three firms licensed for wiring.

Silent, invisible, odourless, electricity is a wonderful servant, but a deadly master. There's no need to be scared of it. It is ready to work for you but, if you abuse it, it can kill you. Treat it with the greatest respect.

Maintenance of doors

Doors should be maintained as they guard the security of the house. The locks should be functional and all doors must close properly. Latches and keys should fit. In case of hinges, grease or oil should be applied. If done so regularly, the noise is taken care of.

Maintenance of windows

Windows should be opened everyday and should also be shut fully. Broken glass panes should be replaced immediately. Window fasteners should be in place to ensure that windows do not slam on their own.

Maintenance of pelmets

Pelmets carry the weight of curtains which are pulled and tugged at everyday. Therefore, one must ensure that pelmets are properly fixed to the wall. The traditional wooden pelmets have been replaced in many homes with curtain rods which are easier to maintain. Pelmets should be painted and polished when the room is painted. Pelmets should normally be painted brown so that they blend with the walls and do not attract attention. Rather the focus of attention should be on the curtains.

Care for Your Appliances

Audio system

Protect from dust.

Use good quality cassettes for better life of the audio-head.

Clean audio-head with standard head cleaner from time to time.

For cleaning the lens of CD player, do not use wet cleaner, use either CD-lens cleaner or ask your concerned service technician.

Air conditioner

Cleaning the filter: Ensure the unit is off before taking off the filter. Clean the filter using a vacuum cleaner or in tap water. Do not use chemical solvents for cleaning. Shake the filter dry. Slide it back into the unit after cleaning.

Clean once every fifteen days or more depending upon the operating conditions. Ensure that the filter is kept clean. It ensures enhanced cooling, lower power consumption and increased unit life.

Cleaning the unit: Periodically clean the unit with a soft cloth dampened with mild detergent, thereafter wipe clean with a dry cloth. Do not use bleaching powder, hot water, thinner or petrol for cleaning. Ensure the power to the unit is off while cleaning.

Service and maintenance: Get your unit serviced regularly from an approved service technician. This is essential for the optimum functioning of the unit and will ensure enhanced unit life and performance. Do not attempt servicing your unit yourself as it can be hazardous due to system pressure and electrical components.

After-season care of the unit: Clean the filter before putting off the unit till the next season. Disconnect power supply to the unit. On a sunny day, operate the unit on 'fan mode' for half day to clean the unit interior.

Precautions: Use the correct voltage. Using voltage other than specified will damage the unit. Install a voltage stabilizer. Check the power plug. If the power plug is not inserted tightly or if there is any damage to the power cord, it could result in leakage or electrical shock.

Use only correct fuses of proper amperage. If using rewirable fuse, use only the correct fuse wire as fire or an electrical accident may occur. Do not put hand or objects into the supply air grill of the unit. These units have a blower running at high speed.

When unplugging the power plug, do not pull it by the power cord. The power cord will be damaged and it will cause electrical shock.

To avoid the risk of serious electrical shock, never wash the unit with water.

Do not obstruct the front of discharge grill. This will block air flow, reduce the cooling effect, and may cause unit malfunction.

Do not use flammable sprays near the unit. The unit can be damaged by gasoline, thinners and other such chemicals.

Do not clean the unit with thinner, hot water or chemicals, use soft cloth dampened with mild detergent.

Before cleaning, ensure that the power supply to the unit is off.

Ensure that the 'activate timer' function is off when you do not require timer function, so that the timer programme does not on/off the unit when not required. When the unit is not in use and timer function is not required, switch off the electrical supply to the unit.

Generator

- Check fuel level before starting.
- Stop engine before filling fuel.
- Filter the fuel before filling into the tank.
- Keep inflammable matter away (1 metre).
- Check engine oil level before each start.
- Use recommended engine oil.
- Change engine oil, first 20 hours of use. Afterwards every 100 hours of use.
- Use choker for cold starting.
- Always connect through changeover switch.
- Switch on appliances drawing higher current first.
- Follow maintenance schedule.
- Always use genuine spares.
- Never connect two or more gensets.
- Never fill less or more engine oil.
- Never connect directly to household wiring.
- Genset should be used inside an enclosed area. Ensure adequate ventilation while genset is in operation.
- Do not put a dust cover while genset is in operation.
- Do not use in wet surroundings.
- Do not touch the genset with wet hands.
- Do not connect pipe to exhaust pipe.
- Do not spill fuel while pouring.

Refrigerator

Follow the manufacturer's instructions to defrost. Generally a chart is provided giving the frequency of defrosting during the various seasons.

The thermostat setting for the different climates are given. As a thumb rule, keep the thermostat at minimum during the winter months and normal during other months. In peak summer, the efficiency is reduced, especially in very hot climates, making it necessary to turn the thermostat to the maximum level.

Periodic cleaning of the interior and exterior of the refrigerator is important to keep up the efficiency of cooling. At least once a fortnight, switch off the refrigerator and remove the plug from the socket. Remove all the contents and take out the racks and the glass cover of the vegetable tray.

Use a liquid soap or one of those cleaning liquids available for this purpose. Spray it and wipe down with a soft cloth. If you are using soap and water, soak a sponge in soap water, squeeze it out and wipe with it. Remove the soap with a wet cloth. You can wash the racks and trays with soap water. Dry well before restoring the contents of the refrigerator. Clean the coils with a duster to remove the dust.

Avoid putting heavy things on the bridge. Spread a cloth or plastic sheet on the top to prevent scratches.

Find out if your refrigerator has a built-in stabilizer and its range. Refrigerators of well-known brands have this feature. If it does not, buy an external stabilizer.

Keep the refrigerator away from moisture and heat.

Washing machine

Washing machines are available in a variety of models. The costliest being the front-loading tumble-wash model which is fully automatic. Next in range comes the top-loading fully-automatic models, then the twin-tub semi-automatic model and finally the washer, which only washes and rinses the clothes.

For practical purposes, the twin-tub semi-automatic model is quite good enough. Though it requires your presence from time to time, it is very efficient. The latest models have the rinse cycle in the dryer itself and consumes much less water than if you were to rinse in the washer. A washing machine is usually quite sturdy and does not give much trouble, but do keep it clean and dry after use. See that the point where you plug in is earthed to prevent shocks.

Vacuum cleaner

It is very useful in cleaning carpets, upholstered sofas, heavy curtains, removing cobwebs, cleaning electronic appliances, etc. Though it does not mop up the floor, it is useful when there are no servants. Vacuuming twice or thrice a week is enough to get the house really clean. A variety of brands are available to choose from.

The various attachments that come with the vacuum cleaner take care of virtually all your cleaning needs. You can dust upholstery, beds, valuable electronic equipment, the cobwebs, fans, etc.

Clean the outer surface of the vacuum cleaner with a sponge soaked in soap water. Take care to see that no water enters the appliance. The dust bag can be changed when the indicator shows that it is full.

Room heater

Compact convection heaters with a blower or fan are the best. These come in both vertical and horizontal models and have automatic temperature and speed controls.

Never leave a room heater on in the children's room the whole night. Switch it off after a couple of hours.

Never close all the doors and windows of the room when you are running a heater. The temperature can become uncomfortable and cause suffocation.

The room becomes very dry due to loss of moisture and can aggravate colds and coughs.

One method of preventing this is to keep a bowl of hot water in front of the heater.

Do not keep the heater on a metal surface.

If you do buy the open coil type of heater, keep it out of reach of small children.

Room coolers

They are less expensive than air conditioners. They work best in the months preceding the monsoons. They consume less electricity than air conditioners and their maintenance is more or less hassle free. Before buying a local brand check out the following:

How to place a cooler

Fix the cooler on a window, from the outside so that evaporation takes place and the cooling is better.

If you are using a desert cooler, select a window or outlet that faces the entire house. This way, the cool air gets circulated throughout the house.

See that there is proper arrangement for filling water.

Coolers that have wheels can be moved from place to place as needed.

How to place a water heater

Wherever there is running water or at least stored water that can be piped, water heaters can be used. Storage water heaters are available from 10 litres to 50 litres. For a family of four members, 25 litres capacity heater is enough. Instant geysers are those where running water gets heated as it passes through the heating coils in the geyser.

These come in sizes ranging from one litre to five litres. The disadvantage of this type of geyser is that hot water cannot be saved and running water is a must. If the water stops, there is danger of overheating and subsequent accidents due to it.

When you fix a storage type heater, select the shape and size according to the size of the bathroom as well as your family. A bathroom where the ceiling is low would do well with a horizontal heater. Similarly, you can buy either a cylindrical or squarish heater depending upon the bathroom and personal preference.

In the storage heater too, the source of the water should be running. You cannot remove the water from a storage heater if the overhead tank which feeds it is empty or if the municipal water supply has stopped. Your plumber will advise you in this matter.

Zinc, brass and copper drums fitted with a heater coil are also used. They have a tap which can be opened for hot water. The danger with these heaters is that they can give nasty shocks if there is some leakage.

Immersion heater

Wherever it is not feasible to have a water heater, an immersion heater is valuable. Copper ones are best as they conduct heat very fast. These are available in 1000, 1500 and 2000 watts rating. Usually, 1000 watts heaters are good enough, but where there is a power problem or when you need water quickly, you can buy one of the higher wattage ones. Check with your electrician to see that the power outlet is capable of taking the excess load.

What to look for in a mixer-grinder

While buying a mixer-grinder, see that the wattage of the motor and its rating. Usually, the better quality mixer-grinders have a 30-45 minute rating.

Do not compromise on quality and buy local mixer-grinder, which burn out with the slightest load.

How to use the mixer-grinder

Put in only quantities specified in the instruction booklet. Never overload the jar.

When grinding very small quantities, use the smaller jar attachment, powder the masala dry, even if you new wet masala because once you add water, the material is likely to stick to the walls of the jar and does not get ground properly.

When wet-grinding soaked dals or cereal, first let the food get ground a little before adding water. Add water little by little, pushing the matter sticking to the walls of the jar by a wooden or plastic spatula.

Care of your mixer-grinder

Never leave the jar of the mixer-grinder to dry after wet-grinding anything. Instead, clean it immediately with water and soap. Dry it instantly, since the central shaft that holds the blade can trap water or food particles and rust. This in turn will jam the blade shaft.

To clean the blade shaft of all its food particles, run the mixer-grinder with some water before removing the blade. This will effectively clean all crevices.

Do not leave the blade on the shaft after finishing grinding. Remove, clean and dry it thoroughly before putting it away.

Keep the mixer-grinders outer surface clean by sponging with a sponge soaked in soap water. Squeeze out the water and clean well. Clean with a clean wet cloth and then with a dry cloth. Use a brush to clean the air vents in the mixer-grinder to prevent clogging with dust.

Keep the mixer-grinder covered when not in use.

Sharpen the blades of the mixer-grinder by running a handful of salt through it at medium speed.

The Kitchen

The kitchen is unfortunately, usually a small part of the house but an average housewife spends a major part of her day over here. The furniture should be arranged in such a way that cooking and preparing meals is made convenient.

The natural work sequence in the kitchen, namely food storage, preparation, cooking, serving, washing up and clearing away is represented today by the refrigerator, cooking range and sink.

The refrigerator, sink and cooking stove or range compose the three work centres in the kitchen. The refrigerator can be placed next to the counter where vegetables are kept. Dishes and dish washing materials should be stored close to the sink. The serving counter should be next to the sink. This should be close to the dining room or serving window between the dining room and kitchen. The three major units, refrigerator, sink and cooking stove/range should ideally be in a triangular arrangement to facilitate handling by the housewife. There should be adequate space for the preparation of food. A wooden inset in the counter top could be provided for cutting and slicing vegetables.

Storage place for utensils should be near the space where they are used.

Kitchen counters and storage cabinets

Storage is a very important part of the kitchen so that all kitchen equipment can be kept conveniently. All things of daily use are stored in the lower shelves. The general principle in planning storage is to store supplies and utensils at their point of first use. Both base cabinets and wall cabinets may be used for this purpose.

Dish washing and cleaning equipment should be kept close to the sink. Clean towels and dish towels should be kept in shelves near the sink.

The garbage pail should be kept covered and placed under the sink.

The shelf for spices should be above the cooking range while the toaster and tea kettle should be kept near the serving space.

While the walls and floors of the kitchen should be tiled so that they can be cleaned easily, the counter should be either of granite, marble or Cudapa stone. The kitchen should have a safe electrical point so that gadgets such as the mixer, toaster, electric kettle, oven-toaster- grill, rice cooker, microwave oven and dish washer can be used.

The refrigerator should have its own power connection. A voltage stabilizer should also be provided for. This could be placed on a wooden plank. Some housewives may use a dish washer and deep freeze depending on their requirements.

The sink

The porcelain kitchen sinks are rapidly being replaced by stainless steel ones. Although this is initially more expensive it is also more durable and causes less damage to crockery during washing. The sink should preferably be connected to a geyser so that hot water can be used for washing.

Safety factor in the kitchen

Due to the presence of fire, safety factors in the kitchen are of the greatest importance. The gas cylinder should be placed in such a way that it is switched off after use. A movable round trolley facilitates easy movement of the cylinder. The height of the cooking counter should be such that it is neither too high nor too low for the housewife.

The modern kitchen uses gas or electricity. Since it becomes very hot, there is a need for just about the cooking area. Cooking smells, fumes and steam makes the kitchen suffocating and an "electrical chimney" or an exhaust fan is essential so that the smells and fumes do not spread to the rest of the house.

Cleanliness requirement

The kitchen should preferably have wire-meshing on the doors and windows so that flies, birds, cats, etc. do not have access. The kitchen must be swept and wiped even thrice a day so that it remains clean after cooking. The garbage pail must be emptied out and washed with dettol from time to time. The pail should also be kept covered at all times and could be lined with a garbage bag to facilitate easy cleaning. Regular fumigation at night and ensuring that no food stuff is left outside will reduce the threat from ants and cockroaches.

The kitchen is the window to our family's health and its cleanliness must be ensured at all costs.

How to wash

Cooking utensils require strong detergents so that the excess oil is removed. Wire scrub or scotch bright may be used for this purpose.

Melmoware on the other hand should not be scrubbed with a strong detergent and wire as they result in scratching the surface. Porcelain should be washed with sponge and can be placed on the plates rack so that it dries on its own. Storing these away when wet can result in water marks. Cutlery must also be washed with a sponge and detergent so that no food particles remain.

Ventilation and lighting

Ventilation and lighting in a kitchen are important. Windows should be kept open to allow free flow of air while the wire meshing will help to keep out insects and flies. The use of exhaust fan or chimney while cooking eliminates extra smoke. A ceiling fan is required but can be switched on when gas is not in use. Tubelights should be placed above the cooking area and at another convenient point depending on the size of the kitchen. There should also be provision for two bulb fixtures which will operate in case of low voltage.

Kitchen woes due to plumbing

"The drains are clogged" is a common complaint all housewives have when it comes to kitchens. In spite of regular care and cleaning of the lint trap of food residues and soap suds, drain flow somehow seems to slow down in a while.

1. Avoid pouring greasy substances down the drains.
2. Grease deposits that collect, nevertheless, may be dissolved by pouring boiling water alongwith washing soda down the drain on a regular basis.
3. It is also a good idea to keep a plunger or "Plumber's helper" handy for quick drain help.
4. However, try not to be too experimental where drains are concerned. Do not mix two different cleaners or use one cleaner after another unless the initial cleaner has been flushed away with gallons of water.
5. Desperate measures such as using a plunger immediately after a cleaner has been used, may cause chemical splash back, so be careful. It's best to call a plumber, when the going gets too messy.

Kitchen sinks

Kitchen sinks are yet another tiresome and possibly the most important areas in the kitchen that need constant maintenance and care. Somehow no matter how much you look after them, there is nothing you can do to prevent drain clogging or discolouration. Home remedies are often the most effective as in cleaning hard water deposits with a solution of white vinegar and water, or removing stains with a paste of lemon juice and borax powder. Cleaning procedures, of course depend largely on the material your sink is made of. If the fixtures are older, chances are the material is porcelain on cast iron, and they may not be as acid and alkaline resistant as the newer porcelain on steel sinks. Cultured marble is also used, and sometimes is moulded into the counter-top for an all-in-one look. Fibreglass marble is now getting more popular in new home construction and remodelling, but they are not nearly as durable as porcelain-coated steel, and need special care to avoid scratching. The most economical cleaning solution for porcelain as well as cultured marble and fibreglass fixtures is a home recipe consisting of 1/2 cup baking soda mixed in a gallon of hot water. However, do be cautioned that this is a highly powerful solution. So it is best to use rubber gloves. Just apply this solution to the areas to be cleaned, scrubbing a bit if necessary, and rinse well with clear water.

Kitchen Hardware

Be it in metal, ceramic or wood, kitchen hardware also need regular care. Faucets, tops, drain fixtures and rods are usually made of chromium or stainless steel. Of course, if your budget allows, you can indulge in brass/copper hardware or any other fancy fittings in antique or modern finish. A quick wipe with a sponge or cloth saturated with the cleaning agent you use is probably the fastest and best way to clean most hardware. Rinse well with clear water and buff shine with dry cloth. Otherwise, baking soda is the cheapest way to clean and polish aluminium and chrome surfaces. Sprinkle some powder on the wet surface making a paste, and use a synthetic scouring pad to spread it. Rinse and buff for a bright finish. Brass tarnishes when exposed to air benefits from a good cleaner/polish. However a paste made of 1 tablespoonful each of salt, flour and vinegar is the most economical method for cleaning brass. Applied with a cloth, the paste is very effective in making tarnish disappear and shine reappear. Dipping a cut lemon in salt and then rubbing it on brass surface is another quick and inexpensive way to clean brass. Be sure to wash in warm soap suds, and buff dry to bring back the shine.

Kitchen equipment

A plethora of high quality kitchen gadgets have ensured that a housewife's task is simplified more than ever. These appliances keep in mind the needs of a modern day woman who has to walk a tightrope between her house and workplace. These equipments are an excellent way to save time.

Liquidizer/blender: A liquidizer/blender is used for emulsifying ingredients for mayonnaise, dips and sandwich spreads. It is excellent for preparing milk shakes and fruit purees which can be poured straight into the serving jug or tumbler. One can buy attachments like a chutney or chopper jar in which small portions of boneless meat can be minced. This attachment can also be used to cut onions, green chillies, tomatoes and other vegetables that don't need uniform chopping. It is excellent for making purees from cooked vegetables or soft fruits for babies who are being weaned. The juicer attachment extracts juice from citrus fruits without crushing the pips.

Food processor: This gadget handles quantities that may be too much for a blender. Its various blades and discs shred, slice, chop and grate vegetables. The food processor also kneads dough for puris, paranthas and shortcrust.

Freezer: The advantage of a freezer is that you can stock up on meats and blanched vegetables so that last minute shopping is unnecessary.

Microwave oven: A great advantage of a microwave oven is that it is automated and one doesn't need to keep watching the time. It's important to use the right containers in microwave ovens. Dishes should be shallow since the microwave cannot penetrate more than four centimetres. Microwaves do not heat food in metal or glass containers. Although some containers have 'microwave safe' marked on them, many don't.

If you want to know whether a container is microwave safe, place it inside the oven next to half a glass of water. Turn heat on high for one to one and a half minutes. If the container is cold then it's microwave safe, but if it's hot, it is not. For more efficient cooking, cover the food or container with plastic cling film.

Mixer-grinder: This is used to grind masalas, rice and dals. These days, mixer-grinders cum food processors are available.

OTGs: Oven-toaster-grills or OTGs are present in most homes. There is little to chose between brands—most are good.

Roti maker: Though it makes rolling pins and boards redundant, rotis made by this device cannot match the hand-made variety. It is excellent, however, for making low-calorie, non-fat rotis.

Tea and coffee makers: Since coffee makers are basically electric filters, they have not become widely popular as ground coffee is preferred only in the south.

Dishwasher: IFB and Videocon offer large-capacity dishwashers. This is a gadget worth investing in. Though the utensils that go on a cooking stove still need to be scrubbed first by hand, tableware comes out sparkling clean.

How to arrange appliances in a kitchen

See how big the kitchen platform is and where the sink is. Let us assume that the platform is on one side of the kitchen and is eight feet long. Use the space by the side of the gas stove to put finished dishes and for preparing the food - like making chapatis, cutting vegetables, etc. You can place a wire basket on one side of the sink to hold the washed vessels. A corner of the platform can house the mixer-grinder.

Keep the refrigerator on the opposite wall or to one side, if the room is big enough. Otherwise keep it in an adjoining room.

Try to keep the gas stove near a window for ventilation and light. If you have poor ventilation in the kitchen, use an exhaust fan.

The shelves should be placed away from the gas stove. If you have shelves running above the stove, you may burn yourself when reaching for something on the shelf. Also, chances of oil stains and smoke spoiling the shelves and their contents are more.

Let the height of the shelves also be at a comfortable level. Keep frequently used items at shoulder height shelves and others at higher or lower levels. Use a small stool to reach upper shelves.

Put up the plate and spoon stands above the sink by nailing them to the wall. They will drip into the sink.

If you have covered shelves, well and good. Otherwise, arrange the tins and bottles in a beautiful manner, so that they do not look cluttered.

Always keep the kitchen bright. Use a tubelight fitting that reflects light in the cooking area. If you do not have a tubelight, at least go in for a 100 watt light bulb that hangs above the kitchen platform. Dark kitchens breed insects and other pests.

The Bathroom

Bathrooms were initially the most neglected part of an Indian house. Today greater attention is being placed on the bathrooms so that they may be well ventilated, easily accessible and aesthetic. While hotel rooms frequently have bathrooms in which there are no windows, a domestic bathroom must be placed in such a way that there is a window which provides adequate ventilation, as well as privacy to the user. In many of the bathrooms in the duplex houses in England, a single bathroom for as many as 3 bedrooms is placed on the landing of the staircase. Not only does this offer any privacy to the user but there is also very little ventilation to remove the steam and air.

The ideal arrangement in any house is to have one bathroom for each bedroom. In some flats, where there are two bathrooms an Indian style toilet is constructed separately from the bathroom to reduce the pressure during rush hours. An area of 5 ft by 6 ft is quite adequate for a bathroom and 3 small bathrooms are better than having 2 large ones. Many people today prefer a bathing area with a shower and taps rather than a tub, as these are generally difficult to keep clean and occupy a large area. These are also difficult for elders and children to get in and out of. A huge mirror, a wash basin with counters, a wall cabinet for toiletries and towel rails should be provided for. The space beneath the counter may either have shelving for storing towels etc. but due to the proliferation of cockroaches and the wood in these cabinets swelling up due to the constant humidity in the bathroom, many now prefer the space to be kept open so that buckets, waste paper baskets can be placed here. The container for clothes to be washed can also be kept here.

Electrical outlets in the bathroom for geysers, electric shavers and hair dryers may be placed above the counter.

Shower curtains are an effective way of keeping the floors dry. The bathroom floors should be kept dry and clean to avoid accidents. This can be achieved with the help of wipers. A fan in the bathroom also facilitates this. A grab or a grab bar in the shower area and next to the toilet are a help for all and are a must for the elderly.

High quality plumbing and equipment should be used in the bathroom as these are more cost-effective in the long run. During construction or when one enters a new home, one should ensure that the gradient of the floor is such that no water collects any where.

Doors and latches should be such that people do not get accidentally locked in. A door knob with an outside lock release would prevent children and elders from locking themselves in. Buckets and mugs should match the colour of tiling in the bathroom and should be cleaned periodically so that fungus does not collect. Shower curtains should also be cleaned from time to time.

CHAPTER-4

How to Wash, Iron and Maintain Clothes

The housewife not only has to maintain her own wardrobe but has the added responsibility of making certain that the whole family is well clad, thus projecting a good image in the public. She also has the responsibility for looking after household linen. Cleanliness is of greater importance in our country due to variations in weather in different times of the year. Perspiration involves both our clothes and us and the quantum of dirt that clothes absorb. It can best be seen if one wears a white outfit for a whole day. This dirt is not as noticeable in coloured clothes as in the white ones. We owe a debt of appreciation to the dhobi, laundry and the dry cleaner for the part they play in keeping our clothes in good condition. They appreciably reduce the work of the housewife but due to the economic and practical considerations, all clothes cannot be passed on to them. The clothes to be washed at home require maximum attention if the quantity is reasonable and can be managed daily. It would be best if a covered basket or basin is placed in the bathroom or outside if convenient so that soiled clothes can be placed in them. Care should be taken to place moist or wet clothes separately as these may run colour. If the housewife is assisted by a maid or servant to do the laundry, a daily routine should be set. However, if she does it alone it may be preferable for her to wash the essentials like undergarments, socks and handkerchiefs on a daily basis. Other clothes can then wait to be washed in lots once or twice a week.

The lifestyle of the conservative, tradition bound Indian family, has, in many ways, evolved beyond belief. The image of a typical housewife in an oil stained saree, hair askew and sweat on her brow has given way to a sophisticated homemaker dressed in sarees or jeans operating electronic gadgets with immaculately manicured hands. One of the magic machines, which have freed women from the shackles of domestic duty, is the washing machine. Electronic gadgets have become indispensable for today's woman who juggles multiple responsibilities, an image reinforced by repeated advertisements. These appliances have become so much a part and parcel of our lives that they are vying with the women for the title of 'homemaker'.

Washing machine is a superior alternative to the cumbersome process of washing clothes manually. The consumer can choose between the semi-automatic and fully automatic machines which come in varying capacities. The buyer also has several alternatives in terms of the various wash techniques made available by different brands such as the pulsator wash, agitator wash, tumble wash, air power wash and so on.

Handwashing

Garment care coding

Most garments and household articles carry a garment care label. Instructions on these labels are there to help and you can't do better than follow their advice. The guide given will assist you in understanding the garment care codes. If a garment care label is not provided, wash under the mildest conditions using the gentlest technique. If the fabric needs ironing, use the coolest setting.

Wash clothes frequently

Modern fabrics, specially man-made fibres, need to be washed, otherwise dirt may set in and become difficult to remove.

Sorting the wash load

Remember, it is the fabric construction rather than the type of cloth that decides the washing treatment. So a single load can be made up of a variety of clothes, provided they are of a similar fabric group. For example, you may sort your wash as cotton, nylon, etc.

Ideally fabric groups should not be mixed in a single wash load unless special care is taken. It increases the risk of shrinkage, dye transfer and discolouration. However, if for reasons of convenience and economy there is no alternative, always select the mildest wash conditions.

It is important to follow the points made above so that:

- You are assured that your fabrics are being washed safely and correctly.
- Colours do not run.
- Extensive creasing and shrinkage is prevented.
- The life of garments and household articles is prolonged.

Sort your washing

- White cottons and linens (natural fibres)
- Colour fast cottons and linens
- Woollens
- Synthetics
- Extremely dirty

Test for colour fastness

Dampen a piece of the hem or seam of the garment. Iron a piece of dry white fabric on to it. If any colour blots off, wash the cloth separately at a cool temperature. If the colour is very loose, drycleaning may be advisable. (check the label).

Pre-treatment and soaking

During the sorting procedure, tough dirt areas or stains should be pre-treated. Ensure the method used is safe for the dye and fabric of the garment.

Sweaty clothes benefit from a soak in cold water before washing. This helps avoid yellow stains of perspiration.

Before soaking any coloured clothes it is important to ensure that:

- The dye is fast and does not come off when soaked. When in doubt don't soak.
- The washing powder is completely dissolved.
- The water temperature is not too high for the fabric or the dye.
- The clothes are not tightly bunched - these should be as free as possible.
- White and coloured clothes should never be soaked together.
- Clothes with metal buttons or fasteners should not be soaked as this can result in rust stains.

The right temperatures for fabric types

If you are using a washing machine, here is a simple temperature guide:

- White cottons and linens very hot, 90°C
- Colour fast cottons and linens hot, 60°C
- White Synthetics, cotton blends Hand hot, 50°C
- All nylons and coloured synthetics warm, 40°C
- Delicate items

Always rinse thoroughly

Thorough rinsing is essential. Some fabrics such as terry towels and nappies may become harsh and scratchy if detergent is left in them (Surf Excel rinses out easily and more quickly). Always rinse twice and when washing baby's clothes, rinse once more just to be sure.

Fabric conditioning

No matter how thoroughly garments are rinsed, after repeated washing they gradually lose their bulk and softness. Comfort Fabric Softener works at untangling matted fibres and restoring natural bulk and bounce to the fabric. Fabric conditioning is not only for towels and woollens: use a softener as an integral part of your wash day routine. Comfort Fabric Softener softens, restores bulk and bounce, removes static, reduces creasing and makes ironing easier. It gently cares for your whole wash load and leaves a delightful fragrance you will enjoy from wash to wash. Follow the dosage instructions on the Comfort pack for best results.

Use of blue/optical whiteners

If you are using a reputed detergent powder, blue or optical whiteners may not be required.

Drying

Certain kinds of fabrics need special care while drying. The conventional wringing and drip drying routine may cause loss of shape and harm the texture of fabrics. Therefore, check the garment label for instructions.

Always dry woollens away from direct sunlight or heat. Lay them flat on a rack to allow circulation of air.

General drying should be in a shady spot, away from direct sunlight which may cause whites to turn yellow and colours to fade.

Tips for handwashing

Start with the whites first. Usually when you soak the clothes in a detergent solution, the clothes get cleaned. All you have to do now is to rub the dirty parts with a little soap. Use a clothe's brush to brush the spot.

It is best to use the rub, squeeze and rinse method to wash clothes by hand. Keep a bucket full of water for rinsing washed clothes. You can brush, squeeze and rinse all the clothes in this water, adding a little as you use it up.

Before rinsing, squeeze out as much water as possible. This will save water, since the water will not get dirty very fast.

Do not try to hand squeeze very heavy linen. Just rinse and hang to drip dry on the tap. In a couple of hours, the water would have drained to the lower part of the hanging cloth. You can easily squeeze that out.

When you have some heavy linen, like bedspreads or bedsheets to wash, you can spread it on the floor and wash the other clothes on top of that. But see that the colour does not run.

When the soap cake or detergent bar you use for rubbing becomes very small to hold, put it in a sock or wrap it in a handkerchief and use. There is no wastage this way. Also you could put the small cake over the bigger one and after some time they form a compact unit.

When clothes need to be handwashed, it is better to wash them everyday or at least on alternate days. Too many clothes on one day will become too tedious unless you have another person or persons to help out. This will show in the clothes which will not wash very clean, since you are likely to get tired after washing some clothes.

Washing in the Machine

Semi-automatic

Select the wash cycle according to the clothes (heavy, regular and delicate).

Remember that half the secret of washing lies in the rinsing. Thoroughly remove all traces of soap and detergent before drying the clothes.

Wash different clothes separately. For instance, do not combine woollens with cottons.

It is safer to wash shirts and T-shirts separately to prevent colour running on to them and ruining them, also to check losing their shape.

Add a few drops of neel (blue or fabric whitener) when you rinse white clothes.

Dry white synthetic clothes in the shade as sunlight makes them turn yellowish.

When you cannot avoid drying coloured clothes in the sun, hang them inside out to prevent them getting bleached by the sunlight.

To prevent petticoat and pyjama strings from tangling with other clothes in the washing maching, make a knot and then push it into the garment.

Button up shirt sleeves to the front holes to prevent them tangling.

Put stuffed toys into pillow covers before washing in the machine.

Do not run blouses with hooks along with delicate clothes, with lace etc. or even with socks. The hooks will create runs in the socks and damage the lace. Alternately, you can fasten the hooks before washing the blouses.

When you only have a washer

This is a basic washing tool which only saves the labour of actual washing— scrubbing, squeezing etc. The rinsing and squeeze drying have to be done by hand. In this case, you will have to depend upon your common sense and experience while washing clothes. For instance, wash delicate clothes separately and do not run the machine for too long. About two to three minutes are enough for delicate clothes. Heavier clothes take longer to get clean. For the rest, follow all the rules of washing with a semi-automatic machine.

Fully automatic

This comes in a variety of models, from front-loading to top-loading models. They are also available in tumble wash and ordinary wash models. Tumble wash models are gentle on the clothes because the clothes are not agitated themselves. The water is agitated by the tumbling of the tub with the clothes in it. A disadvantage of front-loading machines is that they do not open till the entire wash-rinse-dry cycle is over. So when there is a power breakdown, you cannot remove the clothes for a quick handwash. However, the advantages are greater. All you have to do is to put in the clothes, the required amount of soap or detergent and turn the knob on after setting the machine to your requirement. The clothes are automatically cleaned and dried after the stipulated time!

How to get the most from your washing machine

Sort delicate fabrics and lose knits from 'tougher' fabrics. Garments that generate lint, such as fleece sweatshirts and towels, should be washed separately. Before laundering, pre-treat or pre-soak stained articles with liquid laundry detergent.

Adjust the water level of your washing machine to match your load size. Then make your cycle selection. This is the actual washing motion (called agitation) that helps wash clothes better. The cycle selection varies depending upon the clothes you wash.

Hot water is best for whites; items that retain their dyes (colour fast); heavily soiled clothes or greasy stains.

Warm water should be used for permanent press and other 100 per cent man-made fibres, blends of natural and man-made fibres and moderately soiled items.

Cold water will help keep most dyes in dark or bright coloured clothing from running (provided they are colour fast) and minimise the shrinking of washable woollens.

Starching

Starching gives the clothes stiffness and a neater look after ironing. All cotton clothes look better if starched. This need not be an elaborate affair. Nowadays you can buy starch which dissolves in cold water (Revive). Wash, rinse and squeeze all water from the cloth to be starched. Follow instructions on the box of the starch. Take care to open the garment and allow the starch to coat the entire garment. Squeeze out extra starch water and hang to dry, preferably in a single fold to prevent them from sticking after drying.

Silk sarees without zari can be starched at home after washing. Take a tablespoonful of ordinary household gum and dissolve it in warm water. (You can buy this at your grocer). Strain through a strainer and add to quarter bucket of water. Soak the washed saree in this solution turning it well so that the entire saree gets coated. It comes out well starched. The gum gives a shine to the fabric after ironing.

Types of Materials and Their Requirements

Washing machines and modern detergents help in coping with all the pains of washing clothes.

- While washing clothes at home, classify and separate whites from the coloured and printed ones. Dark coloured trousers and socks are more prone to staining the wash.
- Collars, cuffs and soiled or discoloured areas should be pre-treated or pre-washed to dislodge grease or stains.
- Coloured clothes can be soaked in salt water so that the colour sets.
- Heavy cottons and denims, jeans, overalls and uniforms should go into heavy duty cycle of the machine. Alternatively they may be soaked overnight, washed with a clothe's brush and rinsed thoroughly before squeezing out.
- For best results, white linens and heavy white cottons require 110 F hot water, bleaches, blue (ultramarine) or boiling in one metric borax to 2 litres water removes yellowing or discolouration. Today most good detergents contain whiteners, brightners and also stain solvents.

- Synthetic blends and light cottons are easy to care for and dry quickly.
- Silks, crochets, georgettes, chiffons and delicate or other coloured fabrics require cool water, gentle soaps and careful washing. Alternatively, they may be dry-cleaned.
- Woollens should be washed by hand in warm water. The same temperature should be maintained for both washing and rinsing.
- Do not scrub woollens or wring dry but use a good quality detergent. Allow the water to drip out and dry away from the heat.
- Linens, cottons and organdies as also voiles usually require starching. Today starches are readily available in spray form, which make them easy to use.
- For synthetics, woollens, baby clothes and delicate garments, a fabric softener in the final rinse untangles the fibres and adds life, softness, bounce and fragrance to the garments, towels and baby clothes.

Stain Removal—A Guideline

All stains should be tackled soon after they occur or they can set and be difficult to remove.

Check the nature of stain and type of material to try the simplest means of removal first.

When dealing with a delicate or coloured material, first test the treatment on one end.

Thoroughly wash or rinse off the chemical used for treatment.

Handle chemicals and solvents carefully. Read manufacturer's instructions on garments.

If an acid has stained your clothes, sponge with lukewarm water mixed with a little ammonia.

For stains left by candle wax, scrape off surface wax. Place wax stain between clean paper towels and press with a warm iron. Replace paper towels frequently to absorb more wax and to prevent transferring the stain. Place stain face down on clean paper towels. Sponge remaining stains with a dry cleaning fluid; blot with paper towels. Let dry then launder. If any colour remains re-launder with bleach that is safe for the fabric.

To remove blood stains, soak fabric in cold water. Add salt (one teaspoonful to a metric) and leave for about an hour and rinse in cold soapy water. Any stubborn old stains will need to be treated with oxalic acid or salts of lemon solution.

For light butter and cooking oil stains apply a liquid laundry detergent. Place heavy stains face down on clean paper towels. Apply cleaning liquid to the back of stain. Replace towels frequently. Let air dry; rinse. Launder in hottest water safe for that fabric. Before drying, inspect and repeat the treatment and washing if the stain remains.

Coffee, tea or juice stains are also not impossible to get rid of. Flush stain immediately with cool water if possible; or soak for 30 minutes in cool water. Rub the stain with detergent and launder. Launder with bleach that is safe for the fabric. Do not use soap since it could make the stain permanent or at least more difficult to remove.

Gravy and chocolate stains can be sponged off with a grease solvent or detergent and washed in warm soapy water. If the stain remains, re-launder with bleach that is safe for the fabric.

Mildew is a common problem that can cause permanent damage and weakening of fibres and fabric. To treat mildew, first brush or shake off mildewed area. Pre-treat stain with heavy duty liquid detergent. Then launder in hot water with heavy duty detergent and bleach safe for the fabric. Let dry in the sun. Badly mildewed fabric may be damaged beyond repair. Old stains may respond to flushing with dry cleaning fluid.

For stains caused by nail polish, apply nail polish remover to the back of the stain while laying the fabric on white absorbent towels. Replace towels frequently. Then rinse and launder.

Lipstick stains can be treated by placing the stain face down on paper towels. Sponge area with dry cleaning solvent. Replace towels frequently and then rinse. Rub light duty liquid detergent into the stain until outline is removed; launder. Repeat treatment, if needed using an all-fabric bleach because it is less damaging to colours and fabric.

Ink stains are extremely hard to dissolve. Treat immediately by forcing water through the stain before it dries to remove excess ink. Allow to dry. Sponge the stain with dry cleaning solvent. Allow to dry. Rub a liquid detergent into the stain. Rinse. Soak the stain in warm water to which one to four tablespoonfuls of household ammonia have been added. Rinse and repeat if stain reduces. Launder.

Dye stains can be very difficult to remove. Soak the garment in a dilute solution of all-fabric powdered bleach. Check the garment care label and check for colour fastness first. If use of bleach is acceptable, soak and then rinse. If the stain remains and the garment is colour fast, soak the entire garment in a dilute solution of liquid chlorine bleach and water.

For wine stains, soak garment in cold water. Treat with liquid laundry detergent or a paste of powdered detergent and water. Launder in hottest water safe for the fabric, using bleach safe for the fabric. Do not use soap. Reduce the amount of wrinkles from laundering. Be sure you read the care label for the proper ironing procedure and temperature setting to use.

Do not iron items that are dirty or stained. Heat from the iron will set stains.

Some more solutions

Alcoholic drinks (excluding red wine): Dab gently with absorbent cloth to remove as much excess liquid as possible. Sponge the area sparingly with a mixture of warm water and surgical spirit in equal parts.

Black coffee: Mix alcohol and white vinegar in equal parts, soak a cloth in the solution and lightly dab the stained area before pressing gently with an absorbent cloth.

Blood: Quickly dab a damp sponge on the mark to remove excess blood. Dab area very gently with undiluted vinegar followed by cold water.

Butter/grease/sauces: If a greasy mark forms, first lightly scrape the surface of the stain with a spoon or knife to remove any excess oil. Then soak a cloth in proprietary dry cleaning fluid and gently dab the area.

Chocolate/white coffee/tea: Dab gently around the edge of the stain with a cloth soaked in white spirit before following instructions for black coffee above.

Egg/milk: Dab gently with a cloth soaked in white spirit. Repeat with a cloth soaked in diluted white vinegar.

Fruit/fruit juice/red wine: Dab the stain quickly with a mixture of surgical spirit and water (3:1 ratio).

Grass: Apply soap very carefully (using a mild tablet soap or flakes) or dab gently with a cloth soaked in surgical spirit.

Ink/ballpoint pen: Dab gently with a cloth soaked in white spirit. Repeat with a cloth soaked in white vinegar or surgical spirit.

Lipstick/ make-up/ shoe polish: Dab very gently with a cloth soaked in turpentine or white spirit.

Urine: Act as quickly as possible. Lightly blot the mark with a dry sponge to absorb as much excess liquid as possible before applying undiluted vinegar. Then treat as for blood.

Wax: Carefully scrape as much wax as possible from the garment with a spoon or a blunt knife. Place blotting paper over the mark and iron gently on dot 2 setting.

How to Keep or Store Your Garments

- It is advisable to have a cupboard for uniforms, trousers, jackets, suits and sarees. Clothing should be washed, dried and ironed before putting away in a cupboard whose shelves should be lined with white paper, especially if it is a wooden cupboard.

- Dried *neem* leaves under the paper serves as an insect repellant.

- Delicate white silks, organzas, chiffons, or expensive formal clothes like a wedding saree or dress should be dry cleaned and wrapped carefully in muslin and should be kept in a suitcase, tin trunk or cupboard.

- Mothballs should never come in contact with good clothes as they can leave a stain.

- Woollens may be packed in cellophane or plastic with moth balls before storing.

- Separate your clothes into formal and casual wear or what is required everyday and what is required occasionally, i.e. for social or business functions. Formal clothes like embroidered silk sarees need not be washed after each wear unless soiled. Constant washing or dry cleaning can damage the fabric, making them appear faded.

- Sarees should never be folded immediately after use. Rather they should be left on a chair in the bedroom or on a clothe's rack so that the sweat dries out before it is put away in a cupboard.

- Men's suits should be hung on wooden or plastic hangers with the jacket unbuttoned and the pockets emptied out.
- Ensure that there is enough space between the hangers so that the garments are free of wrinkles. Allow your suit to rest at least 24 hours between wearing and try to alternate them. Use a soft clothe's brush to gently remove the hair that sticks to the coats and blazers before putting them away.
- Never mix used clothes with clean ones in the cupboard.
- Always wash or dry clean woollens before storing them away during summer.
- Experienced housewife, Mrs. Ratna Bhattacharya says that monsoon requires extra vigilance. She suggests:
    a) Putting silica gel in little bags and placing them all over the cupboard. These are available freely at chemist shops.
    b) Before putting away suits, brush them and sun them. Then put in air proof plastic.
    c) Wrap sarees in muslin cloth and store in steel cupboards.
    d) You could also place fragrant bars, potpourri etc. in different corners of the cupboard.
    e) Proctor and Gamble fragrance fabric spray 'Fabrize' is ideal for the monsoons.

Ironing

An ironing board would be ideal but if you do not have one, do not worry. A dining or study table would do just fine. Pull it up to the plug point and spread a heavy blanket over it. Cover it with a thick bedsheet and on the top spread a white cloth or bedspread. Your ironing surface is now ready.

Tips for ironing

It is best to iron clothes when they are still damp. If the clothes are very dry, dampen them lightly by spraying warm water over them and rolling them up. Do not make them very wet or they will stick to the iron.

Start with the most delicate clothes first and then proceed to the heavier ones. This is because the iron takes some time to heat up and the delicate clothes require a warm iron, while the heavier clothes require a hot iron.

You can iron a bedspread or saree simultaneously by folding these and laying them under the ironing surface. All they require later is a light press.

Right way to iron

While ironing shirts, start with the collar and the back panel. Then go on to the cuffs and sleeves. Finally begin with the front and then the back. As a final touch iron the shirt as it would hang.

For trousers, begin with the pockets, iron them evenly and then iron the waist band on the wrong side first and the right side afterwards. Now proceed to the waist and press the pleats if any. Lay the trouser with one leg folded over and the other opened out. First iron the insides of the trouser and then the outside. Repeat with the other leg.

Take special care of certain fabrics. Corduroys and velveteen should be pressed on the wrong side with a steam iron.

Woollens need to be pressed on the wrong side with a steam iron using a press cloth. Use a clean, wet handkerchief over the garment if you have only an ordinary dry iron. Do not drag the iron box over the garment since woollens stretch. Set the thermostat to 'wool'.

Silk garments should be pressed on the wrong side using a press cloth, with a moderately hot iron.

Child's puffed sleeve: iron cuff first. Fold sleeve back upon itself, matching cuff opening with arm hole opening. Iron sleeve, cuff side first. Work iron into fullness at cuff. Iron shoulder side, working point of iron into fullness at shoulder.

One seam sleeve with crease: Fold sleeve flat with seam on one crease. Begin at crease, work outward. Turn and iron on opposite side. Touch up cuff and shoulder.

For extended shoulder effect: Iron sleeve first. Fold top of sleeve at shoulder in crescent shape. Place hand through neckline and hold body of garment away from crescent area. Press lightly.

Two seam jacket sleeves: Fold sleeve, underarm side up, narrow panel in centre. Iron. Iron outer arm surface up to where underside of sleeve is attached to garment. Finish top on sleeveboard.

Bias or any uncreased sleeves: Slip sleeve over small end of sleeveboard. Revolve until completely ironed.

Gathered ruffles: Manipulate garment or iron so that point of iron works into the fullness. Use in-and-out strokes. Don't iron over top of gathers.

Bias-cut or circular ruffles: Work point of iron from outside edge in toward heading in oblique, crescent curve. Shift article and repeat until entire ruffle is ironed.

Creased slacks and shorts: Lay one leg on board, inner leg side up, other leg folded back over top. Fold so creases appear in centre front and centre back of leg. Iron. Turn over and iron outer leg up to point where crotch begins. Repeat with other leg. Finish top over end of board. Pyjamas etc. may be ironed with legs folded side to side.

Man's shirt: Iron cuffs first: Inner surface first, outer surface second. Iron body of sleeve, cuff opening side first. Repeat on other sleeve. Iron yoke. Slip one shoulder over end of board. Iron from centre of back to shoulder. Reverse and iron other side of yoke. Iron body of shirt beginning with one front and continuing to other front (or iron both fronts first if fabric is drying out quickly). Iron collar, under surface first, upper surface second, working iron inward from edges. Fold collar down and press over end of board.

Irons and their maintenance

To keep the iron clean, rub the bottom occasionally with wax or paraffin.

If minerals have clogged your steam iron, use a safety pin to get them out. Remember to unplug the iron.

You could fill the tank of your steam iron with water and vinegar (both in equal quantities). Turn the iron on, hold it horizontally, operate the spray and let it steam until the liquid is all used up.

Some more tips

For washing in hard water, use specially formulated detergent powders like Surf Excel.

If the shirt collars, blouse necks, cuffs etc. have become waxy or oily, sprinkle some talcum powder on them. Keep so overnight and wash the next day.

For clothes which lose colour easily, mix two teaspoonfuls of vinegar in soak solution.

When rinsing silks - a few drops of lime juice in clear water gives a delightful shine to them.

On a stuck zipper, rub a wax candle. This helps it open and close easily.

For clothes that are not used frequently, ensure that you change their folds often. This keeps them from tearing along the folds.

Home Crafts

"Mummy my buttons have come off!" "Can you stitch my hem?" are just a few of the common complaints that one has to deal with. To cater to these problems not only saves money but also a trip to the tailor. Increasingly it has become important for every one to know a few basics of stitching.

Sewing has been made easier over the years. New attachments to sewing machines; new electric machines and so on have made sewing easier and a more pleasant task. The first step is to have your own sewing kit. You will need:

Shears: The longer the blade the better your strokes. Old shears should be brightened and cleaned.

a) Sharp, small pointed scissors also come in handy. You can store scissors in unused or old eyeglass case.

Needles: Include several sizes. Needles should suit the weight of the material.

b) A quick way to sharpen your needless is to rub them with an emery board.

c) For smoother hand sewing insert the needle point into a bar of soap every now and then as you work.

Pins: Use pins with sharp points. Get a pins cushion or a clear box with a lid. Use magnet to pick up pins and needles.

Thread: Keep a variety of colours for on hand mending such as black, white and brown.

a) Buy threads that are a shade darker than your material.

b) To prevent a thread from snarling, rub some beeswax or soap along the length of the thread.

c) Cut the thread at an angle, never break or bite it.

d) To facilitate threading a needle dip the thread end into a clear nail polish.

Thimble: Buy a thimble that fits your needle finger. Ensure that there are no rough edges that might tear the materials. If you feel uncomfortable wearing a thimble use an adhesive bandage instead.

Measuring tape is a must.

Tailor's chalk: Get white or coloured chalk. Do not use colouring pencils or crayons as these could stain the fabric.

Embroidery Threads

A wide variety of threads is available ranging from cottons, rayons and silks to wools and metal threads. Suitability of purpose is the most important factor in making a choice. Care should be taken to use threads which are dyed in fast colours for articles which will require laundering or will be exposed to light. Some threads have a dull, and some a shiny finish; some are tightly, and some loosely twisted. Others consist of a number of strands twisted together which can be divided and used as required.

Make a collection of all types of threads, as these will play an essential part in your embroidery.

How to transfer a design

Transparent Material: Place material over the design and pin down. Then outline directly on the material with a hard pencil. For white material, use chalk to prevent soiling.

Lighted Table: Bridge two boxes with a piece of opaque glass (to minimize eye strain) and put a lighted bulb under the glass. Transfer design found in book on tracing paper. Then put tracing paper on glass, lay material thereon, and outline directly on material with a hard pencil.

Carbon paper: Only the specially prepared non-smudge type of carbon paper should be used, such as that produced for dress-making. Trace design on tracing paper. Place the waxed side of the carbon paper down on the right side of the material, which has been pinned on a board. Put tracing paper over the carbon and work round carefully with a pencil.

Prick and pounce: Trace the design on tracing paper, which should be larger than the design so that the pounce will not soil the surrounding material. The pencil lines should be fine and accurate.

Divide both the length and width of the design in half with a pencil line. These lines act as a guide only and will not be pricked.

Place the tracing paper over the tissue paper on the felt pad. The tissue paper under the tracing paper makes the design show up well. Using the pricker in an upright position, prick accurately through all the lines of the design and keep the holes close. It is a help to hold the tracing paper up to the light to see that none of the design has been omitted.

Dip the flat end of the pounce pad in the powder, shake it against the side of the container and then rub it through the holes of the pricking, using a circular movement. Lift the pricking from the material carefully to avoid disturbing the pounce. Paint over the lines of pounce, using a fine paint brush and water colour or oil colour depending on the material in use. Start painting at the lowest edge and work upwards covering the design with paper as it is finished. When the paint is dry, beat away remaining pounce from the surface of the material using a clean dry cloth.

The pricking may be used many times and may also be reversed.

Tack marking: This method should be used for rough fabrics and velvets. Trace the design on to smooth tissue paper and tack this into position at the edges of the background material. Using a thread of contrasting colour (sewing silk will not leave marks), work around the whole of the design through the tissue paper and material. Avoid pressing on the pile of velvet. The tissue paper can be torn away and the design will be clearly marked.

Transfer Ink: With the design on tracing paper, outline with transfer ink using a fine pen nib. Leave it to dry. Then iron off as for a printed transfer. Always making a test first on a scrap of similar material or on the back of which is being used.

How to enlarge or reduce design outlines

To Increase Size: Trace design on tracing paper and draw equidistant vertical and horizontal lines thereon. On another piece of paper draw the same line on a bigger scale. Then draw the outline on this bigger scale. See illustration.

To Decrease Size: Follow same procedure but reduce scale instead.

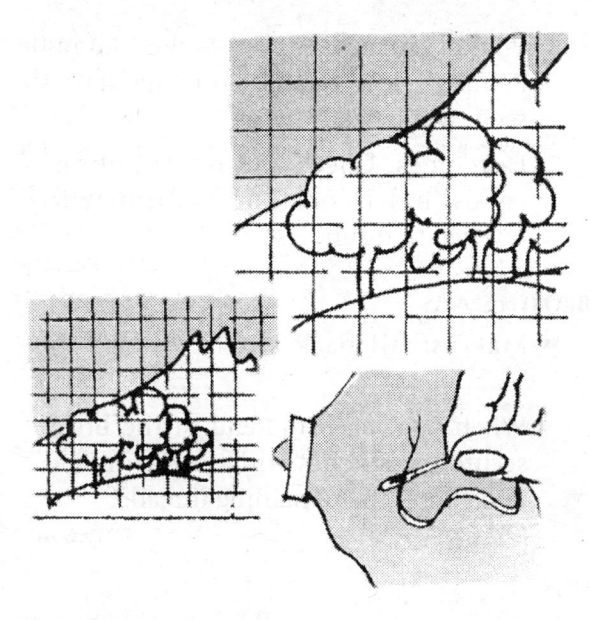

Stretching and pressing

If possible stretch a piece of embroidery rather than press with an iron. Only fabrics and threads which will stand up to a thorough soaking with cold water may be stretched. If an article is already hemmed it should be pressed as the tacks or nails could damage the material.

STRETCHING

Equipment needed:
1. Wooden board or a table top into which tacks can be driven.
2. Rust proof tacks or small nails and a hammer.
3. 'T' square.
4. Clean white cloth.
5. Sponge and a small bowl of clean cold water.

Method:
When the embroidery is finished, cover a wooden board or a table top with a clean white cotton. Place the right side of the embroidery downwards, with one edge parallel and near to the edge of the board. Tack into position, at about one inch intervals. Then, using a 'T' square as a guide, tack one adjacent side at right angles to the first side. Pull and smooth the material until the remaining two sides are squared up, tack into position add the whole surface in taut. The material should be stretched to its original size. Selvedges should always be snipped at intervals to release the tension. Damp thoroughly with a wet sponge and leave until dry. This will take at least 24 hours or more if the material and threads are thick. The work should not be ignored at all. When completely dry, remove the tacks and the embroidery is stretched ready for mounting or making up. Avoid folding the work at this stage as creases cannot easily be removed. If it is not possible to mount immediately, the work should either be kept flat, or rolled round a cardboard tube or around a roll or tissue paper.

PRESSING

Before pressing the embroidery, always test the heat of the iron on a piece of material similar to that which is being used. Also test to see that damping will not leave a mark on the material. Woollen fabrics and linens will usually allow for a damp cloth to be placed over the embroidery and for a hot iron to be used over them. Nylon and some rayon fabrics need only a very slightly warm iron.

Press the embroidery on the wrong side, with the right side down, on a pad of soft material of foam rubber, which should be covered with a clean cloth. The embroidery will sink into the pad and avoid being flattened. Start pressing from the centre outwards, working the point of the iron carefully into any puckering.

MENDING

Useful tips:
1. Seams. Narrow seams may have to be stitched a little deeper to make them hold.

If the edges fray, stitch a line near the edges and overcast them. Two rows of stitching prevent fraying and stretching.

2. Stitching. Rip out and resew broken or drawn stitching.
3. Hems. Rehem when necessary if threads catch or seem unusually loose. Check and restitch hems on household linens also.
4. Dangling threads. Catch and fasten off such threads before further damage occurs.
5. Bindings and facings. See if they are sewed on securely and restitch if necessary.
6. Pocket corners and placket edges. Reinforce with tapes or stitching if they seem weakened by wear.
7. Fastenings. Check and resew buttons, snaps and hooks and eyes. Rework revelled buttonholes.

BROKEN SEAMS

- Make small back stitches along the seamline.
- When you reach the end of the break, secure the stitches with several stitches and cut off the remaining thread.

CHAPTER-5
The Household Budget

It is said that one can never be too rich or too thin and this is especially true with regard to money as no one ever feels that he has enough! This is truer about those who have to live within a fixed salary. They feel the pinch of having a limited income. However, there is little that can be done as even in those families where there are two incomes, expenditure goes up proportionately as the list of human wants gradually become endless. In today's consumerist society, yesterday's luxuries are today's necessity. Ideas on what constitutes a luxury and what is a necessity is relative as one man's idea of luxury may be another's necessity. For example, in the affluent society of Scandinavia's Sweden, even those who are unemployed and on the 'dole' are given enough money to go on an annual holiday. On the other hand in India where a section of the population may not even get two square meals a day, the idea of 'just getting away on a holiday' is limited to those who are in the super rich category.

Since money and finances are frequently a subject of domestic discord it is best for husband and wife to jointly agree on the best way of running the family finances. If it is a traditional single income household, the husband would often discuss with his wife on the amount available for running the house. Where there is more than one income, the couple would jointly have to decide how much of the wife's income would go into the household, what proportion would be saved and what would be "blown up" on luxuries, eating out, clothes, travelling and so on.

Learning to be economical should not be equated with being stingy. Rather it means using the hard earned money in a methodical and sensible way so that every rupee is well spent. If there is no budgeting and one lives beyond one's means through reckless overspending by using credit cards and overdrafts, such extravagance may result in a lot of tension and anxiety.

The purpose of drawing up a family budget jointly is to:

a) eliminate unnecessary squabbling over money which is both undignified and unpleasant.

b) eliminate unnecessary over-spending.

c) derive the maximum benefit from available resources and to get contentment from it.

d) plan the household budget for better utilisation of available resources.

e) take into account some savings for an emergency such as hospitalisation.

Budget can be used to set aside finances for some "extras" which may add grace and spice to daily life, such as eating out, seeing a play or buying something for the house.

The household budget would be divided into fixed costs such as the house rent, electricity, water, telephone and newspaper bills, school fees and servants' salaries. Next there would be expenditure on food and transport and a certain amount for daily requirements. After that would come other necessities such as clothes, entertainment, saving for an important festival or a birthday.

Electricity and phone bills come erratically and school fees often have to be paid every quarter. In order to avoid the strain of suddenly parting with huge sums, it is best to set aside amounts under this head on a monthly basis, keeping the amount in a clearly marked separate envelope. Alternatively, the amount can be deposited in the bank and withdrawn when required.

Tracking One's Money

The domestic budget has to be both realistic and reasonable as setting a too low spending limit is the quickest way of torpedoing the budget.

It is a good idea to have an account book or diary in which the items of daily expenditure are noted down. A simple written account of household expenditure is an asset in the long run as one is not left racking one's brains and memory trying to figure out how the hundred rupee note one had taken to the market got spent so swiftly! A regular day-to-day record with a total at the end of the day would give a good idea of the income and expenses. Later, it can be used as a database for comparing expenditure either on a monthly or yearly basis.

Living Within the Budget

It is not enough to prepare a budget on paper— one has to adhere to it in practice as well. Man's wants and needs are unlimited and the lure of the consumerist culture makes life full of temptations, of never-ending wants and often, consequent dissatisfaction. Hence, every family and the every housewife has to limit wants and strive to live within the available resources. A certain degree of self-discipline and sacrifice is required in order to live within the budget. If one cannot buy something immediately, it should not result in anger and frustration. Instead, one can save and collect money so that the desired item can be bought. Such a purchase would provide lasting satisfaction rather than a quick impulse to buy which could give rise to feelings of guilt for having overspent beyond one's capacity. A certain amount of detachment needs to be developed about material possessions as they are not the only way to peace and happiness.

Organisational Aids

Since pen, paper, notebooks and even computers are readily available, there is no need to strain one's memory. Diaries and calendars are great efficiency aids. Plans for important household work, entertainment, doctor's appointments, messages to be sent on birthdays and anniversaries and dates of due payments of important bills can be entered into a diary for quick and easy reference.

The **telephone** can serve as an important nerve centre for the household. A list of important phone numbers, such as of the family doctor, the police and immediate relatives and close friends can be entered on a big cardboard piece and displayed prominently for use during an emergency. A pen and paper or notebook should be kept for entering important messages. An answering machine may be installed but there is really no substitute for pen, paper and manpower in our country where electricity fails so frequently.

An **address book** listing the names and addresses as well as phone, fax and e-mail numbers of friends, relatives and acquaintances should be placed near the telephone for easy reference.

A **card album** in which cards of people, including tradesmen are kept would facilitate many household activities.

The **call bell** is another efficient aid within the house to summon the servants or for use by the elderly in the house so that one does not have any unnecessary shouting and commotion.

The **mail** that comes into the house should be kept carefully in a central place, such as on the hall table so that nothing is lost or misplaced. Letters should be read, sorted and kept aside for a reply. Those letters which come in the form of advertisements and sales promotion may sometimes be useless to the householder and should, in that case, be thrown away.

The Value of Making Lists

Putting pen to paper helps greatly in organising one's thoughts. By listing the chores of the day or writing down the names of those whom one would like to invite to the next party, a great deal of confusion and time wastage is eliminated.

One should, for example, make a list of things to be brought from the market. Not only does this make shopping more purposeful but also ensures that nothing is forgotten. Listing things down on paper removes a load from one's memory, which in turn leads to less tension.

Another benefit of making lists is that there is a sense of accomplishment as one ticks off the tasks that had to be done once they are completed.

Shopping has become a specialised art in a consumer driven society. We have come a long way from village markets to an era of departmental stores, specialised shops and designer labels. The budget can be efficiently managed and the rupee stretched if one knows what to buy and when to buy and something about the quality of things to buy. Centuries ago the market was a temporary conjugation that blossomed once a week. In city centres or village squares stalls of vegetables, fruits, meat, utensils and fabrics catered to the needs of the local people. For specialised fabrics and weaves one needed to go to a dealer often voyaging for over a week to another city. Today however, time has become a precious commodity and people prefer to save time either by ordering through mail catalogues or going into department stores and specialised shops that cater to specialised needs. Department stores provide a wide choice and variety of products all of which can be found under one roof. There is something to suit every taste and budget. Sales within the stores enable the consumer to buy at reduced prices.

Simple Hints to Economical Buying

a) Compare values - because similar merchandise is priced differently at various stores.

b) Buy according to your own needs and learn what will fill your needs most effectively. Refrain from buying what you don't need simply because the price has been reduced.

c) Buy staples that can serve more than one purpose and more than one season.

d) Avoid fads and extreme styles in either clothes or shoes or decorations.

e) Consider the upkeep required for the item in question.

f) Avoid that which is either too low brow or in the designer category.

g) Goods which are too cheap are often not of durable quality and those which are designer are generally over priced.

h) In shopping for monthly toiletries and other items a larger tube of toothpaste or a larger tin of powder may prove more economical than a smaller one.

i) Limit instalment buying as in the long run it generally costs more.

j) Shop carefully during seasonal and clearance sales as many of these are genuine and can give the consumer value for money.

k) In our country there are many handloom and handicraft fairs in which the consumer is able to buy directly from those who produce the goods. At such fairs one can buy exclusive and well made handlooms and handicrafts without paying either the middle man or the state emporia in terms of sales and other taxes.

l) Our cities are full of wholesale bazaars such as Chandni Chowk and Ajmal Khan Market in Delhi and Bara Bazaar in Calcutta. When it becomes necessary to buy in bulk, as for example during weddings it may be advisable to shop in these markets so that the benefits of bulk buying can accrue to the customer.

Shopping for Foods

Many novices to housekeeping are daunted by the idea of shopping for food stuffs. Most young brides are not conversant with shopping for groceries and fresh fruits and vegetables. Hence they feel ill at ease when this responsibility falls on them after marriage. One has heard of many stories in which young brides are not even familiar with different dals. Food shopping, especially if one has modern conveniences such as a refrigerator and a deep freeze should be limited to one trip per week. The less time one spends in the market the less money one will spend. However, this trip should not be made just before a meal or before guests are due for dinner as the money may result in unwise buying. Monthly requirement of groceries such as rice, wheat flour, sugar, edible oil, detergents, toiletries, and other items should be purchased once a month so that they are stored in the house and used as and when required. A shopping list should be made so that there is no wastage of either time or money.

- Do not buy damaged cans as their contents might be spoilt.
- When buying any packaged goods make sure that the seal has not been opened or tampered with.
- Never buy frozen food covered with frost. It has probably been defrosted and then frozen again which would take away from its quality.

- Always check the dates on perishable foods.
- Do not always buy in large quantities, as they may not necessarily be the best buy.
- Knowing how to read food labels you can compare foods for ingredients, pure quality and nutritious value enabling you to purchase the one best suited to your needs.
- All packaged labels must have the name of the food, weight of the content, name and address of the manufacturer, packer or distributor.
- In foreign countries quality control and labelling of food products is much more stringent. Also for reasons of convenience and the weather most people prefer to shop at either departmental stores or food store chains rather than at the open market. In India however, we have a healthy tradition of buying and eating fresh fruits, vegetables, meats, fish and poultry. Due to our hot and humid climate and the uncertain electric supply this is more prudent and also less expensive. It is, therefore, a good idea to buy fruits and vegetables when fresh supplies come in the late afternoon and early evening.

How can the Housewife be Certain that She is Buying the Correct Quality?

Processed and packaged products by reliable manufacturers speak for themselves. However, it is in buying fresh items in the open market that one has to rely on personal judgement.

Eggs – are fresh when seen against light one should be able to see a large dark highly curved yolk centered in a thick white. The colour of the shell may be white or brownish but this does not reflect on the quality of the egg. The colour of the yolk varies from one breed of poultry to another but this again does not affect its quality. Eggs deteriorate in quality in summer and must therefore be stored in a refrigerator. Grading of eggs, though still not very popular in our country, is done by size.

The traditional method of testing an egg by floating it in water should not be used unless the eggs are going to be used right away as water absorbed by the shell spoils the eggs.

Meat – must be bought from a reliable butcher. Good meat should be bright, dark red, have firm flesh but must be tender and without too many bones. Meat should be bought according to one's requirement. For making *biryani* etc. one may buy meat with bones as this would enhance the taste. On the other hand for curries and roast mutton boneless pieces are required. Meat required for keema should be of the best quality and without any fat so that there is no smell.

Fish – when purchasing fresh fish make sure that the eyes are as clear and as bright as those of a live fish. Also, if the gills do not smell fresh decomposition is on its way.

Poultry – may be purchased fresh from a good butcher or frozen from a store. A dressed frozen poultry is more tender to cook and one is assured of the weight. The chicken must be young and healthy with firm meat with enough flesh on the breast and legs.

Tea/coffee – are available in sealed containers and marketed by reliable companies. Buy loose only if you are certain that the dealer is passing on the correct quality.

Edible oil – is best purchased in sealed cans marketed by reliable manufacturers. It is dangerous to buy loose oil as these are highly subject to adulteration. This was best exemplified by the addition of argemone seeds to mustard oil resulting in a dropsy epidemic.

Flour and pulses – as also whole wheat can easily be inspected before purchasing. One should pay more for a cleaner product that is well-milled and free from grit.

Rice – may be raw milled or par boiled. Par boiled rice is milled out of paddy which has been boiled, is translucent and does not break on cooking. However, it lacks the flavour of raw milled rice. Rice is graded according to the length and thickness of the grain. The longer and finer the grain, the higher its cost especially those that have a fragrance such as basmati. New rice is white, requires less water to cook but tends to be sticky. Old rice is creamish, requires more water for cooking, puffs up to nearly double the amount put in and does not stick while cooking. Old rice is ideal for pulaos and biryanis.

Fruits and vegetables – must be fresh, crisp, and bright in colour and free from blemishes. They should not be over ripe as this renders them limp and fibrous. Old potatoes and onions are better than new ones and hence are more expensive. Old potatoes are recognisable by their characteristic smooth skin. Fruits and vegetables should be bought only in limited quantities as they have low staying quality. While awaiting use in the home when stored in the refrigerator, store in polythene bags and check from time to time otherwise the spoilt portions affect the rest. Potatoes, onions and garlic can be stored in baskets in a well-ventilated corner.

How to Select Vegetables

Cabbages should be green and heavy. It should have shiny leaves. Check for insects. To check if it is fresh, turn the leaves over and look at the stem. It should be white without any spots. Rotten ones have a brownish stem.

Cauliflower should have tightly packed florets and should be white or pale cream. See that the leaves are removed since they add to the weight. The stem should be white too.

Spinach (palak) should have small bright green leaves and thin stems. Some varieties are also dark green and large. Thick stems indicate the age of the spinach. Buy dry leaves as wet ones are likely to have rotten spinach inside the bundles.

Brinjals should be shiny violet. Check for worms. You can see a tiny hole if there are worms. The lighter the brinjal, the less seeds will it have. Weigh it in your hand and select the lighter ones.

Ladyfinger (bhindi) should be tender. You can judge this by breaking off their end. If the vegetable seller does not allow you to snap them off, be safe and select the small ones which have thick skin. Those that show seeds through their skins are to be avoided.

Onions should be light pinkish brown in colour and not dark violet. The latter are wet and not mature.

While buying potatoes look for green parts. Avoid buying such potatoes.

Arvi should not be loaded with lots of soil. It should be dry.

Radish should be white, shiny, soft and firm.

Tomatoes should be bright red, firm and free of blemishes and cracks.

Lemons should be shiny with very thin skins. These are the ones that give the maximum juice. Bright yellow ones are very good. But there are some varieties that have green skins too.

Carrot should be bright and glossy with a firm skin.

Cucumber is of good quality if it is small, green and tender. So avoid the bigger ones which might be bitter in taste.

How to Select Fruits

Bananas should be firm and attached to the stem. Buy bright yellow ones. Those with brown spots are very sweet.

Apples should be chosen according to the variety. Some of them are bright red and shiny and others are dull. Do not buy roundish ones since they tend to be sour. Apples with slightly pointed tops are sweet.

Grapes should be attached to the stalks firmly. Usually one grape from a bunch can tell you if they are sweet. For grapes the best method of selection is by tasting it.

Guava should be yellowish green having shiny skin. Dark yellow ones with strong smell should be avoided since they are over-ripe and have hard seeds.

Storing Vegetables and Fruits

Sort out the vegetables before putting them away. Open the bundle of palak and remove rotten leaves and other weeds. Then wrap them in a double sheet of newspaper. Put it in a large polythene bag and store in the fridge.

If you have the time, string beans and remove the leaves and stalks from cauliflower before putting them away.

Vegetables tend to *sweat* due to the moisture content in them. So if you store them in polythene bags, be sure to turn them inside out or dry them out before storing the vegetables. Do this at least once a day. An easier method is to just store them in the vegetable tray. But spread a newspaper folded at the bottom of the tray and cover the vegetables with a hand towel. This will prevent moisture dripping from the glass cover of the tray and spoiling the vegetables. This way, you can keep vegetables fresh for at least a week.

Store chillies and ginger in plastic or glass containers inside the fridge. Or at least use polythene bags. Remember to change the bags every couple of days.

Coriander can be stored by dipping their roots in a glass of water and standing them up at the back of the fridge. They will keep fresh for a while. Store lemons in polythene bags.

Shopping for Electrical Appliances

Electrical appliances play a major role in our lives, therefore sufficient care must be taken while purchasing them for home use. Electrical gadgets range from refrigerators, washing machines, ovens, heaters and irons amongst others. The quality, durability and safety are a must while buying an electrical gadget and one should check the ISI mark as it is now compulsory for all domestic electrical appliances to carry this mark. If an appliance does not have this mark, do not allow the salesman to smooth talk you into buying the gadget. In buying the electrical appliances it is best to purchase a reliable brand from an authorised dealer. A list of authorised dealers can be ascertained from advertisements, brochures or directly from the company office. If a gadget turns out to be spurious the manufacturer will accept responsibility only if it has been purchased from one of the authorised shops. Lay shops often try to pass off imitations on unsuspecting customers but the manufacturer will refuse to be held responsible for these spurious imitations.

While looking for quality products and reputed brand names one should ascertain that repair facilities are available in the same town. Before buying an appliance and taking it home always check that all accessories, spares, instruction booklet and guarantee card are handed over by the dealer, e.g. a mixie may come with some specified attachment such as a lead wire. A list of the accompanying parts is always provided with the appliance and should be checked carefully. The guarantee card must be stamped by the dealer along with the date of purchase. One should ensure that appliances such as the television, fridge, mixie and V.C.R. have an inbuilt voltage stabilizer so that the appliance can withstand the wide voltage fluctuations so endemic to our electric supply. A stabilizer usually protects from fluctuations ranging from 160v-280v, when the declared voltage for the appliance is 240v. If an inbuilt stabilizer is not provided, the purchaser has to make an alternative arrangement for protecting his appliance with an external voltage stabilizer or such an aid.

Heating appliance like cooking ranges and room heaters must be provided with 2 or 3 elements for stage heating with a thermostat so that the desired heat can be maintained.

All non-current carrying electrical parts of appliances must be adequately earthed. This is especially applicable to room coolers. A three pin plug will prevent shock to the user in case of any leakage. While buying an electrical appliance the functional aspect is very important e.g. a refrigerator should not only look attractive but its capacity and features should be suited to the needs of the family. The size of the family, the space available in the home and the budget should be taken into consideration while buying it.

In buying a geyser, the functional consideration is once again, most important. A storage geyser size should be proportional to the consumption of hot water in the family. Convenience in the usage should be the main criterion. An instant geyser which needs running water supply for its use is impractical in a home where running water is not available at all times. When an appliance like a refrigerator or television is purchased, ask the company mechanic to install it. He will not only do the job well but will also check the house voltage and the plug point and will be able to advise you as to whether it can carry the load.

It is no longer necessary to buy foreign electrical gadgets as they are often unsuitable to the Indian climate and voltage conditions. Moreover repairs are difficult and there is no guarantee provided with the purchase and genuine spare parts are not easily available. It is best to buy fans, fridges, coolers, room heaters and geysers during off-season discounts.

Save Energy to Better Your Budget

It would be necessary to give some hints, at this point, how to save energy, as it would help better your budget. Money saved by saving the energy, can easily be utilized to buy household material. Besides, it could also work to meet out the contingencies, which erupt without notice.

Tips on Energy Conservation

Our vast population and limited resources have made energy conservation, whether of electricity, gas or water, essential. Certain tips on their conservation are given below:

Electricity
a) All electric wiring should be properly checked so that there is no leakage of electricity.
b) All switches should be put off when one leaves the room.
c) Wherever possible, tubelights should be installed as they consume less electricity.

Conserving water
a) All leakages should be fixed immediately, e.g. leaking tanks, taps, etc.
b) Water should be used only when required, e.g. water should not be allowed to run while one is shaving, brushing teeth or bathing.

Saving gas
a) The gas cylinder knob should not be opened fully.
b) The stove should be lit only after one is ready for cooking. Therefore, plan before you start cooking.
c) The use of pressure cookers reduces fuel consumption.
d) While cooking one should not cook continuously on high heat, one should reduce the flame when boiling starts.
e) Use the right quantity of water.
f) Use vessels that do not waste heat and fuel.
g) Soak rice, dal well before cooking so that it cooks faster.
h) Do not use the big burner all the time.
i) It is best to use ISI marked fuel-efficient burners.
j) Food should be covered while cooking so that it cooks faster.
k) As far as possible, mealtimes should be common so that the food is not heated repeatedly.
l) The gas burners should be cleaned regularly so that dirt and oil and spilt food do not clog it and reduce its efficiency.

Tips to save fuel at home
1. Keep the vessel with a lid during cooking—it keeps the heat in and helps cook faster.

2. Don't cook continuously on a high flame. When the liquid in the food starts boiling, the flame size can be reduced. This habit can save as much as 40 per cent fuel.
3. Use the smaller burner of the gas stove whenever possible.
4. A pressure cooker can save up to 75 per cent of the fuel and time spent in cooking.
5. Food cooks faster in aluminium vessels than in stainless steel ones.
6. To achieve better fuel efficiency, ensure that the bottom of the cooking vessel is large enough to entirely cover the burner.
7. For faster cooking, use flat wide-bottomed vessels which expose a larger area to the flame.
8. Turn off the stove a few minutes before the cooking is finished and keep the vessel covered to save fuel.
9. Plan and keep things ready before the stove is turned on to reduce fuel wastage.
10. Get the family to eat together, it saves having to re-heat food several times.
11. Maintain the stove, ensure that the holes are not clogged, that the wicks are trimmed, etc. to increase fuel efficiency. Smokeless *chullahs* (improved cooking stoves) are more fuel efficient than traditional ones.

Coping with power cuts

The state of the electrical supply has become so erratic that in many parts of the country it has become essential to invest either in a battery-operated inverter or in a diesel generator. A battery operated inverter causes less pollution, both in terms of noise as well as emissions. However, in big houses, or in commercial establishments, it may be necessary to use a diesel generator. A battery operated inverter requires the batteries to be serviced at regular intervals by the manufacturer who fills distilled water to ensure its smooth and efficient performance. The battery is charged from an electrical point. In the diesel generator, diesel has to be put in depending on the requirement and hours of use.

Maintenance of air conditioners

Airconditioners must be serviced once a year before the start of the season by an authorised professional who will clean out the air filters and check the electrical wiring and the mechanism. An air conditioner consumes a great deal of power and hence should be functioning properly so that there is no electrical wastage.

Maintenance of fans

Electrical fans must be cleaned periodically, as dust and dirt tend to collect on them while in use. If not cleaned it could cause harm to the health of the users. These could be cleaned with the help of a wet mop and mild detergent. One should be careful to wipe them dry. At regular intervals a professional should be called to check the blades and oil the mechanism.

Maintenance of room heaters

During winters room heaters are essential in some parts of the country. Coil heaters are widely available but are increasingly giving way to convection blowers. Many of these consume considerable amounts of power and hence the wiring and switches should be checked before being put into use.

Solar cooker as a viable option

Though the concept of solar cookers is yet to catch on a wide scale, it has many advantages:

1. The food can never get burnt.
2. No lung damage is caused.
3. No danger of billowing smoke.

However, lack of promotion and doubts among customers have restricted their use.

How to Buy a Mattress

Remember

A deep soft mattress allows the spine to curve.

A stiff mattress does not follow the natural contours of the body.

Hence while buying a mattress, keep these two facts in mind. Hence, you could go in for coir-foam mattress. Though it may be expensive it ensures that your back remains intact.

Some useful tips on buying a mattress

The standard size of a mattress is 75 inches long. Twin widths are available in 80 inches.

The standard width for a twin bed is 39 inches and a double bed is 54 inches. Buy a mattress which is not more than one foot longer than your height.

To select a mattress take off your shoes, lie down on the selected mattress, roll around a bit as you would while you are asleep and then decide whether you want a soft, hard, or an in between mattress.

Remember that double occupancy would require mattress coils with an independent spring action.

If you require a specially firm mattress go in for ones with back boards built into the foundation or one with heavy coils and it should be extra long.

How to Buy a Carpet

The durability of a carpet depends on the knots per cm in a carpet. While purchasing carpets for corridors buy a carpet that has 20 knots per 2.5 cm square. Carpets for bedrooms should have 40 knot per 2.5 cm square. Guestroom carpets should have 50 knots per 2.5 cm square.

Setting up and Maintaining Bank Accounts

At one time, or perhaps even in some families today, banking and financial matters were thought to be the exclusive preserve of the menfolk. An aura of mystery and fear surrounded financial dealings and women were content to leave this aspect of housekeeping to their husbands. However, there is no need for either fear or hesitation in the matter. One visit to the local bank and its manager would divest the procedure involved of any unnecessary apprehension. There are many types of accounts—joint accounts, current accounts, savings bank accounts and single accounts.

A **current account** is an account that does not earn interest. In this account, the holder is permitted to take an overdraft and is generally used for commercial and other related transactions.

A **single account** is one in which salaries could be deposited. However, today banks encourage all account holders to have a nominee who would be the beneficiary of the account in the event of unforeseen circumstances such as death, disability etc.

A **joint savings bank account** with cheque facilities would mean that either husband or wife or, in fact, any two people can jointly operate the account and will be able to issue cheques.

Procedure for Opening a Bank Account

It may be necessary to be referred by an established account holder. Specimen signatures would have to be given so that cheques signed by the account holder could be checked by the bank authorities for authenticity. The specimen signature should always tally with the way one signs subsequently on cheques.

Different banks have different requirements as to the cash balance required for a cheque facility account. While the nationalised banks require a minimum of Rs. 500, private and foreign banks may require the account holder to have a minimum of Rs. 10,000 before giving a cheque facility.

The bank pass book and cheque book should be kept in a safe place to avoid any kind of fraud by unscrupulous persons. Some banks issue an ATM card (Automatic Teller Machine), popularly known as 'any time money', which enables the card holder to withdraw money at any time from the machine. This card may enable the holder to withdraw upto Rs. 10,000 at a time.

When the bank issues the cheque book, ensure that the number of cheques issued is correct and that none are missing.

Types of Cheques

A **self cheque** is one in which one can withdraw the money oneself or it can be withdrawn by the bearer of the cheque.

An **account payee cheque** is one which ensures that the amount indicated (in the cheque) is deposited only in the bank account of the payee.

A **cross cheque** is one in which a double line is put in the top left hand corner so that it is not encashed across the counter but is always deposited in an account (of the payee or beneficiary).

A **bank draft** is one type of cheque by which one party makes a payment to another, In this case, the party making the payment has to deposit the concerned amount at the designated bank counter and request the bank to prepare a draft in favour of the party to whom the amount has to be paid. The draft has to be made payable at the place in which the payee/beneficiary is located. The bank charges a small fee for preparing the bank draft.

Some Banking Tips

While writing a cheque the date, amount and signature should be clearly written. Nothing should be scratched out in a cheque. Should an error occur, one has to sign again over the scratched out portion.

The counterfoil of the cheque should be carefully filled in so that there is no confusion or lapse of memory regarding the person/organisation to whom one has issued the cheque.

The Pass Book of the account must be kept up-to-date so that the account holder has a clear idea of the amounts credited or debited from the account. It devolves on the account holder to carefully scrutinise the figures entered into the pass book and any discrepancies that occur should instantly be brought to the notice of the bank authorities, so that they can be rectified at the earliest.

While issuing a cheque it is imperative to know the previous balance so that one does not issue a cheque that 'bounces'. Apart from the embarrassment, the issue of a cheque that 'bounces' is a criminal offence.

Credit Cards

The use of credit cards or 'plastic money' is so widespread in Europe and America that people there are surprised to see tourists walking around with hundred dollar or hundred pound notes as residents there use their credit card to pay for most things.

The use of credit cards has lately picked up in India and is convenient for emergencies such as sudden hospitalisation, sudden travel or even sudden entertainment. However, one must be extremely cautious about the use of the credit card both for oneself and in case it is lost.

The credit card should be photocopied and kept in a safe place. This would ensure that if lost, one would know the card number and inform the bank so that the account could be 'frozen' to avoid misuse.

It must be remembered that credit card facilities are akin to the services of a money lender, albeit in a sophisticated form, as a substantial amount is paid as interest for availing the credit card facility. Deferred payment may lull one into a false state of prosperity, but ultimately, the bill has to be paid and the accounts reconciled. Hence, although the credit card is useful in certain situations, it must be used judiciously to avoid unwise spending.

Safe Deposit Lockers

Lockers are available in banks for the safe custody of valuables such as jewellery, silver or important documents. Lockers come in three sizes—small, medium and large. The bank deducts the locker rent from the savings bank account under special instructions from the locker holder.

Locker keys must be kept very carefully as its loss leads to a lot of difficulty.

The locker rent must be paid annually or else the bank has the power to seal it for non-payment of rent.

Nomination

Nominations are an essential factor in both bank accounts and in the case of safe deposit lockers as it ensures that they can be operated by the designated nominee without waiting for the succession process to be completed

Wills

Wills are an essential document like birth or death certificates, as it ensures that there is no confusion with regard to movable and immovable property when one is no more.

A will can be written on plain paper or stamped paper and witnessed by two persons who are not beneficiaries (of the will).

In the case of minor children, their legal guardian can be appointed in the event of any mishap befalling the parents.

In order to make the will tamper-proof, it can be registered with a Notary. A will should be carefully and clearly written and one does not have to be rich in order to write a will. However, the will ensures that one's property, both movable and immovable goes to one's rightful or desired successors.

A will may also contain instructions regarding the funeral rites and ceremonies to be performed after one is no more.

CHAPTER-6

A Guide to Home Decor

Everyone wants a dream-house and has done so since pre-historic times. In those days man had to build the house himself, but it was the woman who made the home. In the modern era, it is a partnership. Both the home-makers think, make decisions and carry them out to achieve a home which not only looks and feels good but exudes the very personal aura of its creators.

The in thing is not to yield blindly but to choose whatever appeals to you and then to go about planning it so that one can have different styles from different periods yet live in a fruitful co-existence of styles. Your house ends up being a reflection of your own individual personality.

Some Tips About Vaastu

Along with the revival of the Vaastu concept in Indian architecture, the West has been enthused by the ancient Chinese theory of design called Feng Shui which also stresses on certain architectural planning and aspecting so that the health and welfare of the inhabitants is ensured. A Vaastu perfect construction will have a positive bearing on the thinking, action and fate of people dwelling or working in these places and avoid disorderliness.

Has Vaastu something to do with architecture? Not really. While architecture is the science, art or profession of designing and constructing buildings etc. the definition of Vaastu extends into the realm of occultism.

Vaastu shastra, the edifice science of Bhawan Sthapatya Kala, being the applied aspects of Atharvaveda, is an ancient science and one of the eminent features of our heritage. Indeed, Vaastu is architecture and much more.

In Sanskrit literature, Vaastu means the dwelling of humans and gods. The universe is considered to consist of five elements, the earth, water, fire, air and space and the principles of Vaastu bring balance and harmony among these five elements leading to more flexibility of the body and mind of people enabling them to live a better life. Briefly, Vaastu can make the sweet things in life sweeter and the bitter less bitter. And, if construction is not according to the principles of Vaastu then thoughts and actions of the people dwelling or working in these places will not be harmonious and evolutionary, leading to disorderliness.

Building a house in ancient India was more than just a craft. It was a sacred ceremony where the house was considered a living organism, its spirit was called the Vaastu-Purusha and different cardinal directions and sectors were assigned to different Gods like Brahma, Ishwara, Agni, Varun, Vayu, and Yama. This was due to the belief that waves flowing in a particular direction have a specific influence. Eeshan or north east, for instance, is presided over by god, and is therefore suitable for a prayer room. The central space is Brahma's and should be left open to the Heavens while the head and limbs of the Vaastu. Purusha are to be left alone too. Scholars believe that various activities in a house, shop, office or industry, if directionally channelised as per principles of Vaastu, will begin to draw power from Nature. Once support from this force is forthcoming, all our objectives are fulfilled easily, effortlessly and spontaneously.

Vaastu shastra is being applied not only in the designing and construction houses but in commercial buildings and industries as well. For example, Vaastu assigns the kitchen, chimneys, furnace, boiler etc. to a certain corner on the basis of wind directions to prevent the smoke and cooking fumes from blowing into the living/working area and affecting the health of the residents/workers. This demands that architects and Vaastu engineers co-ordinate their activities. An architect can build a posh house but he cannot ensure a happy life to the people living in the house, whereas Vaastu science assures peace, prosperity and progress to the owner as also the inhabitants.

Many Vaastu rules appear common sense as they relate to ventilation and sunlight. But some like the subtle energy in natural and built environments that affect humans have also been verified and appreciated by those who did not believe in them initially. Here, the sun is the major cosmic entity which radiates light and heat. It is called self of the universe and so the principles of Vaastu allows human beings and society with inexhaustible source of energy and thus make them to live in a fully satisfied manner.

Along with its construction, the internal decoration in the house, shop or factory is equally important. If the settings of things are according to principles of Vaastu, the thoughts, speech and action are supported by nature and lead to health, wealth and happiness.

Vaastu current revival may be confined to human dwellings, but the scope of the shastra, also known as Sthapatya Veda extends to temple-design, isometry, town planning and civil engineering as well.

Most well known temples in South India like the Lord Venkateswara Temple at Tirupathi and the Meenakshi Temple at Maduri are Vaastu perfect. In terms of an entire city, Jaipur was founded in 1727 by Maharaja Sawai Jai Singh II in accordance with the principles of Vaastu shastra.

Vaastu do's and don'ts

Here are some tips and illustrations of the principles of Vaastu. The cardinal points are easily determined with the help of an ordinary compass.

- Plots with round, triangular, polygonal and other odd shapes may constantly lead one into some problem or the other. Square and rectangular plots are good. A family with a round or oblong dining table will suffer disharmony and end up not eating together.
- Blocking off the North-east (Eeshan) portion of the house/industry restricts the inflow of the blessings of God. It leads to tension, quarrel and insufficient growth of the inhabitants; especially the children.
- In an industry, any fault, ditch, broken part in the direction of North-east result in a handicapped child for the owner.
- Having improper position of the entrance/obstruction in front of the gate can reduce the prosperity.
- Improper position of the bed room or bed brings unhappiness in the married life. It also causes disturbed sleep.

- A water body or source should be in the east or north-east of the plot. Having a water body in the South-east/South portion of the house can cause damage to the male child or the wife of the owner. An underground water tank in the South-west can be fatal to the head of the family or the industry's owner.
- More open space in the north or east gives name, fame and prosperity. Leaving more space on the south-west side in the house can adversely affect the male members, whereas in industry it leads to financial loss and disputes amongst partners.
- Having a toilet/fireplace in the north-east corner of the house or industry can ruin it financially.
- A depression in the south-west can result in serious illness to the inhabitants whereas a depression in the north-west causes enmity and litigation. The depression in the south portion of the building restricts growth besides financial problems.
- Extension in the south-west may result in loss of health, money and other insurmountable problems whereas an extension in the south-east may lead to fire, accidents, theft and litigation.
- Heavy machinery has to be installed in the south-west in the factory.
- Finished products are to be kept in the north-west corner. It would help quick movement of the stocks and early recovery there off.
- Transformers, generators, motors, boilers, furnaces, oil engines etc. should be kept in the south-east or southern portion of the plot/ building.
- Central space is better left open or used for rituals. The traditional four-sided houses of Kerala and Rajasthan with a central courtyard and verandahs all around, is a model of Vaastu design.
- Although limited options are available to urbanites, benefits can accrue to the society if Vaastu guidelines are followed. An evenly planned construction of a house or a workplace following Vaastu principles is not possible, because of the levels in and around the plot, the plot's shape, the number of roads and their direction. Hence an architect or structural engineer has to work with the available plot and construct the house or the office to suit one's requirements under the given circumstances to provide maximum benefit to the inmates of the building.
- An architect or builder bestowed with the knowledge of Vaastu, designs the building striking a balance between the two and goes on benefiting society— thereby increasing his practice and acceptability manifold.

Colour

One of the first requisites demanded by everyone is satisfying colour schemes or even re-doing of a scheme which has palled or one which has been a disaster. Colour may be needed to brighten, to lighten a room or to counteract too high a ceiling, or to glamourize ordinary furniture.

Anyway, remember the old Cockney dictum popular in London? "A little bit of powder, a little bit of paint/ makes a girl pretty, even if she isn't!"

One finds in nature the seven colours of the rainbow transformed and transmuted into scores of colours to suit not only the room or the house but also your personality and individuality.

Colour, when correctly chosen and applied, can work miracles. It can make a too large room seem cosy, alternately give a sense of space to a too small one. It can brighten a too dark area and tone down the glare in another.

In short, colour is a highly evocative thing and for home-makers, it can prove to be the most inexpensive ingredient that creates a home to your taste. A home where you can live in comfort and which your friends love coming to.

You are all set for a happy home-making adventure, when you think of COLOUR.

Colour schemes fall basically into three groups: Monochrome, Related or Contrasting.

1. **Monochrome:** This scheme, as the name implies, features one basic colour in a variety of shades and textures.

   This colour scheme is beautifully set off with accents of contrasting bright colours in paintings, flower arrangements or dramatically coloured masks, lamp-bases, throw rugs, or the like.

2. **Related schemes:** These are made up of a combination of colours lying close together in the spectrum of the rainbow or the colour wheel. This is an exciting scheme for the person who has a titillating imagination. It can highlight the decor with one piece of sculpture or a painting.

3. **Contrasts:** These are relevant when the colours or their weights are widely different.

A working break-up to colour scheme

The factors which should be kept in mind while designing a colour scheme are the effect of adjacent colours each other and your own reaction to them.

The golden rule would be, avoid monotony and discord. The total effect should be a harmonious whole which is pleasing to the eye and senses.

Harmony is achieved by a combination of colours where they have something in common. This goes for both a Monochromatic or a Related scheme. For a contrasting scheme however, the apparent discord can be made harmonious by the use of one or more intermediate colours.

Adjacent colours and their effects

Colours influence each other by contrast when adjacent. A colour appears lighter when placed against darker shades.

Colours of the violet to green range, contain a high proportion of blue and appear cooler than the green-yellow to red-violet range, which have a high content of yellow. Green appears cool against a bright yellow but warm when surrounded by violet-blue. An interior has to stick to a natural tonal order. To reverse this is to create colour discord.

The Blacks, Greys and Whites: A cool elegance is achieved by grey walls, skirted at floor level with silver and black. They need a darker carpet. Black furniture set off by silver artifacts completes the picture.

Instead of silver and black braids, white and black ones, pale carpet and chrome furniture should be set off with judicious touches of red. A white wall, white furniture and a pale carpet look distinguished. Add touches of yellow and pink to stimulate the scheme.

The Browns, Beiges and Creams: These colours are easy to live with. Dark brown wall with a beige braid can adapt to any monochromatic scheme. The carpet is lighter and a rich effect is achieved by leather furniture. Brown wall with a darker brown braid calls for cream furniture, interspersed by colourful rugs and cushions.

Beige wall with white braid, a pale carpet and pale coloured furniture is made more delightful with accents of colour in accessories and pictures.

The Blues: Blue, repeated gloriously in sea and the limitless sky, is a moody colour and seems to change according to the way it is used. It can be dramatic when teamed with browns or greens and innocent and fresh when teamed with white. Deep blue wall, light blue and dark brown braids, deep blue carpet and light blue furniture is enlivened with touches of white in props. Use the same scheme with green furniture and touches of white, blue and pink in props. Light blue wall with white braid and dark blue carpet is charming with white furniture and green props.

Fabrics and drapes

Fabrics either mill-made or hand-woven are being manufactured in an endless variety of colour and design in the country.

When buying the fabric, one has to make sure that the colour is fast and that it will not shrink. The salesman will tell you if you want to wash and pre-shrink.

The next step is the hanging of curtains and drapes. Curtains can be hung either to the floor or to the window sill. Remember the hanging fabric is likely to stretch at the beginning, so tack the hem before hanging for the first time and allow a few days before doing the final stitching of the hem.

Methods of hanging curtains are basically two, the invisible track or the visible pole. There is quite a variety to choose from. The method of hanging will depend upon the weight of curtains. Tracks bear more weight easily and do not bend as is the wont of rods.

Curtains are expensive. It is more economical in the long run to line the curtains. Lining protects curtains from fading, when exposed to sunlight. Colours remain brighter and fresh longer.

In modern times curtains and drapes are no longer only adjuncts to privacy or against drafts or too bright sunlight, but very much a potent factor in modern decor.

The Window Treatment has to be studied, before you buy the material. On the visual side consider colour, texture, pattern to complement your colour scheme.

If you have a monochromatic scheme, you could have richly patterned curtains in beige, brown and cream in a room with a stark white interior, with a large window looking out at the front, think of a design with bold bright variegated colours which will look like stained glass with the light shining through it at night.

In a room with a related colour scheme, choose your curtains with an eye to complementing the most dominant colour.

A room with buttercup yellow walls in emulsion paint, natural sisal in curtain material looks well-matched. If your window looks out on a terrace, sheer curtains (sill length) will keep the garden view inside.

Alternately, a window with a depressing outlook would gain airy elegance with floor length sheer net curtains to camouflage the outlook.

In a room which gets too much sun, buy material that is not liable to fade. Big floral patterns or patterns with birds look delightful with the light shining through them. A better idea for children's rooms instead of the ubiquitous characters from comics. The same goes for brightly checked curtains and bedspreads.

With dramatic dark on dark and silver-white schemes, curtains and cushions can effectively repeat the pattern.

Small patterns look good in a room with much of waxed wood on floor and wainscoting.

Gingham, which is comparatively cheap, makes delightful curtains for not only the kitchen but for teenagers' rooms, with bedcovers and throw cushions repeating the colour. Finally, curtain material, be it silk, velvet, hand-weaves, or mill-made, should never be skimped. Enough fullness means elegance in curtains and drapes.

Light is essential

A well set up room done up in a colour scheme of your choice will lose its salient points if there is no proper lighting. A wrongly lit room falls flat.

Natural or artificial light affects colours, forms and textures, so in planning lighting attention needs to be given to both day and night aspects. Light—our friend. Away with the pendent bulb, hanging from the ceiling. Lights are there to serve for the specific purpose you need them and these needs are varied. For reading, for make-up purposes, for reading in bed, for cooking, for sewing, for television, for pictures and sculptures, even for cupboards and closets or those beloved indoor plants, there is the need for different kinds of lights.

Fortunately, the single bulb hanging from a flex has been replaced with a whole array of illuminating equipment in table lamps, standard lamps, picture lights, fluorescent lamps, spot lights, down lights. Your prized possessions, whether a picture, a piece of sculpture or a display can be highlighted to breathe new life into them, with spot lighting. Pictures should be down lighted for the maximum visual value. Lighting can correct the faults of a room, if it is too high, too low, too small or large. For instance an uplighter using a lamp placed on the floor against a wall makes the ceiling appear lower.

Functionally, correct placing of lighting is imperative in the work-areas, the kitchen, the study, the children's room and the dressing table.

Here is a simplified classification for your guidance:

a) General
b) **Directional/Two-directional:** This applies to two-way lighting on the stairs and the porch or hall for safety.
c) **Reflected:** This is particularly useful for relaxed reading. Diffused light reflected from a wall is devoid of glare yet bright for reading.
d) **Spot Lighting:** For getting the most value of your prized collections, sculptures or accessories.
e) **Down lighting:** Essential for the proper display of pictures.
f) **Decorative:** Optional lighting for special festivities.

The choice of lights should therefore depend upon functional aspect and the use of specific places in the house. Lighting is an important element in decor and requires careful planning.

Indoor plants

People had no need of the comfort and joy of indoor plants when urbanisation had not spread. Now it is a must. Foliage house plants need not be confined to the traditional philodendron and money plant. You have an endless assortment of sizes and shapes to choose from, plants of varied textured leaves and lovely hues.

It is best to have crotons, which will lend colour to your indoors or have arica palms, coleus, or exotic varieties like monstera, etc. inside your home.

Plant care

A house plant needs a clean pot, a loose-textured soil mixture and drainage materials such as clay shards of broken pots or large pebbles. Don't be worried if your plant loses a few leaves, because this is essentially a survival mechanism.

Allow the yellow scarred leaf to drop by itself, this way before following it will seal the point so that there is no wound to catch infections.

Watch your plant with loving care, which means adjust your watering to its needs. More house plants die of over-watering. Also sun it occasionally, it may droop with too dark a location.

Light is the power source by which leaves produce sugars and starches to feed all parts of a plant, so see that the plants get their vital food, light. Fortunately, tropical indoor plants need low light levels.

However, the light need of various houseplants vary according to their species. To summarize broadly, the crotons, coleuses and ivies require full sun or the bright reflected light bouncing off a light coloured wall.

The intermediate plants such as Begonias, Dracaenas thrive in partial, shade or light coming through a sheer curtain: Ferns survive in indirect shadowless light. If your plant is near a window, keep turning it to allow it to grow symmetrically.

What Decoration Achieves!

1. The magic of colour, and the effect of lights and lighting creates a mood and atmosphere in the house. It converts the brick and mortar walls into an aesthetic room.
2. Drapes, curtains, upholstery and carpets enhance the decor of your home, giving it an aura of plush comfort.
3. In decoration, the desired effect can be obtained with colour. A small room

looks large with light decorations while deep rich colours contract a large room.

4. A low ceiling will look higher if its in a lighter shade of the wall colour.

5. A room with poor light brightens up when the walls are papered with a cheerful sunny shade with a glossy surface.

6. A room into which strong sunlight pours in may be made subdued by decorating it in soothing shades such as blues and greens.

7. A narrow room will look broader if the ceiling and upper part of the walls are in a deeper shade than the lower portion. This sense of breadth is increased if the floor is covered with a plain carpet and the skirting painted in the same shade.

8. Adding a mirror to one wall of the room gives the illusion of depth.

The Importance of Having a Neat Entrance

In most houses and even smaller flats, there is either a spacious hall or even a small one which serves as the entrance to the house. Everyone from tradesmen to honoured guests enter the bungalow/flat from this entrance, hence it should be neatly maintained.

Both for reasons of security and for ventilation it is an asset to have a double door at the entrance so that one can see the person who wishes to enter. By having a mesh door through which one can see the person who wishes to enter, one can both regulate entry and simultaneously not jeopardise the security of the house by allowing unwanted salesmen or visitors to come in. In case there is no provision for a double door, one would be well advised to have a keyhole or a chain on the door so that the visitor can be identified before granted access to the house.

Keys, umbrellas, raincoats row of untidy shoes on a shoe stand, children's bicycles, cricket bats, and rollers skates, as also school bags and shopping bags are frequently placed at the entrance for convenience.

However, it does not give an aesthetic appearance to visitors. Essentials should be neatly arranged or if they can be stored in a cupboard, that is the best solution to a neat entrance.

While a coir or rubber mat may be placed at the entrance to the house, there should be no loose rugs or small carpets at the entrance as when people are in a hurry these become a safety hazard as they slip.

The walls can be utilised to hang keys and if woollen coats or raincoats have to be kept, a cupboard should be made for this purpose. The walls should otherwise be aesthetically decorated with a suitable painting or statuette so that visitors get a good impression of the house owners.

Managing the exit

The back entrance of the house or flat which is frequently used by tradesmen, domestic help and children coming in from play, should also be neatly kept. Apart from having a mat on which dirty shoes may be wiped, the back entrance should also be organised so that empty crates, bottles, tins, cleaning equipment, and so on, do not clutter the exit. Things should be stored neatly so that they do not pose a hazard to those who are coming in or exiting the house from this point.

The Drawing Room or Living Room

The drawing room or living room is the main room of a house as it mirrors the personality of the owners. The decor of the drawing room, living room parlour or lounge reflects the tastes and interests of those living in the house. It is the one room in the house where outsiders have access as it serves as the centre of social activity. Good decor reflects the personality of the people who live in the home. Just as each person is distinctive, so too, the decor should be distinctive. It is not a mere question of expanse and expensive fittings, furniture and furnishings. Rather the entire room should be in harmony, not only with the furniture and furnishings in this room but also with the rest of the house. For example, if the living room is very small, then the furniture used in it should be light so that the room does not look cluttered with outsized sofas and coffee tables. It is literally a question of cutting the cloth according to the coat, the furniture and the objets d'art should be placed or purchased only after ascertaining the size and style of the room.

There is nothing that makes a room or a single grouping of furniture look more inviting than the appearance for which it is used and enjoyed. To achieve this effect think of the activities that go on in the house and arrange groups or combinations of groups that will take care of all of them. For informal entertaining, chairs should be grouped in a way that two or more can sit easily together. For reading, there can be a lamp, a shelf for books and a place for magazines. A comfortable chair with a reading lamp can be kept for this purpose.

The drawing room should have upholstered furniture sufficient to seat all members of the family plus two to four guests. Each major chair should be within easy reach of a table having an ashtray and should be placed in a way that those entering the room can be seen and welcomed. Tables may contain lamps, books and other accessories both for utility and decoration. Table and chairs should harmonise in weight and style and seating furniture should be arranged either parallel or at right angles to the walls. Chairs and tables may also be placed diagonally whenever possible, units should be balanced with pieces of equal or similar design. Pairs of chairs, table, lamps help in this. The entire room should be linked together by means of something which is in common either by the colour of the wood, the style of the furniture, the colour scheme or some motif which blends the decor into one uniform whole. Even when there are different styles of furniture they should be placed in such a way that it matches with the rest of the pieces in the room.

Lighting

Apart from the natural light which streams into the room it is necessary to have artificial lighting that enhances the furniture and its accessories. There are ostentatious crystal chandeliers which are difficult to clean. There are recessed bulbs placed in the ceiling, standard lamps, table lamps, reading lamps and lamps to highlight a painting or a shelf of objets d'art. Although convenient in terms of the low wattage of electricity, it is advisable not to have tubelights or fluorescent lights in the drawing room as indirect lighting gives a better appearance to the room. The style of the lamps should match with the other decoration. The general lighting should be so designed that by switching them on or off the desired amount of lighting—bright, medium or dim can be achieved.

Floor or table lamps

These should be placed at focal points of interest to attract attention towards some picture hanging on the wall or a flower arrangement. Table lamps can be placed on tables, but if the table is low and only 22" from the floor, the lamps height including the shade should be 32". While high lamps look attractive with open tops so that light can be distributed, lamps that are below the eye level of a standing person should be covered from the top so that the bulb is concealed.

The appropriate material used for lamp shades are fabrics, handmade paper, raffia, reed and even metals and plastic.

Doing it up

Since the drawing room is a place where we entertain friends, it should be done up in pleasing colours with sturdy fabrics. After making a floor plan of the room, it is then safer to decide what to buy, what one already has and the budget for the room. The room should be planned by standing at the entrance as this is the view that all visitors will get on entering.

The drawing room has to be done up according to the needs and available space in the house. For those who have a special study or library, it may be more convenient to install the television and V.C.R, and books in that room. The stereo system, however, can be placed in the living room as gentle music in the background is always conducive to both relaxation and conversation. On the other hand, if the television is placed in the drawing room it may distract visitors and so compelling is its presence, that conversation ceases and all attention is focused on the T.V. screen. Books, while serving as an appropriate component of any living room, are also a source of distraction as visitors frequently get involved in browsing through the books. Sometimes a friend seeks to borrow a book, often it is not returned and then one gets into the unpleasantness of borrowing and securing the return of the book. If one has a library or study room, books and the television as also the computer are best placed in that room.

If lack of space necessitates placing of the television, V.C.R. and stereo system in the living room then it is best to have a wall unit in which these can be placed, along with a book area and a small bar. In selecting a built-in cabinet for the living room it is best to have shelves which are between 12" and 15" in depth.

The bar must be at least 1 ft. high so that large bottles can fit in. There should be a shelf for glasses as well, preferably with a rim, so that they do not slip out.

Upholstered furniture

When buying upholstered furniture, certain features should be carefully checked. Firstly it should be comfortable to sit on and should be the right height to sit on. The cost of this furniture depends on its inner construction. Two identical pieces of upholstered furniture are sometimes entirely different in quality and cost. Upholstered furniture consists of five parts—frame, seat, springs, fillings and fabric.

The upholstery fabric should be bought carefully not only because it is expensive but also because the entire impact of the room depends on it. Fabrics cover a considerable area so they have to be selected on the basis of their texture, colour, pattern and expense. While upholstery fabric and draperies reflect the taste of those who buy them, a simple rule to follow is that if there is a great deal of patterned upholstery, the drapes should be plain and vice versa so that there are no clashing patterns all around. Light coloured upholstery fabrics give an airy and spacious look but light colours are difficult to maintain, especially with houses where there are small children. Earthy colours suggest the outdoors, while dark colours and small patterns give a cosy appearance.

While some people are able to change their furnishings frequently, for those who are unable to, it is best to select durable, natural coloured fabrics for both drapes and upholstery.

Slip covers or chairs which require just a cushion, the rest being wood work can be changed more frequently and also washed or dry cleaned. Different sets of cushion covers can be made for winter and summer so that the living room gets a new look depending on the season.

To obtain a cool look for summer, heavy rugs should be removed and replaced by durries, reed matting or smaller throw rugs. Heavy winter draperies can be replaced with light summer drapes. Slip covers in soothing colours, such as green, blue and white should cover upholstered furniture, both as a summer change as well as to give protection against dust and fading.

Carpets

Whether antique Persian rugs, handwoven Kashmiri carpets, machine-made carpets, durries or jute matting, some form of carpeting is necessary in a living room as it lends a complete, finished look to the room.

A few benefits of carpets are that they absorb noise, make the floor and protect a person from falling down the stairs. The most important impact of a carpet is that it creates an impression of luxury and establishes the colour scheme in a room.

Whereas wall-to-wall carpeting is a necessity in foreign countries to keep out the bitter cold, in India it is not strictly required especially in residential accommodation. Rugs are more easily handled and easier to clean. They can be shifted from room to room and also house to house during transfers.

Whereas wall-to-wall carpeting gives an illusion that the room is larger, covers irregularities in the floor and creates a feeling of luxury, warmth and quiet as it diffuses noise made by footsteps, it is nevertheless difficult to clean and maintain, subject to stains, especially in a house in which there are small children.

A **rug** is a single piece floor covering made with a pattern and which has a border with a fringe.

A **room-sized rug** is one that covers within 12 inches or less from the walls on all sides.

An **area rug** is one which is placed in a large room to demarcate a certain area.

A **scatter rug** is a small rug that is used to complement the decor in a room and is placed in front of the bed or dressing table etc.

An **accent rug** is placed on a wall-to-wall carpet, which is usually plain, to give some colour and complement the colour scheme in a room.

For low budgets felt, jute, coir, cotton or even *chatais* are available to enhance the decor of the room. An advantage of area rugs or scatter rugs is that furniture can be placed around it, rather than on it. When heavy furniture is placed on the carpet it causes a certain amount of wear and tear on it, hence the furniture should be shifted around periodically and the carpet brushed so that it does not get damaged.

Objets d'art in the living room—paintings, sculpture, porcelain and crystal are some of the accessories that are placed in the drawing room. Although tastes differ from person to person, it may be noted that calendars, children's toys, plastic decorations and flowers do not constitute appropriate decoration for living room as these give a tacky appearance to the room. While expensive accessories are not essential, and nor is it necessary to have the room resemble a museum or art gallery, the choice of objects to be kept in the living room should be aesthetic and appropriate. For example, paintings of nude women, sculptures showing an exaggeratedly voluptuous female form are also not in good taste for the drawing room. The right accessories not only enhance the appearance of the room but also reflect the good taste and artistic sensibilities of the owner. The objets d'art and paintings should blend in with and enhance the decor and overall colour scheme of the room.

To avoid clutter, one can rotate the accessories if one has too many so that the visitors are always treated to something new when they come in. The living room accessories can be rotated according to the season with warm-coloured lamps and dark oil paintings for the winter, gay fragile vases and vivid water colours for the spring and crystal flower containers and figurines in white porcelain for the summer.

While accessories lend character and reflect the personality of the owner, too many homes get cluttered after years of random accumulation. Periodical removal of unnecessary objects is wise.

Delicate porcelain, crystal and other fragile items may be placed in a glass covered cabinet or wall shelves with glasses so that they are protected from both dust and damage.

The Dining Room or Dining Area

Whereas some houses may have a separate dining room, which is ideal, others may have a combined drawing-cum-dining room. The dining area or dining room has special decoration requirement from that of the drawing room. Whereas the drawing room is used to entertain visitors the dining room is constantly used by members of the family several times a day. In a house where there are small children there is a constant danger of food spill on the floor, therefore, it is best to keep this area free from carpeting. Even scatter rugs are a hazard as the housewife or servant may slip on it while rushing in and out with the food.

The furniture and decor must be adapted to the size, lighting, proximity to the living room and the amount and type of entertaining contemplated. Expandible tables are available in drop-leaf, extension console or dining room types in which leaves are inserted. Folding chairs may be stored so that the problem of crowding too many chairs into a limited space is eliminated.

If the dining area is connected with the living room, the decor and the rug should blend with it.

Placement of furniture

While the dining table is generally placed in the centre of the room with dining chairs all around it, if the room is very small, there is provision for a folding dining table that would require just 120 cm × 80 cm of spare wall area. The table would seat five people and it can be fixed to the wall with four screws and pulled out whenever required. It becomes a decorative wall piece when not in use.

Dining tables can be wooden, wooden with sunmica top, cane with glass top and a wooden base and marble top table. If there are children in the house it is best to ensure that the table has rounded rather than sharp edges so that it is not a hazard to the child. A marble top table is easy to keep clean and is also durable, though not so easily transportable.

Side boards

Side boards can be used on one side of the wall to keep cutlery and crockery. Alternatively, if there is a wall unit then glasses, plates and decorative items may be placed in them. One drawer can be kept to store placements and other table linen. The top of the side board may be decorated with candle stands, flowers, decanters, silver fruit stands and other appropriate bric-a-brac. Additional storage space may be provided by a corner cupboard. The bar is frequently kept in the dining room. A tea-wagon or tea-trolley placed in the dining room serves as a great serving aid.

Table settings

Table settings will be discussed at length in a later chapter. For daily meals there may be table cloths or table mats. In homes where there are small children it may be more practical to have table mats as a table cloth may frequently be tugged by the child leading to a dangerous situation in which glasses and plates may fall to the floor causing injury and damage.

Table mats are available in all shapes, sizes and materials. Many use plastic mats as these are easy to maintain and, therefore, convenient for daily use. However, when guests come, table mats give a better appearance. Mats can be made of cloth, jute, bamboo and can be purchased to match with the colour of the crockery.

Table decoration

In those dining rooms where the table is placed at the centre, may be decorated with a flower vase placed at the centre. For parties, silver candle stands or porcelain candle stands may be placed on either side of a central floral piece. Small porcelain/pottery animal figures may be placed around this floral centre piece. Alternatively a fruit stand with fruits can form a central decoration piece for change on a daily basis.

The Bed Room

A bed room constitutes possibly the most important element of a house. It is around this space that members of the family unwind after a hard day's work. It serves as a retreat and refuge from the outside world, a room in which one can really be oneself. There are no do's and don't in a bedroom and one can decorate it in any way that one feels like. Comfort and convenience for the user is the chief buzz word for this room.

The main pieces of furniture in a bedroom are, of course, a bed, a side table, cupboards, a dressing table, chairs to enable a seating arrangement, a writing desk and possibly a television and stereo system.

While the bed may simply be of wood, it may also include a frame, headboard, four posts (especially if mosquito nets are to be used), or even a canopy. Some bedrooms have no bed but consist of some thick mattresses placed on the floor. Others have elaborate headboards made of wood and are plain, carved, painted, or even upholstered. The headboard sets the style of the room and may be done in leather, satin, chintz, silk, gingham or rough handlooms. Some headboards have built-in book shelves and a lighting system to facilitate bed time reading.

Dressing tables may be simple or elaborate, with three way mirrors and drawers to keep one's cosmetics and other things such as combs, hairbands, lipsticks and so on.

A full-length mirror on the closet or entrance door facilitates dressing. Lighting in a bedroom should be provided according to one's requirements. There could be some general lighting and then reading lights, lights over the dressing table and at the desk. While floor rugs can be colourful, they should harmonize with the curtains which may be of silk, organdy, handloom or printed floral cottons. The bedspreads add colour and character to the room.

Paintings, posters and a desk calendar where one enters the engagements for the day are useful in the bedroom. Also, an extension of the telephone, along with on address book are often needed in the bedroom.

A seating arrangement with a table can be laid alone the bed and stacked with current newspapers and magazines.

Many beds have built-in storage space which is useful for putting away extra pillows and mattresses. Mattresses and pillows must be chosen with considerable care as a mattress which is not comfortable viz., either too soft or too hard will give rise to back aches. The same is true of pillows. Some people are allergic to the cotton in pillows so they should choose the new ones made of non-allergic foam.

While the earlier trend was to have plain white bed sheets and pillow cases, still followed in five star hotels, floral prints are very attractive and are less likely to show stains and dirt. There is no limit to one's imagination in doing up one's bedroom so that it is both aesthetic, functional and yet a reflection of one's own needs and personality.

Wall cupboards or steel cupboards are essential to keep one's clothes safely and in an organised manner. Some houses have built-in wooden closets in which one portion is made of steel with a safe so that valuables can be kept in them. For men's clothes especially, a cupboard with provision for hanging clothes is essential. Sarees and salwar kameezes may also be hung. The other method is to fold sarees and keep them in neat rows, with blouses and petticoats kept in separate piles. As far as possible, shoes should not be kept in the same cupboard as the clothes, but there can be either a separate shoe cupboard or provision for shoes to be kept under the cupboard.

The Children's Room

Here the colour scheme should be strong and simple and furniture sturdy, accident proof and easy to keep clean. There should be ample provision for keeping toys and books and walls should be painted with washable paint. Paintings can be bright wooden cutouts of cartoon characters and animals can be used. Pictorial charts and maps may be of interest to the child. A large bulletin-board would enable the child to put up interesting pictures and messages.

Rugs in a child's room should be made of easily washable material. Furniture should include a junior bed with removable side rails if necessary. Alternatively there can be a full-sized bed with a firm mattress, a chip proof or inexpensive table and one to three chairs, a clothes chest, closet and desk for the school-going child. A fundamental rule in furnishing a child's bedroom is that children grow quickly and their needs change from year to year. Too many pieces of miniature furniture may be a waste in the long run. In a nursery, the child's cot constitutes the central piece of furniture. A chest of drawers to hold the child's clothes and toys and an easy chair/rocking chair for the mother are required. The furniture and curtains in the nursery can be in gay colours.

As the child grows he can use a bigger bed and toys should be kept within easy reach so that he can keep himself amused. If siblings share a room, bunker beds which are double decker beds are real space savers.

School children will require a study table, a reading lamp and book shelves.

Teenagers have their own ideas about room decoration and may favour posters and pin-ups of their favourite film or sport stars. One should avoid confrontation with the teenager on this subject and can give in to their whims and fancies as long as their suggestions are not outrageous in terms of taste and propriety.

When two siblings share the room there may be a lot of conflict and irritations but there is no better way of preparing the child for the future than by encouraging him or her to share.

The Guest Room

The guest room which used to be an intrinsic feature of all big houses is increasingly rare in small apartment. Hence, it can be a dual purpose room which can be put to use throughout the year. The purpose of the room is to make the guest feel welcome and comfortable. It enables both the guest and the host to maintain privacy.

Furniture for this room should be selected with due care. A sofa-cum-bed is a viable alternative than having two beds. There should be a bedside table with a lamp and if possible a table for suitcases. If there is a built-in cupboard, provision should be made for the guests to hang their clothes. A mirror fitted over a desk should have some letter papers, a pen, a candle stand with candle and matches in case of a power cut and a few magazines.

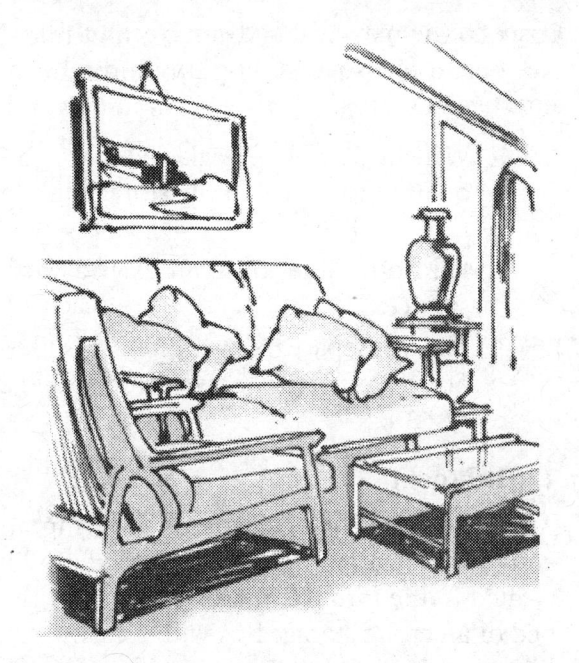

The guest room may have two easy chairs so that the guest feels a gracious welcome.

The drapes, bedspreads and rugs can be in some pleasing colours. A waste paper basket must be placed in the room.

The Study

The study should cater to intellectual requirements of the family members. It should balance the dual needs of relaxation and mental stimulation.

The main pieces of furniture should be:
- a desk
- a straight back chair
- a wall shelving unit
- a diwan

The wall shelving unit may be used for audio-visual equipment such as the television, V.C.R, music system and so on.

The computer may be placed either on the desk or on a separate table. Space for other electronic equipment such as a fax machine can also be provided for.

It is important to pay attention to the electrical connections while installing these so that there are no safety hazards. The wiring should be insulated and placed along the walls so that room looks neat and chances of getting shocks are negligible. If required one should take the assistance of an electrician to install the gadgets correctly.

Bean bags can also be placed to provide seating.

The wall shelving unit should have provision for keeping books, photo-albums, audio and video cassettes and CDs which should preferably be kept covered so as not to collect dust. This unit could either:

- be kept open;
- have sliding glass panes; or
- wooden doors.

Lists of audio-video cassettes, CDs and computer floppies should be made either:

- subject wise; or
- in an alphabetical order.

The walls may either have paintings or family photographs. The floor may be carpeted or have scattered rugs.

A diwan if placed in this room should have colourful cushions and could serve as an extra bed in case of guests.

The Utility Room or Store Room

In earlier houses, every kitchen had a store room. In this room extra rations such as rice, sugar, pulses, etc. were kept. Today not all houses have a store room attached to the kitchen due to lack of space. Kitchen cabinets however are a substitute to the store room. However some houses do have a utility room which can be used for ironing clothes, keeping extra suitcases, extra bedding, children's bicycles and so on.

The rule here is that there should be a place for everything in the house and everything should be in its place, therefore, the store room must be de-gunned at regular intervals. Old newspapers, bottles, shoes, clothing, books etc. must be collected and sold off periodically to the "kabadiwala."

Storage Ideas

Making every inch work

Ingenious storage ideas to make good use of nooks and crannies requires imagination and planning.

With accomodation problems on the rise and more and more people living in cramped apartments, space is at a premium today. Gone are the days of large storage rooms lined with steel trunks and pickle jars. In this world of compact living, even a separate store seems to be an unaffordable luxury. Yet, to use a given space to the maximum advantage, all that we need are a few space saving tips and a bit of effective planning.

1. Wall area, an often neglected space, can be used to create ample storage in the form of shelving.
2. Fold out table tops can extend work surfaces.
3. The dead space below staircases is used effectively with a two-tier storage system.

The bedroom

Apart from built-in cupboards covering an entire wall area and loft, extra storage can be created in the form of drawer units under the bed or an entire storage box with a cushioned lid for seating can be supported on castors.

1. In the children's room, bunker beds use up the floor area of one bed to accomodate two.
2. Shelves and even fold out writing desks could be incorporated along with toy display units and drawers for the usual knick-knacks.
3. Book shelves, too, could find a place in the unit while hollow cubes form a storage unit with the option of adding

up the units in different permutations and colours to add variety. The entire shelving unit in the children's room could be painted over in bright colours with games, cartoons and fairy tale characters stuck on to make an interesting feature.

4. Another space saving device in the kid's room is having two beds of unequal height with one bed on rollers sliding under the other during the day time. During study hours, writing desks could be folded out of the wall shelving unit to use up the empty space.

Bathroom

1. Apart from cabinets below the wash-basin counter, storage space can be created in a number of ways inside the toilet. Because most bathrooms are small to begin with, the storage problems are magnified but with simple additions in the toilet, one could go a long way.
2. Check the unused wall space available. Even the wall area behind the water closet, which we generally give up on, can be used to provide much needed storage space. The entire wall area behind the toilet seat could be converted into a shelving unit with the w.c. itself fitting into a larger size open shelf. Extra rolls of toilet paper, towels and medicines could be stocked here, along with reading material. For those in the habit of reading in the loo, the shelving unit could be converted into a veritable library.
3. Another usable area is the wall above the wash-basin. A dressing cabinet to store cosmetics and medicines with a mirror fixed on to the shutter could be very helpful.

Similar ideas could work wonders in the laundry room.

Not only do they help keep the laundry room tidy, they can also speed up the work and make washing a pleasant job.

1. A shelving unit-cum-hanger rod suspended from the ceiling helps save floor space and provides a unit for hanging up clothes to dry.
2. It could also stock detergents and scrubbing brushes.
3. A wall shelving system could fold out to form an ironing board with an inbuilt plug for the iron. A soft board mounted on one of the shutters could make an innovative tackboard for pinning up messages, monthly planners and important notes.
4. Within the laundry room, a double wardrobe system helps store clothes which are not in season. With one stationary component acting as a cupboard, the other swings in to create a shutter, providing double the storage.

Within the house, effective storage areas could come in the form of wall partitions. Used as visual room dividers and also useful in drawing-cum-dining area, the entire full height partition could be made of shelves for displaying curio pieces. A still more flexible room divider is one which can be taken apart completely and reassembled at a fast pace. Cutting a few notches and grooves into the planks helps the members fit in together to form a wall shelf or room divider as the situation demands.

In rooms with high ceilings, a mezzanine loft can be added to increase the usable floor space. The space below the staircase can be used to stock books in open shelves or just about any extra item through a method of pull out shelving compartment, sliding on rollers.

Inside the kitchen, similar space saving options could come in the form of swing out double shelving units and cabinet shutters opening out to form hinged informal dining tables. When not in use, the table can be folder back and the floor space saved. Magnets help display messages and recipes on the refrigerator door and adding semi-circular shelves to the door of an existing corner cabinet could turn a dead end space into an easy to reach usable area.

Use a counter space for keeping all electrical gadgets like mixers, grinders etc. and provide plug points and overhead cabinets to store the appliances when not in use. Wall mounted shelves could store utensils, condiments and also a few recipe books. Another welcome addition could be a pullout shelving unit on castors to serve as a serving trolley when needed or tucked safely inside a cabinet.

All these units can be made out of 3/4" block board finished with teak lipping and laminated or duco painted to give a sleek look. For areas not prone to heavy usage, fabric could be clad over the board to add an interesting texture in bedrooms and living areas with colours selected to match the upholstery.

In order to economize on space, it is better to use sliding instead of swing out shutters for cabinets as well as doors. Adjustable sizes of shelves too make the entire storage system more effective.

■■

CHAPTER-7

Etiquette for All Occasions

Envisage a scene in which a couple enters a temple dressed in a mini skirt and a suit, screaming and shouting! The scene shifts and a couple sits gloomily at a marriage party. Well what's the common point? They are all doing and saying the wrong things at the wrong place and at the wrong time. People's image of us is formed not only by external appearance (clothes, grooming etc.) but also by our behaviour. This chapter deals with different social situations in which one may be placed and the etiquette attached to each of them.

Marriage Festivities

A marriage is a union between a man and a woman which is socially recognised and established for the procreation of children. It is a joyous occasion and marks the coming together not only of two people but also of two families and sometimes two communities as in the case of intercaste and inter-community marriages. Here are some pointers to be kept in mind while attending or arranging a wedding.

Generally the bride's family decides upon the style of wedding

- A bride's trousseau includes apart from clothes, jewellery and toilet articles, household articles e.g. dinner set etc.
- Invitations for a wedding should be sent at least three weeks in advance to compensate for postal delays.
- A family member or a close friend should be put in charge of accepting and cataloguing gifts. This helps avoiding confusion and makes the task of sending thank you letters easier.
- Traditional attire may be donned by family members for the wedding ceremony.
- The shehnai whether live or recorded sets the mood for the festivities ahead.
- If the marriage is a civil marriage it takes place in the forenoon. Four witnesses are present. However, everyone may be invited to celebrate afterwards.
- A formal wedding reception requires the host and hostess to receive the guests at the entrance. The refreshment stalls should be easily accessible. Provisions should be made for both vegetarians and non-vegetarians.

Paying Condolence

- A member of the bereaved family must take it upon himself to inform all the relatives and friends. This task is made easier if a notification is given in the newspaper.
- If you cannot attend the funeral make it a point to attend the secondary rites which usually take place after 3 to 15 days.
- Somebody should be placed in charge of making a note of the condolence

messages. These addresses should be handwritten.

- All messages of condolence are addressed to the person who is related to the deceased. Avoid using words like 'died', 'death' etc. in a condolence note.
- Floral garlands and offerings symbolise and respect for the deceased.

Man is by nature so tuned that he shuns sorrow, grief or unhappiness. If it lay within his power he would exclude all misfortunes, miseries and unpleasant experiences form his day-to-day life. But sorrow and human afflictions—mental, emotional and physical—are woven fine in the web of life. However unwanted, sorrow is a basic ingredient of man's life. There is no escape from it. Ghalib, the great Urdu poet of the nineteenth century, regarded sorrow so integral a part of life as to be synonymous with it.

Sorrow or pain which one experiences as a result of some sudden calamity or personal loss or bereavement or some unexpected shock that leaves a person totally humiliated and shattered. It might seem unbearable, but such experiences have a positive side to them. They jolt you out of a state of unreality and bring you face to face with the fundamental truth that life is not one extended or rather one uninterrupted, unending melody which you can just sit, listen to and enjoy. Life can hurt.

And the experiences which hurt us most, are really the ones which teach us most. Such experiences bring wisdom though in the process they cause us much hurt. It was the sight of human suffering, pain and the all enveloping sorrow which drove the Buddha to seek enlightenment and it was through long penance that he achieved divinity.

Sorrow is a genuine emotion. Pleasure or joy may have many faces. Sorrow has only one. Because it has a true and honest face there can be nothing pretentious about it. "Behind joy and laughter," said Oscar Wilde, "there may be a temperament coarse, hard and callous. But behind sorrow there is sorrrow. Pain, unlike pleasure, wears no mask."

Suffering has a humanising effect on man. Sorrow and suffering, in fact, break the barriers of the self, cleanse the soul and impart it a touch of divinity.

Why is it, one might ask, that it is mostly good people who suffer most? Why is it that those who are evil have all the pleasures and comforts of life while those who are noble have to eat their bread in sorrow? Why is their lot so full of miseries?

Maybe the bad are bad and having fallen low as human beings, don't deserve to be tested. It is only the good whom adversity tries so that the bad among the good can be segregated, for the true character of a person reveals itself only in times of adversity. A really virtuous person is he who has stood the test of adversity.

Anniversaries

- While inviting people for an anniversary it is not necessary to use a formal invitation card.
- However, the 25th (silver anniversary), 50th (golden) and 75th (diamond anniversary) are milestones and are celebrated on a larger scale.
- The 25th wedding anniversary is usually organised by the couple's children. The invitations to such an occasion may be a formal one. Either a reception or a dinner is organised.

- The golden anniversary is usually organised by the couple's children or the younger colleagues of the couple. The invitations to such an event should be specially designed and engraved.
- Some people might even celebrate their silver, golden and diamond anniversaries as a marriage. The couple is made to go through the marriage rites again.
- Make a note of the anniversaries in your family/friends carefully. Remember to pick up the phone and wish the couple in question. You can also send a bouquet of flowers if it is an ordinary anniversary (i.e. other than the silver, golden and diamond anniversaries).

Correct Telephone Manners

Have you ever been at the receiving end of a loud volley of rude mutterings. If you have dialed a wrong number? Well one might think that while on a phone you are not under scrutiny. This is far from the truth. Your voice on the phone automatically helps the caller form an impression about you, about how you look and about your temperament:

- Make it a point to sound cheerful on the phone as far as possible. Make your first word ëhello' after picking up the phone bright and sunny.
- Do not inflict your moods, depression and problems on the person who is calling.
- Never bang the telephone down.
- If you have dialed a wrong number, apologise. Remember you are the one who has committed a blunder. Avoid being aggressive.
- While receiving a wrong number do not be rude. Listen to the caller patiently and inform him of his mistake as politely as possible.

Entertaining Successfully

Man is a social being, said a famous scholar. Indeed, it is true. All of us form a part of society. Proper, close interaction between members of a group or community help making the society a close knit one. In ancient times people would visit each other's houses on a regular basis. Members of the same village were like family members and would frequently dine together. With advancement in technology and the fast pace of our lives we now have to make time for social interaction. Frequent and informal visits have now been replaced by formal get-togethers and cocktail parties. Informal gatherings have become somewhat infrequent and rare. It is essential thus that one learns not only the art of being a good host but also a good guest.

Entertaining in modern conditions are not only determined by one's own desire but may also be necessitated by one's profession. Whether one is in the corporate sector or in the public sector or a diplomat, entertaining successfully helps one to carve a niche for oneself.

Arranging a Party

To make any event successful one has to plan in advance. Here are some pointers which one should keep in mind:

Select guests who mix well while drawing up your guest list. Ensure that there are people with common interests. Avoid inviting people who are not on good terms.

Your gathering could get extremely boring if there are not enough people around. It is better to have at least one or two couples unless you are very close to the couple or guest invited or you have a special reason for inviting them alone.

While making the guest list limit the number of guests to a number which you can manage comfortably.

Make sure you are able to give each of your guests individual attention.

Dinner for close friends is served in a buffet style while for business associates or while honouring somebody it is a formal sit down meal.

When you plan the seating make sure that each guest has enough elbow room.

Sending Invitations

Now that you have got the guest list out of the way, your next task will be that of sending the invitations. Here are a few pointers:

If they are intimate or close friends then a telephone call is enough. However, a personal invitation is always appreciated.

Invitation cards must be mailed at least three weeks in advance to account for postal delays.

The invitation should include the name and address of the host/hostess, the date and time of the party. If there is a dress code then that too should be specified.

For occasions such as cocktail parties, reception, formal dance, formal lunch or dinner party, wedding a formal invitation which is engraved on white or off-white paper is used. However, increasingly coloured paper with borders are also being used.

All formal invitation cards should have 'RSVP' written on it. This ensures a firm response.

Make sure you give clear directions to the guests. This could be facilitated by giving a map on the card or alternatively putting bright signposts along the way.

Give your telephone number on the card so that your guests can call in case of an emergency.

Planning the Menu

While planning the menu keep in mind the dietary constraints or requirements of the guests.

Make provisions for both vegetarian and non-vegetarian guests.

Do not experiment on your guests. Serve dishes which you have tried and tested.

Your menu should be such that serving is easy.

Prepare as many dishes in advance as possible.

However, perishable dishes like salads, raita should be prepared and served fresh.

The dishes that need to be reheated should be slightly undercooked e.g. quiche, meat curry.

Table Settings/Crockery

Mealtimes should be a pleasant experience not only for parties but for daily purposes also. It is probably the only time the family is together. A correctly set table presents a unified and harmonious picture with all the elements being well co-ordinated. Good lighting if concentrated on the table enhances a well-planned table's beauty.

Dinnerware is the largest accessory of any table and sets the theme for the rest of the table arrangement. It can be of the following types:-

Plastic dinnerware

Earthenware made from a mixture of clays.

Semivitreous ware is opaque and porous

China—real China is superior in beauty and durability to semivitreous ware and earthenware

Fine china—is made of superfine clay. It is thin and appears fragile but is actually hard and resistant to chipping and cracking.

Bone china—is fine China to which bone ash is added to the clay.

Silverware—although it requires less gentle handling than chinaware it should be well taken care off:

* Should be polished regularly.
* Wrap in flannel before storing.
* Do not put too many pieces in a pan for washing as it is liable to scratch other pieces.
* The best care is to use it daily, as daily use prevents the formation of tarnish.

* Do not let silver remain near rubber for any length of time as this results in tarnishing

Glassware—glass is made of white silica sand mixed with a precise amount of potash, lead or lime. Crystal is the finest among glassware and stands out for its transparency and sparkle.

Laying the Table

The rules for laying a table are not rigid. They are followed to facilitate dining and making the table neat:

The place settings should be such that they allow enough space between the diners.

The bottom of the plate, napkin and each place of silver (cutlery) should be in line and all about one inch from the edge of the table. On a round table too, the same is followed but with the plate further away from the edge.

If however the table is small and round one can have the cutlery and plates nearer to the edge.

Forks are placed to the left of the plate in the order in which they will be used. The only exception is the oyster fork which is used for all types of seafood cocktails. This fork is placed on the right side of the plate. The function of a fork is to transfer food into the mouth. When it is used with a spoon its function is to load the spoon. Always keep a fork in preference to a spoon.

Buffet Settings

The tableware and food should be arranged in such a manner that the guests pick up their plates first, then their food, then their cutlery napkins, cups and saucers and finally the coffee or tea.

The utensils for dessert may be a part of the buffet arrangement.

Use a table cloth or keep the table top bare for buffet settings.

Arrange items in such a manner that guests move along without bumping into each other.

Arrange the cutlery in attractive patterns. Do not stack one on top of the other

The centerpiece should be placed towards the back or end of the buffet or table

Arrange the veg and non-veg dishes together on either sides of the table. The seasoning such as raita, salads, chutney can be placed in the center or around the centerpiece.

If you have a large dinning area then place the dinning table in the center of the room. However, if the room available is limited place the table on one side of the room.

One can place the plates, and cutlery, drinks coffee, tea and glassware on a separate table to save space.

Table Service

Sit down meals

At a sit down meal, the food should be served from the left of the guest.

Water and wines are poured from the right.

Do not garnish more than one or two dishes.

Serve coffee after dinner in small cups (coffee cups).

A finger bowl should be filled with warm water. Do not overfill.

English serviceó The host carves out slices of meat with a carving set from a platter placed by his sides. The plates are now passed to him one by one to be served. This is however never practiced at a formal dinner.

Indian style - The food may be pre-served in thalis. Paans are usually passed around after the meal.

Russian style - No serving dishes are placed on the table. The serving dishes are passed around accompanied with the proper implements. No food is passed around a second time. While serving a Chinese meal use Chinaware. An interesting variation would be to provide chopsticks.

Hold the dishes containing food low to enable the guest to served himself with ease.

Hold the serving dishes on a folded napkin in you left hand and never with both hands.

Remove dinner plates with the right hand and bread and butter plates with left hand.

Do remove water glasses from the table to refill.

Always serve the guest of honour first. He should be seated on the right side of the host.

The dishes should be passed in the following order:

a) Main dish
b) Vegetable
c) Sauces
d) Bread/rolls

Hold the napkin in a square while placing or removing dishes.

Serve the dessert whole at the table so that the guests can help himself.

Serve the dessert only after individual dessert spoons or forks and plates have been placed.

If the service is being done without any help then:

a) plan a meal with only three courses
b) serve the main course from one platter
c) Remove the used plates by passing them from one to another and finally to the hostess who can then place it on the trolley.

To serve wines at a sit down meal:
a) The host could either pass or pour the bottle around the table.
b) Allow guest to see the label.
c) The host should always pour his own glass first to avoid any sediment. He should then fill the guest glasses (3/4) full.
d) To avoid droplets the host should hold a folded napkin under the mouth of the bottle.
e) Now place the bottle on the serving table. Wrap the bottle with a napkin.

Serve:

Desert wines in a cocktail glass.

While wine in medium size glass

Red wines in a goblet

Sparkling wines in stemmed glasses.

Ensure that toasting glasses are thin and not very large

Serve:

Aperitifs (Sherry, Dubonnet) before meals.

Cocktails (e.g. Martini) should be served before meals.

Serve white wines with fish, poultry or shellfish.

Sweet wines and cordials are served with dessert or after the meal.

If serving several wines then serve the younger or newer vintages first and the older bottles later.

Dry wines should be served before sweet wines.

White wines should be served before red wines.

Light wines should be served before heavy wines.

Serve aperitifs, white wines, sparkling wines, beers and cocktails cold.

Serve red wines sherry, spirits taken neat, gin, rum, whisky and brandy at room temperature.

All the above, however, are the general preferences, individual tastes and preferences may vary.

To open a wine bottle:

Cut and remove the capsule below the bulge.

Wipe off old dirt with a wet cloth.

Drive a corkscrew into the center of the cork as far as it can go.

Now lever out and even motion. Avoid jerking.

With a T-corkscrew hold the shoulder of the bottle in the palm of the left hand. Pull slowly and evenly with the right hand, turning slightly to the right.

Finally wipe the mouth of the bottle thoroughly

Etiquette at the Table

Do not talk with your mouth full

Do not place your elbows on the table while eating.

Never use tooth picks on the table.

Do not tilt soup plates to scoop out the last remains.

Ask for the dish you want. Do not reach across the table.

Do not play with the cutlery.

Place the teaspoon in the saucer and not in the cup.

Wait till everybody is served before you start eating.

Use a handkerchief to wipe your lipstick. Do not substitute a handkerchief with the napkin.

Do not chew with your mouth open.

Avoid eating too fast.

Do not shove large amounts of food into your mouth.

Do not swallow with gulps

Do not lick fingers.

Do not use your napkin as a face mop.

Do not spit out hot food.

Do not tip your chair at a table you could lose both your balance and your dignity.

Being a gracious host /hostess
Make sure you are ready at least half an hour before the guests are expected.

Generally the host takes care of the drinks and the hostess of the food.

Make sure you circulate.

The trademark of a good host is to be able to attend to everyone.

If a guest arrives unexpectedly at a meal time, always invite him to join you on your table. If he arrives in between the meal make sure you offer him some refreshments at least.

Greet your guests at door with the traditional 'namaskar' or a modern hello.

In case some of your guests have got intoxicated do not allow them to drive back. Either ask his/her partner to drive back or call a cab. Another alternative could be to ask him spend the night.

Do not be too rude to guests who won't leave. It is advised that if their presence is annoying you make excuses such as you to have to go out, start taking glasses to the kitchen, close the bar etc.

Be a good guest
Reply to an invitation within two-three days of receiving it.

Do not break an appointment. If you have to for unavoidable circumstances inform your host.

If you are going to be late or want to leave early inform your host in advance and specify the reason.

Never accept or refuse invitations by fax or e-mail. These are work tools. Such devices are okay only if you are very intimate with the host.

Develop a sense of timing. There is no set time to leave a party. But when you leave do so quietly and quickly without breaking up the party.

For informal gatherings, it would be a good idea to carry flowers, wine or a champagne bottle.

Remember always try to return the hospitality.

If you are staying at somebody's house overnight or longer, tip the servants.

Send a letter of thanks to your hosts within two or three days.

As a house guest, try and avoid borrowing things from your hosts.

If you have a baby make sure you take all its paraphernalia. Take adequate precautions so that the baby does not soil the host's furniture.

Different Kinds of Parties

Cocktail parties

The usual time for cocktail parties is from 7 p.m. to 9 p.m.

Some cocktail parties are held in the morning but are called ó . The time for such a gathering is from 11 a.m. to 1 p.m.

While attending cocktail parties remember that they may be held outside. So dress accordingly. Make sure you wear comfortable shoes as it may entail standing for a long time. Queen Elizabeth II of England had a very valuable suggestion. She said never stand with your feet very close together. Keep a distance of about a 1/2 inch between them. Balance your weight evenly on both sides. This makes the long hours of standing less tiring.

If you invite very few people for a cocktail party then you could provide some seating arrangements.

Clear the room of fragile objects which could be knocked down by guests while circulating.

Prepare platters of canape before the guests arrive.

Place ashtrays and coasters at strategic places.

The bar

If your gathering is a large one (about more than 20 people), then hiring a bartender is advisable.

Give your guests a fresh napkin with every drink.

Make sure you have enough ice.

Make provisions for both alcoholic and non-alcoholic guests.

Formal lunch

Keep the cocktail hours short

A formal lunch could consists of:

Three courses (which include 1st course and dessert).

Four courses which include a first course, salad and then dessert.

Five courses which include a first course, fish, salad and then dessert.

You can serve ethnic meals for e.g. a wholly Indian meal pre-served in thalis or a Thai meal served in bone China etc.

You can use lace tablecloths for formal lunches.

Formal dinner

There are no bread and butter plates at a formal dinner.

The rest of the pointers are more or less the same as a formal lunch. However the center piece of a formal dinner is usually flowers. Candles could also be placed.

Tea parties

Tea parties are held from about 5 p.m. to 8 p.m.

One can serve the following kinds of tea- black tea, milk tea, lemon tea, iced tea, jasmine or Chinese tea.

Include a wide variety of snacks e.g. samosas, sandwiches, pastries, patties, small squares of fried bread with baked beans on them, etc.

Keep the dietary consideration of your guests in mind.

Give your guests quarter plates with napkins and a spoon before serving the snacks.

The snacks should be arranged on a tray and served. Cover the tray with a napkin before placing the dishes on it.

Similarly, the tea could also be pre-served or alternatively can be placed on the table and guests could help themselves.

Often the guests may ask for cold drinks or coffee, so be prepared for individual variations.

Theme parties

While organising theme parties ensure that your guests are aware of the theme. An easy way to ensure this would be to have it engraved on the invitation card.

Make sure that the decor and food are in co-ordination with theme. e.g. if you are arranging a Japanese dinner use Japanese dinnerware. Make provisions for chopsticks. Another interesting variation would be to have a Japanese flower arrangement at the center of the table.

Organising parties outside the home - hotels, clubs

The situation sometimes makes it necessary for us to arrange parties outside our home. The reasons are many for example a wedding. Also when the guest list is large (60 or more guests) than the space in our homes may be inadequate and the staff required also large. Hence many people go in for hosting such gatherings outside the home.

Handy hints

Make sure you make the bookings in advance. So not leave booking the venue to the last minute especially in peak seasons, e. g. marriage seasons.

Give specific instructions on the kind of decor that you want.

If you hire a caterer always sample the food.

Make sure you order enough food (keeping the number of guests in mind) accommodating the dietary preferences of your guests.

If you want to cut down on costs avoid serving hard drinks.

Picnics

Handy hints

Carry disposable plates, spoons and glasses.

Do not forget to carry a bottle opener, a tin can opener and a pair of scissors.

Invest in a water carrier and a picnic basket.

Make sure you include paper napkins.

Plastic boxes with good quality seals make the task of packing easier. However, if these are unavailable one could use tiffin boxes, casseroles and even foil paper.

Even if you use plastic boxes, repack with foil for double protection.

Carry cans for drinks instead of glass bottles. You could also make use of the ISC plastic bottles.

Carry a few plastic bags along for mopping up.

Avoid littering the places you visit. Throw your waste in a bin or carry it back with you.

Dry cooked foods are the most convenient to serve and eat on journeys, e.g. paranthas, sandwiches, boiled eggs etc.

Vegetables, which stay for long, include potatoes, cauliflower, carrot, peas.

However cook fresh and do not re-heat before packing.

Barbecued meats are the best to carry e.g. chicken tikas, grilled chicken.

Take along packets of tomato sauce, salt, pepper and sugar.

If you are travelling with children take fruits and some snacks, e.g. biscuits, nuts, cakes.

Take along flask of hot water, tea bags, small packet of coffee and creamer, in case you are unsure of getting tea or coffee in that surrounding.

In summers, carrying ice tea is also refreshing.

Proper Social Attitudes

Many people have a negative attitude towards entertaining and socialising. They feel it is a waste of time to interact with people whom they may meet for just one dinner or cocktail party. They consider such social gatherings to be superficial and a waste of time and effort. This is an unfortunate attitude to adopt as many friendships, business opportunities and lasting relationships can arise from such occasions. To those who say that they are too tired after a hard day at work to dress up and make inane conversation with strangers, the retort is that would one really be better off staying at home in one's own company? It would really require considerable ego to even think that one's own company is superior to that of others. There is so much to see, learn and savour and one should respond graciously to all invitations that come. Remember that when one is sick or retired or old or even all three, such occasions would rarely arise and that time one would have all the opportunity of being alone and at home.

The entire process of dressing up and going out to meet people should serve as a mood elevator rather than a depressant. Do not think that dressing up is too much of effort and that the weather is an impediment, as it is either too hot or too cold to put on one's finery.

There are many ladies who use their health, their work, their children or fatigue as an excuse not to accompany their husbands to parties. They should later not be surprised if other women 'hang around' their husbands all evening and even after!

For those men who are workaholics or social recluses, they would be well advised to rethink their strategy. A gregarious and sociable man is always more popular than an anti-social one. This is particularly true of the corporate sector where entertaining and socialising is practically part of the job as it is in diplomacy.

The worst problems arise when husbands and wives have opposite views about socialising. If one wants to party and the other does not, then fights and long faces along with frustration are bound to result. Many overpossessive husbands try to stifle their wives by virtually keeping them in 'purdah' and shun going out as their insecurity makes them feel that she may be attracted to someone else during these gatherings. Such antediluvian thinking only results in frustration, as it is not possible to 'police' one's spouse.

Make adequate provision for children and elders who may be at home, but do not turn down invitations and become prematurely old. The children do not appreciate constant supervision and moreover seeing parents who do not interact with their friends provides a poor role model for them.

Etiquette for Children

Habit is a most important factor in human nature, and therefore it is necessary to get children into habits of good manners from a very early age.

One of the earliest things which a child should be taught is to say 'Please' and 'Thank you'. He must never be allowed to snatch things from people's hands and leave out this essential courtesy. Small children should not be allowed to 'boss' their ayahs and bearers. Most Indian servants are very fond of children and rather encourage the little ones to give them orders in a high-handed manner, but if this is allowed, the child will never learn that he must always defer to older people.

Children should be encouraged to be considerate to their parents and adult friends. They should not be allowed to loll in a comfortable chair while a grown up sits on a hard stool. When a visitor enters a room, Children must always stand up and offer a chair to the newcomer.

Children should be encouraged to talk freely to their parents' friends. Nothing is so awkward as a shy, tongue-tied child, and children are not naturally afraid to talk. Parents must be careful of 'squashing' children who are open and friendly as his would undermine their self-confidence and produce a social awkwardness which may take years to dispel. On the other hand, children who are constantly interrupting adult conversation and insisting on all the attention being concentrated on them are an unmitigated nuisance. Parents should try to teach a happy medium.

Little boys can be taught to be small gentlemen from quite an early age. When walking with his mother, he should open doors for her and wait for her to go in first. It adds to a boy's dignity if his mother allows him to pay bus fares (of course, giving him the money to do so) and he will then take an interest in behaving as courteously as possible.

Children's parties

Children's parties are delightful functions if they are organised properly but can degenerate into a riot if not held together by a competent adult.

Invitations are usually sent out on special party invitation cards with pictures and decorations. Invitations must, of course, be answered and as soon as the child is old enough, he should answer them himself. Most children are anxious to do this and the principle of prompt replies to invitations is thus inculcated into them at an early age.

Most parents find it very trying to entertain mothers and children at the same time, unless they have a very good governess, or a sister or friend who will take over the entertainment of the children; for while they are being polite to the mothers, the children are getting out of hand. It is, therefore, kinder to send your children alone or with an ayah than to accompany them yourself.

At a birthday or Christmas party, the cake is the principal feature, and there is quite a little ceremony connected with it. When all the guests are at the table, the parent lights the candles (one for each year of the child's life) and when the effect has been admired for a few moments, the child whose birthday it is blows them out, trying to do so in as few puffs as possible.

The little host should be encouraged to see that his guests are looked after and offered all the delicacies provided. After tea, it is best to organise games as small children do not know how to occupy themselves. If there are children of widely varying ages, two or more groups should be arranged. If a little cinmea show or puppet play can be arranged, this is an ideal way of entertaining guests, since it keeps their interest without causing them to get hot and rowdy.

If a Christmas tree is part of the entertainment of a Christmas party, the distribution of the presents should be left till the end. This is preferable for two reasons: first, that it is a good way of breaking up the party and arriving at a climax, and secondly, if little children are given their presents too early in the proceedings, they will probably lose or break them before the end and go home disappointed.

Children should be made to take leave of the little host and his mother, and to thank them for their hospitality. The mother and child usually stand near the door so that there is no dofficulty in finding them.

School etiquette

Children at school are usually very quick to learn what is done and what is not done is their particular school, and they conform readily to custom, as children never like to be considered queer, or different from the general run. But parents who have not been to school themselves or have forgotten school etiquette, often cause their children to be remarked upon by the odd things which they themselves do, or which they cause their children to do.

Parents should always uphold the discipline of the school and help their children to keep its rules. They should see that the children are enabled to arrive at the proper time for school in the morning, and should not ask for them to go away before the proper closing time. If the school has a uniform, the child should always wear it. Uniforms are worn in schools to avoid invidious social distinctions and to provide children with a healthy convenient costume in which they do their work. Girls should never wear jewellery in school. It distracts their attention, causes them to 'show off' and often, owing to the carelessness of the wearer, causes a great deal of trouble to the school authorities when it gets lost or broken.

Parents should avoid visiting the Principal too often or sending notes on every possible occasion about their child. This merely causes the child to become a nuisance. Letters about a child should never be sent to individual members of the staff but always to the Principal.

It is very foolish, as well as being in bad taste, to dispute the decisions of the Principal as regards a child's school career. If, for instance, the Principal advises that the child should spend a second year in one class, it is very bad form to go and make a scene and insist on the child being promoted. Teachers as a rule know their job, and many a child has been in the top ten of a class for the rest of his school career after spending a second year in one of the lower classes. Teachers do not keep a child down out of spite or prejudice.

If a child is ill, or suffering from any nervous or mental disorder, the parent should write to the Principal and let him know. If you intend to keep your child from school for any period longer than one day, you should write and give the reasons to the Principal at once; you should not wait until he is ready to return. This is particularly important in the case of infectious diseases, as it gives the school authorities a chance of taking precautions against the spread of the disease.

When writing to the school about your child, refer to him or her as 'my son' or 'my daughter'.

Avoid discussing the teachers unfavourably in the presence of children. You may have reason for disapproving of some things which a teacher has done, but if you let the child know this, you will at once undermine the teacher's authority and the child will cease to respect him, and therefore will reap no benefit from his instructions. The proper thing to do in such circumstances is to go to see the Principal and state your complaint politely.

When you visit the school on occasions when there is a function, do not monopolise the attention of the Principal. Remember that all the parents have to be noticed too.

If you are a person of some social importance, or are very rich, do not expect your child to be given preferential treatment. Remember that a good school is the most democratic institution in the world.

Miscellaneous Hints

Appointments

Be most meticulous about keeping all your appointments punctually. If you have a bad memory keep an engagement book and consult it regularly.

Buses

A gentleman never pushes in front of a woman in order to get on to a bus first. If there are only a few people waiting, he should let a woman get in before him. If there is a queue, he should enter in turn in an orderly way. Young and healthy people of either sex should be ready to give up their seats to old or ill people or to a mother with a baby. A young girl should not accept a seat from an old man even though he offers it.

When travelling in a crowded bus with a very small child, do not allow the child to take up a whole seat. It is quite easy to put him on one's knee, thus making room for another passenger.

Chewing

No well-bred person would ever allow himself to be seen chewing in public. The chewing habit whether of sweets, gum or 'paan' is most objectionable. One has only to watch the grotesque motions of the jaw of the person who is indulging in this cow-like pleasure, to understand why it should be avoided.

Contradiction

It is very bad manners flatly to contradict a person with whom you are in conversation. If you think any statement he has made is incorrect, let it pass for a moment, and then say quietly: 'I think you must have been misinformed about this. I have reliable information that_____' and then proceed to explain your point. On no account should you burst out with 'that's not true,' or worse still, 'that's a lie.'

Doors
Never allow your servant to shut the door in the face of a caller. If he cannot admit the caller immediately, he should leave the door open while he goes to enquire what to do.

Eyes
When you are talking to people, look them straight in the face. People whose eyes are always wandering from one thing to another are soon labelled as shifty and unreliable.

Fidgetting
Avoid nervous movements of the fingers when talking to people. Do not continually move small articles like ashtrays about the table or constantly smooth your hair or adjust your tie. This suggests lack of confidence in yourself.

Name
Never introduce yourself to anyone by saying 'I am Mr. _____'. Say, 'My name is___'. Married ladies only are permitted to use their courtesy titles when introducing themselves. They may say 'I am Mrs ____'. It is particularly bad for a young girl to call herself 'Miss'.

A parent should refer to his children as 'my daughter_____' or "my son ___.'

Noises
Avoid making unpleasant noises in company. Do not clear the throat loudly, or belch. On no account spit except in the bathroom. If you have to blow your nose, do so as quietly as possible into your handkerchief. When coughing, always hold a handkerchief or the hand before the mouth.

Notepaper
Be careful to have good quality notepaper with envelopes to match. The paper should be white, grey, or bluish and should not have any decorations or fancy edges. The address may be stamped in the top right hand corner.

Ostentation
Ostentation or showing off, in any form, is very bad taste. A well-bred person avoids at all costs dress, behaviour or speech which draws attention to himself or herself.

Pipes
When you are in a house other than your own, ask permission of the hostess before beginning to smoke your pipe or cigarette.

Rubbish
It is a most objectionable habit to dispose of your rubbish by throwing it out of the window or dropping it in the street or in any public place. Take care also that your servants do not do these things.

Safety pins
Safety pins should never be used as a visible part of a person's attire. To use one instead of a button which has come off is a sign of slipshod habits.

Servants
A well-bred person is always courteous to servants. If you have to reprimand one of your servants, do so in private after your guests have gone. Never speak sharply to anybody else's servant.

Staring
It is extremely bad manners to turn around and stare as a person, either in the street or in any public place.

Teeth
Never pick your teeth or clean your nails in public.

Unkindness

A lady or gentleman does not make unkind remarks about people merely for the sake of being clever. It is always better to take the charitable view of another person's conduct.

Goodbyes

If you have been to a party in a flat and are going home very late, do not shout 'goodbye' to your host or your fellow guests on the staircase or in front of the entrance or you will disturb all the sleeping occupants of the other flats. Go home quietly and unobtrusively.

Grumbling

Don't grumble at your wife or husband in the presence of other people, or about her or him to others when the person in question is not there.

Husbands and wives

Do not talk of your wife as 'Mr. X'. Say, 'my husband,' or 'my wife', as the case may be, unless you know the person you are conversing with well enough to use your partner's first name when talking.

Interruptions

It is very ill-mannered to interrupt another person in the middle of a speech. However, eager you are to make something known, you should restrain yourself until person speaking has finished.

Jokes

A gentleman never makes a joke of a doubtful nature in the presence of a lady. Such jokes are rightly called 'Smoking room' stories, and should be kept for purely male gatherings. A lady should avoid such stories altogether

Knowledge

Do not try to show off your knowledge on any subject when in company. If people want your expert opinion on something, they will ask for it. Nothing is so deadening to a conversation as to have someone holding forth at great length on his pet subject.

Language

Never, under any circumstances, use bad language in public, or in place where ladies are present. Such behaviour would brand you at once as having no breeding. A lady should never use swear words under any circumstances.

Laughing

The poet Goldsmith remarked: 'The loud laugh bespeaks the vacant mind.' It also betrays the ill-bred woman. No lady shrieks with laughter especially in a public place. Restraint in all things is the mark of the gentlewoman.

Make-up

Although make-up is universally used nowadays, there are many woman who use it very badly. A lady never attempts to make herself look startling. She should choose cosmetics which are as near as possible to her natural colouring when she is in her best state of health, and she should apply them in the places where nature intended her to have colour. No human being, for example, has a high colour just in front of the ears. Yet how many women daub their faces with rouge in this position. The effect is to make them look ridiculous and ill-bred.

20 Things You Must not Do!

'The difference between a well-bred and an ill-bred man is this: one immediately attracts your liking and the other your aversion. You love the one till you find reason to hate him, you hate the other till you find reason to love him.' Thus wrote Samuel Johnson in an era when it was truly believed that manners made a man. In order to survive in society, the lubrication of good manners is as essential to man as engine oil is to a car.

Etiquette has evolved over time and to some who are newcomers to the ways of polite society, rules and decorum may appear to be arbitrary and unnecessary. However, most rules and conventions have come about for the general convenience of all concerned. A truly courteous man or woman will consider the effect of his or her words and actions on the person with whom he or she is dealing. Natural courtesy is of immense value and one must always try to do and say the correct thing and behave in an appropriate and becoming manner at all times.

A well-brought up person should be aware of what is socially unacceptable behaviour.

1. Comb hair, cut nails, dig their nose, clean their ears, scratch or spit in public.
2. Chew with an open mouth.
3. Sit down to meals without washing one's hands.
4. Sneeze or cough without holding either one's hand or a handkerchief to the mouth.
5. Fail to greet guests.
6. Skim doors and go up and down noisily.
7. Use bad language.
8. Enter a room which is occupied without first knocking on the door.
9. Interrupt while others are specaking
10. Speak unnecessarily loudly.
11. Behave conspicuously in a public place.
12. Order other people's servants about.
13. Read letters addressed to others.
14. Boastful behaviour about one's wealth, position or looks and figure.
15. Fail to acknowledge gifts and thank the giver.
16. Not responding to invitations by either accepting or writing a polite letter of regret.
17. Address ladies and elders in an impolite manner.
18. Monopolise the conversation at a social function.
19. Making sexist and racially or religiously discriminatory remarks or even jokes at a social gathering
20. Telling off-colour jokes at a social gathering.

CHAPTER-8

Health & Nutrition

Life today has become very demanding. Juggling the pressures of the work place along with responsibilities of the house poses an enormous strain on us. In the process we tend to neglect our bodies. Blood pressure and diabetes are just some of the common ailments which are a result of this high pressured life style.

Although cases of polio, leprosy, typhoid, cholera and tetanus have gone down in India, HIV/ AIDS, malaria, asthma, cancer, tuberculosis are on the rise. While the concept of "Health For All" is undoubtedly a laudable goal, our efforts to achieve it have not been totally successful. While painstaking research by medical doctors and scientists have helped to develop new techniques and products in surgery, pharmacy and social and preventive medicines, our lifestyles and the polluted atmosphere in which we live have given rise to new diseases. The stresses and strains of fast-paced modern living has brought in its wake attendant medical and physical problems. In addition, there is a wide range of psychosomatic stress related diseases and not even children are exempt from these traumas. A World Bank and Harvard University report says that depression is set to sweep the world as the second largest cause of death and debility.

Health is not mere absence of disease but a state of physical, mental, social, spiritual and environmental well being. The western science basically deals with the physical health. Mental health is dealt by a psychiatrist and not by a common general practitioner. Spiritual health finds no place at all in spite of widespread spiritual rituals and beliefs. The eastern science on the other hand deals much more comprehensively and covers all aspects of health as defined but unfortunately lacks technologies and advancement especially in the field of emergency care.

According to the concept, mind and body are spiritually one. Each and every disease for practical purposes can be traced to an emotional imbalance. Research has shown that emotions like fear and anxiety are associated with high blood pressure; anger and jealousy with heart attack and paralysis; and greed and possessiveness with obesity, diabetes and heart failures.

According to the Upanishads, the classical eastern philosophical teaching, "You are what your deep rooted desires are". We are infinite choice makers and by changing our perception and our choices, we can change our reality and hence ultimately our body and our health. Instead of worrying about the past or having anxieties of the future, we should learn to live in the present. The body is not a fixed structure but a thinking organism. Each and every of the three trillion cells in the body are thinking cells. However, most of them are concentrated in the heart, stomach, kidney, colon and bronchial tubes. According to the eastern philosophy, the mind is not confined to the brain but is present in each cell of the body. Many of these cells are even more reliable thinkers than the brain.

Disease occurs when we do not live according to our inner intelligence known as the Dharma. The responsibility for the illnesses and cures resides within us. Living with the law of nature and understanding these laws can help in preventing most of the diseases.

Today the western approach is geared for advances in the treatment of acute illnesses which of course is life saving but when it comes to chronic illnesses the western approach does not have much to offer. The western model has been framed on the concept of understanding the mechanism of disease while the eastern model is based on the philosophy of understanding the origin of the disease.

The mechanism of the disease deals with identifying the organisms or an outside influence. Understanding the origin of disease deals with eating, breathing, digestion, metabolism, eliminating thoughts, feelings, emotions, desires, memories, sleep and relational aspects of a human being. By concentrating on the genesis of a disease one can influence 90 percent of the outcome of a chronic disease.

Ayurveda, prominent name in the eastern system, is a science with a difference. The word Ayurveda is the combination of two Sanskrit words meaning life and knowledge. The 6000 year old holistic system of healing and prolonging life considers all aspects of a person's existence from life and environment through mind and consciousness.

While dealing with addiction the western model for example will ask the patient to quit smoking. On the other hand, the eastern approach deals with the origin of addiction at the mind level itself and motivates the circumstances by which the person himself will give up the addiction.

Heart attack, paralysis, high blood pressure, diabetes, insomnia, cancer, acid peptic disease, infertility, dysmenorrhea etc. now are classified into lifestyle disorders. To a large extent these can be controlled and prevented by changing the lifestyle the body-mind way. The lifestyle disease is nothing but the manifestations of the mind. By improving the power of interpretation and analysis, and by cultivating good thoughts one can change the present situation and alter the occurrence of a disease. By combining the eastern philosophy with the western technologies and advancement one can prevent the disease, control the ongoing biological process, regress the damage done, curtail the dose of various medicines and even avoid using these medicines in future.

Meditation is, in fact, a very good way of balancing oneself against the onslaught of stress. It has been proved beyond doubt that meditation in any form is very good for the body. The inward journey from the disturbed state of consciousness to the undisturbed state of consciousness. When this is attained with the help of primordial sound, it is called Primordial Sound Meditation (PSM).

Meditation is not acquiring Samadhi or a thoughtless state of mind but is the process of attaining that state of mind. The silent spaces in between the thoughts are sources of a pure potentiality with infinite possibilities. Inserting intents in that state of mind (sutra of advance meditation) increases.

According to the eastern philosophy, the body can be defined as made up of three components. The physical body consisting of food and pranic layer, subtle layer consisting of mind, intellect and ego and lastly the casual body consisting of soul, consciousness or the spirit. The soul can be equated to the undisturbed state of consciousness and subtle layer to the disturbed state. It is like an ocean where superficial layers represent the subtle body and the calm and still bottom the consciousness. Yoga is nothing but the union of physical body with the casual body which can only be achieved by controlling the subtle body.

The first basic principle of yogic meditation involves acquiring efficiency in any action performed and be consciously aware of the present. The conscious awareness leads one away from the miseries of the past and anxieties of the future. To give one example while eating breakfast one should concentrate on the meal and not think about something else. Practising conscious awareness of each and every action is the first step in acquiring spiritual health. Breathing awareness, eating awareness, thinking awareness etc. all are the practical ways of doing the same thing. The second step in Yoga is to balance yourself between loss and gain and to maintain tranquillity of mind at all times, places and situations. Every opportunity good or bad should be taken as an opportunity to learn for the future betterment. Various mental exercises are taught to acquire this state of mind. Let go of the attachment, to the results of an action is what the third step propagates for acquiring internal yoga.

Repression and suppression of the thoughts are the fundamental causes of diseases. Fear, doubts and attachment are the three basic fundamental root causes for the development of diseases.

According to the *Bhagwad Gita*, five gateways to hell or acquiring a disease are **attachment, anger, greed, desire and ego.** Many scientists considered doubts, expectations and denial to be the root cause of a disease. Persistence of negativity in the mind is what is responsible for most of the disorders.

According to *Yogasutras* of Patanjali, to remove the negative thoughts of mind, opposite thoughts should be cultivated. The eastern philosophy basically teaches the ways to acquire and cultivate these opposite thoughts of love, compassion and happiness.

The Weather and Health

The weather undoubtedly has the power to affect our moods and health, both psychologically and physically. Psychologists have long proved that our mood is affected by dark clouds and rain, that long dreary winters when the sun is not seen causes depression and that bright sunlight causes mood elevation.

While one has to guard against waterborne diseases and flies during the monsoons as these cause stomach ailments, one has to be careful to protect oneself against chills, draughts and colds during winter. Adequate warm clothing is an essential feature of this season.

However, since ours is a predominantly hot country in which some parts do not even experience winter, given below are a few tips to cope with the summer heat.

With atmospheric temperatures rising, the number of deaths attributed to excessive heat exposure goes up. But most tragedies can be avoided by taking a few precautions, according to physiologists.

1. While the human body tends to adjust to the heat, sometimes, the sudden rise in temperature doesn't allow enough time for the body to adapt to it. When the body is unable to cope with excessive heat, the result is heat exhaustion or heat stroke.
2. Under normal circumstances, humans need about two weeks to acclimatize to a dramatic change in temperature.
3. Symptoms of heat exhaustion include fatigue, nausea, cramps, headache, dizziness and uncoordinated movement. People with heat exhaustion should stop working or exercising; move into shade or air conditioning or take a cool shower; drink fluids to replace lost salt; and rest. If left untreated, heat exhaustion can progress to heat stroke, a more serious condition that can be fatal.
4. With heat stroke, the body simply shuts down the mechanisms for cooling. It stops sweating, so the skin becomes dry; the blood vessels close to the skin constrict, not allowing blood flow to the skin, so there's less cooling. The temperature rises to over 104 degrees, which can cause brain damage that interferes with breathing and circulation. Common symptoms of heat stroke include dizziness, confusion, unconsciousness, rapid and strong pulse, and hot, dry skin. Children, older people, and those engaged in heavy physical labour are most vulnerable to heat exhaustion or heat stroke.
5. The elderly do not feel as thirsty as younger people do with the same amount of fluid loss, so they are more vulnerable to becoming dehydrated. People on diuretics or tranquillizers are more susceptible to heat exhaustion, as are those with high blood pressure, diabetes or an overactive thyroid.

For people dealing with hot weather, physiologists offer the following tips:

Drink plenty of fluids, but avoid alcohol and caffeinated drinks because they promote dehydration.

Find shade or air conditioning if possible. Even two hours of air conditioning each day can significantly reduce the risk of heat-related illness.

Use common sense.

Avoid strenuous jobs and exercising in the heat.

Do not leave children, pets or anyone who has difficulty caring for themselves in a car without ventilation.

Ask children to rest after 30 minutes of outdoor play.

Check periodically on elders and others who live alone.

Consult a pharmacist about medications because some can inhibit sweat or aggravate heat-related conditions.

Food, Dieting, Anorexia and Bulimia

The Bhagvad Gita says that "a man is what he chooses to eat".

All foods are characterised by four basic sets of distinct features. There are three Guna's (nature) present in food- *Sattvik*, *Rajasik* and *Tamasik*. Food has two qualities, hot and cold. The three *Doshas* or humours namely, *Pitta* (bile), *Vayu* (air) and *Kapha* (phlegm). The six *rasas* (tastes)- sweet, sour, pungent, astringent, bitter and salt.

In a traditional home, pungent foods are recommended in summer, sour during the rains, salty in the autumn, sweet for winters, bitter during the frost and astringent in the spring. These combinations had medicinal considerations in order to maintain equilibrium between bile, phlegm and air. Food and pleasure, food and the seasons, food as a metaphor for seduction has long been written about in literature and in the epics. In fact, food is the raison d'etre of our lives, the reason why we live and work so hard. Yet today it appears that every mouthful that we ingest is adding to our weight, causing us ill health and more importantly, a great deal of guilt. As gay fashion designers stride across the fashion world decreeing what should be worn and what should not, they have taken their revenge on the world by deciding that women should forsake their curves and be presented as flat-chested, with no derrieres and decidedly underweight. As teenagers strive to reach the proportions of the models on the ramp, they cannot live up to either Kate Moss or Twiggy and are falling into depression and eating disorders, chief of which are anorexia nervosa and bulimia.

Anorexia, which is also striking Indian teenagers in the big cities as they fit themselves into the tightest of jeans, is a state in which the teenager feels that she will gain love, attention and success only if she is slim. She, therefore, starves herself and insists that she is fat even when she is reduced to skin and bone.

Dieting loses its magnetic draw when you accept and appreciate your physical body as it is instead of focusing on improving it.

The key is to focus not on the calorie burning effects of exercise but on the enjoyment and sheer pleasure of being active. Celebrating your body through physical movement whether it's a four mile run, a gentle stretching session or a hike in the park enhances self-esteem and promotes self acceptance.

Eat sensibly, eat with a relaxed mind and don't feel guilty. Eat junk food too once in a while if it makes you happy.

Exercise and Good Health

Modern conveniences make it essential for us to go to the gym, take a walk, do yoga or any other form of aerobic exercise. Working in an office, sitting in front of computer screens or even house work does not give the body enough exercise to keep fit and trim. The easy availability of exotic, mouth-watering foods in our fridges or at the supermarket will be our undoing if we do not consciously balance our intake with the outflow.

Regular exercise brings sound health to people of all ages. Pick up any book or health magazine and you will find pages about the other benefits of exercise. Undoubtedly, exercise can work wonders.

You will sleep better, wake up fresh, feel more alert, walk erect and look very much younger than your age. Those who have been exercising regularly can appreciate the difference. There are many others who wish to start exercises but do not find the right occasion.

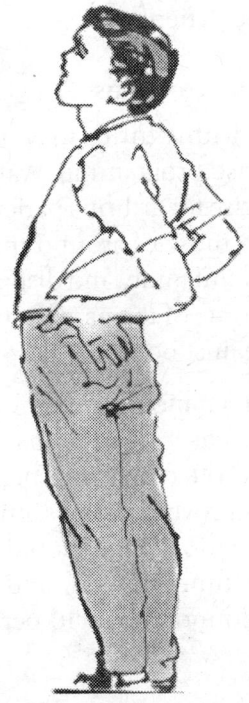

In the first place, people hesitate to start exercising. Once they start, they tend to overdo it so as to get quick results. Some take up strenuous exercises in the beginning itself. This group of people often land in trouble.

Are there many points to be remembered before taking up any strenuous exercise? Should one consult a doctor? The answer is yes. Here are some of the situations where you need to take a doctor's opinion:

1. If you are over 60 years of age and have been doing mild exercises like walking and suddenly plan to take up strenuous activity like tennis, cycling and swimming.

   After a certain age there are many degenerative changes occurring in the body. When the body is put under stress, bones and joints may get stretched causing injury. Besides, the blood supply to heart and brain is compromised and this may have grave consequences.

2. If you are over 40 and have never done any exercise throughout your adulthood.

   After 40 years, several diseases go on for years together without any obvious symptoms or signs. Once the body is put under stress these become manifest, e.g. coronary artery disease.

3. If you are a heavy smoker; smoking more than 20 cigarettes a day.

   Smoking makes blood vessels hard and narrow and therefore the circulation to vital organs may be reduced. While taking up any stressful exercises all of a sudden, some organs may fall short of blood supply. It is always better to build up the level of exercise gradually.

4. If you are overweight, take a doctor's opinion before starting any exercise programme. Obese individuals are a storehouse of many diseases. It is better to undergo a thorough check-up before any exertion to avoid sudden shocks.

5. If you have been suffering from high blood pressure, heart disease or kidney disorders.

6. If you are pregnant, you should not undertake any strenuous exercise as it enhances the chances of abortion in the early stages of pregnancy. However, regular walking should be encouraged as it enhances the sense of well-being and relieves aches and pains associated with pregnancy.

Walking your way to good health

After injuries suffered during jogging and the undue strains of doing aerobic exercises, doctors are increasingly supporting walking as the panacea for many ills. It can be undertaken safely by all age groups and the end results are highly beneficial.

For those who ignore walking as mundane, this is the time to break the myth and discover its benefits. It is an easy path to recovery and also a prescription to healing at times. Walking is a miracle treatment that can alleviate heart diseases, diabetes, arthritis, obesity and depression- a simple remedy of putting one foot in front of the other.

As life becomes hectic by each passing day, some simple activities can help sustain daily pressures. Not many people realise that if in a day, we sit or lie down for more than 15 hours, it is harmful for our posture. Here is a list of a few diseases that can be warded off with just a walk.

Walk away from heart diseases

Heart specialists prescribe walking to heart patients as it may help prevent cardiovascular diseases and in making the heart muscles stronger. Walking also oxygenates every part of the body. The blood-fat level changes to a healthier balance; the levels of artery-clogging blood fats decrease with walking.

One may have to reduce the intensity of an exercise but with an increase in duration and frequency, walking works well as jogging does for the body. "Every step you take, is a step towards a stronger heart and a longer life Walking also helps prevent a second heart attack in people but they should get the doctor's permission.

Walk away from diabetes

Walking is also strongly recommended to diabetics. It increases the energy level and enhances the ability of the muscles to rake up blood sugar, as a result of that, the requirements for insulin in most people decreases. Walking after a meal is beneficial for most diabetic patients.

Walk away from arthritis

Most people with arthritis may benefit from a regular exercise programme. Walking may be the best exercise for arthritis patients as it helps to strengthen muscles around the joints. This may prevent joint injury and disfigurement and also relieve some of the pain that occurs when bones rub against bones.

The natural tranquillising effects of walking also help to ease arthritic pain. Its mood elevating effect offers an added benefit. Walking can greatly improve a person's attitude but one should not overdo it. One should start walking three or four times a week, and increase the distance by no more than 10 per cent every 2 weeks.

Walk away from obesity

Obesity is always a problem and can lead to other ailments. It is always good to maintain the body weight throughout one's life and walking is one of the best ways to do it. It shoots up your metabolic rate and you burn more calories.

Walking helps the burning of body fat, building muscle tissues at the same time. As a result, you look much better at a given weight.

Also it increases the muscle mass, has higher metabolic rate than fat, which means that it continuously burns more calories.

Walk away from back pain

Walking can help relieve back-pain by strengthening and toning muscles that make the spine more stable.

Though the general view is that a person should rest when he has back-pain, if a person walks slowly and does not put any strain on his back while walking, it is an effective remedy.

Health Check-Ups

Earlier it used to be said that one should go for a health check-up after the age of 40. But, with the changes in our lifestyle body resistance is lowered these days. Health check-ups can be undertaken from the age of 35.

The frequency of check-ups can be planned as follows:

Up to 35 years - every 3 years

36 to 40 years-every 2 years

After 40 years- Yearly

Most hospitals in big cities have health check-up schemes.

Requirement of an annual health check up?

IMPORTANCE

To know your health status.

To have base line information about your biochemistry.

To know about any systemic problem.

Early detection of any incipient disease.

Primary and secondary preventive measures to be adopted.

Lifestyle intervention strategies to be adopted.

Helps early diagnosis and early treatment and may cure the disease.

Prevents complications.

Improves prognosis.

Determines the frequency of subsequent follow up.

Annual health check up after the age of 20 is a must to keep you healthy and fit.

Sustain health and fitness.

Clinical examinations

Pulse: Normal pulse is 60-80 per minute.

Tachycardia: If pulse is faster (more than 90 per minute)

Bradycardia: If pulse is slow (less than 60 per minute)

Irregular: If there are missed beats or irregular rhythms.

This can be prevented by appropriate life style interventions and necessary medical treatment if detected well in time.

BLOOD PRESSURE

Normal systolic (upper) blood pressure is 110-140 mmHg.

Normal diastolic (lower) blood pressure is 70- 90 mmHg.

HYPERTENSION

Mild when diastolic blood pressure is 90-99mmHg.

Moderate when diastolic to 100-109 mmHg.

Severe when the diastolic blood pressure is more than 110 mmHg.

Systolic Hypertension - when the systolic blood pressure is more than 160 mmHg.

Hypertension is a silent killer. 15-80% of the population after the age of 20 is hypertensive. It is usually detected on routine check up or otherwise. It has been estimated that 60% patients are unaware that they have hypertension, since it does not produce any symptoms in the early stages. Various predisposing factors responsible for hypertension are stress, consumption of excess of salt, consumption of excess of alcohol, fat rich diet, smoking, obesity, lack of exercise, environmental pollution, family history of hypertension, consumption of oral contraceptive pills in women and some of the pharmaceutical preparations containing ephedrine or adrenaline.

Lifestyle intervention such as regular exercise, meditation twice a day, abstinence from smoking, alcohol, ideal body weight, consumption of fresh vegetables and fruits and avoidance of saturated fat can control hypertension to a very large extent.

Every individual should know his/her base line blood pressure after the age of 20. If normal, they should get it checked on a periodical basis once in a year. If hypertensive with or without risk factors then blood pressure may checked, monitored and treated on an individual basis by the treating doctor.

HEART

Heart is evaluated to detect first, second, third or fourth heart sounds or presence of any abnormal murmur, thereby suggesting narrowing or leaking of the valves or presence of any hole in the heart. It is also evaluated for presence of any pericardial rub.

LUNGS

Lungs are evaluated for normal vesicular breathing and for the presence of any abnormal adventitious sounds such as rhonchi (sound produced by narrowing of breathing, tubes bronchioles) usually heard in bronchitis or for presence of any crepitations heard in lung congestion or infection such as pneumonia, tuberculosis or bronchitis. Lungs are also evaluated to find out any evidence of fluid in the pleural cavity (pleural effusion) commonly due to tuberculosis.

LIVER

Liver is evaluated for any enlargement such as fatty liver, hepatitis, alcoholic liver disease and various other disorders. Liver span may reduce in shrunken liver.

SPLEEN

Normally spleen is not palpable. If enlarged it suggests disease process.

KIDNEY

Kidneys are normally not palpable. If enlarged suggests disease process such as infection or malignancy.

INTESTINAL SOUNDS

Normal and abnormal intestinal sounds can be evaluated. Abnormal intestinal sounds may predict intestinal obstruction.

PERIPHERAL VESSELS

Peripheral vessels are evaluated for normal circulation in the periphery. This is of tremendous clinical help in evaluation of blood flow in smokers, diabetics and individuals with narrow peripheral arteries.

PERIPHERAL NERVES

Are evaluated clinically for presence of any motor/sensory neuropathy, especially in diabetics etc.

BONES AND JOINTS

To find out any deformity, arthritis etc.

EYE, ENT AND DENTAL CHECK UP

To evaluate any disease process in eyes, throat, ears, nose and oral cavity.

Investigations

HAEMOGLOBIN

Usually by a drop of blood to find out anaemia (normal haemoglobin is 13-14 gm% in men and 11-13 gm% in women)

TOTAL LEUKOCYTE COUNT (TLC)

This can also be tested by a drop of blood. If the white count is increased we call it as leukocytosis which may suggest infections or malignancy. If the count is very low we call it is leukopenia which suggests compromised white cell count due to various disease processes (normal white cell count is 4000-11,000 per cubic mm).

RED BLOOD CELL COUNT

This reduced in anaemia and the shape of red cells may be microcytic or normocytic. If the red blood cell count is increased we call it as polycyathemia suggesting a disease process. Differential count (DLC) may decrease or increase depending on type of infection or malignancy.

ESR

Erythocyte Sedimentation Rate suggests the time taken by red blood cells to settle down. It may increase in chronic infection, malignancy or anaemia and may reduce when the red blood cell count is high.

BLOOD SUGAR TEST

Normal fasting blood sugar should be 60-100 mg% and post prandial (2 hours after meals) is usually up to 140 mg%. If the reading is above these values an individual is labelled as a diabetic. It also helps us in regular follow up of diabetic patients who are on oral antidiabetic drugs or Insulin.

LIPID PROFILE (CHOLESTEROL)

Normal blood cholesterol is 150-250 mg%. If the cholesterol is more than 250 mg%, then one has higher risk for heart attacks/ strokes. If the cholesterol is low or below normal it increases proneness to malignancy and depression.

Good cholesterol (HDL-High Density Lipoprotein) are protective for heart. Normal HDL is 40-50 mg% in men and 50-69 mg% in women. If HDL is 35% it is a risk factor for heart attacks/ strokes.

BAD CHOLESTEROL (LDL-LOW DENSITY LIPOPROTEIN)

Normally levels are up to 160 mg%. High levels of LDL is a risk factor for premature heart attacks/ strokes.

Triglycerides: normal level of triglycerides are 200 mg%, levels between 200-400 mg% is border line high risk, levels between 400-1000 mg% is high risk and levels above 1000 mg% are very high risk for heart attacks.

Cholesterol fitness can be achieved by regular exercise for 30 minutes daily, abstinence from smoking, alcohol in moderation, (not more than 1 or 2 ounce per day), meditation for 20 minutes twice a day, having diet less in saturated fat with cooking oil having more of poly unsaturated fatty acids and mono unsaturated fatty acids, having optimum body weight, avoiding pot belly obesity and caution for the use of oral contraceptive pills, may increase HDL and reduce LDL, TG.

Have periodical check ups of cholesterol profile as recommended by the doctor.

LIVER FUNCTION TEST

Include serum Bilirubin, SGOT, SGPT and alkaline phosphate to find out any abnormality in the liver function.

BLOOD UREA AND CREATININE

To evaluate kidney functions.

URINE EXAMINATION

To find out presence of protein, sugar, casts, crystals, white blood calls and red blood cells.

X-RAY CHEST

To evaluate any evidence of fluid in the pleural cavity or lung parenchymal disease such as tuberculosis or pneumonitis or malignancy and assessment of heart size.

ELECTROCARDIOGRAM (ECG)

To find out any abnormality in the rate, rhythm and electrical activity of the heart, assess ischaemia, infarction and heart blocks etc.

TREADMILL (STRESS TESTING)

Is a method of making you walk on a machine with graded exercise to evaluate the effort tolerance and assess the reserve of coronary arteries. If the test is positive it suggests a lack of circulation to the heart muscle (ischaemia) thus giving information about the line of treatment. Left ventricular angiography evaluates the status of coronary arteries, LV function and valves. It helps in further management such as CABG, angiography, stenting, valve repair or valve replacement.

COLOUR DOPPLER ECHOCARDIOGRAPHY

Usually required to evaluate heart functions including the status of hole in the heart and other abnormalities.

PULMONARY FUNCTION TEST

To evaluate functional capacity of lungs.

PAPSMEAR

For early cancer detection in women.

Hence, to remain fit and healthy, one has to get annual check ups periodically.

Good Health and Water

Water is an essential component of life. Every cell in our body depends upon water to function properly. Without it we would die in days. Most of us don't understand the role of this vital nutrient. The human body consists mostly of water. Blood is 83% water; muscles 75%; bones 22%. In fact 55-65 % of a woman's body and 65-75% of man's body is made up of water (men generally have more water retaining tissue than women). The average adult body holds 35-50 litres of water, 2.3 to 2.8 litres of which are lost every day through excretion and perspiration.

Some seemingly solid foods are mostly water. Fruits and vegetables are more than three-fourths water. Green beans, for example, are 89% water and lettuce is 95% water. Both of these are actually wetter than milk, which is 87% water. Even meat is about half water and bread about one-third water by weight.

Though thirst is your body's way of signalling you to consume more water, it is an imperfect signal that may turn off before you've drunk enough to satisfy your body needs. Water helps you digest and absorb all nutrients and get rid of both liquid and solid wastes. In fact, inadequate liquid intake may be one factor in chronic constipation.

Water, as an essential component of blood, transports oxygen as well as infection-fighting to where they are needed in your body. It lubricates joints, keeps internal organs from sticking together and skin from shrivelling and drying out. Salts dissolved in water, maintain the proper electrolyte balance inside and outside cells. Water is also part of the body's air conditioning system - the water lost through your skin helps to cool your body. During pregnancy, it provides a protective cushion for the foetus.

To maintain the proper amount of water in your body, you should consume at least six to eight glasses of clear liquids each day and more if you are physically active or sweat a lot. Most people don't consume nearly enough water, particularly in the warmer months when large amounts of body water are lost through perspiration. Pregnant women need extra fluids, and women who are nursing should drink extra liquids daily to help maintain their milk supply. Infants also need more water than adults realize, and in warm weather babies should be offered water in between feedings.

Water comes from many sources - from other liquids such as coffee, tea, milk, beer and soft drinks; from the content of many solid foods; from the body's own metabolic processes. However, the caffeine in coffee, tea and some soft drinks has a diuretic effect that ultimately causes your body to lose (through urination) more water than you consume.

Alcohol too tends to dehydrate, which is why you may wake up thirsty after a night of drinking.

Many people confuse "water weight" with fat. The weight you gain after a big meal is usually almost entirely water that you will lose in a few days.

When you go on a diet that produces rapid weight loss - especially one that is high in protein, low in sugars and starches - most of your initial weight loss will be water, not fat. As soon as you slip back into your usual eating habits, you will "gain" back about a kilo of water (not fat, which all you should be losing and all you should be worrying about). While you are losing weight, its important to drink plenty of water to help your kidneys eliminate the toxic wastes produced by the breakdown of body fat.

Diuretics, commonly prescribed to treat high blood pressure and congestive heart failure, are sometimes recommended for women who gain more than 1.5 kilos just before their menstrual periods. However, diuretics should never be taken without a doctor's approval, because in addition to ridding the body of water, they wash out needed salts, sometimes resulting in potassium deficiency. Never use diuretics to try to lose a few kilos quickly. You will lose water, not fat, and that loss is temporary, and you may seriously dehydrate your body.

Some people believe that drinking liquids with meals dilutes digestive enzymes, preventing the body from digesting and absorbing some of the food eaten. It's not true. Water does not rush undigested foods through our digestive tract. In fact, it facilitates digestion, since enzymes work best in a fluid environment. Drinking water or other low calorie liquids before or with your meals can also help you control your weight by creating a sensation of fullness.

Inadequate or inappropriate liquid intake is a common problem among active people, and it contributes to muscle fatigue and poor performance. In extremely hot weather, or during strenuous exercises such as running a marathon, insufficient water intake may actually be life-threatening.

Water is by far the best liquid to drink before, during and after any activity. If after strenuous exercise you need to drink more than three litres of water to replace lost fluid, add a little salt to any additional water you consume. Salt tablets, however, can be extremely dangerous and should not be taken unless they are administered by a doctor for symptoms of salt depletion.

Very sweet drinks draw water into the intestinal tracts (at the expense of our muscles) and may result in cramps during exercise.

On an average, one requires 10-12 glasses (1glass= 200ml) of liquids every day. Hence you need 1.5-2 litres of liquids daily.

Constipation

The Indian systems of medicine, be it ayurveda, naturopathy, or homoeopathy lay a great deal of emphasis on proper elimination. Good health and happiness are closely connected and naturopathy emphasizes that "constipation is the mother of all diseases." Good health encompasses not only proper digestion but its assimilation and the excretion of waste. While the body has two channels by which air and food enter, namely the wind pipe for air and the food pipe for food, there are four outlets for the excretion of waste materials - the lungs, the kidneys, skin and bowels. It is therefore that Mother Nature has designed the body is such a way that outgo should be more than the intake.

Lifestyle diseases such as diabetes, acidity and even asthma and blood pressure can be traced back to improper diet and excretion. Constipation can also aggravate some diseases such as hernia, piles and fissures. So constipation must not be ignored. Today, the problem has even gone down to little children who literally have "no time" to go to the loo as they are yanked out of bed at around 6 a.m. or so and dragged off to catch their school buses. Added to this is the regular intake of processed and refined "junk" foods that are good to taste but which do nothing for one's health.

Some common causes of constipation
Low fibre diet.

Drinking less than 8-10 glasses of water daily.

Emotional stress and anxiety.

Frequently ignoring the call of nature.

Lack of exercise.

Pregnancy.

Regular intake of medicines like pain-killers and antacids.

Frequent travel.

Certain chronic diseases.

Cures

Taking laxatives is not a permanent cure of the problem. Rather it should be tackled by having a proper diet with a high fibre content, drinking adequate water and taking exercise.

Ayurveda recommends a wide range of simple and compound medicines. One of the simple medicines is fruit pulp of cassia, which is to be taken with water twice daily. This softens the stools and increases movement of the intestines which helps evacuation of the stools. Triphala Churna, a compound medicine prepared from three plants, is also very effective for chronic constipation.

According to homoeopathy, long-standing constipation can have several major consequences such as lowered resistance to various diseases, discomfort in the stomach due to flatulence, allergies, migraine and diseases of the digestive system. It recommends an increased intake of water and drinking warm fluids such as warm milk, honey or lemon in warm water as important for controlling constipation.

Non-vegetarian food should be avoided and smoking stopped. Homoeopathic medicines for treatment of constipation depend on the combination of the symptoms. Commonly used medicines include Nux Vomica, for constipation associated with fissures.

Nature cure also considers constipation to be root cause of several diseases such as appendicitis, rheumatism, arthritis, high blood pressure and cancer. This is based on the fact that poison is formed from constipated stools. Drinking at least 10-12 glasses of water everyday is considered to be the most important measure to control constipation.

Other options for the treatment of constipation offered by nature cure include mud packs, cold towel packs, cold hip baths, abdominal packs, enema and regular toilet habits.

The easiest way to deal with and avoid constipation, however, is to:

1. Pay attention to one's diet. A high fibre diet that consists of 70 per cent green leafy and other vegetables.
2. Cereals should form almost 30 per cent of every meal. Three tablespons of wheat bran added to the wheat flour helps maintain normal bowel movements. Further a high fibre diet is effective only if every mouthful of food is chewed at least 15 times.
3. All fruits except banana and jackfruit will relieve constipation. Bael, citrus fruits, grapes and prunes are the best when it comes to relieve the constipation.

How Yoga Fights Stress

Stress has been directly linked to a variety of prevalent ailments such as heart disease, memory loss, migraines, peptic ulcers, faulty child development during pregnancy, diabetes and viral infections like common colds, acidity, impotence and skin diseases. It has been labelled the millennium plague.

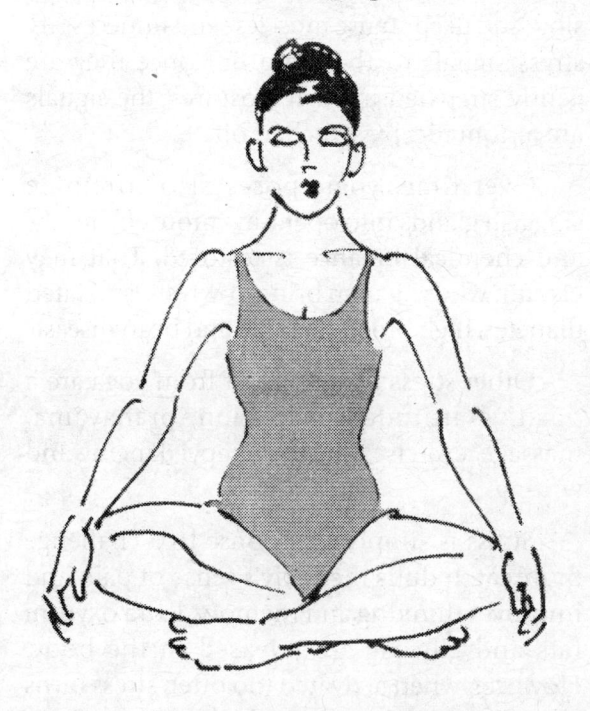

It is an accepted fact that yoga contributes to health and peace of mind. But not many know just how it works. Ancient yogis said that yoga increases life force, which does not explain much. But modern research is slowly uncovering the mechanics of yoga and explaining it in terms that can be understood. A person's mental and physcial health depends on brain and body chemicals. Regular practice of hatha yoga actually alters brain chemistry. It slows down the action of the sympathetic nervous system. In practical terms, this means your body does not get flooded with stress hormones as quickly, your blood pressure does not rise everytime you have an argument, and your heart does not start pounding for fear of missing the bus. Regular yoga practice also improves the functioning of the parasympathetic system which controls your ability to relax. Even after a period of stress, you are able to relax and normalise quickly. Blood pressure comes down, the heart rate rerturns to normal and breathing becomes slow and deep. Tense muscles send unnecessary stress signals to the brain but once they are gently stretched in yogic postures, the signals are automatically switched off.

Over time, yogic poses also stimulate sluggish glands into operating more efficiently, and chemical balance is restored. That may explain why yoga can bring down stress related diabetes, high blood pressure and heart disease.

Other stress busters apart from yoga are a positive attitude, meditation, pranayama, massage, exercise, music therapy, dancing and writing.

Stress is simply a response to a challenge or threat. It dulls the body's sense of pain and improves thinking and memory. Extra oxygen, fats and glucose are released in the body. However, when activated too often stress turns chronic and burns down the immune system and turns the body into a hot bed of disease.

The human body has not been designed to drag around frustrations, anxieties, overwork and bad thoughts. The ambitious, the hostile and the competitive sort of people are more susceptible to stress related disorders.

Breathing Correctly

Breathing correctly is an important way to combat stress, disease and the ever increasing pollution. Yogic breathing systems or pranayama can be undertaken by all age groups for a healthier lifestyle.

Sleep and Sleeping Disorders

"Sleep is related to man's deeds", says an old proverb. But today with the late night on all night working and partying syndrome, sleep is at a premium. One of the reasons for disturbances in one's sleeping patterns is the computer which has encouraged people to remain awake till the early hours of the morning while they "surf the net". The presence of electricity no longer makes it necessary for a man to rise and sleep with the sun, but as in everything else by upsetting the body's natural rhthyms man has created his own problems. In many, insomnia has become a disease that must be treated by taking sleeping tablets and tranquillizers, which in turn give rise to their own problems.

Sleeping disorders or insomnia are the result of:

- Anxiety or tension.
- Environment change such as constant travel.
- Emotional arousal.
- Phobia against sleep or fear of insomnia.
- Pain or discomfort.
- Caffeine and alcohol.

While the days of the legendary Kumbhakaran and Sleeping Beauty are behind us, a good nights sleep is essential to function properly as sleep is indeed the wonder drug that causes the body and mind to heal themselves. A good night's sleep has always been considered a panacea for many ills.

Sleep Well-Hazards to Our Health

Most people know when they have had a perfect night's sleep. They rest without a break and wake up renewed, with a sparkle that lasts the day.

Such nights often follow being stretched to the limit physically or mentally, or accomplishing something. Pleasure is important - a convivial evening often precedes good sleep. And the environment matters: to some people, a dreary bedroom takes a toll on relaxation.

So, if you sleep less soundly than you would like, it is time to improve the quality of your rest - and inject more energy into your day.

Golden rules

A good night's sleep is as important to life as exercise and healthy eating. Go to bed and get up at about the same time most days. Then you can enjoy the occasional late night or early morning without suffering ill effects. For weekend late-nighters, "Sunday insomnia" can put a blight on Mondays. One solution is to forgo a late lie-in on Sunday morning so that you are tired by bedtime. Plan pleasurable wind-down activities on Sunday evening.

Avoid heavy, rich meals and foods high in calcium and magnesium, such as nuts.

Bedtime rituals

Try the following:

Along, warm bath with soothing aromatherapy oils, candles and music.

Read a book in the bath.

Try hot milk, which contains tryptophan, a natural tranquilliser, or yoghurt.

Take a five-minute, leisurely walk.

Treat yourself to a night cap, but only if you have not had a drink all day.

Mattress support

Support without sag is the key, says physiotherapist Wendy Emberson.

"When lying on your side, the bony bits - hips, shoulders and knees - should sink in so that the waist and spine are supported. This does not happen with an "orthopaedic mattress', which means your spine and joints are under strain."

When buying a new bed, don't just lie flat on it for 30 seconds, looking embarrassed. Try each bed for five minutes or more, in a variety of sleeping positions. The average weight difference between men and women is 25 kg, so you might prefer two single mattresses that bolt together. Mattresses should be turned regularly. If you have a bad back or arthritis, a good mattress can vastly improve the quality of sleep. You will also feel less stiff in the morning.

Pillow talk

One pillow only is the general rule. One man began to suffer such bad headaches that he feared a brain tumour. He had been sleeping on his front with five pillows; after changing to one, his 'headache" vanished. Nerve compression when the neck is under strain can also lead to the frightening sensation of a "dead" arm.

When lying on your back, a good pillow should fit into the nape of your neck. When sleeping on your side, the pillow should fill the space between your ear and shoulder; scrunch it up if necessary. People with broad shoulders sometimes prefer a high, harder pillow. To avoid neck problems on a holiday, take your pillow with you.

Some people, because of heartburn, breathing problems or snoring, like to sleep propped up. Rather than adding pillows, it is best to raise the head of the bed by placing the legs on a brick. This keeps the neck and spine straight.

The best position

Whether flat on your back, curled up in a foetal position or on your front with arms splayed like a windmill, sleep position is largely a habit. In fact, we change positions is largely a habit. In fact, we change positions about 60 times a night.

Hazards to Our Health from Pollution

Water pollution

Considering a WHO study pointed out almost a decade ago, 80 per cent of the deaths in our country are caused by water-related diseases every time we drink a glass of water".

Our drinking water comes from two sources: surface water and groundwater. After surface water - rivers, lakes and canals - was declared polluted some decades ago, there was a race to switch to 'safer' groundwater. But the bad news is that today surface water is more polluted than ever and groundwater is far from safe. Scientists at the National Environment Engineering and Research Institute have concluded that 70 per cent of the available water in India is polluted.

The three main sources of water pollution are industry, agriculture and municipal users.

"Waste from our households accounts for almost 80 per cent of all pollutants." So in the absence of proper sewage and water treatment facilities, people across the country are consuming their own rubbish and excreta.

Add to this the agricultural waste that trickles into the surface water in and around cities. Nitrates, sulphates and fluorides - poisonous components found in fertilisers and agrochemicals - flow down in large quantities into rivers and canals from fields surrounding them. Excessive accumulation of nitrates give rise to cancerous growths in the human gastroinstestinal tract. Sulphates attack the alimentary canal and fluorides teeth.

Pesticides, handy tools for suicide scenes in Hindi films, get washed down by rain and collect in low lying areas near a river and seep into it. Pesticides and fertilisers manufacturers play a major role in poisoning us. Although the Water Act (1974), makes dumping of effluents into water illegal, a few large and most medium and small scale units indulge in it regardless. Other high-polluting industries - distilleries, tanneries; pulp and paper, electroplating, textiles and dyeing units - pump in heavy metals, phenols, cyanide, oil and grease, which are extremely difficult to treat. Their accumulation in the human body over a long period can be fatal.

Most of them don't bother to install mandatory treatment plants and some which do, don't operate them as the costs are huge.

The main reason for groundwater pollution is the culture of over dependence on it. Industrialisation and the population explosion has dried out the shallow layers and in the absence of regular regeneration, the concentration of pollutants have become abnormally high in the ground-water.

Apart from the pollutants which percolate and seep into the groundwater from the top, its excessive mining has lead to a relatively new problem - widespread poisoning of arsenic, a known carcinogen - in West Bengal and more recently a calamity situation in neighbouring Bangladesh.

At an international conference on arsenic poisoning of groundwater in Dhaka in February, global experts discussed ways to combat what is possibly the largest mass poisoning case in the world with more than 50 million people at risk.

The calamity has occurred due to large-scale withdrawal of groundwater - 97 per cent of Bangladesh uses groundwater - which gradually denuded the arsenic deposited under the fertile Bengal delta which found its way into drinking water by leaching in shallow aquifers causing arsenicosis. The problem has reached such alarming proportions because of late detection of the problem as the toxicity may take 8 to 14 years to manifest itself.

If you now think only bottled mineral water is safe - think again. For, experts claim that many quick buck seekers in every corner of the country are simply drawing out groundwater into bottles, adding a bit of carbon-dioxide to it for sparkle and flooding the market.

Food pollution

The manufacturer doesn't care about what he's putting into your food, and neither does the government

Before you bite into that *jalebi*, think a moment. You know, of course, that it is filled with oil (which will clog your arteries) and sugar (which will interfere with your metabolism). But those aren't the only poisons that *jalebi* contains. The oil has probably been hydrogenated which can cause cancer. Look at the maker of the jalebis. Do you think he cares what colouring agents he puts in? Do you think he's bothered about the possibilities of adding carcinogenic properties?

But then the jalebi-maker is not alone. You might even say you're taking your chances eating his wares from an uncovered stall on that dirty thoroughfare. But what do you do when some of the reputed brand names are also in there, popping a poison or two into their preparations?

Consider this list of horror stories from the mouth of hell:

In 1995, the government banned candy floss, on the grounds that it contained cancer-causing agents that harmed the liver, the spleen, the kidneys and the brain. Candy floss is back. Are the contaminants back too?

The food colouring often used in *sevganthia*, *jalebis* and Mughlai *pulao* is Metanil yellow which has been proved to cause cancer, anaemia, paralysis and even mental retardation in the young. That could, of course, be the result of the turmeric powder used which is often contaminated with Metanil yellow so that the manufacturers can stint on the amount of turmeric they put in.

Or you could find that the red chilli powder you're using has Sudan red in it, another colouring chemical that causes paralysis and cancer.

Deep-fried samosas, stored ketchups, cheese and mushrooms, sausages, salted fish and seafood are rich in nitrosoamines which can give you cancer.

Any baked crunchy is likely to overdose you with salt and give you hypertension and even kidney problems.

So what's safe? Fruit? Not unless its organically grown. If its been sprayed with DDT, you'd better wash it or you'll choke to death. DDT accumulates in the system and prevents the body from absorbing oxygen, which eventually causes asphyxiation. But even washing may not do it because DDT can penetrate the top layers of thin-skinned fruit and dissolve into it. And if you suddenly find an apple or a melon that is sweeter than normal, it might have been injected with a banned carcinogenic sweetener, many of which are cheaper than sugar and have 500 times its sweetening power.

Various bodies have tried to control and moderate the use of these poisons but the problem has always been policing. There are laws, there are penalties but we still haven't cracked the problem of putting them into practice.

Air pollution

The poisonous air in Indian cities has set a new record in WHO reports. And it's killer.

Millions of Delhiites suffering from respiratory disorders, cannot deny that there is something wrong in the composition of air in their metropolis. Instead of the regular 20-79-1 per cent ratio of oxygen, nitrogen and other gases, there are large quantities of oxides, suspended particles and toxic compounds which play havoc with our lungs. The situation is no different in Mumbai, where breathing is equivalent to consuming 10 cigarettes a day. Or in any other Indian city. Spiralling levels of air pollution - that urban curse - have made gas chambers of our business hubs.

"The main culprit as far as air pollution in cities goes is exhaust from vehicles, followed by industries, and lastly, burning of refuse".

Even as new urban centres and mini-Mumbais spring up all over India, a study by a Delhi-based NGO, the Centre for Science and Environment, revealed a shocking figure: there are an estimated 51,779 deaths every year in Indian cities because of air pollution.

Indeed, pollution was never so assisted as in an urban set-up. To beat the heat, you travel in an AC car, but in the process you aid the production of ozone, which can damage the respiratory cilia and cause chest pain.

We might as well rework the standard line taught to Class I students: polluted air is everywhere. The levels of sulphur dioxide, carbon monoxide, hydrocarbons and suspended particulate matter (SPM) in Indian cities far exceed the limits set by the World Health

Organisation. Consider SPM pollution levels stated by a WHO/UNEP study in 1996. Delhi ranked fourth, while Calcutta was sixth and Mumbai thirteenth. Ahmedabad, Calcutta, Kanpur and Nagpur too find a mention in environmental impact studies.

Ultimately, it is the human body which has to pay the price for man-made pollution. Increased levels of sulphur dioxide, particulate matter and ozone can lead to irritation in the eyes, nose and throat and frequent colds, to serious ailments such as asthma, chronic bronchitis, lung fibrosis and cancer. Taking in carbon monoxide reduces the amount of oxygen reaching the brain, thus causing angina, giddiness and confusion. Lead, which is released from petrol-run vehicles, affects the liver and brain and leads to learning disabilities in children. A World Bank study in 1992 had stated that 40,351 permature deaths in 36 Indian cities were due to ambient air pollution levels exceeding WHO standards.

Dust pollution

All the dust that we inhale does not produce disease because there is an inherent protective mechanism in the lungs and respiratory tract.

Dust may be fibrogenic, irritant, inert and allergic. The ability of dust to produce adverse health effects depends on:

i. Nature of dust and its physio-chemical properties.
ii. Concentration of free silica in the dust.
iii. Duration of exposure.
iv. Health status including presence/absence of tuberculosis, asthma, bronchitis, etc.
v. Individual susceptibility such as bronchopulmonary clearing mechanism, genetic disorders and smoking habits.
vi. Use and efficiency of the protective equipment.

Health Effects

i. Dust may aggravate already existing respirator illness such as asthma, bronchitis and tuberculosis.
ii. Respirable particles may get deposited in the lungs and depending on their nature may produce a type of lung disease generally known as Pneumoconiosis, which means presence of dust in the lungs and the tissues, reaction to its presence.
iii. Among the different types of Pneumoconiosis we are more concerned with silicosis. It is a progressive disease and may be associated with tuberculosis. It may take 20 to 25 years for the individual to develop the disease. There may or may not be symptoms. The symptoms, if present, are dysponea (breathlessness), dry cough, feverish feeling and chest pain.
iv. Coal dust produces coal workers pneumoconiosis, and aggravates the existing chest diseases.
v. Inhalation of iron oxide particles or iron dust produces sclerosis which is a mild pneumoconiosis and reversible condition.
vi. Nuisance dust may also irritate the eyes, the upper respiratory tract and skin.

You can help yourself

a) Ensure proper maintenance of in-built ventilation system. Inform supervisors of any failure of dedusting mechanism.
b) Maintain good housekeeping and ventilation.

c) Do not smoke! Smoking is known to increase respiratory illness.
d) Please bring to the notice of the doctor any chronic respiratory illness such as tuberculosis, bronchial asthma, bronchitis, etc. Use appropriate dust masks and replace filters at periodic intervals.
e) Do not confuse dust masks with gas masks. These cannot be interchanged.

Food and Nutrition

Human nutrition is the study of how food affects the health and survival of the human body. Without food our bodies cannot stay warm, build or repair tissues or maintain a heart beat. Eating the right foods can help us avoid certain diseases. These and other important functions are fuelled by chemical substances in our food called nutrients. These are classified as:

Water helps the absorption of the food materials through the digestive tract. A person can survive only 8-10 days without water. Water also maintains a natural balance between dissolved salts and water inside and outside of cells. While water has no calorific value without it in our diet we cannot digest or absorb the foods we eat or eliminate the body's digestive waste.

Carbohydrates are the human body's key source of energy providing 4 calories of energy per gram. When carbohydrates are broken down by the body, the sugar glucose is produced. Glucose is critical to help maintain tissue protein, metabolise fat, and fuel the central nervous system.

Proteins help build and repair body tissues from hair and fingernails to muscles. In addition to this proteins speed up chemical reactions in the body, serve as chemical messengers, fight infection and transport oxygen from lungs to the body tissue. Although protein produces 4 calories of energy per gram, the body uses proteins for energy only if carbohydrates and fat intake is insufficient. When tapped as an energy source protein is diverted, from the many critical functions it performs for our bodies.

Fats provide 9 calories of energy per gram. They are the most concentrated of the energy producing nutrients, so our bodies need only very small quantities. Fats play an important role in building the membranes that surround our cells and in helping blood to clot. Once digested and absorbed, fats help the body absorb certain vitamins. Fats stored in the body cushion vital organs and protect us from extreme cold and heat.

Vitamins and minerals are needed by the body in very small amount to trigger the chemical reactions necessary to maintain good health.

Storing Food

It is necessary for every housewife to have a fair knowledge of the purchase and storage of food. Given below are a few helpful hints—

Rice, pulses and legumes should be stored in air tight tins.

Flour and *maida* can be stored in air tight polythene bags and kept in the fridge. Alternatively one could use air tight containers. Keep whole grain flours in cool and dry place.

Fruits and vegetables
Keep all vegetables in the fridge in separate polythene bags.

Cut lemons and grapefruit will keep moist if placed cut side down on a saucer.

Wash and trim fresh green vegetables before storing.

Fruits should be ripened at room temperature and then put away in the refrigerator.

Do not cut fruits until ready to use.

To keep asparagus fresh, cut a small amount off the bottom of each stalk. Stand the stalk upright in a container in a small amount of water, cover with a plastic bag and refrigerate.

Before storing root vegetables e.g. carrots cut off their leafy green tops.

Sorting out vegetables before putting them away is a must.

Open bundles of palak, remove rotten leaves and other weeds. Then wrap them in a double sheet of newspaper. Put in a large polythene bag and store in the fridge.

Remove leaves and stalks from cauliflower before putting them away.

Ensure to turn polythene bags inside out or dry them out from time to time as vegetables tend to sweat due to the moisture content in them. This will prevent moisture dripping from the glass cover of the tray and spoiling the vegetables.

Store chillies and ginger in plastic or glass containers inside the fridge.

Dhania can be stored by dipping their roots in a glass of water and standing them at the back of the fridge.

Store lemons in polythene bags.

Keep vegetables and fruits in the fridge because there are certain enzymes in the fruits and vegetables which combine with oxygen from the atmosphere and destroy the vitamins present in them. These enzymes are inactive when food is kept chilled, so fruits and vegetables should be kept in the fridge immediately.

Bananas, oranges and potatoes, are usually never kept in the refrigerator because the reason is simple. These fruits and vegetables have a thick peel which protects the vitamins.

Dairy products
Paneer will keep fresh longer if it is refrigerated upside down in original carton

Before putting away an opened carton of ice-cream in the freezer press plastic wrap on to the surface of the ice-cream.

To check freshness of an egg put in a container of cold water, if it floats to the top its too old to use.

To preserve left over egg whites pour into plastic ice cubes tray and freeze.

Milk and cream should be covered properly. Remove only amount to be used at one time, keep away from foods and flavours.

Use soft cheese quickly. Wrap left over cheese tightly in waxed paper.

Fish meat and poultry
Wrap poultry and meat loosely in wax paper to allow air to circulate around the flesh.

Freeze chicken broth in ice-cubes trays. When frozen store in plastic bags.

Wrap bacon in wax paper. Remove only amount to be used at one time.

Wrap fish tightly or leave in store wrapping, cook as soon as possible.

Freezing food

Clean your refrigerator and freezer at regular intervals to control odour.

Prevent odour from spreading by making all food wrapped and covered.

Before refrigerating any liquid ensure that it is in a tightly sealed container.

To cool food quickly before freezing set hot pans in ice water. Wrap the food and freeze it at once.

Maintain a list of frozen foods. This would enable you to cook the older items first.

Frost-free refrigerators have made the task of keeping the fridge clean much easier. However, if you still have a fridge that is not frost free make sure you defrost it. When the frost is 1/4 inches thick, use a dull plastic scraper. After defrosting dip a cloth in glycerine and wipe the freezer coils with it. This will make your task easier the next time over.

How to Buy Medicines Over the Counter

These medicines are available at chemist shops, supermarkets and other stores and do not require a prescription. Nevertheless certain precautions should be taken before buying medicines.

- Read instructions about the dose
- The drug dose is according to the body weight
- If someone between the age of 12-15 is underweight he should be given the dosage for a 12 years old
- Start with smaller doses in old people

Medicines for colds—many types of medicines are available for curing colds. Asthma patients or peptic ulcer patients should refrain from buying aspirin containing cold cures.

Cough syrup—if you have a dry cough with minimal white sputum, you require a Cough suppressant. If you have a cough with sputum you require expectorants. If you have a dry cough with minimal sputum following an attack of cold you can choose any commercial cough syrup, but in case of yellow sputum, never take an over the counter preparation.

Pain killers—are of two kinds paracetamol and aspirin or sometimes both as a combination. Paracetamol is the safest pain killer. Old people, asthma, peptic ulcer and hyperacidity patients should avoid aspirin.

Menu Making for Daily Meals

Increasingly today, members of the family have to rush in different directions be it school or the workplace. Thus the breakfast becomes a meal that is had on the run. Similarly lunch may be had out of a packed tiffin box or bought from the canteen. We seem to forget that in the process we are completely neglecting our bodies. The housewife thus should ensure that while planning for the day, menu making for the day should be the highest on her priority list. The menu should be so planned as to include all the essential nutrients. Balanced meal at least twice a day is a must. Here are some tips:

Turn menu making into a family project.

Try unfamiliar fruits and vegetables.

Try out new recipes. Exchanging recipes with your neighbours and friends or consulting books goes a long way.

Change your meal pattern e.g. instead of serving rice and dal everyday try out a baked dish.

Notice what your family enjoys at restaurants, try to duplicate those dishes at home.

Vary the shapes and colours of vegetables.

Try to liven up the meal by adding a crunchy vegetable salad or raita.

While serving leftover dishes e.g. chicken curry, don't just repeat it - instead reform it e.g. make it into kathi rolls or dry the gravy and use it as a filling for samosas.

Try and include high fibre foods in the diet especially if catering to elderly people.

While cooking red meat ensure that the fat is trimmed properly.

One can serve fresh fruit for desert.

Instead of butter, season foods with lime juice, vinegar or spices.

Pureed vegetables make excellent sauces for fish, poultry and vegetables.

Menu Making for a Party/ Party Cooking

Plan your menu so as to make it interesting, but do not experiment on your guests.

Select dishes that go together in balanced diet formality etc.

Plan your menu so that serving is easy.

Prepare as many dishes as possible ahead of time. Choose recipes that can be made a day or two in advance.

If you cook in advance remember that dishes to be re-heated should be slightly underdone.

Choose dishes that do not call for last minute attention.

If you hire outside help, hire a caterer in advance and always ask to sample his food.

Be aware of your guests' diet, any needs and preference, e.g. vegetarians may prefer salads, dals or raita.

While planning your menu balance rich foods with light foods.

Avoid serving white or light coloured foods together.

Buy the best meat and other foods, do not stinge.

Select fruits and vegetables that are in season as these taste better.

Health Watch

Under this section we will examine the values of food, colour in food, ways of fighting cancer, and water.

Let us first begin with salads. Yes salads. Most doctors and nutritional experts suggest green leafy vegetables as a cure for almost all diseases. But here's the catch, did you know that salad could also kill you!

Salad vegetables are grown in soil which is prone to faecal contamination by animals and humans. It is prone to infestation of worms. Thus chances of contamination are high. These worms work their way from the intestine to the brain. The larvae burrow through the stomach walls and enter the blood vessels from where they are disseminated to tissues, including the central nervous system. Although they remain harmless in muscles, in the brain or spinal cord these cysts degenerate, their outline becomes irregular, fluid oozes out and the content of the cyst becomes turbid. This can result in swellings in the brain or spinal cord. This causes disorders like fits, motor impairment and even paralysis. Eventually, these cysts degenerate and many of them calcify. If these cysts degenerate completely, the swelling may also disappear, this leads to the disappearance of the symptom as well. However, chances of permanent damage cannot be ruled out.

Despite development of technology the endless micro-organisms cannot be put to an end. The increase in the storage life of chilled foods presents the problem of low temperature bacteria such as listeria. Listeria is a resistant bacterium and is responsible for food poisoning from cooked and chilled chicken products which are heated in the microwave. This bacteria also grow on vegetables, e.g. cabbage, cauliflower. Frozen shrimps are also a source of this bacteria. Listeria may also be present in ice-creams.

Hence, prevention is better than cure. Always take the following precautions:

a) Never munch mooli or gajar without first scraping and washing thoroughly.
b) Wash each cabbage separately. Wash the cabbage again after cutting it.
c) While stir frying vegetables, cook it slightly more to kill the parasites.
d) Ensure that children wash their hands before eating.
e) Ensure that your servants follow hygiene rules.
f) Avoid salads at parties and restaurants.
g) Cook all vegetables and meats at high temperatures to destroy listeria and other pathogens.
h) Always pasteurise milk.
i) Disinfect dish cloths in a sodium hypochloride cloth at regular intervals.
j) Clean and disinfect work surfaces, chopping boards and tap handles in kitchen.
k) Keep your fridge clean and cold (between 0-4 degree celsius).
l) Store cooked meat and raw meat separately. The former should be kept in the bottom shelf of the fridge.
m) Clean and disinfect moist surfaces like sinks, toilets, etc.
n) Pregnant women and senior citizens should avoid all soft cheese and pre-packed ready to eat foods.

■■

CHAPTER-9

First Aid

Before rushing to the doctor, all households should have an emergency medical kit which should be kept in an accessible place. It should contain the following items:

- Oral and rectal thermometers
- Flashlight
- Dosage spoon, eyedropper
- Hot water bottle
- Ice bag
- Blunt end scissors
- Tweezers
- Cotton swabs
- Safety matches
- Adhesive bandages in assorted sizes
- Roll of absorbent cotton
- Painkiller
- 3% hydrogen peroxide solution
- Antacid
- Antibiotic ointment
- Decongestant
- Antivomiting compound
- Burnol
- Balm

Work, Emotions and Mental Health

Five out of ten leading causes of disability worldwide are psychiatric in origin. In embracing a materialistic system with its bagful of unfulfilled aspirations and expectations, people complain of feeling brittle, fragmented and tired of the intolerable mercenary routines of life.

The West and the Japanese as also those in Singapore have influenced the world with their concept of the work ethic. A man was expected to work long hours in the office and be virtually wedded to his work rather than to his wife! This gave rise to a new expression "workaholic" in which men put their personal lives on the backburner in order to work, get ahead and achieve success. One's success at work determined one's self-confidence and self-esteem.

Family relationships, romance, sex, children and even one's health took second place to one's all consuming obsession with work. Even today, there are law firms and investment banks in the U.S. where management recruits earn a million but work from 8 a.m. to 11 p.m. Six days a week! By thirty five they have earned enough to retire. In India too, many corporate executives are wedded to their companies, working long hours, travelling endlessly, chasing "targets". Many die premature deaths as they drink, smoke and suffer stress due to this unnatural lifestyle and unrelenting pressure and competition to achieve and succeed.

Achieving the right balance between the workplace and the home or one's personal life is essential to both the well-being of the individual and the organisation. For too long people have been programmed to regard their company's products and services as more important than themselves and their personal lives. In doing so, one not only loses the correct perspective between work and home but often in losing one's spouse or the children, work suffers. Peter Bolt, an American management consultant today emphasises, that if we live to work, rather than work to live, our lives will be out of balance and we will fail on all fronts!

'Don't worry, be happy' say the lyrics of a hit song and it was popular because most people want to be happy. Happiness, high self-esteem, optimism are all linked together and contribute towards our physical and mental well-being. If you are happy there are more chances that you will be healthy and not suffer the pangs of ulcers or the trauma of insomnia.

Rules for mental health

- Postpone until tomorrow what you are worrying about today.
- Don't brood over the past, plan for the future.
- Make the best of any situation.
- Limit your desires to things which are reasonable and attainable.
- Cultivate a tolerant attitude.
- Develop a sense of humour.
- Find a hobby to occupy yourself. Try and keep busy at all times.
- Share whatever is troubling you with others it will lighten the burden on you

Saving energy

- Plan your work so that you do most of it while sitting.
- Stand straight with your weight borne by the bony framework. This puts minimum strain on muscles and ligaments.
- Stand straight from hips to neck.
- To save your back, bend at the ankles or hips.
- Use whole body at centre if any weight to be removed.
- Take a break after every hour of work.
- Have tables and working surface at the correct height.
- While carrying packages hold the body in balance.
- Use labour saving devices when you can

Caring for the Sick

When somebody is ill in the house the doctor may want a record of the following:

a) Temperature.
b) Quality and duration of sleep.
c) Frequency and quality of bowel movement.
d) Quantity of urine passed in 24 hours.
e) Items and amount of food consumed.
f) Amount of liquids taken.
g) Mood of the patient.
h) Complaints that a patient may have.
i) Ensure that the patient has fresh and clean sheets everyday.
j) Do not allow any wrinkles to be left, smoothen the sheet and tuck tightly on the head and foot of the bed.

- Brush the patient's hair, wash his hands and face. A daily spongie bath is refreshing.
- If the disease is communicable ensure that all eating and drinking utensils are

washed with soap and water. Scald with boiling water after each use by the patient. Keep the patient's utensils separate from the other members of the family. In case of an extremely contagious disease the linen, mattress, and clothing should be burned.

Advice to the person taking care of the patient

- The person should maintain a cheerful and sympathetic attitude.
- Wash your hands with soap immediately after each handling of the patient.
- The attendant should strictly obey all orders of the physician regarding the care of the patient.

Food needs of the patient

Liquid diet—Includes milk or milk drinks, fruit and vegetable juices, soups, coffee, tea or cocoa.

Soft and bland diet includes—any of the above plus pureed vegetables, toast, cereals, custard, eggs, ice-cream.

Light diet—includes any of the above plus baked or steamed fruits or vegetable, chopped chicken.

Diabetic diet—includes minimum sugar and calories and limited protein.

Cardiac diet—minimum salt

Anti constipation diet—Bulky foods, food rich in fibre, whole cereals, fruits, vegetables and fluids.

High calorie diet—large portion of starches and fats.

Low calorie diet—minimum fats, starches, sugar, leafy green vegetables.

Alternative Therapy

Reiki

Reiki is a complete system for activating and putting to use natural energy to promote healing, personal growth, transformation, and enlightenment.

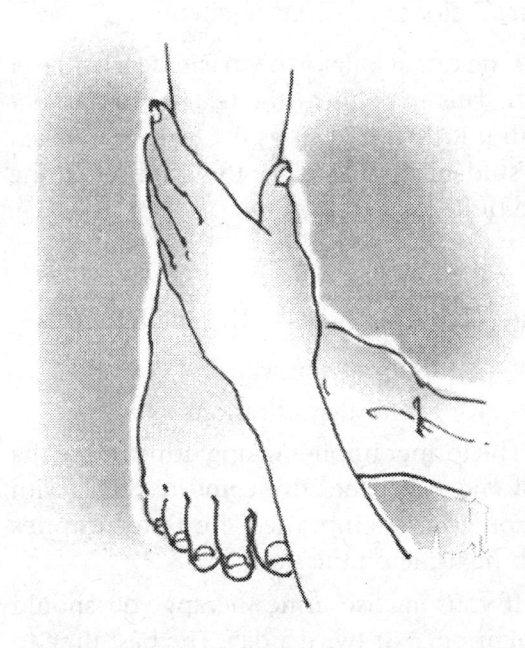

What is Reiki: 'Rei' means 'universal', 'ki' means 'life force'. A method of self-healing founded by a Japanese missionary Mikao Usui. It is not a religion.

Who can learn Reiki: Anyone, including children. It can be taught in any language.

How does Reiki Heal: By flowing through the affected parts of the energy field and charging them with positive energy. The energy flows just by placing your hands. However, some Reiki masters can heal over distances too.

What can be Treated: Almost every illness or injury. It is almost always beneficial and has no side-effects. It works to improve the results of other types of medical treatment, reducing negative side-effects, shortening healing time, reducing or eliminating pain, and lowering stress and creating optimism.

Third degree Reiki: This is also called the maxey degree. At this level the person is ready to learn the intricate process of passing Reiki energy and activate it in others through transmissions called 'attunements'.

One can also take the master teacher level Reiki. This introduces the teacher to another symbol RAKU. It enables the teacher to teach the student now to place the symbols in the field of Reiki.

Urine therapy

Urine Therapy consists of two main parts :

  a) Internal application
  b) External application

The former implies taking urine inside the body and letting the urine come in contact with the mucous membrane. The latter implies rubbing urine on the skin.

If you practise urine therapy you should drink it once or twice a day. The best time to do so is in the morning. If you are suffering from some disease then drink it several times a day including the first urine of the day.

Water therapy

To maintain the proper amount of water in your body consume at least 6-8 glasses of clear liquids each day and more if you are physically active or sweat a lot.

Pregnant women need extra fluids. Infants also need more water than adults. In warm weather babies should be given water between feedings.

Acupressure

It is an ancient and simple oriental therapy which is prevalent even today. Though accupressure is easy and simple it is an effective treatment and can be taken by an individual in the privacy of his own home. This treatment can be taken as often as possible.

Home Remedies

Anaemia

Vitamin B 12: Vitamin B 12 is needed for preventing or curing anaemia. This vitamin is usually found in animal protein, especially in meats such as kidney and liver. There are, however, other equally good sources of Vitamin B 12 such as dairy products which also contain some B 12.

Beetroots: Beetroots are very helpful in curing anaemia. Beet juice contains potassium, phosphorus, calcium, sulphur, iodine, iron, copper, carbohydrates, protein, fat, vitamins B1, B 2, B 6 niacin, and vitamin P. With their high iron content, beets help in the formation of red blood cells. The juice of red beet strengthens the body's powers of resistance and has proved to be an excellent remedy for anaemia, especially for children and teenagers, where other blood-forming remedies have failed.

Fenugreek: The leaves of fenugreek help in many ways. The cooked leaves should be taken by adolescent girls to prevent anaemia, which may occur due to the onset of puberty and menstruation. The seeds of fenugreek are also a valuable cure for anaemia, being rich in iron. The leaves and seeds are useful for diabetic patients.

Lettuce: Lettuce is another effective remedy for this ailment as it contains a considerable amount of iron. It can, therefore, be used as a good tonic food for anaemia. The iron in it is easily absorbed by the body.

Spinach: This leafy vegetable is a valuable source of high grade iron. After its absorption, it helps in the formation of haemoglobin and red blood cells. It is thus beneficial in building up the blood, and in the prevention and treatment of anaemia.

Asthma

Honey: Honey is one of the most common home remedies for asthma. It is said that if a jug of honey is held under the nose of an asthma patient and he inhales the air that comes into contact with it, he starts breathing easier and deeper. The effect lasts for an hour or so. One to two teaspoonfuls of honey provide relief. Honey can also be taken in a cup of milk or water. Honey thins out accumulated mucus and helps its elimination from the respiratory passages. It also tones up the pulmonary lining and thereby prevents the production of mucus in future. Some authorities recommend one-year old honey for asthma and respiratory diseases.

Figs: Among fruits, figs have proved very valuable in asthma. They give comfort to the patient by draining off the phlegm. Three or four dry figs should be cleaned thoroughly with warm water and soaked overnight. They should be taken first thing in the morning, along with the water in which they were soaked. This treatment may be continued for about two months.

Lemon: Lemon is another fruit found beneficial in the treatment of asthma. The juice of one lemon, diluted in a glass of water and taken with meals, will bring good results.

Indian Gooseberry: Indian gooseberry has also proved valuable in asthma. Five grams of gooseberry mixed with one tablespoon of honey forms an effective medicinal tonic for the treatment of this disease. It should be taken every morning. When fresh fruit is not available, dry gooseberry powder can be mixed with honey.

Bitter Gourd Roots: The roots of the bitter gourd plant have been used in folk medicine for asthma since ancient times. A teaspoon of the root paste, mixed with an equal amount of honey or juice of the tulsi leaves, given once every night for a month, acts as an excellent medicine for this disease.

Drumstick Leaves: A soup prepared from drumstick leaves, and taken once daily, has been found beneficial in the treatment of asthma. This soup is prepared by adding a handful of leaves to 180 ml of water and boiling it for five minutes. After being allowed to cool, a little salt, pepper, and lime juice may be added to this soup.

Ginger: A teaspoonful of fresh ginger juice, mixed with a cup of fenugreek decoction and honey to taste, acts as an excellent expectorant in cases of asthma. The decoction of fenugreek can be made by mixing one tablespoonful of fenugreek seeds in a cupful of water. This remedy should be taken once in the morning and once in the evening.

Garlic: Garlic is another effective home remedy for asthma. Ten garlic cloves, boiled in 30 ml of milk, make an excellent medicine for the early stages of asthma. This mixture should be taken once daily by the patient. Steaming ginger tea with two minced garlic cloves in it, can also help to keep the problem under control, and should be taken in the morning and evening.

Bishop's Weed: The herb bishop's weed has been found valuable in asthma. Half a teaspoon of bishop's weed should be mixed in a glass of buttermilk and taken twice daily. It is an effective remedy for relieving difficult expectoration caused by dried-up phlegm. A hot poultice of the seeds should be used for dry fomentation to the chest, twice daily. The patient can also inhale steam twice a day from boiling water mixed with ajwain. It will dilate the bronchial passages.

Safflower: Safflower seeds are beneficial in the treatment of bronchial asthma. Half a teaspoon of powder of the dry seeds, mixed with a tablespoon of honey, can be taken once or twice a day in treating this disease. This acts as an expectorant and reduces the spasms by liquefying the tenacious sputum. An infusion of five grams of flowers mixed with one tablespoon of honey, taken once daily, is also useful in this disease.

Linseed: A decoction of linseed is also considered useful in curing congestion in asthma and preventing recurrence of attacks. The decoction prepared by boiling a teaspoon of linseed powder and a piece of palm candy in two cups of water till the mixture is reduced to half. This decoction taken with a tablespoon of milk once daily, will provide relief from chest congestion. Simultaneously, a linseed poultice should be applied externally during the attack, at the lung bases.

Mustard Oil: During the attack, mustard oil, mixed with a little camphor, should be massaged over the back for the chest. This will loosen up phlegm and ease breathing.

Copper: One of the preventive measures to stop attacks of asthma is to drink water which has been kept overnight in a copper vessel. This water, with traces of copper in it, is believed to change one's constitutional tendency to get respiratory problems.

Backache

Garlic: The most important home remedy for backache is the use of garlic. Two or three cloves should be taken every morning to get results. An oil prepared from garlic and rubbed on the back will give great relief. This oil is prepared by frying ten cloves of garlic in 60 ml of oil in a frying pan. Any of the oils which are used as rubefacients, such as mustard oil, sesame oil, and coconut oil can be used according to one's choice. They should be fried on a slow fire till they are brown. After the oil has cooled, it should be applied vigorously on the back, and allowed to remain there for three hours. The patient may, thereafter, take a warm-water bath. This treatment should be continued for at least fifteen days.

Lemon: Lemon is another useful remedy for backache. The juice of one lemon should be mixed with common salt and taken by the patient twice daily. It will give relief.

Chebulic Myroblan: The use of chebulic myroblan is beneficial in the treatment of backache. A small piece of this fruit should be eaten after meals. This will give quick relief.

Vitamin C: Vitamin C has proved valuable in case of severe backaches. About 2,000 mg of this vitamin should be taken daily.

Bronchitis

Turmeric: One of the most effective home remedies for bronchitis is the use of turmeric powder. Half a teaspoon of this powder should be administered with half a glass of milk, two or three times daily. It acts best when taken on an empty stomach.

Ginger: Another effective remedy for bronchitis is a mixture comprising of half a teaspoon each of the powder of ginger, pepper, and cloves, three times a day. It may be licked with honey or taken as an infusion with tea. The mixture of these three ingredients has also antipyretic qualities and is effective in reducing fever accompanying bronchitis. It also tones up the metabolism of the patient.

Chicken pox

Brown Vinegar: The use of brown vinegar is one of the most important among the several home remedies found beneficial in the treatment of chicken pox. Half a cup of this vinegar should be added to a bath of warm water. This will relieve the irritation of the skin.

Oatmeal: A bath of oatmeal is considered a natural remedy for relieving the itch due to chicken pox. This bath is prepared by cooking two cups of oatmeal in two litres of water for fifteen minutes. This mixture is then put into a cloth bag, preferably cotton, and a string is tied tightly around the top. This bag is allowed to float in a tub of warm water, and swished around until the water becomes turbid. Precaution should be taken to ensure that the bag is not torn. The child with chicken pox can splash and play in the water, making sure that water goes over all the scalds, while the pouch of oatmeal can remain in the tub.

Pea Water: Green pea water is another effective remedy for relieving irritation of the skin. The water in which fresh peas have been cooked can be used for this purpose.

Baking Soda: Baking soda is a popular remedy to control the itching in chicken pox. Some baking soda should be put in a glass of water. The child should be sponged with this water, so that the soda dries on the skin. This will keep the child away by this application.

Honey: The use of honey as an external application has also proved valuable in chicken pox. The skin should be smeared with honey. It will help in the healing of the disease within three days.

Carrot and Coriander: A soup prepared from carrots and coriander has been found beneficial in the treatment of chicken pox. About 100 gm of carrots and 60 gm of fresh coriander should be cut into small pieces and boiled for a while. The residue should be discarded. This soup should be taken once a day-decreases toxicity and reduces the duration of the illness. One lemon should be diluted in a glass of warm water, and a teaspoon of honey should be added to it. This should be taken once or twice daily.

Garlic: Garlic soup is an old remedy to reduce the severity of a cold, and should be taken once daily. The soup can be prepared by boiling three or four cloves of chopped garlic in a cup of water. Garlic contains antiseptic and antispasmodic properties, besides several other medicinal virtues. The oil contained in this vegetable helps to open up the respiratory passages. In soup form, it flushes out all toxins from the system and thus helps bring down fever. Five drops of garlic oil combined with a teaspoon of onion juice, and diluted in a cup of water, should be drunk two to three times a day. This has also been found to be very effective in the treatment of common cold.

Ginger: Ginger is another excellent remedy for colds and coughs. About ten grams of ginger should be cut into small pieces and boiled in a cup of water. It should then be strained and half a teaspoon of sugar added to it. This decoction should be drunk when hot. Ginger tea, prepared by adding a few pieces of ginger into boiled water before adding the tea leaves, is also an effective remedy for colds and for fevers resulting from cold. It may be taken twice daily.

Lady's Fingers: Lady's fingers are highly valuable in treating irritation of the throat and a persistent dry cough. This vegetable is rich in mucilage and acts as a drug to allay irritation, swelling, and pain. About 100 gm of lady's fingers should be cut into pieces, and boiled down in half a litre of water to make a decoction. The steam issuing from this decoction may also be inhaled once or twice a day to relieve throat irritation and a dry cough.

Turmeric: Turmeric is an effective remedy for colds and throat irritations. Half a teaspoon of fresh turmeric powder mixed in 30 ml of warm milk, and taken once or twice daily, is a useful prescription for these conditions. Turmeric powder should be put into a hot ladle, milk should then be poured in it and boiled over a slow fire. This mixture should then be drunk by the patient. In case of a running cold, smoke from the burning turmeric should be inhaled. It will increase the discharge from the nose and provide quick relief.

Tamarind and Pepper: Tamarind-pepper *rasam* is also considered an effective home remedy for a cold in South India. Dilute 50 mg tamarind in 250 ml of water. Boil the diluted tamarind water for a few minutes with a teaspoon of hot ghee and half a teaspoon of black pepper powder. This steaming hot rasam has a flushing effect, and should be taken three tines a day. As one takes it, the nose and eyes water and the nasal blockage is cleared.

Vitamin C: According to Dr. Linus Pauling, a Nobel prize winning scientist, the regular intake of vitamin C-75 mg for adults and 35 mg for children-will prevent the common cold. If, however, a cold has already appeared, large doses of this vitamin will relieve the symptoms and shorten its duration. He estimates that one to two grams (1000 mg to 2000 mg) per day is approximately the optimum amount of this vitamin for this purpose. His advice is to swallow one or two 500 mg tablets of vitamin C at the appearance of the first sign of the cold and continue the treatment by taking one to two 500 mg tablets daily.

Headache

Apple: An apple is valuable in all types of headaches. After removing the upper peel and the inner hard portion of a ripe apple, it should be taken with a little salt every morning on an empty stomach in such cases. This should be continued for about a week.

Henna: The flowers of henna have been found valuable in headaches caused by hot sun. The flowers should be rubbed in vinegar and applied over the forehead. This remedy will soon provide relief.

Cinnamon: Cinnamon is useful in headaches caused by exposure to cold air. A fine paste of this spice should be prepared by mixing it with water and it should be applied over the temples and forehead to obtain relief.

Marjoram: The herb marjoram is beneficial in the treatment of a nervous headache. An infusion of the leaves is taken as tea in the treatment of this disorder.

Rosemary: The herb rosemary has been found valuable in headaches resulting from cold. A handful of this herb should be boiled in a litre of water and put in a mug. The head should be covered with a towel and the steam inhaled for as long as the patient can bear. This should be repeated till the headache is relieved.

Other Measures: Other helpful measures in the treatment of headaches are a cleansing enema with water temperature at 37°C, a cold throat pack, frequent applications of towels wrung out from very hot water to the back of the neck, a cold compress at 4.4°C, to 15.6°C, applied to the head and face, or an alternate spinal compress. Hot fomentation over the abdominal region just before retiring relievs headaches caused by stomach and liver upsets.

Hot foot baths are also beneficial in the treatment of chronic headaches. The patient should keep his legs in a tub or bucket filled with hot water at a tempeature of 40°C to 45°C for fifteen minutes every night before retiring. This treatment should be continued for two or three weeks.

Yogic kriyas like *jalneti* and *kunjal*; pranayamas like anuloma viloma, shitali, and sitkari; and asanas such as uttanpadasana, sarvangasana, paschimottanasana, halasana, and shavasana are also beneficial in the treatment of headaches.

High blood cholesterol

Lecithin: Lecithin, also a fatty food substance and the most abundant of the phospholipids, is beneficial in case of increase in cholesterol level. It has the ability to break up cholesterol into small particles which can be easily handled by the system. With sufficient intake of lecithin, cholesterol cannot build up against the walls of the arteries and veins. Lecithin also increases the production of bile acids made from cholesterol, thereby reducing its amount in the blood. Egg yolk, vegetable oils, wholegrain cereals, soyabeans, and unpasturised milk are rich sources of lecithin. The cells of the body are also capable of synthesizing it as needed, if several of the B vitamins are present.

Vitamins: Vitamins B6 choline, and inositol are particularly effective in reducing the level of blood cholesterol. Wheat germ, yeast, or vitamin B extracted from bran contain high quantities of these vitamins. Vitamin E also elevates blood lecithin and reduces cholesterol.

The patient should take liberal quantities of vitamin E rich foods such as sunflower seeds, safflower, soyabean oils, butter, and sprouted seeds and grains.

Sunflower Seeds: Sunflower seeds are valuable in lowering high blood cholesterol. They contain a substantial quantity of linoleic acid which is the fat helpful in reducing cholesterol deposits on the walls of arteries. Substituting sunflower seeds for some of the solid fats like butter and cream will, therefore, lead to great improvement in health.

Menstrual problems

Parsley: Parsley is one of the most effective among the several home remedies in the treatment of menstrual disorders. It increases menstruation and assists in the regularisation of the monthly periods. This action is due to the presence of apiol, which is a constituent of the female sex hormone oestrogen. Cramps, which are a result of menstrual irregularities, are relieved and frequently corrected entirely by the regular use of parsley juice, particularly in conjunction with beet juice; or with beet, carrot, and cucumber juices. The recommended quantity is 75ml of each of the four juices.

Ginger: The use of ginger is another effective home remedy for menstrual disorders, especially in cases of painful menstruation and stoppage of menstrual flow. A piece of fresh ginger should be pounded and boiled in a cup of water for a few minutes. The infusion, sweetened with sugar, should be used thrice daily after meals as a medicine for treating this condition.

Sesame Seeds: Sesame seeds are valuable in menstrual problems. Half a teaspoon of powder of these seeds, taken with hot water twice daily, acts excellently in reducing spasmodic pain during menstruation in young, unmarried anaemic girls. Its regular use, two days prior to the expected periods, cures scanty menstruation. A warm hip bath containing a handful of crushed sesame seeds should be simultaneously taken along with this recipe.

Papaya: The unripe papaya helps the contractions of the muscle fibres of the uterus and is thus beneficial in securing a proper menstrual flow. Papaya is especially helpful when menstruation ceases due to stress or fright in young unmarried girls.

Bengal Gram: A bath prepared by putting an entire Bengal gram plant in hot water is beneficial in painful menstruation. The plant also may be used for a sitting steam bath.

Marigold: The herb Marigold, named after the Virgin Mary, is useful in allaying any pain during menstruation and facilitating menstrual flow. An infusion of the herb should be given in doses of one tablespoon twice daily for the treatment of these disorders.

Banana Flower: The use of banana flower is one of the most effective home remedies in the treatment of menorrhagia or excessive menstruation. One banana flower should be cooked and eaten with one cup of curd. This will increase the quantity of progesterone and reduce bleeding.

Coriander Seeds: Coriander seeds are also beneficial in the treatment of excessive menstruation. Six grams of these seeds should be boiled in half a litre of water. This decoction should be taken off the fire when only half the water remains. Sugar candy should be added to it and the patient should drink it when it is still warm.

Mango Bark: The juice of the fresh mango bark is another valuable remedy for heavy bleeding during menstruation. The juice is given with the addition of white of an egg or some mucilage - a kind of vegetable glue obtained from a plant, and a small quantity of the kernel of a poppy. As an alternative, a mixture of 10ml of a fluid extract of the bark, and 120ml of water may be given in doses of one teaspoon every hour or two.

Ashoka: The bark of the Ashoka tree is an effective remedy for excessive blood loss during the monthly period which occurs due to uterine fibroids and other causes. It should be given in the form of decoction in treating this condition.

About 90gm of the bark should be boiled in 30ml of milk and 360ml of water till the total quantity is reduced to about 90 gm. This quantity should be given in one day, in two or three doses. The treatment should commence from the fourth day of the monthly period and should be continued till the bleeding is checked. A fresh decoction should be made for use each day.

Indian Barbery: The herb Indian barbery is also useful in case of excessive bleeding. It should be given in doses of thirteen to twenty-five grams daily.

Rough Chaff: The herb rough chaff is also valuable in excessive menstruation. An infusion of the herb should be prepared by steeping 15gm of rough chaff in 250ml of water and used for treating this condition.

Hermal: The herb hermal is useful in regulating the menstrual periods. It is especially beneficial in painful and difficult menstruation. Two tablespoons of the seeds should be boiled in half a litre of water, till it is reduced by one - third. This decoction should be given in 15 to 30 ml doses.

Hemp: Hemp can be successfully used when menses do not start at the scheduled time. Five large heads of hemps should be boiled in half a litre of water till the water is reduced to half. It should then be strained and drunk before going to bed for two or three nights. This remedy seldom fails.

First Aid

1. Do first things first quickly, quietly and without fuss or panic.
2. Give artificial respiration if breathing has stopped - every second counts.
3. Stop any bleeding.
4. Guard against or treat for shock by moving the casualty as little as possible and handling him gently.

5. Do not attempt too much - do the minimum that is essential to save life and prevent the condition from worsening.
6. Reassure the casualty and those around and thus help to lessen anxiety.
7. Do not allow people to crowd round as fresh air is essential.
8. Do not remove clothes unnecessarily.
9. Arrange for the removal of the casualty to the care of a Doctor or hospital as soon as possible.

Shock

Shock is a condition of severe depression of the vital functions. It is associated with changes in the circulatory system varying from temporary weakness to complete failure. Its severity varies with the nature and extent of the injury and it is a common cause of death following severe injuries.

Type of shock

There are two types of shock:

1. Nerve Shock.
2. Established Shock.

General signs and symptoms of shock

These may vary from a transient attack of faintness to a state of collapse, and there may be:

1. Giddiness and faintness.
2. Coldness.
3. Nausea.
4. Pallor.
5. Cold clammy skin.
6. A slow pulse at first which tends to become progressively more feeble and rapid.
7. Vomiting.
8. Unconsciousness.

General treatment of shock

1. Reassure the casualty.
2. Lay him on his back with the head low and turned to one side unless there is an injury to the head, abdomen or chest when the head and shoulders should be slightly raised and supported. If he has vomited or if there is interference with breathing, place him in the three-quarter prone position.
3. Loosen clothing about the neck, chest and waist.
4. Wrap him in a blanket or rug.
5. If he complains of thirst he may be given sips of water, tea, coffee or other liquid but not alcohol.
6. Do not apply heat or friction to the limbs. Hot water bottles should not be used.

Special treatment of established shock: Proceed as already described but bear in mind that in severe cases, transfusion and surgery are matters of grave urgency if life is to be saved. It is therefore unwise to delay transfer to hospital for as long as even five minutes except to deal with failing respiration, to stop severe bleeding, to dress a sucking wound of the chest or to secure a limb badly broken.

7. Do not give anything by mouth (the casualty may require an anaesthetic).
8. Tilt the stretcher so that the level of the head is lower than the rest of the body, except in cases of head, chest or abdominal injury.
9. Remove urgently to hospital.

Asphyxia

When the lungs do not get a sufficient supply of fresh air vital organs and the important nerve centres in the brain which regulate their activity are deprived of oxygen and this causes a dangerous condition called Asphyxia.

Causes of asphyxia

1. Causes affecting the Respiratory Tract
   (a) Fluid in the air passages as in drowning.
   (b) Harmful gases or fumes in the air passages, e.g. coal gas, motor exhaust fumes, after-damp, smoke, sewer gas, ammonia.
   Note: Some gases affect the respiratory centre in addition.
   (c) Foreign bodies in the air passages causing choking, e.g. portions of food, artificial teeth, vomited matter in the case of an unconscious person (owing to failure of the action of the epiglottis), tongue falling back in the case of an unconscious person, blood collecting from a fractured jaw.
   (d) Compression of the windpipe, e.g. hanging, strangulation or throttling.
   (e) Smothering, e.g. overlaying an infant, an unconscious person lying face downwards on a pillow.
   (f) Swelling of the tissues within the throat as a result of burns, scalds, corrosives, stings (wasp or bee), or from some diseases affecting the throat.
2. Causes affecting the Respiratory Mechanism
   (a) Pressure on or crushing of the chest resulting from accidents in mines, quarries, sand pits or demolitions, or from pressure in a crowd.
   (b) Spasm of respiratory muscles in the case of certain poisons, e.g. Strychnine, or diseases, e.g. Tetanus (lockjaw).
   (c) Nervous diseases causing paralysis of the muscles of the chest wall or the diaphragm, e.g. Poliomyelitis.
   (d) Electric shock
3. Causes affecting the Respiratory Centre
   (a) Electric shock.
   (b) Stroke by lightning.
   (c) Poisons such as prussic acid and Morphine.
   (d) Some gases.

Signs and symptoms of asphyxia

Early stages:

1. Dizziness and weakness.
2. Shortness of breath.
3. Rapid pulse.
4. Partial loss of consciousness.
5. Swelling of the veins of the neck.
6. Congestion of the face with blueness of cheeks and lips.

These signs and symptoms may vary with the degree of asphyxia present.

7. The lips, nose, ears, fingers and toes are bluish-grey.
8. Breathing intermittent or absent.
9. Pulse slow and irregular.
10. Complete loss of consciousness.

General rules for treatment of asphyxia

1. Remove the cause if possible or the casualty from the cause.

2. Ensure that there is a free passage for air. In an unconscious person the tongue may fall back and obstruct the air passages. This possibility should be kept constantly in mind if the casualty is lying on his back.
3. Apply artificial respiration immediately. Artificial respiration must be continued until natural breathing is restored, if necessary for a long time unless a doctor decides that further effort will be of no avail.
4. Utilise any help available to:
   (a) Provide warmth, e.g. blankets.
   (b) Provide shelter from the elements.

Treatment in special cases

Drowning: While artificial respiration is being performed, instruct bystanders to remove wet clothing as far as practicable and wrap the casualty in dry blankets or other dry clothing.

Strangulation: Cut and remove the band constricting the throat.

Choking: To dislodge the obstruction bend the casualty's head and shoulders forward, or in the case of a small child hold him up side down, and thump his back hard between the shoulder two finger right to the back of the casualty's throat.

Swelling of the tissues within the throat: If breathing has not ceased or when it has been restored give ice to suck or, failing ice, cold water to sip. Butter, olive oil or medicinal paraffin may also be given.

Suffocation by smoke: Protect yourself by tying a towel, handkerchief or cloth, preferably wet, over your mouth and nose. Keep low and remove the casualty as quickly as possible.

Suffocation by poisonous gas:
 i. Before entering any enclosed space known or suspected to contain poisonous gas of any kind, take a deep breath and hold it.
 ii. Ensure a free circulation of air by opening or if necessary by breaking doors and windows.
 iii. If the gas is lighter than air, keep low; if heavier, remain in the upright position. Remove the casualty as quickly as possible.
 iv. In cases where ventilation is not possible and the character of the gas is known to be deadly a suitable gas-mask must be worn. An additional safety precaution is a lifeline.

Miscellaneous conditions

FOREIGN BODY EMBEDDED IN THE EYE

1. Prevent the casualty from rubbing the eye. In the case of a child it may be necessary to get help to keep him still.
2. Seat the casualty facing the light and stand in front of him. Pull down the lower eyelid.
   (a) If the foreign body is seen and does not appear to be embedded or adherent to the eyeball, remove it with the corner of clean handkerchief, preferably white, twirled up and moistened with clean water.
   (b) If the foreign body is embedded in or adherent to the eyeball, do not attempt to remove it but instruct the casualty to close his eyelids. Apply a soft pad of cotton wool and secure it by a bandage. See that medical aid is obtained.
   (c) If the foreign body has not been found and is suspected to be under the upper eyelid, instruct the patient to blink his eyelid under water.

Alternatively, lift the upper lid forward, push the lower lid beneath it and let go both eyelids. The lashes of the lower lid brush the inner surface of the upper one and may dislodge the foreign body. Should the first attempt be unsuccessful, repeat several times. If the foreign body is not dislodged, see that the casualty obtains medical aid as soon as possible, but when medical aid is not available:

i. Seat the casualty facing the light and stand behind him, steadying his head against your chest.
ii. Place a matchstick on the base of his upper eyelid, press it gently backwards and instruct the casualty to look downwards. Take hold of his upper eyelashes and pull the lid over the matchstick, thereby averting the eyelid.
iii. Remove the foreign body with a corner of a clean handkerchief as described in (a) above.
(d) When a corrosive acid or alkali is suspected, instruct the casualty to blink his eyelid under water or flush the eye with copious supplies of water. Apply a soft pad of cotton wool over his eye and keep the pad in position by a shade or bandage applied lightly, and see that he obtains medical aid as soon as possible.

Foreign body in the ear channel

If an insect has entered in the ear channel fill the ear with olive or salad oil or insert a few drops of surgical spirit; the insect will float and may be removed.

All other foreign bodies should be left in position and the casualty warned not to interfere with them.

See that medical aid is obtained.

Foreign body in the nose

Instruct the casualty to breathe through the mouth. Do not interfere with the foreign body. See that medical aid is obtained.

Foreign body in the stomach

Pins and other small objects such as coins or buttons may be accidentally swallowed. Smooth objects need not necessarily cause alarm.

Do not give anything by mouth. See that medical aid is obtained without delay.

Fish bone in the throat

These incidents can cause great discomfort with continued retching, coughing and even vomiting. Usually the casualty's alarm is very much exaggerated and not justified by his actual condition. Do not attempt to remove the fishbone but try to allay panic and seek medical aid.

Emergency resuscitation

BACKGROUND TO MOUTH-TO-MOUTH (OR-NOSE) RESPIRATORY AND EXTERNAL CARDIAC RESUSCITATION

1. If the brain is deprived of oxygen for four minutes irreversible changes take place in it. The aim of respiratory resuscitation is the immediate oxygenation of the blood in order to forestall such changes.

   The urgent need for oxygenated blood is such that the lungs should be inflated, if possible, even before attempting to remove debris from the mouth or air passages.

2. The method of choice in respiratory resuscitation is mouth-to-mouth (or to-

nose). Its main advantage is that it can be for example, in case of drowning while the casualty is still in shallow water, or to an individual who is trapped by a fall of earth and who cannot be immediately released. Other advantages are:

(a) It gives the greatest ventilation of the lungs and oxygenation of the blood.

(b) The degree of inflation of the lungs can be assessed by watching the movement of the chest.

(c) It is less tiring, does not require strength, and can be applied by a child.

Difficulty in employing this method, in cases of injury to the mouth or face and for other reasons, is recognised. Alternative methods of resuscitation.

Respiratory resuscitation

3. The first aider must realise that the vital need is to inflate the lungs even though the air has to be blown past an obstruction in the casualty's throat or windpipe.

Delay of one or two seconds may prove fatal.

If in doubt start mouth-to-mouth (or to-nose) inflation.

In such serious emergencies the first aider's equipment is his hands, his mouth and his lungs. For efficient use they must be co-ordinated by training and practice. The well-trained first aider will be conditioned to take the immediate action of inflating the casualty's lungs while simultaneously positioning his head and lower jaw to open the air passage.

(a) Conscious person in upright position, showing open air passages.

(b) In the unconscious casualty lying on his back, the tongue may fall backwards and block the air passages.

(c) If the neck is extended, the head pressed backwards and the lower jaw pushed upwards, the tongue moves forward thus opening the air passages.

Mouth-to-mouth method

4. Depending upon the position of the casualty, whether lying on the ground, supported in shallow water, or on a bench or table, take up a convenient position such as lying, kneeling or standing and work from the side. With the casualty on his back, hold his head in both hands, one hand pressing the head backwards and the other pushing the lower jaw upwards and forwards Open your mouth wide, take a deep breath and in the case of:

(a) An infant or young child - seal your lips round his mouth and nose, blow gently until you see his chest rise then stop and remove your mouth. Repeat this procedure at the rate of twenty times per minute.

(b) An adult - seal your lips round the casualty's mouth while obstructing his nostrils with your cheek; it may be necessary to pinch the nostrils with the fingers. Blow into his lungs and watch for the chest to rise, then remove your mouth. Inflation should be at the rate of ten per minute.

The first six inflations should be given as quickly as possible.

Method of improving the air passage

5. While continuing mouth-to-mouth inflation of the lungs, in the case of:

(a) An infant or young child- place one hand under his neck and raise gently. With the other hand extend the head backwards.

(b) An adult-grasp the back of the head between the hands with the fingers gripping the angles of the jaw. While extending the head backwards push the jaw forwards and upwards.

Not infrequently it will be found that as soon as the air passage is clear and the lungs have been inflated, the casualty will gasp and start to breathe spontaneously.

Gurgling or noisy breathing indicates the need to clear the throat of fluid or debris.

Mouth-to-nose method

6. Should the casualty be in a state of spasm or convulsion and his mouth cannot be opened, or if he has no teeth, it will be necessary to inflate the lungs by the mouth-to-nose method.

Again work from the side of the casualty with his head extended. Open your mouth wide, take a deep breath, and seal your lips widely on the casualty's face around the nose. Make sure your lips do not obstruct his nostrils. Close the mouth by placing your thumb on his lower lip.

If the head is not sufficiently extended, the soft palate will allow inflation through the nose but may prevent expiration. If this happens, press the casualty's lips with your thumb after each inflation.

Obstruction in the air passages

7. If efforts to inflate the lungs by mouth-to-mouth or mouth-to-nose methods fail, make sure that there is no obstruction in the mouth or throat. If a foreign body or other obstruction is found, remove it (turning his head to one side if necessary), then restart inflation.

If the obstruction is thought to be in the windpipe, in the case of:

(a) An infant or young child—lay the child prone with his head downwards over the knee and give three or four sharp slaps between the shoulders to dislodge the foreign body (Fig. 8), or hold the child up by his legs and then smack him smartly three or for times between the shoulders.

(b) An adult—turn the casualty on his side and strike him three four sharp blows between the shoulders. Check if any debris has come into the throat by feeling with the fingers. If seen remove it and start inflating again.

External cardiac resuscitation

8. The value of Respiratory Resuscitation is greatly reduced.

Oxygen cannot be carried rapidly by the circulation of blood to the brain. Should the heart cease to function it is essential that external cardiac resuscitation (an immediate method of restarting the circulation) be combined with respiratory resuscitation. It is possible that this will cause the heart to function. In some cases, external cardiac resuscitation will have to be continued until the casualty reaches hospital.

External cardiac resuscitation is not without its dangers and a first aider should only use this technique if he is sure that the heart is not functioning.

It is an advantage if two first aiders are present, one to undertake respiratory resuscitation and the other to carry out external cardiac resuscitation, working alternately.

Method

If the casualty is not breathing, mouth-to mouth or mouth-to-nose resuscitation must be performed. If after ten to twelve breaths into the casualty's lungs there is no apparent change in his condition, such as improvement in the colour of the skin, lips, or conjuctive, feel for the pulse in the neck (at the carotid pressure point). If there is no pulse external cardiac resuscitation should be started.

While continuing mouth-to mouth (or-to-nose) resuscitation the casualty should, if possible, be placed on a firm surface such as the floor, the ground, or a table. Feel the chest and locate the lower half of the sternum. In the case of:

(a) An infant or young child—with two fingers on the lower half of the sternum apply quickly six to eight sharp but not violent presses at the rate of one per second between each inflation.

(b) An adult—having located the lower half of the sternum, place the ball of the hand on it with the second hand covering the first. After each inflation of the lungs apply six to eight sharp presses at the rate of one per second.

If there are two first aiders available the person at the head should be able to feel a pulse in the neck with each pressure by the other on the sternum. He should also check this pulse periodically to see if the heart has resumed its normal beat. If so, external cardiac resuscitation should stop, but respiratory resuscitation should be continued, if necessary.

First aiders should practise on each other to feel the neck pulse at the carotid point and the position of the lower half of the sternum.

The revised silvester (chest pressure-arm lift)

METHOD OF RESPIRATORY RESUSCITATION

This manual method can be combined, if necessary, with external cardiac resuscitation.

1. If there is any obvious obstruction to breathing, remove it with your fingers or with a cloth wrapped round your fingers if it is in the mouth. Several sharp blows between the shoulder-blades may help to dislodge an obstruction.
2. Lay the casualty on his back, put something under his shoulders to raise them, and allow his head to fall backwards. The head should if possible be a little lower than the trunk. Remember that speed is essential.
3. Kneel at the casualty's head and grasp his arms at the wrists. Then cross them and press them firmly over the lower chest. This movement should force air out of his lungs.
4. Release this pressure and pull his arms with a sweeping movement upwards and outwards above his head and backwards as far as possible. This movement should cause air to be drawn into his lungs.
5. Repeat these movements rhythmically about 12 times per minute, checking the

mouth frequently for obstruction. Each cycle therefore takes five seconds -two seconds for chest pressure and three seconds for arm lift.

With the casualty on his back, there is danger of aspiration of vomit, mucus or blood. This risk can be reduced by keeping his head extended and a little lower than the trunk.

Colour Therapy

Colour therapy is based on the principle that when the body is subjected to strain, there is an alteration in the functions of somatic vibrations. The solution is to strike a balance which would make it return to the right frequency. This treatment is based on the rainbow spectrum (which consists of 12 colours). Each colour consists of different elements and minerals. This system enables you to replenish the minerals and elements that your body lacks by intake of colours that contain those minerals. Given below is the mineral and element list of various colours.

Red is composed of the gases hydrogen, cadmium, krypton and neon. Red energizes the liver, builds haemoglobin. Being a senory stimulant, it can also be an irritant. The liver, seen as the seat of emotion, needs a boost of red when a person receives a shock of any sort. Eating beetroot can help restore the balance.

Orange is good for the lungs. Preponderated by aluminium, it works as a respiratory stimulant. It depresses the parathyroid and stimulates the thyroid gland. Its silicon content makes it work as an aromatic and xenon makes it a lung builder. Eating orange coloured foods can help strengthen the respiratory system. The intake can be combined with exposure to orange light and wearing pearls, which are said to radiate orange colour.

Yellow is a motor stimulant because of its carbon content. Sodium works as a digestant and other elements in yellow can strengthen your nerves.

Gold activates the thymus gland, what this system believes to be the source of energy. So wearing the metal next to your skin improves your vitality. You can soak a gold ring or any other gold article in a glass of water, place it in the sun for a while and then drink the water.

Green stimulates the pituitary gland and its chlorine content makes it a disinfectant. It is also known to have purificatory and antiseptic properties. The radium in green makes it a muscle and a tissue builder.

Turquoise contains zinc and tantalum, which work as skin builders. Burns when exposed to turquoise light heal faster. On the other hand, its chromium content makes it a cerebral depressant.

Blue works as a cooling agent. Blue induces perspiration. Feeling itchy? It's blue you need. The colour blue works as a pain killer and a softening, soothing agent.

Scarlet—Imagine sitting in a scarlet room, dressed in scarlet robes, sinking your teeth into squashy tomatoes. Besides making your head spin, what do you think this colour will do for you? It increases your blood pressure. Scarlet works on the kidneys, its dysprosprum content being a renal energiser. The colour is also an aphrodisiac and builds sex drive.

Food Poisoning

Symptoms

Abdominal cramps, starting from an hour to 4 hours after eating tainted food and lasting up to 4 days, usually indicate bacterial food poisoning.

Abdominal cramps, headache, fever and chills, beginning from 12 to 48 hours after eating the contaminated food particularly seafood usually indicates viral food poisoning.

Sweating, dizziness, tearing in the eyes, excessive salivation, mental confusion and stomach pain beginning about 30 minutes after eating contaminated food are typical indication of chemical food poisoning. Food poisoning needs immediate attention of the doctor if there is partial loss of speech or vision and muscle paralysis, as it may be botulism poisoning. It is a life threatening illness. If the vomiting or diarrhoea is severe and lasts for more than 2 days, it's best to consult the doctor.

Treatment

a) Vomiting and diarrhoea are the body's way of flushing poison out of the system.
b) No solid food or milk should be eaten until the diarrhoea and vomiting has stopped.
c) Drink plenty of clear fluids to avoid dehydration.
d) Once you can retain the fluid in your stomach drink clear liquid.
e) Then eat bland foods like rice, cooked cereals and clear soups for a full day. If diarrhoea and vomiting is severe or prolonged, intravenous fluid may have to be taken to the hospital.
f) If your symptoms last beyond 2 days getting your stool, blood or vomited material tested can help to identify the cause of your illness.
g) Chemical food poisoning can usually be diagnosed by the description of symptoms and by testing the food potentially responsible for the poisoning.

Precautions

Never use food from containers that are leaking, bulging or damaged.

Clean utensils and cutting boards thoroughly with soap and hot water after preparing meat.

Wash fresh fruit and vegetables in cold, running water.

Store raw meat away from all other types of food.

Keep the egg dishes in the refrigerator.

Don't eat any food that looks or smells spoiled.

Avoid keeping the food near the doors, under the rotating fans or direct sunlight, to prevent the temperature changes.

Sterilise the food properly before storing it. Canned goods, especially home canned food products can harbor bacteria that need no oxygen to multiply and is not destroyed while cooking. To preserve food, sterile it in a pressure.

Thaw frozen meat or poultry completely before you cook it.

Always wash your hands before touching any food, especially after handling the raw meat.

Eat meat as soon as it is cooked. Cover up left-overs; cool, refrigerate within 90 minutes.

Store fish in the coldest part of the refrigerator.

Reheat meat quickly and thoroughly.

Foods that Will Fight Cancer

Oncologists and cancer researchers are quite firm in their opinion that certain foods have the capacity to fight cancer. From the garam masala found in the Indian spice collection to broactive compounds-enriched vegetables such as cabbage and cauliflower. Exposure to the wrong food can be carcinogenic.' According to the World Cancer Research Fund, nearly 30 to 40 percent of all cancers have a link with the food we eat, our physical activity and our weight control. And when these diet and lifestyle preferences are combined with the absence of smoking and chewing tobacco and paan, as much as 60 to 70 percent of all cancers can be prevented.

The best way to prevent cancer is to have salads, fruits and vegetables, nuts and sprouts or a natural low fat diet. Diets high in vegetable and fruits and the intake of foods rich in broactive compounds may trigger detoxification enzymes which in turn reduce the exposure of DNA to carcinogens.

Antioxidants in carrots include alpha-carotene and beta-carotene.

The indoles in cauliflower promote the production of enzymes that make the hormone estrogen less effective, reducing the risk of breast cancer.

Caffiec acid in apples increases the production of enzymes that make carcinogens more soluble in water and ultimately ejects them from the body.

Grapes contain ellagic acid, scavenger of carcinogens.

Ginger has mechanisms that suppress the creation of dangerous adducts, formed by the reaction of chemical carcinogens with DNA.

Terpenes in oranges may prevent lung cancer; while beta cryptoxanthin is an anti-cancer carotenoid.

The phytochemical phenethyl isothio-cyante in cabbage, in turnips, hampers the development of lung cancer.

Allium vegetables like garlic contain organosulphides that lower the risk of gastrointestinal cancers.

Alcohol may promote cancer. Excessive drinking can cause cancers of mouth, throat, oesophagus and liver. However, wine contains resveratol, a protective chemical.

Tomatoes get their colour from lycopene, which neutralises cancer-causing substances. The vegetable contains an estimated 10,000 plant chemicals. Ten servings a week may help reduce risk of prostate cancer by half.

Water

Water forms one of the essential components of our body. It is indispensable for our survival. However, if the water is not purified properly it can cause more harm than good. Here are a few facts about water:

Water contains three types of impurities:

Physical impurities—such as mud, dirt, soot, filth, riffraff and other dust particles which can be easily seen by the naked eye.

Chemical impurities—invisible organic salts that smell bad, and add a bad taste and colour to the water.

Germs—disease causing bacteria and viruses, which are again invisible to the naked eye. It is these impurities which are highly responsible for all kinds of water-borne diseases.

Methods of filtering

Membrane/cloth filtration: Method can remove only the physical impurities.

Candle water filters: Can remove germs and physical impurities. However with the accumulation of organic growth inside the candle pores, within a very short time, the candle easily becomes a breeding ground for disease causing germs.

Vaccum filtration: This eliminates only physical impurities. It adds an unpleasant taste to the water.

Boiling: Boiled water can be totally safe only when it is boiled continuously for 15 minutes after reaching the boiling point. But subsequent cooling and handling often leads to recontamination. Moreover, certain essential elements present in the water are either destroyed or broken down while boiling. Besides, boiling also alters the natural taste.

These days many companies offer water purifiers which solve all these problems.

Everyone is aware that boiling water destroys harmful bacteria and viruses. However, what is not known to all is the actual length of time for which the water is to be boiled.

Most people put off the gas as soon as water starts boiling. This is absolutely wrong. To make water 100% safe, it should be boiled for a full 20 minutes. This means that the time should be noted when the water starts boiling. Switch off the gas only 20 minutes after this point. Many micro-organisms do not get killed if the water is not boiled for 15-20 minutes.

The greatest loss in cooking is discarding the water after boiling the vegetables. All minerals, sugars, vitamin C, and vitamin B complex can pass out of cell walls of food into water even when food is simply cut and kept in water. Further, when these fruits/vegetables are cooked the cell walls break down.

Therefore, other nutrients which do not naturally dissolve in water pass into the cooking liquid. Hence the cooking liquid should never be thrown away. There are nutrients which dissolve in water but do not get destroyed by heat. So it is the cooking water which acts like a tonic and should be used in soups, etc.

■■

CHAPTER-10

Making a Home Happy!

Be Happy, Be Positive

The four walls, adorned with costly paintings, valuable rugs on marble floor and expensive crockery and cutlery do not necessarily constitute a happy home. A happy home consists of happy family members who have adopted, cultivated or are imbued with certain correct attitudes which contribute towards making theirs a happy home. In the ultimate analysis, happiness is a question of perception and one can always see a cup as being either half full or half empty. When travelling abroad, one is often asked how it is that Indians are always smiling and talking even though they are either very poor or atleast surrounded by poverty. All the material goods and individual liberty have not made westerners a happy lot.

Traditional Indians are happy with their position in life, because of the philosophy of Karma which is based on the belief that one's deed's in a past life influence the present. Hence one has to work hard so that one does better in the next life and in the meanwhile one must accept and make the best of what one gets. Joys and sorrows, good health and illness, success and failure are all part of this cosmic reality.

Modern thinking, particularly in Europe and America, places a lot of emphasis on the individual, his effort and his hardwork. Not much emphasis is placed on the elements of luck, chance or fete and no quarter is given to the possibility of failure. Hence when things don't go their way, as they planned or worked for it, they get depressed, pressured, anxious and require 'counselling' so that they may come to terms with it. Too much emphasis is placed on success and material prosperity and individual self-worth is linked to the trappings of either power, success or riches. With increasing consumerism and an admiration for Western values, people in India, particularly in the corporate sector where there is a great emphasis on targets and their achievements, people are beginning to suffer the same syndrome of performance, success, targets and also unhappiness, depression, stress, anxiety, panic attacks and low self-esteem. This is quite at variance with our traditional values in which the man of spirituality and learning was placed at the top of the hierarchy, the man of action or the warrior was placed next and the man of business placed only third. It is only with Westernisation that mammon worship has caught on and the abbreviations that have crept in with it, would now to put any Westerner to shame.

The problems of success and plenty may have appeased a material hunger in the west but it has brought in it's wake a realization that there is a great emptiness in their life. Individual quest and success has increased selfishness and has alienated him from the family system. Rushing from one transient relationship to another has only increased their insecurity but they are now too used to the impermanence and freedom that such relationships offer. Hence, unhappy people flit from one person to the other causing themselves more trauma and low self-esteem.

You can achieve whatever you think you can as consciously and unconsciously you will work towards your mission. Life is full of obstacles, failures and bad health and no one is free of this. The only difference between those who succeed and those who don't is that the positive individual knows how to cope with the hurdles and accepts them as part of life enabling him to cope with adversity and coming out stronger.

Never get tripped or fazed by the problems that come your way. Take it as a challenge to prove yourself and adopt the resilience of a bouncing ball. Negative thoughts and negative thinking do not help in any way but only make things worse. Also remember that every problem is transient and recall the old adage 'This too will pass.' Depression arises when one feels that one is helpless and that the situation in which things are going wrong will last forever. It happens with everyone but can be tackled if one says 'that I am emotionally drained and need to take better care of myself and rest so that I can feel good tomorrow this'. If one thinks in manner the depression will ease and disappear.

Negative thinking breeds depression and is contagious. If one is living with someone who is gloomy and critical, it is contagious as one gets depressed not only by being around such a person but also because one gets depressed thinking about the other's unhappiness. Moreover, negative thinking kills the present and the future because of thinking that the worst may happen. Better to think that nothing bad will happen!

Tips on Positive Thinking

1. If you are feeling negative do something to change your mood by going into a new environment, by visiting a friend, going shopping or going to a cinema or play.
2. Do things that make you happy—watch TV, read a book or go for a walk.
3. While neither the past nor the future can be changed. C, change the present by having a positive approach.
4. Get some exercise as exercise releases certain chemicals that are mood elevators and which destroy tension. Even cleaning out cupboards is fine.
5. Rest, sleep and relaxation afford a respite from fatigue that in turn encourage positive thoughts.
6. Refuse to think negatively when things don't go your way so that you avoid self-pity. Never say
    I have no will power.
    I did a bad job.
    I look terrible.
    I hate myself.
7. Concentrate on your achievements rather than your drawbacks.

8. Believe in your successes and your accomplishments and give a boost to your self-esteem.

Laughter Banishes the Blues

The proliferation of laughing clubs in our cities goes a long way in proving that laughing has now become a serious matter. One may notice that as one grows older one laughs less and this in turn increases one's stresses and strains. A hearty laugh not only dispels gloom but acts as an antidote to depression and enhances good health.

In many ways laughter seems to have gone with the joint family. Today, even children do not laugh as much as they should, burdened as they are with unwieldy courses, early competition and the constant pressure to excel. Said one dour parent, 'It's a question of laughter versus starving! We have no time for laughter anymore. It has to be hard work. I have worked every minute of my life to see that my children succeed.' Little wonder that heart attacks, diabetes, stress, anxiety and depression are rising steadily.

Thus laughter clubs have come up and January 10 is celebrated as world laughter day. The endeavour of its members is to remind the world that human beings are the only species blessed by the Almighty to laugh.

Laughter has been synonymous with the sound of happiness, a touch of joy and the wisdom of ages enjoins that it is the best medicine for healthy and harmonious living. Laughter is said to have a powerful healing effect on many diseases and women rate a good sense of humour as one of the important attributes in a man.

A healthy laugh is said to trigger off life—enhancing hormones that are so powerful that a person's entire immune system can help it to ward off diseases even helping to fight cancer.

A professor of psychoneural immunology at the New York State University, who has been a pioneer in laughter research has provided the most conclusive evidence yet of a link between laughter and immunoglobin A, an antibody which helps fight illness by marking out harmful invading bacteria and viruses. Another vital chemical triggered by laughter is cytokines, dubbed the 'happy hormone' which promotes the activity of white blood cells which specialise in fighting off invading bacteria and viruses and destroy potential tumour cells.

It is an unequal world and life is often unfair. We cannot always get what we want, but that does not mean we cannot be happy. There is no better way than to laugh our way to happiness and by facing our adversities with a smile.

What better way to heal a person than to make him laugh since laughter is the best medicine?

Laughter is one of the best medicines in tackling lifestyle diseases such as stress, high blood pressure, depression, psychological problems and even heart disease. All these troubles arise out of the modern syndrome of taking oneself and one's problems too seriously. Some specialists have equated laughter with meditation—you not only lose track of time but you emerge a more relaxed and carefree person later on.

The best form of humour is the ability to laugh at yourself and your own mistakes, and to make light of your personal problems.

So, if you thought humour was a funny business, think again. There is nothing more exhilarating in life than having the last laugh. Don't take laughter for granted but cultivate it as the great tension releaser and dispeller of gloom and doom.

Never consider laughter as frivolous and unbecoming as many serious minded peopled appreciate laughter and use it to win friends.

Adjustment is Necessary

'Adjustment is necessary' insisted our mother and to make any relationship work and to achieve success one must adjust to the situation, to different circumstances, different environments and different people.

Today the theme is 'I', ' Me', 'My'—everyone believes that he or she is the centre of the universe and that the world and everyone in it should function according to what we want and expect. The western concept of stressing on the individual has percolated down to us also and the women's lib movement in particular has emphasized that the onus of adjustment has always been on the woman and she has thus lost her individuality. This is a concept for theoreticians but in real life one will notice that everyone has to adjust and they have—be it men to women, husband to wife, parents to children, children to parents, daughters in law to mothers in law and sons in law to fathers in law.

The spirit of adjustment and accommodation must be inherent and cultivated so that living and working with others becomes easy. In many ways, the ego is inborn and we many tend to put ourselves above all else. However, this instinct has to be kept in check so that we can live and function with others in society as well as in personal relationships. We should promote mutual harmony'. Harmony and adjustment are virtually two sides of the same coin. We have to take into consideration another person's needs, habits, temperament and mould ourselves to accommodate the other person.

In a marriage situation for example, two people are required to live together and share everything from morning till night—one bed, one bathroom and one house has to be shared. Therefore, we must adjust or modify some of our habits and needs to harmonise with our partner. Why is it that many marriages crumble even after a couple has known each other for a long time? This is often because when called upon to spend 24 hours together under the same roof, each person may find the habits of the other intolerable!

The concept of sharing of putting others before yourself, sometimes if not always, must be taught to our children and must be practiced by us. By adjusting with others we do not become lesser individuals, rather we become supreme and superior, managing in every situation and with every type of person and their individual idiosyncrasies.

Patience is a Virtue

In a life of instant, the fact that patience is a virtue is no longer reiterated. However, we need to remember that patience is a fruit of the spirit just as love is. Patience does not mean inactivity—it means that people are to go on with their work and duty without necessarily getting their instant rewards. In a world of desperate and irrational haste, patience is the art of pacing.

The beauty of patience is that it helps to still a restless mind in its haste to seek appreciation, gain success, reap rewards and achieve goals. The world does not move as we want it to and hence we must steel ourselves to be patient and inculcate in our children the notion that instant gratification is not always possible. If a person has not learnt to be patient, he has learnt very little.

Tidiness is a Must

Although our burgeoning population has not yet forced us to live in tiny spaces as in Tokyo, dwellings are no longer as spacious as what they used to be. Our cities in particular, which have increased in size and numbers, now boast of huge populations which have to be accommodated within a limited space. Flats and houses are getting smaller and space is really at a premium. In Tokyo, people live in miniscule flats and visitors have to check into 'capsule' hotels in which most of the furniture folds into the wall or projects from it at a height. At the same time, the demands of a materialistic and consumerist society are such that we are buying and accumulating more than what we can use. Along with this comes a frenetic pace of life in which we are always rushing in and out of the house on errands, work or social obligations. More than ever before it is essential for us to be tidy as too many people in too small a place with too many things leads to untidiness. The need therefore is to have a space for everything and everything in its place.

No matter how busy one is or how tired, tidiness has to be maintained, particularly in small apartments where every room is on display and where neatness is an essential prerequisite. The easiest way to be tidy is:

1. To have a place for shoes, newspapers, clothes and toys. All family members should cooperate in keeping the place tidy by putting things back in their right place.
2. Once there is a place for everything then putting things back where they belong is a matter of ten minutes everyday, whenever one has the time.
3. Children should be encouraged to put their clothes, shoes and toys back in their appointed place.
4. No matter how beautiful the decor and how costly the furnishings, neatness has its own beauty and an untidy room is an eyesore. Therefore ensure that beds are made, that bedcovers and carpets are not crooked, that curtains are properly pulled and cushions are plumped into shape. Tidiness enhances the decor.
5. If your house is enough or if there is a corner of your room which can accommodate a chair, place your 'extras' on it and put it away as soon as you have time in their appointed place in your cupboards.
6. Tidiness also ensures order and eliminates time that is wasted in looking for things amidst clutter.

Anger—A Volatile Emotion

While some believe that to discharge one's feelings is beneficial, and that people should hit out when frustrated, others are of the view that uncontrolled expression of anger is detrimental to health. Anger is one of the most awesome emotion felt by a human being, yet one which can cause widespread disturbance—both in an individual and where collective anger is involved such as in strikes and riots, looting and arson—to society in general. This primeval emotion has been responsible for wars and persecution of racial groups such as Hitler against the Jews, or whites against blacks in South Africa, and in the US. Anger may be thought of as a great motivating emotion, as it can spur on an individual to prove oneself in an endeavour to combat past humiliation, hurt, insult or man-made impediments in one's path towards a particular goal. One may cite the examples of those individuals who have undertaken the cause of the downtrodden, or women leaders who have taken up the fight against the torture and humiliation of women in this country. It was the emotion of anger against the treatment meted out to individuals or group causes which have spurred them on.

There are certain physical accompaniments to anger. When aroused, the pituitary glands release a hormone called adrenaline which fills the blood stream and ignites the chemistry of the human system. As a result, every sinew, nerve and muscle is filled with a sort of super power which instantly endows us with a strength which is beyond our normal capacity.

Certain people are always raging about something - from being held up in traffic to waiting in queues. They shout and rant and blame others when things go wrong. Constant hostility of this type leads to high blood pressure, which again is linked to coronary heart diseases and strokes. Such personality types are frequently able to channelise their anger into political movements, social work or business, frequently rising high in the organisation due to their heightened competitiveness. However, those around them who are less vocal or powerful may have to bear the fruit of their anger, such as subordinates, spouses, servants and children. This presents a no-win situation as repressed anger can lead to depression, arthritis, asthma, blood pressure and ultimately heart trouble. If negative feelings are expressed as they are experienced, there is no destructive rage, since feelings are not bottled up.

The ability to express anger has much to do with preconditioning during one's childhood. A small child who is constantly nagged by the mother, severely punished for throwing tantrums or rebuked by an older sibling is more likely to develop into an easily angered adult. Suppressed anger can lead to suicide, depression and violent behaviour ranging from physical violence and drug taking, to murder.

A growing child or a teenager has to cope with emotions as well as frustration in various spheres of life as part of the growing up process. Careful guidance and an abundance of love from parents, especially the mother will go a long way towards helping the child to cope with feelings of anger and aggression. With maturity some measure of control comes in. Hence, Yogic meditation is highly beneficial as it helps to still the mind and bring mental peace. It also encourages reflection which is essential for every adult, as the fast pace of modern life leaves no time to ponder over, or analyse one's drawbacks, ambitions, frustrations and goals. Reflection and self-analysis is essential to cope with anger.

Dealing with Anger: It has to be understood that like joy and sorrow, anger too is a natural emotion and should be dealt with as such. One must remember that it is possible to love and hate somebody at the same time. So one need not feel guilty about being angry with them. One should go straight to the cause of one's anger without misdirecting it into distant objects or those who are powerless. Encourage children to talk about their hurts and resentments so that they become communicators rather than suppressed individuals. Most of all self-control, reflections and self-analysis must be done to analyse the cause of one's anger. By this method we can make anger work for us in a positive way and hence it can spur us on to positive improvements rather than negative destruction. With a bit of self-restraint, we could look back on anger as something we have conquered rather than the reverse. It should be remembered that over the centuries angry men and women have maimed and murdered, destroyed cities and exterminated civilizations. In an increasingly violent society it is imperative that we understand and control this emotion.

The Power of Love

A new field of research called psychoneuro-immunology (PNI) reveals a link between the brain and the immune system. Laboratory tests have revealed that married women had stronger immune systems and that happily married women had the strongest immune system of all. Studies with men produced similar results. Contact and warm personal relationship with others contributed to health and longevity. Today, western research is corroborating what our forefathers already emphasized when they stressed that the mind and body were closely connected. Homeopathy and Ayurveda take into consideration the mental and emotional state of a person when treating illness.

It is the power of love that enables children to grow. An experiment was conducted on babies who were fed and then cuddled by their mothers. Another group of babies were fed and then put back into their cradles without either being cuddled or held closely. The growth in the babies who were cuddled was much faster than those who were merely cleaned, fed and put into their cots. Can love, that ephemeral thing of the mind, contribute to our physical well-being. All religions, most singers and many poets have long since waxed eloquent about the power of love.

The mandate to love your neighbour as yourself is not just moral but also physiological.

Love, caring and closeness have the potential of being stress relievers as those who are loved feel less alone, less threatened and more confident of facing stress because they know they have someone to turn to. The feelings of security, optimism and hope are great antidotes to success. Holding close, hugging, snuggling, petting, stroking, touching—is all good for your health, your heart and of course, your relationships.'

Unconditional love is the medicine for today's stress and tension burdened society. Love is soothing, physically, mentally and emotionally and the lack of it can make us physically sick, create emotional imbalance and disharmony. Adults too need love as nourishment as much as children and elders too need to be loved and felt loved so that they do not fall into the degenerate diseases of the aged.

Nobody can live wholly in his job. Although too many workaholics are trying to do, thinking that they can dispense with intimate relationships and get along with the casual personal contacts of the job and the club. It would be better if we acknowledged our need for love and affection and then tried to build up these relationships in the full light of self-knowledge. No one can really thrive in a wholly institutionalised environment or in a purely intellectual career. Personal attachments are necessary. Love is not the mere play thing of romantic dispositions but belongs to the realities of daily life where a loving word, touch or gesture goes a long way towards making us feel whole and satisfied.

The Power of Communication

In today's world, the power of communication is essential. At the same time, the art of conversation to have been forgotten and often people have reduced themselves to a limited vocabulary of monosyllables such as 'yeah', 'no', 'fine', 'ok', 'hi' and so on. The taciturn Englishmen, the voluble French, the inscrutable Chinese and the garrulous Indian—these are racial stereotypes that exist but as the world gets linked through the internet, both written and verbal, communication is essential. The power of communicating means expressing your thoughts and feelings effectively and putting your point of view across in a pleasant way. Whether it is business negotiations, international diplomacy or even a family interaction, it is important to put your viewpoint across pleasantly. Sometimes things are better left unsaid, but sometimes one may feel regret at not having expressed oneself adequately at the right time. To be Ms Malaprop is unfortunate and can have disastrous consequences as people are judged not only by their actions but by their words.

Improve Your Communication Skills

1. Children are encouraged to speak up in class, participate in debates and take up public speaking so that they learn communication skills early in life. Such exercises give you the ability to think on your feet and keep your wits about you.
2. Whenever you speak you are revealing something about your own personality and background. As Prof. Higgins in *My Fair Lady* would find out, your education, your place or country of origin, your status in society is unconsciously being expressed every time you speak. Your conversation will reveal to others whether you are kind or selfish, rude or polite, open minded or rigid, cheerful or morose, humorous or dour.
3. In order to say pleasing and tactful things which come across as being sincere, you have to cultivate such traits as alertness, kindness, tolerance, cheerfulness and an ability to appreciate another's point of view. People have so many hidden woes you never know when your words touch a sore spot. Hence cultivate kindness and be gentle in your speech.
4. A skillful communicator or conversationalist is one who has something to say, but his success lies in making others want to talk as well as to listen.
5. Communication does not mean a monologue in which one person monopolises the conversation.
6. Communication means the ability to draw out others into the conversation on topics of common interest.
7. 'Small talk' is a phrase which is used to denote that people exchange when they are getting acquainted or when they are thrown together for a few minutes of conversation. To be ready with such conversational fillers, you do not have to be blessed with unusual gifts. Feel a friendly interest in others without being pryingly inquisitive, notice what is going on around you, give yourself upto the enjoyment of the moment and you will never be tongue-tied.
8. Be a good listener and pay attention to what the other person is saying.

medicine. The need of the hour is to try to blend together the benefits of instant technology with the timeless human qualities of close family and friendship bonds, tolerance, compassion and non-violence. There has to be a conscious effort to eschew the seductive lure of a money-oriented consumer culture. Once acquired, wealth and possessions offer little lasting mental peace or satisfaction.

The entry of spiritual gurus who offer instant *nirvana* through the chanting of magical *mantras* are yet another aberration of the instant culture which seeks a short cut to contentment. The instant slimming pills, aerobics and exercise contraptions are another hoax perpetrated by this philosophy. Modern day eating disorders such as anorexia nervosa and bulimia are manifestations of a restless and rudderless generation which follows the dictates of fashion creators, blindly. The obsession with one's looks and figure and equating one's self worth with these has lead to the ruination of both health and mental balance.

The theory of instant, which is influencing too much of our present day lifestyles, needs to be closely examined and analysed so that one can pick the best of that which is traditional and that which is current or even futuristic. Human beings have been endowed with a brain and emotions. They cannot and should not become robots and automatons mindlessly following the herd. Instant fame, instant wealth and instant emotions are all too brief and the instant fall or letdown that invariably follows, brings in its wake feelings of rejection and insecurity. These feelings play havoc with a person's psyche and the ever-growing numbers who need to be treated for psychological disorders are proof that wealth, fame and possessions do not ensure mental well-being. Perhaps it is time to introspect, and rationalise one's goals and expectations. Traditional values such as happiness, peace of mind and family ties, along with such qualities as patience, tolerance and self-restraint need to be cultivated instead of blindly groping for a materialistic, consumerist and instant lifestyle.

Curbing Materialistic Values

Don't keep up with the joneses

If one sits dawn to analyze the reasons for one's restlessness, unhappiness and anxiety one will find that discontent is at the bottom of it. Today very few bother to count their blessings and appreciate what they have. Everyone is looking around, seeking to acquire, grasp, accumulate and outdo others. In this quest for happiness, man feels happiness lies in chasing shadows of pleasures, possessions and power. Happiness actually lies in contentment and being loved as well as loving others. The philoshopy of the day seems to be 'If only I had more....'. A sticker at the back of a car states 'he who dies with the most toys, wins'.

Our clocks, notepads, utensils, clothes and crockery all carry the logos of the latest 'in products'. While our T-shirts parade their designers, or carry the logos of tobacco, soft drink or sports equipment. Our athletes are less worried about winning national or international laurels on the sports field. Rather once they become 'names' they are awarded commercial contracts to wear conspicuous brand-name labels. Entertainment anywhere is punctuated by advertisements. How can one concentrate when every segment of film or a sporting event telecast is sponsored by a product? India is no longer a country of spiritual values but one in which mammon worship and greed has led to innumerable girls being dowsed with kerosene because they failled to bring in a scooter, a television set, a fridge or a cash settlement.

Possessions have become our masters and we are slaves to them. Technology is pushing us into multiplying our needs. For example, the children are no longer content with books and marbles—they want their own rooms, computers, CD-Roms, laser toys, video games..., the list is endless and frightening. If we do not curb this desire for consumerism and keeping up with our neighbours in a game of materialistic oneupmanship, we are doomed to a life of unhappy discontent.

While it is true that we can no longer go back to the era of a loincloth, thatched roof and the Vedas, we must intelligently plan our lives so that consumerism does not consume us. Learn to say no, to do without and to live within your means. Do not be lured by the trap to spend more on your credit card so that you get a free gift and are then left frantically striving to earn more, by fair means or foul, to pay off your debtors.

While poverty is depressing, so is the mad scramble after wealth and material possessions. One should try to keep one's wants within reason and strike a right balance between earning enough for necessities and needs and not for greed. Since the dividing line between a man's need and greed is thin, unless he learns the virtue of contentment, desires can change and corrupt a person's outlook.

Indeed it gives us much to think about and strive to put into action. One should learn to want what one has rather than long to have what you want.

Don't Neglect the Children

The Indian social system has always placed a great emphasis on children—having them, providing for them, helping them to grow up, guiding them into careers and finally into marriage. In fact, having children and raising them was the raison d'etre of most people's lives. Today as the corrosive trends seep in from the west, there are DINK (double income, no kids) couples and many others who are pooh-poohing the obsession with children, saying that too much time, energy and, most of all, money goes into having children. In an article titled 'More expensive than a Porsche - Are children worth the cradle?' Margarette Driscoll writes about the cost of raising children in England. In an indepth study entitled 'What price a child', consumer journalist Jan Walsh carried out a comprehensive survey commissioned by ASDA, the supermarket chain in England. 'Low cost' children on welfare or 46 per cent of two-parent families spent pounds 26,128 on their children by the time they are 21. Mr and Mrs Ordinary in their three-bedroom, semi-detached house spent pounds 100,000 while the snooties of Kensington spent pounds 295,000 on their children, inclusive of nannies and school fees.

Today with the man, woman relationship in decline in the west and with so many marriages crumbling, children are low priority and hence their declining birth rate. They feel that children are not a worthwhile 'investment'.

In India, we are still natural enough to want marriage and children. After all the childless may have all the money, but they have only half the fun. The zeal to have children often comes in when it is already too late and when career satisfaction does not fulfill all that one craves for in life. Many westerners adopt children or opt to have children out of wedlock - the single mothers of the west try to emphasise that there is no need to have the support of a man. After having studied the effects of close to 50 years of high divorce rates in the west it is evident that a disturbed childhood results in disturbed adolescence and adults. There is really no substitute for a stable two-parent household.

The extremely callous attitude that parents can have toward their children is exemplified by the article 'Baby left on a pavement as parents dine in style in New York' in which a 14-month was left unattended on a New York pavement while the parents dined in style at a Manhatten restaurant. The parents were jailed for neglect but the mother Annette Sorenson, who hailed from Denmark, asserted that in Denmark it was quite common for children to be left unattended while their parents shopped or dined. The waiters had suggested that the couple opt for a larger table which could have accommodated the stroller but the couple declined!

Lest we complacently point fingers at others we would do well to remember the large number of children who got lost during the recent trade fair in Pragati Maidan as their parents shopped mindlessly! The reason shootouts in England and America by deranged men with guns in schools and churches should serve as an eye opener to us.

In India also we have millions of street children who are victims of the worst type of exploitation and child abuse, drug addiction and child prostitution. Let the educated middle classes not add to these numbers by neglecting their children. Becoming a parent is a serious business which requires a sense of commitment and responsibility. Parenthood is not all drudgery - it gives you a great sense of security, of love, joy and hope. Parents are called upon to teach the children such timeless values as integrity, responsibility, loyalty and building up a value system which is your child's greatest asset as a future citizen. Their best moral compass is you and your spouse.

One of the biggest myths about parenting has been the 'buzzword' of 'quality time'. As far as babies are concerned, there is no such thing as quality time - it is just quantity as the child gets up, feeds, bathes, is put to sleep, wails, gets up and has to be fed and changed again. In order to convince women that they do justice to their jobs outside the home if they devote 'quality time' to their children is one of the many misleading concepts of today's generation. Were our mothers uneducated doormats to have spent all their time in raising children? An answer to this is to study the steady increase in juvenile crime rates and teenaged insecurities and abberative behaviour. As Swami Chinmayannanda once told and audience of ladies, 'children are not bad - mothers are, as they are more selfish and less devoted to their children than the previous generation. Ten minutes a week from a busy mother is certainly not what a baby deserves for growth.' Author and psychologist Ronal Levant asserts, 'children need vast amounts of parental time and attention. It is an illusion to think they are going to be on your time-table and that you can say `okay, we've got half-an-hour, lets get on with it".

Experts agree that many of the most important elements in the children's lives - regular routines and domestic rituals, consistency, the sense that their parents know and care about them - are exactly what is jettisoned when quality time substitutes for quantity time. Moreover kids do not shed their need for parental time when they become teenagers. At this stage they may get into drugs, bad company and feel reluctant to study, to subtly monitoring them is essential. When parents come home at 7.30 pm, and then head straight towards their fax machines and computers they are scarring the children by showing where their priorities lie. Neglected children show deviant behaviour and indiscipline in schools. They are crying for parental attention which they have not got due to work pressures on working parent.

A solution is to slowdown and take a break when you have children. If one is unwilling to put children before career, don't have them, as modern birth control methods make family planning a matter of personal choice and timing.

Also don't substitute neglect by overindulging them by giving them money and material possessions in lieu of your time and affection. A case in point is the lawlessness exhibited by 'rish brats' in our cities who have become role models for the poorer kids down the road. A major problem with these youngsters is that their prosperous parents are too busy with their business and socialising and leave raising of children to *ayahs*. They do not get the necessary guidance and values that must be instilled by the time the child is three or four. Child psychologist Gurmeet Kaur, who counsels children Delhi's elite schools, says 'in many cases where parent don't give time, I find the kids grow up with misshapen personalities, they are prone to violence if they don't get what they want.'

The absentee parents assuage guilt by giving the child anything they want. Love, discipline and time is essential for child rearing. Substituting these by giving the child unlimited money, fast cars, guns and a licence to do as they please is asking for trouble as children will then not obey the law and will expect their parents to bail them out when they are in trouble.

Some parenting tips
1. Low marks in school does not necessarily mean that the child has not made an effort. Both Einstein and Bill Gates did not excel in school.
2. Emotionally loaded and unkind words or cutting remarks scar the child.
3. Leniency does not necessarily make a child 'soft' but may make him more

responsible in the future. Harshness should not be equated with being a good parent.

4. Discipline the child judiciously, consistently and never in anger.
5. Don't swamp your child advice - it is boring and may cause him to revolt.
6. Do not go on comparing your child with other 'good' children as this will only make him feel jealousy and rivalry.
7. Do not scold the child or point out his shortcomings in front of teachers, friends or relatives. Remember that children have feelings and they should not be hurt by your insensitive conduct.
8. Do not nag children about their studies. The curriculum in our country is so overloaded that children suffer from 'burnout' right from class X. Parental nagging just adds to child's woes and will not ensure success.
9. Today's parent should neither by authoritarian nor too indulgent and permissive. Children need to be guided to be democratic in approach. Deal with your child coolly and in a mature fashion and encourage the child to express his opinions but also help him to recognise his responsibilities. Children brought up in a democratic manner tend to be socially responsible, self-confident, able to control aggression and have high self-esteem. They are also able to make social and personal adjustments easily.
10. Due to the overloaded curriculum and competitive environment our children have to sacrifice their childhood at the altar of studies and academic achievement. Until this system is modified, never grudge them their playing time as play is therapeutic for children.

Take care of your children for they are your richest treasure and your greatest contribution to society.

Doing one's Duty-Caring for the Aged

Life is a duty: dare it!
Life is a burden: bear it!

The cultures of Asia have long had a veneration for elders and filial piety was considered one of the main duties of a householder in Confucian China. Indian culture also enjoins on us to look after the lederly and to be respectful towards them. In the joint family system, the elders had a special place as the head of the household.

In a unique experiment conducted by 26 year old Pat Moore in New York in 1985 who disguised herself as an 85 year old to see how the elderly were treated and the problems they faced. At the end of the day, she was angry because she had been 'condescended to, ignored, counted out... people, I felt, really judged a book by its cover.' During this experiment, she was mugged and robbed and dealt with rudely. The entire experiment was a revelation of how the elderly could be ill-treated but there were also some instances of people being kind and helpful.

In view of the large segments of the greying population in the world, we must do our duty towards our elders. The western world has its own set of values in which independence and individuality are the cornerstones of their society. They find it humiliating to be a 'burden' on their children and remain alone as long as possible. When they are no longer self-sufficient they are institutionalised by their children.

India too has witnessed a burgeoning of the elderly population and some states such a

Himachal Pradesh have made it mandatory by legislation to look after elders. It is a sad fact that what was once a part of our culture now needs to be legislated.

The break-up of the joint family, increasing urbanisation, children working abroad have all contributed towards the problems of the aged, e.g. 72 year old Laxmi Iyer is many miles apart from her only son. Mrs Iyer is alone in an old age home. My son takes good care of me and I am happy, she says. However, the expression on her face has a different story to tell. She showed all the signs of a neglected and lonely person. Hers is not an isolated instance. Another example are the homes of non-resident Indians in Tiruvalla in Kerala. The aged parents here struggle to cope with the problems of infirmity and loneliness. Most parents admit that though their children urge them to accompany them abroad, they are reluctant. Life there, according to them is even more lonely. All this has led to the sprouting up of old age homes all over the country. However studies have shown that most of the inmates in these homes suffer from depression.

Plan your old age

Retirement can come as a intimidating but welcome time. The days of living on your pension have gone. Instead one has to give careful thought and considerartion as to how and where one would spent their fragile years. Questions such as how will I take care of my monthly expenditure? What if my children view me a burden for the rest of my life? also cause increasing concern. To deal with all these questions, it is advisable to start planning early. Take the example of Mr Chari, aged 45. He has to provide for the education of his children, marry his daughter and buy his dream home. How should he go about it? One of the many options in front of him would be to invest Rs 30,000 per annum for 15 years in PPF (self) or alternatively he could invest in UTI Child Gift Growth Funds of Rs 10,000 per annum for 20 years which will yield adequate funds for the education of his child. The point to be noted here that planning early always works to your advantage. Its not enough to save, you must invest and its not enough to invest but invest wisely. Once one has ascertained his needs, one can make planned investments. One should remember to take the money's maturity value and the time period of investment in consideration says Sushil Chandra Chopra. 'I always knew that I would'nt be able to manage in this money (pension). So I put my money in other instruments like life insurance schemes, fixed deposits, property, stocks and shares, and national savings certificates...' Senior citizens should ensure liquidity. Bank deposits serve this purpose.

Thus, the moral of the story is to plan 10-15 years ahead of your retirement. Otherwise you will see your living standards plummet, this would increase hardship dependence and depression.

The government on its part is trying to come up with a national policy for older persons. Some of its provisions are:

Policy proposals

Economic measures: A significant expansion in the ambit of the old age pension scheme for the poor, with the ultimate objective to cover all elderly persons below the poverty line.

- Revision at intervals of monthly pension and sensitivity in taxation policies with a view to ensuring that inflation does not deflate actual purchasing power.
- Tax-concessions including higher standard deduction and a son/daughter whose aged parents stay with them.

Health care: Affordable health services, heavily subsidised for the poor and with a graded system of user charges for others.

- Development of health insurance.
- Directives to public hospitals to ensure that elderly patients are not subjected to long waits and visits to different counters for medical tests and treatment.

Housing: Earmarking 10 per cent of houses/house sites under urban and rural housing schemes for lower-income segments for elderly persons.

- Easy access to loans for purchase of housing and major repairs.
- Special consideration in matters relating to transfer of property, and property tax.

Legal: Introduction of special provisions in the IPC to protect older persons from domestic violence and a machinery to attend to all such cases promptly.

- Review of tenancy legislation so that their rights of occupancy are restored speedily.

Special focus: To identify the more vulnerable among the aged-the disabled, the infirm, the chronically sick and those without family support, and provide welfare services to them on a priority basis.

- Institutional care only as a last resort when personal circumstances are such that staying in old age homes becomes absolutely necessary.

Implementation mechanism

- To ensure effective implementation the government plans to set up a National Council for Older Persons headed by the minister for Social Justice and Empowerment with representatives of relevant central ministries, the Planning Commission, NGOs, media and experts.
- Targets to be set within the framework of a time schedule.

Responsibility for implementation of action plans to be specified.

- Detailed review every three years.
- An autonomous National Association of Older Persons (NAOP) be set up to mobilise senior citizens, articulate their interests, promote programmes for their well-being and to advise the government on all matters relating to older persons.

Though this scheme may have several pitfalls, the experts point out that governmental effort can only supplement and not replace family support and caring for the elders. The elderly may appear to live in the past and may seem boring to you. It is only when you make an effort to talk to them that makes you realise how receptive they are to the changes around them.

The modernity in their thinking may come to you as a surprise. All of us feel the need to be wanted and loved. Elders too feel this need. Be sensitive towards them, take their advice and help and watch them grow. The youngsters often use the phrase 'you don't know anything' little realising how much this hurts the grandparents or parents. Always remember that they are the ones who taught you to speak in the first place.

Allow the older people to initiate their own decisions after considering the options.

Always involve them in decisions regarding their future.

Services which are usually available on payment are:

a) Home help—assistance with household tasks.

b) Trained nurses

In the case the situation makes it imperative to put the elderly in a home always check the following:

1. Does the home have diversional and physiotherapy programmes.
2. Do community groups visit
3. Are services from hairdressers, dentists, optometrists and podiatrists available.
4. Are the residents treated as individuals with courtesy and respect.
5. Are residents allowed to keep personal possessions, e.g. pictures.
6. Does the home cater to special diets.
7. Are the cooling systems adequate.
8. Is their a garden and an outdoor area.

However, always remember that putting them in an old age home is not the end of your duty. There are many sad instances of people in these homes who never have any visitors. Hence, make it a point to keep in touch by writing letters or sending e-mails. Visit your parents as frequently as possible. Remember you may be in the same boat one day.

However, the situation in India is not yet so bad. Have you heard of modern day joint families? Yes! Joint families are now being recast and remoulded to suit the modern day demands. The sheer difficulties of managing both the economic and domestic fronts have prompted younger generations to review the joint family system. The system that has evolved is a two-way one, where the younger generation has the comfort of knowing that they are well looked after, the elders feel more secure and will get moral and physical support in times of illness or just loneliness. However in this situation also, both sets should be given ample breathing space. Do not interfere too much or dictate terms in each other's lives to keep the system functioning smoothly, e.g. each unit takes care of its own day to day expenses - one may also have separate kitchens.

Thus the modern day joint family is a place where the youngsters can draw from the wealth of wisdom and experience of the elders and the latter can remain active by contributing their advice and guidance to the household. The grandchildren may also often shower more love than the children and this works wonderfully for the psyche of the old people.

How to Make Friends

Blood is no longer thicker than water. Changing patterns of life and urbanisation have necessitated close associations between people. Friends now do what family once did. They cook together, holiday together and even buy property together. They have become an essential support system in tragedy and celebration thus spawning its own custom and value system.

The new family is a family by choice and not just genes e.g. the Aligan family who are a group of 8 families living in a building called Aligan in Calcutta. This group functions as a joint family. All the rites of passage from birth till death are a group affair. Their exists a traditional division of labour between them. The process of urbanisation mutated joint families into extended families and extended families into nuclear units. Lost in big cities, these units are starved for company and companionship. They now look for new families and new moorings.

The institution of marriage has also undergone a change. Couples today have more equal relationships. The division of labour is clear-cut. Anthropologists point out that there is an absence of generalised exchange where one person may do more than the other. However there is tension in equality and hence couples need other couples. The increasing divorce rates and single parents also make friendship a valuable commodity. Friends are not as judgmental as the family, says Arpita, a 35 year old single parent.

Thus the new Indians make their friends through work, friendship and even common hobbies. With more income at their disposal, these new groups can even go out together or plan holidays together.

Here are a few ways in which you can start your 'new family' or in other words, make friends:

1. Smile and project a relaxed body language
2. Cultivate a genuine interest in people.
3. Make it a point to remember people's names.
4. Be a good listener.
5. Get over your fear and half the battle is won.
6. Start the conversation about general topics like the weather, work etc.
7. Make compliments sincerely.
8. Since everybody enjoys the opportunity to talk about themselves, allow the other person to talk.
9. Keep the conversation lively.
10. Avoid ignoring people.
11. Cultivate a good sense of humour.
12. Give the other person a feeling of importance.
13. Respect the other person's opinion.
14. Graciously end the conversation when you have nothing more to say.
15. Maintain contact.
16. Always remember that friendship is always around the corner but waiting for you to make the first move.

Home and Family as the Basic Unit of Society

The family is the primary social structure of human society and fulfills many needs which are indispensable for the continuity, the change, and the stability necessary for human existence. The family fulfils a multifarious and multi-dimensional role as it takes care of the emotional, physical and financial needs of human beings.

Traditionally, agrarian societies all over the world had a predominance of extended families. These families were generally patriarchal and authoritarian with all members being guided in their activities by an elder family head. Women, generally had a subordinate position and marriage was guided by rules of kinship rather than those of courtship. The family was an important unit of economic, cultural, religious and even political activity. The economic structure of such societies was closed and exposure to technology or mass media rare. Hence the total volume of knowledge in the form of mythology folklore and folk songs was handed down by the elder generation to the younger, by oral tradition. Primarily due to this reason, age was an important element governing status and privileges in such societies. Feelings of individuality and personal freedom was alien to this type of family structure.

Such a society existed in England and in Europe until the beginning of the Industrial Revolution.

The concept of the family as being nuclear is not an Indian concept, and family jointness continues to be a major sociological phenomenon in the Indian social structure.

By the term 'nuclear family' one denotes a couple and their unmarried children, but there are many variations, such as a supplemental nuclear family, in which widowed divorced or aged relative or relatives live together. Aged parents may also join one of their sons, or even daughters, to form an extended family. Nor can one state categorically that joint and nuclear families are either rural or urban as case studies have revealed that joint families predominate in even larger numbers in urban and semi-urban pockets. If the rural joint family stayed together because of agricultural and allied pursuits, the urban joint family may thrive due to a common family business, a profession, such as the legal or medical one, and due to common housing.

In its transition into modernity Indian society has been careful to preserve a great deal of that which is positive in its culture. The care, concern and sympathy for the aged, and for the very young, is widespread. Under this transition has evolved the 'new joint family' in which the older generation strives to be more accommodating and less authoritarian and lives in harmony with children and grand children.

The traditional joint family in which three or four generations lived under one roof had both its advantages and disadvantages. There was no feeling of alienation in the old and the needy. Children were brought up in an atmosphere of warmth and emotional stability. However this form of living together in an extended family situation called for a lot of mutual adjustment and consideration and resulted in a lack of individual initiative and freedom. Moreover, domestic strife due to competition and the unjust victimisation of the daughter-in-low for bringing inadequate dowry, are frequent in joint families and often lead to its disintegration.

Status is achieved, rather than ascribed, in an industrial society, and the isolated nuclear family is best suited for such a society. Moreover the nuclear family is able to achieve geographical mobility without being unduly tied down to a binding range of kin a obligations to them. In addition, a wide range of specialised institutions such as schools, hospitals, business firms and even the Church, Creches and the police step in to perform the duties earlier done by the family.

The 70's and 80's saw women stepping out of their homes in ever increasing numbers, not only to supplement the family income but also to fulfil their individual career aspirations. Without the support of kin, beyond that of the nuclear family, the conjugal bond is often strengthened and women are given a great deal of scope to exercise initiative, regain their individuality and remain independent.

However, some reservation has to be exercised in adopting the nuclear family as the ideal since this new family system has given rise to set problems and drawbacks in the relationships between the older and younger generation and between parents and children.

Since the nuclear family is a manifestation of the achievement-oriented, status conscious society, there is less time and energy for bestowing attention and care on individual members. The stresses and strains imposed on the individual is considerable, as it calls for a great deal of self-sufficiency, independence and self-reliance. Aged parents can no longer expect to depend financially on their sons who have to fulfil the demands of their own immediate family and social environment. With women working, and domestic help being scarce and unreliable, children are brought up in a more matter-of-fact and less loving style than the generations before. The creche and the nursery school are the modern-day substitutes for grandparents, aunts, uncles and a plethora of servants. Both at the creche and at the nursery school the infant faces competition and consequently has to build up resilience and toughness in order to cope with the pressures of the environment. The problems do not stop with childhood as younger children and adolescents often become victims of the 'latch-key syndrome'. Each child has the house keys and after school is expected to return home, eat and study till their parents return in the evening. Returning to an empty house and remaining unsupervised for many house leads to loneliness, boredom and mindless viewing of the 'idiot box 'or television and endless hours on the computer and internet. Many teenagers find warmth and sympathy amongst peer groups or in casual relationships with the opposite sex.

What About the Position of Women?

Having achieved a measure of independence and initiative, and the freedom to pursue an individualist path, unfettered by the demands of the authoritarian older generation, is life a bed of roses for her? Perhaps not always so, for she is under severe pressure to achieve excellence in all roles—that of a home maker, a parent, a wife and a worker outside the home. The pace of this continuous pressure often results in psychosomatic stress ailments, tension and insecurity as doubts creep in as to whether she is indeed able to fulfil adequately the demands placed on her and juggle her multifarious roles to become 'superwoman'.

The modern man also is no longer monarch of all he surveys as his writ does not always run unchallenged on the domestic front. Not only is he expected to achieve success in his career but he also has to lend a hand to domestic chores, help out with children, and adjust to the schedule of his working wife. He can neither expect to be waited on hand at and foot, nor can he expect his decisions to be blindly accepted by his family, as that perhaps of his father and grand father were before him.

The compulsions of the nuclear family extract a certain response from its members and has a consequent impact on society.

The positive impact has been that men, women, and children have become more self-reliant, self possessed and independent. However in the absence of the cocoon of warmth and security which the joint family offered, there has been some unsettling repercussions such as neurosis, emotional instability, selfishness and excessive materialism. The preoccupation with success, achievement, status are western ideals which success, achievement, status are western ideals which seem worthy of emulation, but which once achieved often result in emptiness, loneliness and insecurity.

In the west, and indeed in some segments of our society, the nuclear family has yielded to its logical successor, the atomised family or the single parent family. The psychological and emotional scarring of the children of such families is too well-known to reiterate. An extreme concern with oneself, one's goals and aspirations detract from the general need to adjust and he sensitive to the needs of another. For all its infringements on personal liberty, the joint family offered a great deal of emotional and psychological sustenance which cannot be measured by any materialistic yardstick.

One can only conclude that so far the impact of the nuclear family on Indian society has not been unfavorable. But one would have to continuously guard against those aberrations of selfishness, greed, materialism and rigidity which crept into the western nuclear family to render it virtually obsolete today. Whereas it may be necessary for us to improve our social welfare system by having creches, old age homes and women's shelters, let not the existence of these institutions lead us to an attitude of indifference and irresponsibility to what must be our filial and social duties. We must not and do not want to reproduce western society with all its attendant problems of alienation depression, divorce, drug abuse and violence.

Be a Good Member of Society

We do live in our houses in isolation. We are part of a family, part of an apartment building, part of a society, part of a city. People often say how can one man make a difference? Of course, he or she can—did'nt Mahatma Gandhi, Swami Vivekananda and Mother Teresa move whole generations and countries? Apathy and indifference to our surroundings have made our cities into living hells, full of dirt and garbage. Everyone looks to another to clean up the mess. Look around you and at the end of everyday look at one action of yours that has been for someone other than yourself - your good deed for the day.

Some tips

1. We live in a multi-religious and multi-lingual society. Do not vitiate the atmosphere by making communal statements and derogatory comments about other communities.
2. Encourage your children to celebrate all festivals—Id, Diwali, Christmas and any other that they may want to.
3. Keep the environment clean. Do not litter, spit or urinate in public places. These habits and an absence of civic sense have made us highly unpopular when we go abroad, apart from the scathing comments from foreigners about the state of our cities.
4. Inculcate civic consciousness in children. The best way of doing this is to observe the correct norms yourself.
5. Do not get de-nationalised and forget our traditions of love, tolerance, patience and respect for elders. These should be passed on to the children through you rather than through the media.
6. Avoid adding to the corruption around us and do not bribe public servants if you are caught violating the rules. Pay the penalty instead.
7. Drive carefully and ensure that your car is finely tuned so that it is not adding to the air pollution.
8. Alert the authorities when there is traffic hazard on your road or if stray animals have become a nuisance.
9. Make sure that your name is included in the electoral role and make sure you vote during elections. There is no sense in grumbling about the state of affairs if one does not even bother to exercise ones franchise.
10. People avoid getting involved because they feel they will be victimised by the authorities. However, if one tackles all issues judiciously there is no reason why this should happen.

CHAPTER-11

Travel and Transfers

From the era of bullock carts, stage coaches and passenger trains we have reached the jet age where time and distance are swallowed up as one moves from country to country and continent to continent. A significant percentage of the family budget is devoted to travel and holidays, particularly in the west where even those who are on the dole or social security get an allowance for travel and holidays! In India, our travel is more geared towards family occasions such as attending marriages, helping out a sibling during child birth or emergency trips when there is a bereavement. Younger people however have been bitten by wanderlust and would like to travel. They do not always want it to be family related. Today an increasing number of well-off people are seeking new destinations to see and savour and to indulge themselves in. All manner of travel guides, travel agents and even internet services are available to facilitate travel but the concept of travel for pleasure is still a concept in gestation for the large mass of Indians.

Choosing A Destination

Choosing a travel destination is entirely a matter of personal task and requirement, both in terms of the budget, the time factor and one's interest and convenience. While westerners in Europe flock to the East, to South in the sun, savour the exotic foods and cultures of Asia and do sight seeing. Indians may want to visit Switzerland to see the snow or London and New York to witness the fast pace of life. A family elder may want to go on a pilgrimage to Kedarnath, Badrinath or Vaishno Devi while youngsters may want to go off on trekking holidays in the hills of northeast India.

Choosing a travel destination therefore is entirely up to the individual or the family and their proclivities. There are no hard and fast rules that can be made towards this decision except that it must suit one's budget, one's interest, one's time and one's health to the travel destination towards which one is headed. For example, those suffering from high blood pressure or heart problems are not advised to go to Leh and Ladakh where the altitude poses a problem to those who are less than fit. Similarly if one has a very short period of leave it is not advisable to head towards a distant place where travel time would eat into the holiday period.

Hence in choosing a travel destination one needs to take into account many factors of personal choice and convenience. Travelling is fun and with a little planning and thought it can be a wonderful experience that allows one to get away from the monotony of daily life. Travelling can mean picnic, a weekend away from home or a long trip abroad or to a holiday resort. Whatever it may be, even doctors agree that an occasional change from the normal routine is good, for both body and mind.

Advance Planning and Its Benefits

While spur of the moment decisions are fun and lend a great deal of spontaneity to any outing, it is necessary to plan for longer holidays or overseas visits. Advance planning ensures that one has a place to stay at the other end, that railway or air tickets are booked and that there is no wastage of either time or resources. During the festival season in India, that is between Dussehra and Diwali and during the school vacations, it is virtually impossible to get a train reservation unless one has booked in advance. Advance planning also eliminates the possibility of disappointment on not being able to undertake the journey. In case one is visiting friends or relatives, advance planning is required so that one ensures that they will be available and ready to receive you. Particularly in travelling with the family, advance planning is a necessity as chaos would reign supreme with wailing babies, fretful children and grumbling elders if foolproof arrangements have not been made in advance.

Advance planning would ensure that monetarily one does not suffer as there are many holiday 'packages' in hotels and in the airlines sector which offer valuable discounts and other services to the traveller.

There are also rail and air concessions that are given to children below 5-12 years to students and elders over the age of 60. Since rules keep changing from time, the details can be verified at the various agencies or through a good travel agent.

Travelling by Car

In travelling by bus, air, rail or sea, one has to worry about little except to make the necessary reservations. However, in travelling by car, one must ensure its road worthiness and also have a good road map to the destination.

Prior to leaving check

1. That the spare tyre is in good condition and that there is a jack and other tools in the car.
2. A spare distribution point, a fan belt and an extra tube are good standby assets during a long trip.
3. Check the engine oil while refuelling.
4. Do not overload the car with extra luggage.
5. Travel at a comfortable speed and take a break every two hours so that both the driver and passengers do not suffer from fatigue.
6. Road conditions in India make night driving hazardous, hence it is best to make an early start and reach one' destination during day light hours.

Packing Correctly

For most people, packing for a holiday is problematic as one must carry a restricted amount of luggage yet at the same time there should be enough clothes so that one is comfortable, and yet smartly clad throughout the holiday. One must also take one set of formal clothes in case one is invited out to a hotel or for a formal function. The main purpose of packing in advance is to ensure that one packs only that which is required as travelling with too many loose packages are difficult to keep track of.

To pack correctly

1. Ensure that your suitcase suits your travel requirements. For air travel a light suitcase is required since the luggage has to be weighed. If one is travelling by the Rajdhani or Shatabadi trains, the space for luggage is limited hence one should travel with smaller suitcases rather than a huge one which is cumbersome to lift and take down from the luggage rack. For bus and rail travel it is essential that one has a sturdy suitcase that will bear frequent handling. For those travelling by car, the suitcases should be small and lightweight as they will be put in the luggage boot and it should not add towards overloading the vehicle.

   The markets are flooded with suitcases of every size and description that will suit specific travel.

2. Packing must be done in a way that they do not get crushed. Clothes should be ironed before packing and there are travelling irons now available which can be taken along to literally iron out the creases. For short holidays one can pack a single suitcase for the family or have one for the children and one for the husband and wife. However, for longer holidays it will be necessary for everyone to carry a separate suitcase.

3. While grown up children may be able to do their own packing, younger children may need assistance. However, it may be advisable to check that the children are taking along suitable clothes, both for the weather and for other occasions.

4. Before packing, one should go through one's wardrobe and take out the dresses, pants, salwar kameezes, sarees and sweaters and assemble them on the bed. One should check to see that every item is in good condition and that there are no tears or missing buttons. Ensure that nighties, underclothing, handkerchief and so on are there so that nothing is forgotten. A little bit of initial thinking saves a lot of effort later and things are not left behind.

5. Place a towel on the bottom of the suitcase as a lining and let the ends come out so that the clothes can be covered after the packing is done. This towel not only provides a soft padding on all sides but also protects the clothes from dust during travel. If worse comes to the worst, the towel can also be used if they are not clean or readily available at the other end.

   Place clothes on top of the towel and ensure that matching ensembles are placed together for convenience. The sides may be packed with nightwear, handkerchiefs, socks and shoes. Make sure that the packed clothes are level so that they do not crease unduly. Sweaters and cardigans can be placed on top.

6. If one is accompanied by small children it is best to keep a towel, drinking water, toys and some reading material for them

in a separate bag which they can carry themselves.
7. While travelling always make sure that the suitcases are labelled with your name and address and mentally make a note of the number of pieces you are travelling with.

Emergency Travel Kit

While a change is good for most of us, one has to take along certain amount of necessary medication as well as one's regular medicines while travelling. Children in particular are prone to illness during a change of place hence their medication for cold and cough or an upset stomach must be taken along. It is difficult to look for the same medicine at different places where they may not be available.

For those who suffer from motion sickness, there are both allopathic and homeopathic medicines which can be taken prior to a journey.

Adequate pre-departure preparations and information regarding health hazards in the area you are about to visit will go a long way in ensuring an illness-free stay. Making sure that you are healthy pre-travel medical check is a must- get that tooth filled and keep an extra pair of spectacles with you. Looking around for a dentist or ophthalmologist in a strange place can be daunting. Also, if you are on regular medications for an ailment such as hypertension or diabetes, take adequate stocks along to cover the period of your stay. The brand of medicine you are used to may not be available everywhere.

A small, simple medical kit is wise in addition to your luggage. This should include:

- Antihistamines such as Benadryl or Cetrizine useful for colds, allergies, itching from insect bites and stings. Marzine and avomine are especially good for travel sickness. Take a tablet about 45 minutes before starting your journey. Remember that antihistamines cause drowsiness and alcohol should be avoided.
- Painkillers and medicines to bring down fever, such as aspirin. The safest of these is Paracetamol (Crocin). Brufen is useful in body-aches and joint pains. These medicines should never be taken on an empty stomach.
- Antibiotics- keep a full course of these handy, but only after advice from your doctor. If you are allergic to any of these (such as sulphas and penicillin), ensure that this information is carried on your person at all times. Antibiotics are necessary in case of mild infections (sore throat, infected cuts), and medical help should be sought for more serious ailments.
- Dehydration mixtures for diarrhoeas especially while travelling with children, as even seemingly mild diarrhoeas can cause serious loss of fluid in them. Follow the instructions on the packet to make up the solution. Lomotil or Imodium can be used to relieve symptoms, but only if absolutely necessary. In all circumstances, fluid replacement remains the mainstay of treatment.

Antiseptics, such as Betadine, which are available as swabs lotion or ointment. These are used to clean cuts and grazes. Dry antibiotic powders such as Neomycin may also be sprayed on the area after cleaning it well with an antiseptic.
- Calamine lotion eases irritation from stings and cuts. It also helps to soothe sunburned skin.

- Bandages, band-aids, crepe bandages (for sprains) are a must. Scissors should be carried in the kit, and tweezers often come in handy in pulling out thorns, glass shards and other foreign material. A thermometer is always useful, but mercury thermometers are not permitted on airplanes.
- Insect repellents, especially mosquito protectants are invaluable.
- Last but not least, always carry sterilised disposable syringes of varying sizes (2 ml and 5 ml) along with needles. About two of each should be enough for a short stay. With the AIDS epidemic on us, this is a wise precaution, should in injection become mandatory.

Arrangements to be Made Before Leaving for a Holiday

Certain arrangements must be made before the house is closed prior to a family holiday. If all members of the family are not going then there is no need to lock up the house. However, if the whole family is travelling together certain precautions must be taken prior to departure.

Handy tips

1. Do not leave the entire house open and in the charge of servants as they may be tempted, or forced by their friends, to avail of the facilities in the house. Many a householder has returned unexpectedly to find even an old and trusted servant having a party of his own while his employer is away! It necessary, keep only a restricted portion open and lock up the rest.
2. Check all the lights, taps, doors and windows.
3. Inform your neighbours that you will be away and give them your holiday address so that you may be contacted in an emergency. You may leave a spare key with either a neighbour, friend or relative during your absence.
4. If you stay in an independent bungalow it may be a good idea to employ a guard to look after the premises.
5. Remove all valuables from the house such as jewellery and put them in the bank locker.
6. Have your house and belongings insured against theft.
7. Instruct the newspaper about not delivering newspapers but do not inform him about the exact days of your absence. Do not give the exact dates of return to such people as information may spread to unsavoury elements that the house will be vacant during a specified period during which they may plan a burglary.

Tips About Foreign Travel

As airtravel connects more and more countries together, foreign travel has now become a part of life. For those who work in offices of the private sector, or even those in government, foreign travel has become quite frequent. A few handy tips before one embarks on a journey abroad will ensure that the itinerary goes through smoothly.

Before going abroad

1. Ensure that you have a valid passport and make sure that you obtain viasas for the countries to which you are travelling to. On account of the large number of Indians going abroad, many of whom go with invalid documents, the authorities

in foreign countries thoroughly scrutinize the documents of Indians entering their country. Even in countries where Indians were initially warmly welcomed, as in Thailand they often ask to see one's return airticket at the immigration counter!

2. Make sure that no vaccinations are to be taken prior to departure as some countries have yellow fever (Africa and South America) and hence one has to be inoculated or face being quarantined.

3. Dress adequately for the weather and make sure that you have enough warm clothing to stave off the cold. A lots of walking is necessary in foreign countries so ensure that you have comfortable and durable shoes. Take an umbrella along.

4. Try to have a confirmed ticket and confirmed hotel or other accommodation at your destination.

5. Make sure that you carry enough money. The main international currency being US dollars, one would have to check the exchange rate and take money according to the duration and destination of one's travels. An international travel or credit card is useful. Travellers' cheques afford protection against theft but a certain commission is charged to encash these locally.

6. While travelling abroad be conscious of the fact that you are an envoy for your country. Due to the deeds of uneducated Indians who have gone abroad, our world image is not always a good one. Resist the temptation to bargain aggressively. While shopping, do not ask to see every item and then refuse to buy as foreigners are short of both time and patience and often refuse to show Indians their merchandise because they know that they will not buy. Such episodes frequently occur in Thailand, Hong Kong and the African countries.

7. Be careful of pickpockets and smugglers abroad. India is not the only unsafe country - infact violent crimes are even more prevalent abroad. Italy for example is thoroughly unsafe and pickpocketing is rampant. Racial insults may be hurled in Germany and England. Mugging is a possibility in New York and Washington. Hence always be alert and avoid the more crime infested places in town.

8. Foreigners expect others to be self reliant hence you will not find passerbys helpful in terms of telling you directions and so on. At the same time, since these places are thoroughly organized, maps and guides along with Information Counters in public places are set up to handle all queries.

9. Remain polite and smiling in a foreign country where the rules and regulations and precision technology offers a frightening contrast to our country.

Every country and culture has their own etiquette and since business travel is frequent it is a good idea to be aware of which one is going so that there is no faux pas.

Given below is a list of some major countries and the demands of the local culture there.

Hopefully these tips will ensure that you have a bon voyage and that you become a good ambassador for India abroad. If in doubt during formal dinners, just observe the host or hostess before digging headlong into the food and drink.

What Happens When You're Jet-lagged?

Your sleep-wake cycle gets interrupted.

You arrive at your destination confused and depressed.

Reduced physical and mental activity.

Poor memory.

Your appetite does not coincide with the local meal times.

Constipation is a very common occurrence.

You may experience mood-swings.

Travelling eastward is worse than travelling westward as the former reduces the traveller's day.

Tips to reduce jet-lag blues

ON ARRIVAL

Eat a high protein breakfast that includes egg, cheese, curd, pulses, chicken, fish, nuts etc.

Have a high carbohydrate dinner that includes rice, potatoes, whole grain or pastas.

Avoid sleeping the '40 winks' during daytime.

Research has shown that physical activity like a swim, jog or a brisk walk reduces the effect of jet-lag.

Light has an important role to play in reducing jet-lag too. So, go ahead and spend a good deal of time in light.

BEFORE COMMENCING YOUR JOURNEY

If you are travelling eastward, try sleeping earlier than usual a few days before your date of departure. Conversely, if you are travelling westward, just do the opposite - stay up late.

If possible, try to reach your destination in the evening and go to bed early or try taking a stopover.

Before your flight do a little exercise.

Drink a lot of water and fruit juices.

Avoid drinking alcohol—the cabin pressure reduces the ability of the liver to process alcohol. This increases the chances of a hangover.

Move around the aircraft as often as you can.

Wear loose-fitting clothes for travel.

Sitting encourages water retention—do neck, ankle, and wrist rotations as many times as possible.

Remove your contact lenses before the flight. Use special drops to keep the eyes moist.

Dehydration is very common in a pressurised cabin increase your fluid intake.

The skin tends to get very dry. Use a moisturiser every four hours.

Travelling is supposed to be one of life's great pleasures. But instead if you feel sick in a car/plane, your hair feels dry and your feet swell or your skin breaks out, you may wonder why. Whether you travel by air or by road here are a few tips to help you travel beautifully.

FEEL FRESH

Keep yourself cool and calm while travelling by road by placing two cotton balls on the window shelf of the car, one with a drop of eucalyptus and the other with drop of peppermint oil. These oils are not only antibiotic and antiseptic but soothe the nerves and keep you fresh.

TRAVEL SICKNESS

Travel sickness is to a large extent caused by conflicting messages reaching the brain from the eyes and the balancing mechanism of the ears and stomach. It helps to close your eyes while travelling or fix your eyes on an object in the distance.

While flying the pressurised cabins, air causes dehydration, dry skin, swollen feet and ankles, cramp, headaches and painful knees.

DRY SKIN

Before starting out on your journey have a shower after which you use a light body moisturiser to which a few drops of any calming essential oil have been added such as lavender or geranium. Remove your make-up, splash with water and apply an emollient cream. If you prefer not to take off your make-up, use a night cream under your make-up. Spray your face regularly with mineral water. Invest in a mini plant spray bottle to carry in your hand luggage.

WHAT TO DRINK

Avoid alcohol when travelling by air to ward off the exhausting effects of dehydration from alcohol. Hangovers in the air can be bad. Try to avoid coffee and tea also as these are diuretics. Instead try to have a cup of peppermint tea before you leave the house—one drop of peppermint oil mixed with a teaspoon of honey in hot water.

WHAT TO EAT?

As you take longer flights, jet lag is one of the problems you face. When you need to sleep you may crave for food at odd times or may feel too sick to eat. So the best solution is to eat less than usual and try to eat healthy food such as vegetarian or low-sodium meals. Another solution is to massage a few drops of peppermint and eucalyptus oils throughout your body, or you may even add them to your bath water after the flight.

SWOLLEN ANKLES

Sitting for long periods in a train, car, bus, or while flying the speeded-up gravitational pull of the aeroplane affect circulation and cause your feet to swell up. So try to massage your legs in an upward direction to the bottom of the calf with a few drops of pure lavender oil and try to wear loose fitting shoes.

CRAMPS

If you are prone to getting cramps while travelling, make a compress by using geranium oil and hold the compress over the affected area, usually the calf of the leg or the foot. Also try the old Chinese trick of holding your big toes tightly between the thumb and forefinger. This treatment will alleviate the symptoms of jet lag but for the best results it must be continued.

Before you set out on a journey make sure your handbag is well-stocked with the things you need. BONVOYAGE.

Coping with Transfers

Sher Shah Suri has always been regarded as one of the finest administrators in Indian history. In fact, many of the systems followed by subsequent rulers had their foundations in the administrative philosophy of Sher Shah. A keystone of Sher Shah's system of governance was the system of transfers. He believed that since a lot of power was invested in the hands of lower functionaries, it was best to move them around from place to place before they developed an equation with the local vested interests. This philosophy pervades our administrative set-up even today. Whether in the government or in the private sector organisations, the armed forces and now, even in the higher rungs of the judiciary, there is a system of transfers whereby the employee is shifted from one place to another, either within a particular state, a zone or even overseas. Whereas many private and public sector organisations bear the cost of this movement in financial terms, it is not always possible to calculate the exact psychological and physical strain and the consequent mental adjustments which have to be made in facing a new environment.

Those in our country who are in 'transferable' jobs, must have or acquire, a 'gypsy' mentality. Since many tenures are of a fixed duration of two, three or five years, families become restive once the tenure goes beyond the stipulated deadline. Perhaps to retain their mental and emotional equilibrium, many look forward to the challenge of facing a new environment, making new friends, decorating a new house or the exposure to a new culture. Apart from a flexible mental attitude, numerous other points should be kept in mind so that transfers, which are a hazard of the job in many professions, do not lead to financial, educational or material losses of an overwhelming proportion.

A person in a transferable job is bound by certain transfer rules, in which the benefits and facilities provided to him by the organisation are clearly formulated. The amount of leave or joining time available, the air or train fare given to the employee and his family, the packing allowance and the transit or other accommodation given at the new place of posting all come within the purview of these rules.

In case both husband and wife are working, often in the same office or frequently in different professions, there is the additional problem of securing a simultaneous transfer to the same place at the same time. Frequently the wife opts to stay back rather than follow her husband to the new place of posting, either for professional reasons or because of the children's schooling. Boarding school or hostel facilities are not always readily available, especially for school going children. In the case of the Armed Forces, the families are often separated due to Non-Family Stations, which are located in the border areas or in troubled areas within the country.

Since we function in a 'paper raj', it is essential to ensure that all one's important papers and documents are in order. Passports, ration cards, school Transfer Certificates, Birth Certificates and papers relating to the return of gas cylinders must be kept carefully. The bills pertaining to the payment of house rent, vacation of the house or government accommodation, electricity and water bills, insurance and bank accounts should be cleared and the receipts maintained in a folder. To safeguard against loss or damage during transfer, these should be photocopied and kept in a safe place.

Some government and private organisations allow their employees to pay a visit to the new place of posting so that it becomes easier to apply for children's admissions to schools, secure appropriate accommodation, meet one's predecessor and get a general idea of the new environment to which one has to shift. Of course, in the case of Foreign Service officers or the armed forces, this is not always possible so one would either have to contact friends who had been posted to these places earlier or read up from books about the new city or country of posting.

Moving house

Not all jobs provide furnished accommodation, so it is often imperative to move with the entire complement of furniture, along with one's clothes, objets d'art, crockery, kitchen utensils, linen, refrigerator, television, VCR and stereo system and car.

For an overseas transfer, the luggage could either go by air or by sea. For movement by air, one's personal effects would be packed in cardboard cartons. Movement by sea would require either a liftvan or big wooden crates so that things are not damaged during loading and transhipment. There are many professional companies which provide facilities for packers and assist in moving one's personal effects both within the country and overseas. However, not every employer gives complete reimbursement for these frequently exorbitant charges.

If one is in a job in which one is frequently transferred, it is best to keep the general quantum of luggage down. Items such as books are difficult to cart around as they are weighty. Delicate crockery and paintings are also fragile and hence have to be very carefully packed in order to avoid breakage. It is best to keep a few wooden boxes and steel trunks as well as the original packing cartons of items like televisions and stereos, clocks and crockery so that they can be easily packed during transfers. It is also helpful to number the boxes, either with a felt pen or with paint, and enumerate the contents in a notebook or diary, so that at the time of unpacking it becomes easier to locate things without undue strain on one's memory.

Packing Materials

For those who are able to engage the services or professional packers there is no problem, as they assess the quantum of luggage and provide the requisite packing materials. They provide the required number of cartons and crates, plastic and string, along with corrugated paper and gunny for heavier items.

As mentioned earlier, if one is unable to avail of the services of professional packers, either due to financial constraints or because they are simply not available in smaller places, one should keep packing boxes and some packing materials of one's own.

Along with insulation against the weather and damage during movement one also has to protect one's belongings against insects such as silver fish, moths, cockroaches and white ants. If boxes are made of wood, they can be attacked by white ants during storage, a sprinkling of gammaxene powder at the bottom of the crate will offer protection for some time atleast. Trunks and suitcases should have naphthalene balls so that silver fish and moths do not damage the clothes. Dried 'neem' leaves are also a great insect repellent and can be used not only for clothes, but while packing carpets also.

All suitcases and trunks should be locked and separate key rings should be made of original and duplicate keys. It is advisable not to use brass or even brass coloured locks as these attract thieves who break locks so that brass can be melted and sold. Even the wagon or container, if one is sending luggage by train, should not have a brass or brass coloured padlock. This was he advice given by seasoned railway officers as protection against luggage breakers'!

Transporting Luggage

Packing and transfers is literally, a herculean task. For international transfers luggage is transported either by sea or by air, and has to be packed accordingly. Lists of the goods have to be maintained for custom's clearance, and for these transfers it is best to secure the services of professionals who are familiar with the procedure and formalities involved in such movements.

For transfers within the country also, goods must be clearly listed so that there is no problem at the octroi check posts which are located throughout the country. The railway container service is 'door-to-door' one, but if one sends one's luggage by EVK, luggage has to be arranged therefore, along with 'coolies' to transport the goods from the residence to the station. At the station, there are railway labour contractors with whom one can negotiate for loading the wagon. These loaders are professional and experienced, and are able to stack the luggage in such a way that there is minimal damage during 'shunting'. The car can also be transported if both the car as well as the luggage are tightly secured with or coir rope so that there is no movement.

It is also possible to transport luggage as well as the car by truck. This mode of transportation gives rise to a few apprehensions however. Firstly, one should deal only with established or reliable truck owners. Due to bad roads, there is a lot of jerking, which may damage fragile items. Secondly, there are dangers of accidents and transhipment. Seasoned 'transfer victims' therefore, often send a known member of their personal staff in the truck so that the above-mentioned liabilities can be taken care of.

It is also advisable to get the luggage insured for the period of transit. A Transit Insurance must be taken out atleast two days before the luggage leaves from one destination to another.

Although transfers are a matter of routine in some professions in this country, it often becomes the cause of physical, mental, emotional and financial hardship. An example of this is the use of transfers as a method of punishment for being uncompromising or intransigent towards the powers that be. However, this trauma can be partially reduced if one is organised and mentally and physically equipped to face the challenge which a change of residence inevitably poses on all one's resources.

CHAPTER-12

Personal Grooming

In an increasingly fashion conscious world, grooming has become essential for both men and women. An individual today should be aware of his/her own worth, send out right signals and make the most of him/herself. With a little bit of effort one can easily bring about a role reversal and be at the receiving end of those admiring looks.

Exercise

Do not be put off with the term exercise. Women get their fair share of exercise doing housework, but the advantage of doing specific exercises are many. Regularity in exercising is more important than anything else. For instance if you go for a half-an-hour walk everyday, it is better than doing vigorous exercises once a week or less. Similarly, do a few specific yogasanas regularly, and feel the difference. By exercise, one does not mean anything fancy like dance aerobics or going to the gym for a workout. You will be amazed at how many calories you can burn off by just changing your way of sitting, walking and doing ordinary chores.

Calories

What on earth are calories? They are nothing but the amount of energy produced by the food you eat. Though generally, every calorie is supposed to produce energy, there are some calories that do not produce any energy and are hence called empty calories. Refined sugar and high cream desserts fall into this category. These foods produce calories that get accumulated in the body as fat when consumed in excess. In short, you can avoid them, with no loss of energy.

The calories you consume every day should be in proportion to your level of physical activity. For instance if you do not do any physical work at home and also hold a desk job, the calories you expend per day are reduced very much, thereby making extra calories turn into fat that shows up in your waistline, hips, arms and thighs. Likewise, if you do a lot of physical work, the calories spent by you will be more. If you reduce them, you may feel weak and tired.

This chart only provides an approximate estimate of the ideal weight, since it can vary a little depending upon your build: whether you are a large, medium or small built person. An honest look at yourself in the mirror will tell you all you need to know.

How many calories do you need?

As explained earlier, the calories you require depend upon your activities or lack of them. On an average, though, the following chart is a good guide.

The wide variation is to allow for difference in the level of activities. You can assume that you require only the minimum calories if you do not do any vigorous housework or even exert yourself while doing the chores. A lot of bending, pushing and pulling of furniture, carrying heavy shopping up the stairs, walking up and down stairs at least two three times a day, briskly, all qualify as some form of exercise.

Which type of calories do you need?

Our food consists of three broad food types: carbohydrates, proteins and fats. Unless the food combines all the three in the right quantities, your meal will not be a balanced one and provide you the right type and number of calories you require.

Carbohydrates are required for providing energy to the body. They are the fastest to leave the stomach, since they are quickly broken down into glucose to provide energy. Rice, bread, potatoes, refined sugar and sweets are some carbohydrate foods.

Proteins are necessary for the growth and repair of cells in the body. They are present in dals, whole pulses like rajma and chana, eggs and meat.

Fats are high sources of energy and therefore, one must be very careful of the quantity one consumes. This is because, unless the person eating a high-fat diet is extremely active physically, the excess fat tends to get accumulated in the body, especially around the tummy and hips. Butter, oils, ghee, cheese and other milk products are some forms of fats. For an average adult, the maximum fat requirement per day can be about 10 gms including cooking fats.

Plan your diet to suit your calorie requirement

This may require some effort on your part, but having a food-calorie chart and planning the menu accordingly is a sensible way of losing or maintaining weight. Combine and discard food groups from this chart and you can achieve a balanced diet for your level of activity.

All vegetables have relatively fewer calories. They are highly fibrous and therefore necessary for digestion. Sweet potato is one root vegetable that is very high on calories. It provides 120 calories per 100 gms. Potato provides 94 calories. So when these are combined with fats like oil or cream and butter, their fat content goes up very high. Similarly, among fruits, banana (153 calories) chikkoo or sapota (94 calories) and mangoes (80 calories) are the high calories fruits. Watermelon (tarbuz) and white melon (kharbuj) are among the lowest calorie fruits.

Things to remember while dieting

- Note that the oil allowed for the whole day is about 2 tsps. only. Reduce salt intake since fresh vegetables and fruits have a lot of natural salt in them. Rest assured that you will not suffer from any deficiency or weakness due to less salt. According to several studies, the amount of salt a person requires in a whole day is as low as 3 gms, provided he or she consumes a lot of fresh fruits and vegetables.
- Remember to take at least 8 glasses of water in a day.
- Never drink water during the meals. However, if a large appetite is a problem with you and you tend to overeat, sip a glass of hot water half an hour before the meal.
- Chew each mouthful slowly and do not gulp down the food or wash it down with cold drinks or water. The process of digestion is upset by this method.
- According to studies, a person feels satiated 20 minutes after eating food.

So it is important to make each mouthful last by chewing thoroughly and eating for at least 20-25 minutes. This will prevent the urge to snack after a meal.

- Avoid pickles and sauces since these contain preservatives and high quantities of salt, both of which are bad for dieters.
- Do not go on fad diets, like an all fruit or all milk diet. Also, never eat unappetising food thinking that it will help you reduce. Chances are, you will put the weight you may lose double fast once you go back to your original diet. There is also the danger of deficiencies and sudden collapse.
- Slimming concoctions and pills are best avoided because their efficacy is not proven.
- Exercise is very important. Set aside at least 15 minutes a day for some form of exercise—walking, yogasana, skipping, etc.
- When you go for parties, have something at home to take the edge off the hunger. Try to stick to salads and vegetables as far as possible. Avoid the sweet dish or go in for fruits if there are.
- If you are planning to lose weight, think in terms of vegetarian food and that too simple dishes that do not require too much frying. Meats if you must take, should be lean (fat removed) and boiled as far as possible. Western cooking is best in this respect.

Myths about dieting

Eating less will **not** make you lose weight. I know of women who literally starve to become thinner, but find themselves getting fatter. Even if you do, you will regain it soon. Exercising is a better way to lose weight.

Not all the calories are the same. calories from carbohydrate foods like whole wheat bread (roti, brown bread), boiled or baked potatoes, pasta, etc. are burned for energy. But excess fats get stored in the body.

Starches are **not fattening.** But if you add fats like oil, ghee or butter, cream, etc. it will add to the calories and turn fattening. For example, potatoes when plain boiled or baked is a good source of energy, but when fried, turns fattening. Making parathas in vanaspati or ghee is also the same.

The most difficult task that faces a dieter is eating out. It is here that he loses the battle of the bulge. However, occasional treats are not harmful to healthy eating habits. It is better to eat in small quantities foods that you crave, e.g chocolates, rather than allowing build up to unmanageable heights. Here are a few choices you can make at a restaurant:

Healthy eating habits should be inculcated as early as possible. Here are a few suggestions for a healthy diet for children:

a) Make use of non-stick cooking utensils to reduce fat while cooking.

b) Use vegetable oils for cooking instead of ghee or butter.

c) Increase their consumption of high fibre whole grain cereals such as whole wheat flours, brown rice and potatoes. Use a mixture of whole meal and white flours for baking cakes for young children.

d) Make all the changes gradually.

e) Eat food which is as near to the natural state as possible, avoiding foods with artificial additives and colours.

f) It is not necessary for children to have large amounts of potato wafers, chocolates and sweets in the lunch box. Try to avoid sugary or fried snacks as they destroy appetite, but a fruit or salad to chew on is a good idea.

g) By weaning children straight on to the healthy diet that is great fun. Your kids will enjoy it as much as you do. And before you know it, you have prepared the foundation which will ultimately set your child in good stead for a healthy life in the future. They will be free from modern day scourges of poor dietary habits and poor nutrition.

Although the problem of over-weight people has been addressed widely, those who are underweight rarely find material on how to put on weight. Here are a few tips:

a) Eat a balanced meal which is slightly high in calories.

b) Concentrate on workouts to tone your body and build muscles.

c) Remember that weight gain should be slow. Sudden weight fluctuations cause immense harm to the body.

A few more tips for a healthy life

Give attention to your hand, feet, nails.

Weight is not a criteria to judge your fitness. It is a free fat percentage.

Do not take any food for 1/2 hour before exercising.

No food is fattening; it is either too much or too little.

Fat is equally essential in the diet as Vitamin A, D, E and K is absorbed through fat only.

After 30 years of age, exercise is must for calcium deposition in bone, otherwise osteoporosis sets in.

As eyes are the mirror of your face, skin is the mirror of your health.

Vitamin C increases your body response and is available in plenty amount in Amla, Guava, Lemon.

Roughage should be the important part of your diet and it is found in whole grains, fruits and vegetables.

Laughter is the best medicine as it exercises all the muscles of your body in a positive direction.

Fresh fruits and vegetables are the main source of vitamins and minerals.

Dieting doesn't mean starvation it means balanced diet.

Balanced diet means combination of carbohydrates, proteins, fat, vitamins, minerals and plenty of water.

As calcium and phosphorus are main minerals for bone formation, iron and zinc are main minerals for blood formation.

Losing weight through starvation leads to many medical complication like anaemia, low blood pressure, weakness and giddiness.

To keep your skin glowing use choker, kacha *dudh* and *haldi* instead of soap.

Massage

Massage should be applied at such regular daily time as suits the mutual convenience of patient and operator. The purpose of massage is to increase and perfect nutritive activity in special designated parts, which implies unequal distribution of its processes.

The commencing processes should usually be at the extremities, more frequently the lower.

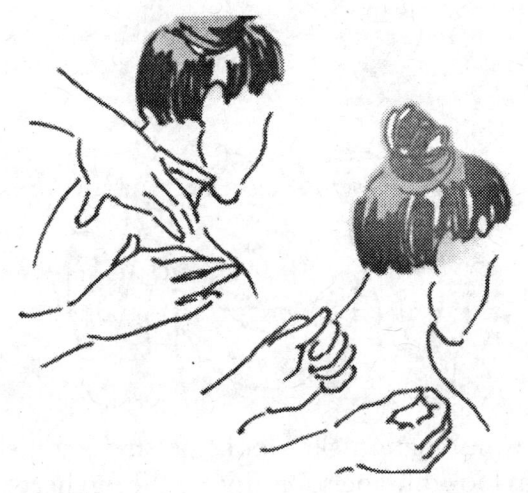

The degree of force of the processes applied must be apportioned to the degrees of irritability of the different parts of the body, and must be greatest to the least irritable parts. Sensitiveness to impressions is an approximate measure of irritability. With the processes properly adjusted, the irritability and liability to local pain disappears as the local diseased organs are approached, and no other than agreeable sensations are evoked by the processes.

An hour or two spent in the application of the processes, with their intervals, is quite sure to superinduce a feeling of, and a desire for, repose, which often culminates in sound sleep.

Good Posture

Whatever your height, walk straight and tall. One way to do this is to imagine someone pulling you up with strings from your shoulders. Slouching will not only make you look shorter but also make your shoulders look round and your neck sunken. Square your shoulders, look straight and you would have added inches to your height. Good posture also makes you feel more confident.

The right sitting posture

Make it a habit to sit with a straight back. This may sound difficult and to begin with, you may sit with drooping shoulders, but if you remember to straighten your shoulders and back, soon, you will find yourself improving your posture. This is very important for people who have a desk job or do a lot of work on the computer or typewriter. You will actually find back pain reducing, by sitting straight. If you do not believe me, try this. Sit slouched at the table for 15 minutes and then straighten your back and shoulders. The nagging pain in the back will reduce. If it returns again, it means that you have slouched again!

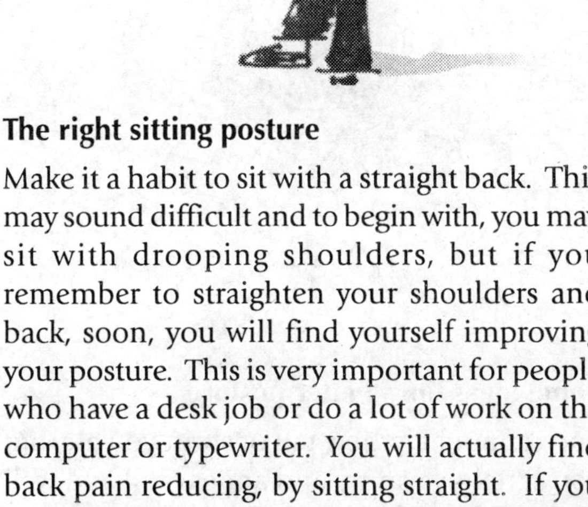

When you are simply sitting, say, at the doctor's, do not fidget while standing or sitting. Fold your hands on your lap if you are sitting. If you feel restless, you can always hold a book or newspaper or even knit. Cracking fingers, biting nails and fiddling with the hair, are all signs of agitation and best avoided.

Some ideas for a better posture

You cannot help how tall or short you are, but you certainly can try and **appear** tall and well proportioned, with the help of dress, make-up and accessories like shoes and jewellery. It is not difficult to make a thin person appear fatter, a fat person to look thinner and so on.

Skin Care

Find out your skin type

Before you pick a skincare regime it is important to know what your skin type is.

Oily Skin feels greasy on the surface and is prone to breakouts and blemishes, enlarged pores and a constant shine.

Normal skin is soft and supple with a smooth feel.

Dry skin appears dull and flaky. It is also likely to feel tight and rough after being outdoors.

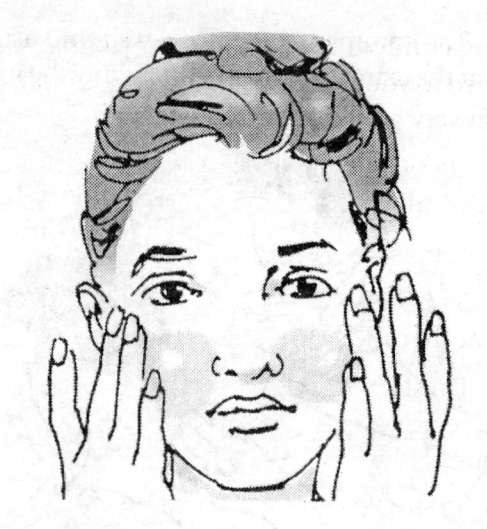

Combination skin looks patchy— some areas look oily and some dry e.g. the forehead, nose and chin known as the "T-Zone" appear oily and shiny while the skin on the cheeks are dry.

Skin routine for different skin types

CLEANSING - TONING

Teenage: Clean your face regularly and use a sunscreen lotion during the day.

If you are prone to pimples, get a dermi-check and follow the routine for oily skin.

Clean your face of all dirt and make-up every night before sleeping.

Get into a regular skincare routine that is suited to your skin type and always handle your skin very gently.

20s: Check your skin for superficial fine lines and wrinkles. Use moisturisers regularly.

A sunscreen is a must for daily use.

By now you should be following a regular skincare routine.

This is the age where you experiment with make-up, so cleanse off all make-up thoroughly.

30-40: Check your skin for superficial fine lines, wrinkles and sagging skin.

Visits to a beauty therapist for facials is advisable.

Follow a regular skincare routine and add on a Skin Replenishing Night Cream or Skin Revival Lotion/System to your regular moisturiser.

40-50: During these years your skin needs extra care since a lot of skin changes occur, e.g. change of skin type from oily to dry or vice-versa, breaking out into pimples, sudden sagging around the jaw line, wrinkles due to sun damage in the earlier years.

Keep a watch on your skin, and visit a beauty therapist if required.

50s and beyond: Normally skin tends to get drier after 50 and needs a lot of nourishing and moisturising for which Skin Revival Lotion/System is ideal.

Facial

Facial is a process of complete cleansing, toning and tightening the facial skin and muscles. If you have the time, you could go to a beauty parlour, but having a facial at home is not at all difficult. You do not even require fancy equipment for it. You will need:

1. A big bowl of boiling water
2. Cold cream or olive oil
3. Face pack
4. Lots of cotton
5. A little rose water
6. An astringent lotion

First of all, start with creaming your face. Take generous quantities of cold cream and apply over the face and neck, massaging it well into the skin. While massaging, use upwards strokes. Massage around the eyes and between the eyes using upward and outward strokes. While doing the neck, use a downward motion. Massage for at least 10 minutes.

Wet a piece of cotton and remove all the grime and dust from the massaged areas. Boil a large bowl of water. Bring it to a table. Bend your face over it, with a thick towel covering your face and head to keep in the steam. Stay like that till the water becomes warm. By now, your face would have begun to "sweat". Lightly dab with some cotton.

Next, remove the blackheads and tweeze the eyebrows.

Do not use soap or any other cosmetic on the face for at least 12 hours, to allow the skin to breathe.

Go to a beauty parlour at least once every two or three months to get a professional facial. Keeping your skin clean with home facials is a good idea, even if you do go to the parlour.

When you have absolutely no time, you can quickly steam the face and wipe well with cotton to remove the dirt and grime.

Blackheads and whiteheads

These are impurities that enter the skin through the pores and get settled. Generally, oily skins are more prone to blackheads and the nose and forehead are the main areas where these are found. By steaming the face, these can be loosened, since the pores get enlarged. Use a blackhead remover to gently remove these from the face. Be careful to avoid injury. Never try to squeeze them out with your nails since they may get infected that way.

Face packs

Dry skin

1. Mix the yolk of one egg with a teaspoonful of almond oil, adding the oil drop by drop to the yolk, and stirring constantly. Apply to the face and neck and leave for 15 to 20 minutes. Remove with warm water.
2. Add olive oil drop by drop to two tablespoons of white flour (maida) until it is the consistency of a soft porridge. This pack should be kept on for half an hour if possible. Remove with rain water or rose water.
3. Mix one tablespoon of pure butter or ghee with half a tablespoon of cocoa. Leave on the skin for 15 minutes. This pack does not have a very pleasant smell, but has a wonderfully softening effect. Remove with warm water and soap.

Normal skin

1. Boil two tablespoons of white flour with milk to make a soft consistency. Add a little rose water and spread over the face and neck while warm (not hot). Leave on for 15 minutes. Remove with warm water.
2. Mix some whole wheat flour (atta) with a little water. Cook on a low heat for about 5 minutes, stirring all the time. Add one teaspoon of honey and mix well. The pack should have a soft, porridge-like consistency and should be applied to the face while still warm. Leave it on for 15 to 20 minutes. Remove with warm water and soap.
3. To one teaspoonful of honey, add a few drops of almond oil. Spread all over the face and neck. Leave for ten minutes, then remove with rain or softened water. This pack has an excellent softening effect and is especially useful for removing fine wrinkles.

Oily skin

1. Mix together equal parts of cornflour and talcum powder. Add a little cold water and mix until the pack has the consistency of soft porridge. Spread over the face and neck and leave for 20 minutes. Remove with cotton wool which has been soaked in astringent lotion.
2. Beat the white of an egg until it is quite stiff. Spread lightly over the face. Leave till dry, then remove with astringent lotion.
3. Grate some cucumber (Kheera), add a few drops of lime juice and a teaspoonful of rose water. Place between two pieces of gauze or fine cloth and apply to the face. Leave for 15 to 20 minutes.

It is important to remember that face packs should not be left on the skin for more than the stipulated time. And never apply a pack to the fine skin under the eyes.

Each skin type needs different care

Dry skin

Cleanse: Give up washing your face in soap and water for a while, and cleanse your skin with cold cream or cleansing milk only. After a week or two of this treatment, you may wash your face with soap and warm water, but only just once a day, preferably at night before your skin care routine. At other times during the day you may cleanse your face with cream or cleansing milk, and after doing this you may splash your face with cool water to give you a fresh feeling.

Tone: Immediately after cleansing, tone your skin. Take a small piece of cotton wool, soak it in water, wring it out and moisten with a little skin tonic. Pat gently all over your face and neck. Do not apply to the skin under your eyes.

Nourish: A dry skin needs plenty of oil, as an over-dry one inevitably leads to premature wrinkles. There are plenty of expensive skin foods for women with dry skin, but there is no need to spend a great deal of money. Nothing can rival almond oil for improving dry skin. Apply it lightly, using upward and outward strokes. Using the third finger of your left hand, pat it in very gently under the eyes.

Normal skin

Cleanse: First wash your face with soap and water, then give it a thorough cleansing with cleansing milk.

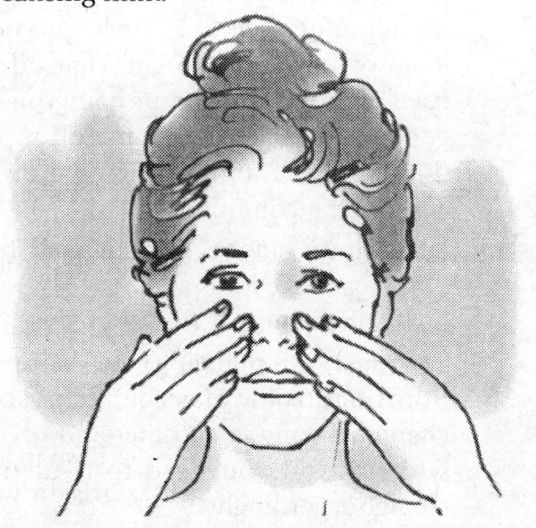

Tone: Your skin with skin tonic (rose water is fine for this purpose) or a mild astringent lotion. Apply the tonic or lotion with a small piece of cotton wool. Pat it into the skin: don't rub. Do not apply to the skin under your eyes.

Nourish: A nightly application of almond oil is very effective in guarding against wrinkles and for nourishing the skin. However, if your skin shows signs of becoming oily after starting this treatment, stop it immediately and nourish with a light cream instead.

Oily skin

Cleanse: Soap and water is ideal for a greasy skin. Wash your face as often as possible—three or four times a day-using a medicated soap. Never use cold cream for deep cleansing. You should, of course, use a cleansing milk, for soap and water alone can not penetrate into the pores to clean away every trace of grime and stale make-up. But remember to rinse your face in tepid water after using cleansing milk.

Tone: Your skin with a good astringent lotion (see Astringent).

Nourish: Nourishing the skin means replenishing the natural oils that are lost during the day and when the face is washed. Since your skin is already oily, you will not need to do this. However, as you get older you may, if you wish, use a reliable hormone cream with a non-greasy base.

If you have "combination" skin

Some women have "combination" skin. This means that part of the face is one skin type, part another. For example, someone with a predominantly dry skin may have an oily patch down the centre of her face. Another woman may have greasy skin with a dry patch on her chin or forehead. If you have "combination" skin treat the different parts of your face according to type.

Fruits and their use

Oranges: Orange juice makes a fine skin tonic. Dip a piece of cotton wool in equal parts of orange juice and water. Dab it on all over face and neck.

Water melon: Water melon has been described as "nature's own moisturizer". Cut off large, thin slices from the fruit and lay them over your face and neck. Leave for about 20 minutes.

Grapes: Mix the juice of ripe grapes with half the amount of rose water. Use as a skin tonic.

Tomatoes: Boil some ripe tomatoes in a little water. Strain the liquid and use it to wash your face.

Peaches: Grate the fruit finely and place between two layers of fine cloth. Now place the compress over your face and leave for 20 minutes. If possible, chill the compress slightly before use.

Strawberries: Cut a big strawberry in half. Rub the cut side of the fruit all over your face and neck.

Bananas: Mash a ripe banana. Mix with two tablespoons of wheat flour and spread all over your face and neck.

Hair

It is rightly called the crowning glory of a woman. You need to pay a lot of attention to it. The foremost rule of hair care is to keep it scrupulously clean. Shampoo at least once a week if the weather is cold and twice if it is warm. Hair tends to collect a lot of dust and grime due to the pollution in the air and the sweat on the scalp. When it becomes dirty, it sticks to the scalp and looks dull and flat.

Hair facts

- Having your hair swinging glossily over your shoulders is a very sensual image. But only well-conditioned hair does this. In fact, long hair alters a woman's whole body language.

- Knowing when to stop: Long hair like short hair, needs regular trimming to look its absolute best.
- Knowing what suits you: Long hair can be ageing. Those who have long or thin faces, in particular, should avoid growing their hair long.
- Its colour: Brown and black hair are thickest and grow the longest;
- Hair grows at the rate of 2.5 cm in a month-until it gets to 25 cm long, when it slows down to 1.25 cm. Hair oil in itself does not make your hair grow. A good oil massage makes the oil reach the hair roots, thus inducing growth and general conditioning.
- Hair colours cannot grey your hair. They don't reach the roots and hence cannot be held responsible for the greys.
- You must keep changing your shampoo from time to time. Hair conditions keep changing - oily in summer and dry in winter - and you need to treat this change accordingly.

darkener. Regular use of this herb will delay the greying process. When the hair is light in colour, it gives a dark reddish tint to the hair. However, if you want to avoid the red tint, use amla along with it.

You can use any of the store-bought hair dyes and follow the instructions given in it. Godrej hair dye is a good brand as is also Bigen.

Home-made dye

Take half a cup of henna powder, mix a quarter cup of amla powder and make a paste with curds. Apply this paste to the hair. Make partings close to each other and apply the paste in such a way that the roots are covered well. Coat the hair strands too. Let the dye soak for at least two hours. Wash with warm water and a mild shampoo.

Precaution

While using hair-dyes, wear rubber gloves to protect the hands. Also take care not to accidentally apply the dye on the skin since it is very difficult to remove. Wear old clothes to prevent them getting stained.

Go grey gracefully

It is certainly not compulsory for everyone to dye their hair if they grow grey. A shock of grey hair or a patch of grey can look very attractive. Do you remember the famous grey patch of Mrs. Indira Gandhi? Sometimes it may be wiser to let the grey be. Nothing can look sillier than a wrinkled face sporting a shock of jet-black hair! But dye by all means if grey makes you feel old and self-conscious.

Manicure and pedicure

These are also possible at home with a little effort and practically no expense. You require:

1. A basin of warm water each for hands and feet.
2. Some liquid soap.
3. Cotton buds.
4. Nail clipper.
5. Fleer for filing nails.
6. Hand cream.

Soak your hands and feet in the basin of warm water, to which some liquid toilet soap has been added, for at least 15 minutes. Gently knead and squeeze the muscles of the hand and feet, working off the accumulated dirt and grime.

Pat dry with a soft towel. Clip the nails of fingers and toes, cutting straight across the toe nails to prevent in-grown toenails. If you want to grow your fingernails long, shape them accordingly and file them smoothly. With the cotton buds, gently push back the cuticles of the nails. Clean the inside of the finger nails with a cotton bud. File the clipped nails with an emery board for a smooth finish.

Massage hands and feet with cream, pressing the soles of the feet and the palms as you do, to remove the tiredness and also the roughness out of them. Apply nail varnish or polish after the manicure and pedicure.

Nail polish

- Select the shade of the nail polish that will match with your dress and lipstick. Going for bright red nail polish while applying a pink or orange lipstick will clash.
- Take care to see that the toes are separate by putting small balls of cotton between the toes to prevent the nail polish from smudging. Allow to dry under a fan.
- Apply the polish in single strokes, beginning from the cuticle and going to the top of the finger/toe. Apply a second coat after the first one dries, for an even, smooth finish.

- Never scrape off old polish. Use a nail polish remover.
- Do not grow nails too long.
- Remember to keep finger nails clean. Dirt under the nails is more ugly than chipped nails.
- Nail polish comes in plain as well as frosted shades. The latter are better in terms of finish and give a pearly glow to your nail polish.
- Wear the same shade on your toes and finger nails.
- Match nail polish exactly to the of lipstick: pearl and natural shades however, can be worn with any shade of lipstick.
- Remove chipped nail polish.

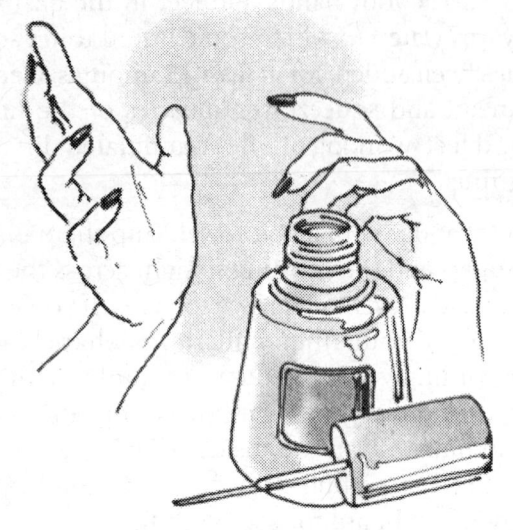

Eyebrows

You can shape your brows with a tweezers or by threading. When you have very thick brows that need to be trimmed, threading is better as it is faster. It is better done by a beautician, while you can use the tweezers yourself.

- Before beginning, wipe brows with a piece of cotton soaked in Eau de Cologne.
- Stretch the skin taut with left hand and begin tweezing.
- Always tweeze by grasping as near the root of the hair as possible and pulling along the growth of the hair.
- Keep the thickness the same till you reach the arch and then slowly taper it off.
- Do not make the eyebrows longer than the end of the eyes.
- Always tweeze from below.
- Keep the natural arch at the top, as far as possible.
- If you have thin brows, use an eyebrow pencil, using short, light and feathery strokes upward and outward.
- Very thin eyebrows are out. The look is more natural nowadays. So all you may need is a few deft strokes of the tweezers.
- While tweezing eyebrows, go slow and carefully. You can tweeze an extra hair later, but you will not able to grow instant hair if you over-tweeze by mistake.

Make-up

Make-up is an art. It adds a touch of glamour to the face. It highlights your good features and helps camouflage the bad ones. However, one should keep in mind that it should look as natural as possible.

Basic requirements

PRODUCTS
- Foundation
- Under eye concealer
- Contouring brush
- Check contour
- Highlighter

- Mascara
- Lip liner
- Lipstick
- Lip gloss
- Face powder
- Eye shadow
- Eye liner

TOOLS

- A large long handled soft brush for applying blushes and powder
- A child tooth brush to brush up brow
- Slant tipped brushes for applying eye shadow
- Tapered up brush
- Brow brush angled
- Tweezers
- Pencil sharpener
- Stiff brush for applying brow contour

SUPPLIES

- Tissues
- Cotton
- Q-Tips
- Make-up sponges

What kind of a face do you have?

KNOWING YOUR FACE TYPE

Oval: The widest area will be around the eyes and ears with gradual curves towards the forehead and jawline.

Pear: Your face will be close to the vertical lines at your forehead and wider than the lines at your ears and jawline.

Square: There is same amount of your face outside the vertical sticks, all the way down the jawline.

Rectangular or oval: There is very little of your face outside the two vertical sticks, with virtually the same width top, middle and bottom.

Heart: A great deal of your forehead is visible outside the two vertical sticks, a little less at the ear area and very little if any at the jawline.

Diamond: There is very little face visible outside the two vertical sticks and this will be close to the ear area, tapering sharply towards a narrow forehead and chin area.

Round: The widest points which overlap the vertical sticks will be around the ear area with a gradual curving up to the forehead and down to the jawline, creating an almost round shape.

Step by step guide to makeup

- Start with a clean skin. It is a must to have a freshly cleaned skin before putting on any type of make up.
- Now apply a skin covering: this could be in the form of a foundation (liquid or cake) loose or pressed powder or a blusher. Foundation is the base of the make up. Carry the foundation right from the hair line down under the chin. Put it on lightly and work it into the skin until it has a sheer over all look. Remember that your foundation should match your skin shade exactly.
- For greasy skin: use liquid or pancake foundation.
- For normal or dry skin: use cream foundation. This gives a smooth matte finish.

Rouge

Should be applied next. Cream rouge for dry skin and powder rouge for oily skin should be used. Use your rouge as follows:

Square face: Place rouge down the sides of your cheeks and blend over back point of jaw bone.

Long face: Place rouge at a point under the triangle of your cheek bones and blend out no further than the corner of your eyes.

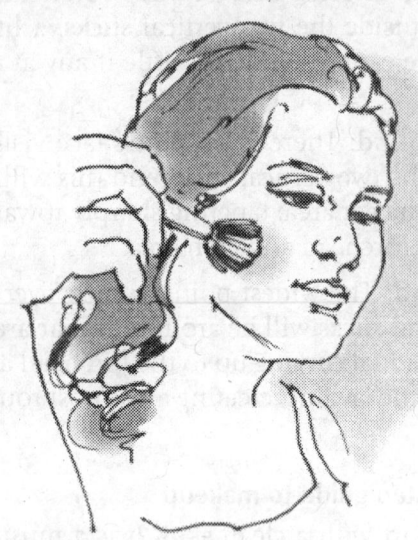

Round face: Place rouge in a long triangle at the sides of the face. The corner of the triangle should almost touch the outer corner of the eye.

Heart-shaped face: Place rouge high over your cheek bones. Sweep back and upwards towards the hair line.

Face powder

Should be exactly the same shade as your foundation. For a more translucent look choose one shade lighter than the foundation. Apply with a smooth powder puff. Brush off excess with a fluffy powder puff or a facial brush.

Lipstick

Lipstick not only gives colour and shape to the mouth, but also protects the sensitive skin of the lips from cracking in strong winds and cold.

Applying lipstick:
- First outline the lips with a lip pencil or brush. The colour should be a shade brighter and darker than the lipstick itself, with which you will 'fill in'. Remember that they should be of the same shade.
- Fill in with a soft lip brush. This is better than applying the stick directly, since the cracks are filled in and also makes the lipstick last longer.
- Let the colour set for at least three to four minutes before blotting with a tissue. Apply another coat and blot with tissue again. This will 'set' the colour properly.
- Apply lip gloss for the natural look.

HOW TO MASK DEFECTS

If lips are too thin: While drawing the outline, draw it slightly above and below the normal lip line. Fill in.

If the lower lip is too full: Draw a line inside the natural shape of the lip. Fill in and blot well.

If the mouth is very small or narrow: Extend the corners of the lips on both sides, keeping the natural shape of the mouth in mind. Fill in and blot.

- While choosing the colour of the lipstick, keep in mind your complexion. Dark skinned people should avoid using bright pinks and reds. Very bright shades are better suited for the evenings, while milder shades look good during the day. Roll on lip gloss can be used to highlight the lipstick or even used by itself, without using lipstick.
- Colour or lipstick should match the colour of Bindi worn.

Some make up hints

Receding chin: Apply highlighter across the chin line blending it under the jaw.

210

Double chin: Apply shadow across the lower part of the chin blending it under the jaw.

Protruding chin: Highlight the area around the mouth to make the chin look as if it is receding.

Pointed chin: Highlight both sides of the pointed chin and shade the tip.

Receding forehead: Apply highlighter straight across the forehead blending it into the hairline.

Protruding forehead: Apply shadow straight across the bulging part of the forehead and blend into the hairline.

GIVING A SHAPE TO YOUR NOSE AND BLUSHING YOUR FACE

Nose type:
Prominent: Apply highlighter starting from either side of the nose and extending just beneath the middle of the eye. This will make the nose appear to recede, thereby making it less conspicuous.

Short: To give illusion of greater length, apply highlighter straight down the centre from the bridge of the nose to under the tip. Pluck eyebrows to give a wider space between them and a longer line to the nose.

Curved: Apply shadow to the high point of the curve, then carefully blend highlighter both above and below the shadowed area.

Upturned: Apply highlighter straight down the centre from the bridge of the nose to under the tip, then shadow the turned up portion and blend downwards.

Broad: To make the nose appear narrow in width, highlight down the centre from the bridge to the tip, then shadow on either side to create a "diamond" pattern of correction.

Protruding: Shadow down the length of the bridge and highlight on either side. Be careful not to bring the highlighter over the nostrils.

Long: To cut down the apparent length of a nose apply shadow on the tip, blending it under the nose.

BLUSHING THE FACE

Face type:
Oval: Apply blusher high on the cheek bones in a triangular shape, and blend into the hairline.

Round: Apply blusher in a wide triangular pattern, blending into the hairline and over the earlobe.

Diamond: Apply blusher in a wedge-like pattern on the highest point of the cheekbone, being careful not to blend the blusher into the hollow of the cheeks.

Rectangular: Apply blusher to the cheekbone in a rectangular pattern, keeping it very narrow. Do not run the blusher down the length of the face.

Pear: Apply blusher in a wide triangular pattern. Do not blend the blusher close to the nose area.

Heart: Apply blusher in a narrow wedge-like pattern on the highest point of the cheek bone.

Square: Create a triangular pattern on the cheekbone. Blend downwards over the earlobe.

Eye make up

Eye brow contouring: is applied first. Keep the line of the brow subtle and graceful. If your eyebrows are scanty or fair, emphasize them with a dark brown or black pencil used in short feathery strokes. Ensure that the pencil is well sharpened before use.

Eye shadow: is the next step. For day wear, one should avoid bright colours.

i) **Dark eyes:** brown, beige, green and mauve.
ii) **Blue or grey eyes:** light grey, blue or mauve.
iii) **Hazel eyes:** green and dark grey are most suitable.

The eye shadow should be blended in carefully.

Eye liner (liquid): to apply pull up the outer corner of the eye and with a quick, firm stroke outline the edge of the upper lid keeping close to the line all the way to the outer corner but not beyond it. If you have small eyes, you can continue all around the eye with the liner.

Mascara: makes the eye lashes appear thicker. Apply with quick short strokes from the base to the tip of the lashes. To make the eyes appear larger, apply mascara on both upper and lower lashes.

Handy hints

1. If you want to emphasise the eyes, you can use eyeliner on the base of the upper and lower lashes. Start from the inner eye and proceed to the outer portion, drawing a thin line.
2. Eye shadow gives the eyes a dramatic effect, especially in the evenings under artificial light. The shade used has to harmonise with the colour of the eyes, clothes and the time of the day. You can use the frosted variety for the evenings and the matte variety during the day. Highlighting with gold or silver is also reserved for the evenings. A general rule while applying eye shadow: use a colour to blend with your dress, especially if you have dark eyes.
3. If your eye colour is black or dark brown, you can use a wide variety of shades from mauve to brown.
4. While wearing eye shadow, remember that the darker shades with a touch of gold or silver are best for the night. Day make up should be simple and subtler.....

Hide flaws

To hide flaws, two shades of foundation are used: one light and the other darker. The light foundation is used to enlarge or bring forward and the darker is used to make smaller or recede. Always use darker foundation over the lighter one blending the edges well so that no dividing line is visible.

To thin down a too-round face: Use the shadow method. Use a shadow-base, orange-brown blusher or brown or charcoal grey powder eye shadow (depending on your skin tone) and brush softly down side of face, starting from just below temple to beginning of jawline. Blend in hollow of cheeks.

To play up cheekbones: Use a lighter tone of base or powder than your skin tone (white, dry eye shadow works well) and apply lightly under your cheekbone, then cover your face with your regular foundation or powder, blending very gently. Take a darker tone blusher or shadow and brush on cheekbone itself. This will mould your facial bones which can be one of your most attractive features.

To thin down or shorten nose: Use a darker shade of base or a touch of dark brown cream eye shadow and blend it along sides of your nose. Add a dab beneath tip of nose for a turned-up look.

To give wide-eyed round look to eyes: Make your liner heavier at centre of eye than at the outside corners. If Eyes Are Too Close Together: Blend a light shade of eye shadow from centre of lid to outer corner. If eyes are too far apart, apply shadow at corners of lids nearest nose.

To thin down lipline: Using a lipstick brush, draw outline slightly under your natural lipline. If mouth is too wide, concentrate the application of lipstick to the centre of it, blending lightly to the outer corners. Keep away from chalky-pastel shades.

To create a smile effect: Apply your lipstick with a smile in your mind. Translation: bring corners up and out- never turned down.

A note about highlighting and shadowing: "Highlight" means to use a lighter shade of your own skin tone on areas you wish to play up. "Shadow" means to use a darker base, powder, or blusher on areas you wish to play down.

Clothes and Jewellery

It is often said that, "clothes maketh a man". The first impression that one creates is established by the way we dress and what accessories we use. It is thus important for men and women to dress right: both for their age and the occasion. The following factors can be kept in mind:

The cut of your clothes is a vital component of dressing well.

a) **Women:** who wear western outfits should pay attention to neck lines, sleeve lengths, waist and hip detailing and the length of the skirt. If your hips are heavy, wear a stunning blouse with a comparatively sober shirt or a pair of trousers.

b) **Men:** should also choose their clothes according to their body shape.

- Those with long necks look good in mandarin collars, while those with short necks look good in buttoned down collars with pointed ends.
- Heavily built men should wear single breasted jackets while those who are underweight should wear double-breasted jackets.
- Well tonned men look good in collarless T-shirts and shirts with pleated or embroidered fronts.
- If your physique needs something to be desired, go in for sports shirt with collar.

While choosing the colour of your clothes, keep in mind your complexion.

a) **If you have a wheatish complexion:** you would look best in earth tones like olive, green, khaki, rust and mushroom.

b) Fair complexion will look good in almost any colour.

c) Make sure that the most arresting colour is worn on top or bottom, depending on which part you want to highlight.

Dress to suit the occasion. There are four broad categories though the boundaries between them can be blurred:

- Formal day wear
- Informal day wear
- Formal night wear
- Informal night wear

Keep in mind the fabric that you choose and the accessories that you choose.

Make sure that you smell good. There are many ways of combating body odour:

i) **Soap:** is vital to keep clean, however it has a short term effect and should be supplemented with other products.

ii) **Talc:** Talc works by absorbing the sweat and keeping the skin surface dry.
iii) **Perfumes/after shaves:** are essentially enhancement products that mask the body odour temporarily.
iv) **Deodorants:** are the most effective way of keeping body odour away. They should be used daily.

To choose the fragrance that is right for you, two factors are important:

a) The image you like to project
b) Your mood

The fragrance should suit and enhance your personality, e.g. floral scents are blended with sweet romantic notes, woody notes project an aura of sophistication and sensuality.

Know Your Body Type

To determine your body shape you need to consider your height, frame, the widest and the narrowest points of your body and their relationship to each other. Use a full-length mirror to examine your figure. Commence with your shoulder bone and visualize a vertical line running straight down your body from your armpit crease. Now, assess your body shape following the undermentioned table:

BODY SHAPE

Angular: Body appears broader above the waist than below it. Straight, broad sometimes bony shoulders. Rest of the body falling at a rectangular slope to the waist.

Heart: Body is wider above the waist than below it. Upper forearms wider than the shoulders with the bust coming close to or over hanging the imaginary line (mentioned above).

Pear: Body hangs over the imaginary line below the waist and the upper part of the body stays inside the imaginary line.

Curvy pear: Thighs and hips hang over equally.

Straight pear: Thighs hang over more than the hips.

Ellipse: Body runs parallel with the imaginary line from the bust area down to hips and then slopes towards a slimmer thigh area.

Curvy ellipse: Waist hangs over the imaginary line between the bust and the hip area thereby resulting in very little or no waistline.

Straight ellipse: Shoulders narrower than the waist resulting in waist seem high or nonexistent.

Hourglass balanced: Slim waistline irrespective of the proportionately curvy area below and above the waist. Body may hang over the imaginary line at the bust and hips.

Curvy: Extra weight accumulates across the bust upper forearms waist and the hips.

Straight: without a waist Balanced shape above and below the waist and in line all the way down the imaginary line.

With a Waist: Narrow-boned and rectangular or broader and squarer body profile.

Knowing your body balance

You can find out how balanced or in proportion your body is, by looking at where certain points fall in relation to your height. The ideal is when your waist falls halfway between your shoulder line and your bottom. If your waist is higher than the midpoint, you are short-waisted. If lower, you're long-waisted.

Undoubtedly a balanced figure looks pleasing to one's eyes but for those who don't have a balanced figure there are ways in which an illusion of balance can be created. To be able to do this, you need to understand the concept of "Line". The term refers to the outline of a up. A line will lead the eye and can be used to create an optical illusion. Following are the tips to balance a short waist:

- Wear a belt which is the same colour as your top.
- Choose a coloured top which you can blouse over a contrasting bottom giving the impression of a lower waist line.
- Choose dresses with tapered skirts, with either a drop-waisted style or no waist detail.

To balance a long waist

- Wear a belt of the same colour as your skirt or trousers.
- Choose designs that give the illusion of a higher waist, such as skirts with broad waistlines.
- Choose designs that miss the waist and emphasize other parts of the body.

Body shape and balance of body

Here are some guidelines for using both line and colour to great effect for each figure type:

HEART TYPE

- Shoulder pads allow the fabric to hang free and clear of the wider part of the arm.
- For wide waist and trunk use a slightly looser style line.
- Centre detail and cut-in sleeves divide your upper body making it look smaller visually.
- A dress with shoulder pads, creative button placement and the centre detail provided by the heart-shaped neckline all take the eye from the heavy forearms and balance the heart-shaped figure.

STRAIGHT TYPE

- Shoulder pads can be used to balance a tunic or dress in semi-fitted A-line kurtas.
- A dress with shoulder pads, short sleeves and horizontal pockets (if you want) gives width to the top half of the body making the waist, hips and things look smaller and more shapely.
- For a broad straight figure the clever use of colour in patterns can focus attention on selected areas of the body as well as making it look slimmer.

ANGULAR TYPE

- A low-yoke design with sleeves and yoke picked out in a non-advancing colour will take the focus away from the shoulders.
- An unusual line-design features and fabric mixes can focus the eye to the centre, away from the broad shoulder.

PEAR TYPE

- Use of shoulder pads and a light colour on the top half will visually give you more width and will make your waist appear smaller.
- Wearing dark and subdued colours on the bottom half will minimize your thigh area.
- A dress with a low, curved, dropped waist is another good choice as this emphasizes your smooth waistline.
- Perhaps a white dress with black background leads the eye away from the thicker areas of the thigh. The white in the jacket may be expansive making the top half of the body look wider thereby creating a balance.
- Cut away jackets break up the horizontal line and give length to the bottom half.

ELLIPSE TYPE

- Choose a dress with yoke to create width, centred buttons for interest.
- Use shoulder pads and line design, to bypass your waist and to emphasize your well shaped thighs and hips.
- Straight ellipse figure may put on a plain and patterned fabrics worked together.
- Whereas a curvy ellipse figure could wear the above mentioned by reversing the fabrics.

HOURGLASS TYPE

- Dress with sleeves and outside panels in a non-advancing colour and centre panels in an advancing colour would suit this figure type the most.
- Semi-fitted dress with shoulder pads gives smooth emphasis to the waist and the thighs.
- The dark coloured for the bottom half balances a heavy bottom particularly the colour worn on the bottom half is incorporated into the top half.

Fashion and You

Everyone, regardless of size, can develop a personal style that makes the most of their positive features and minimizes the negative ones. All you need to do is to keep the following in view

Average figure

- Always match or tone shoe and hose colours to your hemline colour to lengthen your legs.
- Select neutral and basic colours for business wear.
- A short or long coat can add a contrasting colour effect.
- Wear colours which are close in colour value that is, wearing a single colour from head to foot. Match shoe and hose colours to outside and/or inside garment colours.
- A contrasting jacket should finish in the area between your natural waist and above your full hip.
- Avoid hemline patterns and frills or any straight horizontal lines from the hipline downwards.
- Avoid overwhelming details such as extra large collars and belts; over sized sleeves; big bold prints; bulky fabric; too many collar breaks; excessive fullness and garments that are too long.

Short, broad figure

- Wear a single colour from head to toe or add a contrasting colour at the neckline. For instance if you're wearing a sari with lot of blue you should choose blue for your blouse too. Suits should be of a single colour.

- Keeping shoes, hose and dress in the same colour, add another colour in your jacket, cardigan or coat.
- Keeping shoes, hose, skirt and jacket in one of your best neutral colours, a multicoloured blouse in a lightweight fabric in your best basic colour.
- To look taller and narrower, avoid fitted curvy lines, too much fullness, too many details, large fussy sleeves, horizontal stripes, heavy-looking fabrics and over use of colour breaks which create straight, horizontal lines.
- Go in for suit designs that taper towards the bottom. A lot of pleats and flounce will make you look fatter and wider.
- Select fabrics with tiny prints, flowers or designs.
- Avoid heavy or wide bordered saris. A thin border is the best. Same goes for *pallus* too.
- Do not wear blouses with a gather at the arms. Also avoid tight fitting suits. They will show off the bulk.
- Wear high heels.

Tall, thin figure
- Use shoulder pads to help create a waist.
- Though heavy fabric for skirts can add width to your body, but mind you, this can overwhelm your boney structure thus making your legs and arms look thinner.
- Add a built to pick up the colour of your skirt or blouse to create break.
- To create interest at the neck area, use a contrasting colour for a collar or deep yoke.
- Avoid straight, vertical lines, a monolook, clingly designs and fabric.
- Horizontal stripes in saris or dresses give the appearance of fullness.
- Straight hemlines add width to the body.
- Brightly patterned dresses and saris will give you some fullness.
- Kurtas should be full with a lot of gathers. A skirt type kurta with a wide belt would look very good on you.

Tall, broad figure
- Select designs with vertical lines, or lines that close asymmetrically. These have a slimming effect and create interest.
- Choose loose-fitting, semi-fitted or flared garments.
- Break up vertical lines on the top half of the body by wearing more than one colour.
- Pick out one of the darker or more subdued colours from your top and use it as a block colour for your bottom half.
- Choose a one-piece dress with a big collar in a contrasting colour which extends down the middle.
- Use deep yokes, provided your bust line can stand them.
- Use diagonal and asymmetrical lines with two tone colouring.
- Wear elasticated waistbands for comfort.
- Avoid clingy fabrics, fussy sleeves, horizontal stripes and short jackets.
- Also avoid lines that are too curved or have too much fullness, and small design details which appear out of proportion.
- Balance head size with a soft medium-volume hairstyle.
- Wear designs that have vertical lines. There designs will create the illusion of thinness. Horizontal stripes on the contrary make you look more rounded and heavier.

- Don't wear large prints or pastel shades. These will only make you look fatter.
- When you wear dresses, go in for A-line cuts. These will make a person look taller and take the attention away from the figure.
- Dark shades should be worn more than light or pastel shades. The best colours are black, navy blue, bottle green, brown, rust etc.
- If your upper arms are very heavy, avoid sleeveless blouses. They will focus attention on the rolling fat.
- Two colour suits, with the kurta in a darker colour will also help.
- When you buy or make suits, avoid patterns with lot of *kalis*, which add to the bulk. Simple straight cuts should be preferred.
- If you want to take away attention from your heavy hips, do not pin the sari up. Instead, leave the *pallu* loose, flowing over your left arm.
- Wear fabrics which do not stand away from the body, like organza, organdy etc. When you wear cotton, starch the garments mildly. They will cling closer to the body.
- Jewellery should not be large, heavy or chunky. A single strand of small pearls, a thin golden chain with a small pendant, or a couple of long chains of gold will look good. Avoid chunky necklaces,
- Wear several thin bangles instead of one heavy *kada*.
- Rings in the ears will make your face look thinner.
- If your face is large and fleshy, avoid huge bindis. Either reduce the size of the round bindis or go in for the various fancy shapes that are vertical in design.

Colour Aesthetics and You

Most people can choose a simple colour that looks good on them, but few of us can combine colours that make us look especially attractive, or choose colours that are appropriate for our life style. Like other swift changes in life our likes and dislikes, norms and values about the use of colours have undergone a drastic change.

The colour one unconsciously chooses to wear are vital clues of one"s inner personality and can help one discover oneself. Colours have personalities too, and knowing what they're helps one to select the right colours for the message someone wants to convey. Always choose colours that feel good on you, and are appropriate for the occasion. For our convenience we divide the colours in two broad categories, viz. advancing and non-advancing. By the former we mean the ones that seem to advance towards you when you hold your colour wheels up at arms length. Whereas the latter is just the opposite of the former in its approach towards you. To comprehend the "language" of colours we assist you by providing the meanings of the expression displayed by these colours:

Advancing	Non-Advancing
Active	Passive
Analytical	Intuitive
Animated	Quiet
Assertive	Submissive
Direct	Subtle
Dramatic	Reserved

Men

Dressing for work

a) Casual clothes should be clean, pressed and well fitting.
b) Never outdress your boss.
c) Keep a blue blazer and tie in your office for unexpected appointments.

d) Pay attention to your physique and physical appearance.
e) Invest in high quality separates, e.g. double breasted blue blazer over a white buttoned down shirt always looks great.
f) When wearing a bow neck, mock neck, or turtle neck unit shirt with a suit or sport coat it should be tucked into the trouser.
g) When wearing a belt, it should be colour coordinated with the shoes.
h) Trouser length should at least touch the top of your shoe.

Formal wear
a) A blazer teamed with trousers and shirt is ideal for a cocktail party.
b) For dinner, a full shirt with a black tie is ideal.
c) For formal occasions during the day, the nature of the occasion dictates how to dress e.g. a dark suit is the most festive.
d) If one has received an invitation beforehand, dress festively.
e) In case of parties, events at night, dress shirt, e.g. Knighthood teamed with dark trousers and a blazer is most appropriate.
f) An all time outfit for an evening out is a kurta pyjama.

Tie
- The quality of a tie is judged by its fall. Drape the tie across your waist and it falls down as it does from the neck. It should fall down straight without twisting.
- Tie's texture should be smooth to touch.
- Check the back side of the tie for its bar tack which is the short horizontal strip that keeps the two sides of the tie together.

Summer Clothes

The weather does not allow for any other clothes than cotton or cotton-blends. Pure cottons and handloom are the best for the hot humid months of summer. But if you have no time for starching and ironing the cottons, you can go in for blends of cotton where, synthetic content keeps the fabric from getting crushed as much as pure cottons. Even if they do, all you may need to do is iron the dresses lightly. These dresses and saris have the advantage of being cool and elegant too.

Children will be happy wearing cotton T-shirts, frocks and skirts. Or maybe Bermudas (loose half-pants) and a coloured vest.

- Get them cotton socks to be worn under their sneakers. These absorb perspiration and prevent rashes.
- Generally buy dresses that are loose fitting since tight fitting ones can be hot and uncomfortable.
- Go in for light shades since dark shades absorb heat.
- Avoid wearing shoes if you can. Wear sandals or chappals instead. Where the dress code of the office demands that you wear shoes, wear cotton socks. Let children wear open sandals that let their feet breathe.
- Keep aside your heavy silks and brocades for the summer months.
- The make-up should also be light. Too much of foundation and creams will make you sweat inside them and ruin your skin.

Winter
Winter clothes consists of sweaters, shawls, warm underclothes and coats. Children need

more than a few sweaters since they get them dirty very fast. These should preferably be in darker shades since lighter shades show up dirt.

These are the basic winter clothes you need to buy:

- A pair of woollen socks/stockings.
- A couple of warm banians/chemise and pyjamas.
- At least two sweaters for daily use and one or two for outings.
- A couple of shawls at least. You can buy more to match with your dresses, if you so desire.
- If you have to bear severe winters, go in for an overcoat. When you are at home, you can wear kurtas or housecoats made of warm materials like flannel or wool.
- One firan made of wool.
- One woollen or silk scarf.
- If you go out very often or drive a vehicle then you must have a pair of gloves.

You need not have a dozen shawls or sweaters to match every sari or salwar suit. Buy one or two in neutral colours like maroon, off-white, brown or grey. These colours go well with other colours. For special occasions you can have matching shawls and sweaters.

Tips for buying clothes

- Avoid buying clothes off the pavement stalls since the quality is quite bad. Even though you may feel you are saving money, you will end up spending more since the colour may run or the fabric may lose shape or even tear. You may say that not all clothes are like that. But it is very difficult to make out the good from the bad.
- Watch out for sales in well known stores. Every shop has a clearance sale just before a season sets in or at the end of the season. In direct company sales or factory sales, the stock is fresh and can be safely bought.
- Another event you can look out for, is the "seconds" sale of reputed mills. However, look very minutely for the flaws in the fabric before buying. Sometimes it may be an irregular print that can be hidden in the folds of the sari or an unprinted section that can be cut and discarded while stitching the garment.
- When you buy readymade clothes, look out for the fabric, the stitching, the other trimmings used and colour fastness. It is a good idea to reinforce the stitching by putting a second stitch either over the original one or very close to it. Also secure hooks, buttons, etc.
- When you buy a sari, buy two blouse pieces of different shades. This not only gives a different look to the same sari, but also prevents one blouse from going dull if used alone.

A word about accessories

- The belt should never be so wide or tight that it pulls in the flesh, causing a bulge above and below.
- The shorter the skirt, the narrower the belt and vice-versa.
- If you want to wear a belt but do not want to draw attention to your waist wear it loose with an unbuttoned jacket or cardigan, allowing just a small part of the belt either side of the buckle to be seen.
- Before adding a handbag, briefcase etc. to your look ask yourself what look you're trying to achieve.

- A scarf can give a favourite old garment a more fashionable look.
- Also a scarf can lift, tone or change the look of a garment colour.

Some handy dressing tips

- Avoid wearing dark colours, especially midnight blue or black during an afternoon party or celebration. Reserve these for the nights.
- Dress your forehead with some of the exotic and beautiful bindi available in the market. They can liven up your dress.
- Many women wear their party dress while going to work if they have to attend a party after office. This may be inconvenient and crush the dress by evening. To avoid this, keep a change of blouse—preferably a dressy one that can go with the sari you are wearing. Take some costume jewellery along. Change in the evening for a jazzed up look. To complete the party look, open out your hair and give it a good brushing, apply some make-up and you are all set for the party!
- Avoid wearing dresses made of flimsy stuff in the rainy season. Because if you happen to get wet then they get dressed very soon and make you feel uneasy. Some clothes require lining and if they don't have one, don't forget to wear a chemise inside.
- Always keep safety pins with you, so that whenever, if at all, stitches go undone you can use a safety pin right then and thus can avoid an embarrassing situation.
- In the summers try to wear cotton dresses because they are climate friendly for Indian conditions further they help you soak sweat, keep you free of rashes. If you wear a dress with lining that is an obvious choice for summers.
- If being a working woman you are hard pressed for time, choose saris of drip-dry materials or of the material which as far as possible is crease resistant, non-ironing type.
- While buying saris always check the length and width and never buy a sari which's less than 5 metres.
- When choosing a sari never pick the one which"s been displayed in the shop because constant exposure to light makes such pieces faded and almost lustre less. So ask for the fresh one.
- Don't show off your preference for any dress, no matter how much do you like that particular piece. Because judging your weakness the shopkeeper might quote a higher price.

Short, broad figure

- Wear a sari with small prints, narrow borders and vertical stripes.
- Avoid wearing sari or salwar suits with a pattern of horizontal strips and try to wear footwears with some heel.
- Also avoid too many pleats around the waist, and starch in clothes which add to the width.
- Preferably wear prints which are small in pattern and have vertical stripes.
- If you are going to wear salwar suits remember not to wear a very long kurta. Kurta should be near or just below the knees. If possible wear salwar with vertical stripes.
- While wearing sari tie it above the navel to give the lower part of your body a length.
- Don't wear very dark colours.

- Wear dresses made of the stuff which have good fall e.g. chiffon, wrinkled cotton.

Tall, thin figure

- Wear the dresses which add width to your body—like organdy, organza, tissue, tusser silk etc.
- Wear long kurta with some zig-zag patterned stripes on it, while wearing sari tie it below the navel.
- Avoid wearing heels.
- Wear dark and bright colours.
- If possible wear well starched clothes.
- Preferably avoid wearing churidar pajamas and tight jeans in particular and well-fitting dresses in general.
- Avoid wearing stuff which clings to the body.
- Wear saris with bold prints, big skirt borders and horizontal design because these will enhance your look.

Tall, broad figure

- Tie your sari just on where your navel is so that you can balance your stature.
- Break the colouring of your dress, that is, preferably avoid wearing single coloured or patterned dress. Wear contrast and combination.
- Avoid wearing very bright colours.

Chiffon

Chiffon saris are light and lovely - ideal for the hot, summer evenings. French chiffon saris are difficult to get these days, so look after yours carefully to make them last. Chiffon saris are now being manufactured in India and some of them are very attractive.

Never try to wash chiffon at home. Always send your chiffon garments to a reliable dry cleaner.

Chin

If you have a large or prominent chin, or if your chin is too "weak" you can disguise the defect with the clever use of cosmetics (see cosmetic modelling).

If a double chin is your problem, you can banish it by doing these exercises every day, and by sleeping without a pillow:

Exercise 1: Sitting in an upright position, bend your head back as far as it will go, then bring it slowly back to position. Repeat five times, gradually increasing to ten.

Exercise 2: Sitting at a table, rest your elbows on the table top and slap the fat under your chin with the backs of your hands.

Cholis

Since your choli is the garment nearest your face, do choose yours in colours that flatter your complexion.

Here are a few hints to help you choose the choli style that's most becoming to you:

Neckline: A high neckline covers up scrawny shoulders, but should never be worn by someone with a short neck. A V-neckline makes a stubby neck look longer. A wide "off-the-shoulder" neckline should only be worn by someone with pretty shoulders.

Sleeves: Sleeveless cholis are suitable for short girls, as they give the impression of added height. They may also be worn with good effect to show off pretty arms. Sleeves ending just above the elbows are most flattering to women with plump arms. Little cap sleeves, ending an inch or two below the shoulder are suitable for young girls and women with slender arms.

Length: The length of cholis seems to be getting shorter and shorter! While it's fashionable to display a wide strip of bare midriff, it is better to keep the choli slightly longer unless you are very slim because a "spare tyre" bulging out beneath a short choli looks very ugly.

To spark off your own creative ideas about good combinations for salwar-kamiz here are some suggestions to build on:

For morning wear

1. White churidars, blue and white paistry patterned kurta, matching blue dupatta.
2. Pale yellow salwar, printed kamiz in shades of yellow, green and white. Dupatta made from the same printed material.
3. Pale pink churidars, checked gingham kurta in pale grey and white with pink embroidery around the sleeves and neckline.

For afternoon wear

1. Cyclamen churidars. Slim, full sleeved kamiz, richly printed in shades of cyclamen, green and slate. Green dupatta.

2. A bold, burnt orange and black kamiz, teamed with black churidars and dupatta.
3. Pale coffee churidars and kurta with elaborate embroidery in leaf green and white all around the yoke and sleeves. Pale coffee dupatta.

For evening wear

1. Copper coloured satin churidars. Natural raw silk kamiz with zari embroidery work around the neckline. Old gold dupatta in fine chiffon.
2. Black silk churidars. Mandarin-style kamiz in white, black and red. White dupatta.
3. White satin salwar. White silk kamiz with silver zari butis. White dupatta sprinkled with tiny silver sequines.

Sari

Saris are the most beautiful and graceful of all garments. They suit all women and cover up a multitude of figure faults. So give the sari its due by wearing it well.

1. Tuck in the inside edge of your sari, taking care to see that the length is correct. About 1" from floor level is the right length (nothing looks worse than an ankle-high sari) If you are going to wear high heels, put on your sandals before tying the sari, as your heels can make quite a lot of difference to how long your sari will look.
2. Tuck in firmly, all the way round, gathering it up a little in the centre back, so that the fabric will not "seat".
3. Take the pallu across the back and place it on the left shoulder to the desired length. The length may be:
   (a) Very short—known as the "duster" style in which the pallu is only about

12" long. (In this case the sari should be tightly draped across the front, tracked into the waist at the back, and then placed over the arm.)

(b) Average length—this is worn hip length and is the most usual length, as well as being the most practical for everyday wear.

(c) Full length—here the pallav is worn long and flowing, until it almost touches the floor. This looks very elegant and is suitable for formal evening wear.

4. Take the remaining material to form the front pleats. Starting from the right, first make a broad, deep pleat about 5" wide. Then go on making pleats about 3" wide until all the material has been pleated.

5. Holding the pleats tightly together, neaten them out, pressing them firmly to keep them in place. Now tuck in the pleats, taking care to see that the edge of the sari is 1" from the floor. When tucking in the pleats, see that they lie flatly and neatly under the petticoat so that they will not look bulky.

6. Finally, drape the pallav neatly across the front and over the arm.

Jewellery

There is nothing to beat the charm of gold, pearls or diamonds when it comes to jewellery. These can be either simple or elaborate, delicate or chunky, depending upon the occasion.

A simple strand of pearls combined with delicate chiffon gives a grand appearance. Likewise a diamond jewellery set looks stunning with a heavy silk sari. Take care though not to look like a jewellery stand, wearing a lot of them.

With the fear of robberies and chain snatching on the rise, costume jewellery is getting to be very popular. These come in a wide range of materials and designs and can go with any dress and be suitable for every occasion. The best thing about costume jewellery is that they come in a variety of colours to match your dress. Moreover, they are inexpensive and therefore you can have several sets to go with various dresses. American diamond is another inexpensive substitute for real diamonds. Anyway most women keep diamonds safely in their lockers to avoid theft.

Care of pearls
- Keep pearls in a separate pouch to protect them from being scratched.
- Don't let pearls rub together.
- Take care to ensure that the pearls are not crushed.
- Don't wear your pearls when they might be splashed with ammonia, ink, vinegar or acids that can damage them.
- To clean pearls, wipe them with a cloth moistened with mild soap and water.
- Rinse, then dry the pearls with a soft cloth. Never use jewellery cleaner on pearls.
- Have pearls restrung regularly.

Gold
- To clean gold at home use soapnuts (ritha).
- Beware of vendors who come home and offer to clean your gold.
- These people have special chemicals which help them steal gold while cleaning.

Silver
- Wash the item in warm soapy water.
- Polish with silver polish and a soft cloth.

- Store in a dark place.
- Exposure to humidity and sunlight causes metal to tarnish.
- Silver zari work can be polished by a dry cleaner.

Diamonds: while selecting diamonds one should remember

- Go to an experienced and trusted jeweller.
- The quality and size of the stone determines its value.
- Diamonds should be set in platinum.
- The worth of diamond depends on 4 Cs.

i) **Colour:** The best colour is colourless. However, they may be of several colours including blue.

ii) **Cut:** A good cut is what gives a diamond its sparkle and fire. A well cut diamond usually has 58 cuts.

iii) **Carat weight:** A carat is divided into 100 points so that a diamond of 25 points is described as quiquarter of a carat or .25 carats.

iv) **Clarity:** refers to the diamond's purity. Some black spots known as nature's vinglipunts are found in the diamonds. The fewer such spots, the more valuable the stone because the flow of light is less obstructed.

Handy hints

- Do not wear very heavy jewellery or diamonds during the day. They look better in the evenings.
- Sometimes wearing just a thin chain of gold around your neck will make you look more stunning than loading up on jewels, especially if you are wearing a simple chiffon or silk.
- A thumb of rule is to avoid loads of jewellery, especially if they clash. For example, a ruby necklace will look awful with an emerald pendant. Pearls worn with diamonds will be a real disaster.

Handbags and footwear

These are as much accessories, as part of your personality. So be careful while choosing a handbag.

- Have at least a couple of roomy handbags with a lot of storage space for your daily office use. You can alternate them. Keep them large because you never know if you will need to pick up something on the way home from work—a kilo of apples, a packet of tea or maybe the painting box that your son wanted.
- However, if you believe in keeping home and office separate, carry a nylon shopping bag, folded, in your handbag!
- While buying a bag, remember to go in for usefulness rather than just appearance. A narrow-necked bag may look beautiful in the shop but may not accommodate your folder or lunch box. It would be better to invest in a single leather bag that will be sturdy and look good too. A shoulder slung bag is more convenient especially if you have to hang on to the strap in a crowded bus.
- For parties and other special occasions, you can carry a small purse or sling bag, in which you can keep your powder compact, lipstick and comb or even your make-up kit.
- Shoulder-slung briefcases are both sleek and sophisticated. If you have files and folders or lots of paper, go in for one of

these. The advantage is that, you can even carry it like a briefcase.
- Denim and suede are both sturdy and sophisticated. You can buy good handbags in one of these materials.

Footwear

Footwear should be comfortable and easy to walk on. This is more important if you are going to be on your feet all day at work. Unless they are comfortable, you will end up with a bad strain on your legs. For daily use, go in for simple footwear—sandals that buckle up or chappals that are soft and flat. As a rule, avoid wearing stilettos to work if you have a lot of walking to do. Anything more than a two-inch heel would be uncomfortable when you have to wear it the whole day.

Slip-on shoes (bally) are most comfortable and can be worn with any dress—be it a sari or salwar-kameez suit. These are available in leather, suede and canvas, and come in a wide variety of colours and designs. If you wear jeans and shirt to work, you can wear sneakers (sports shoes). They are very comfortable on the feet.

Very high heels are fashionable, but are not good for your back. If you have any problem with your back, avoid wearing high heels. Pregnant women should strictly avoid high heels.

CHAPTER-13

Gardening

Any house is incomplete without some kind of greenery. Traditionally every house had large spacious lawns. However, today because of the rapid rate of urbanisation these are becoming a rarer occurrence. The layout of any garden depends on the individual's taste. The garden furnishes the setting of a house and enhances its architectural beauty. In this chapter we will discuss the various ways in which you can plan and improve your garden.

The Soil

There are three types of soil

Sandy Soil: looses water quickly, absorbs heat, holds excessive air and draws out fertilizer elements quickly.

Clay soil: has very fine particles. It holds too much water, and thus remains muddy after the rains. It lacks air.

Loam: is the type of soil between sand and clay. It is suitable for most plantings.

Thus, all types of trees, plants and shrubs cannot be grown in all types of soil. Hence, it is essential to ascertain the soil type in your garden before you start plant.

Other Pointers

- Sunlight - requirement varies from plant to plant
- Aeration
- Drainage
- Suitable temperature

Formal gardens usually have – a centre of interest and symmetrical arrangement of walks and planting trees – trees are an essential part of the garden. The following factors should be kept in mind before planting them:

a) The shade of the tree though desirable, is harmful for the lawns and flower beds. Hence care should be taken.
b) Evergreen trees may be planted maintaining a safe distance from the building.
c) The final size of the full grown tree must be kept in mind as these must be in proper scale with the house.

Planting Trees

The best time to plant trees is in spring or fall but after leaves have fallen.

Method

- Dig a hole that's roughly twice the diameter of tree's root ball and $1^1/_2$ times as deep.
- Loosen bottom soil. Crumble the soil you have dug up together with compost.
- Refill the hole until the tree can sit on its own at the same level as the surrounding ground. Finish refilling.
- Make depressions for holding water. Fill it with water and let it soak in.

The lawn and its maintenance—lawns are made by two methods:

- From cuttings
- From seeds

Preparing the site

- clear the debris.
- dig at least one feet deep.
- ensure that all perennial weeds are burnt.
- if the soil is heavy wood ash, sand and peat should be dug in to make it porous and light.
- sprinkling of bone meal encourages root growth.
- After digging the soil should be allowed to remain fallow for a few weeks. It should then be raked to reduce it to even tilth.
- the ground is then flooded with water and then after drying the surface levelled. This process is repeated again.
- the soil should be rolled with a garden roller to make it even.
- weeds may come out in a few days due to manure or foreign soil which should be removed from the roots.
- the level of the lawn is kept about two inches below the garden path.

Maintenance of Your Lawns

- The best time to prepare a new lawn is either during summer or during the rains—grass stops growing in October.
- Annual timing of the lawn is essential. It should be given before the monsoons.
- Daily watering is necessary only in summer seasons otherwise once in two days is sufficient. Do not flood the grass.
- During winters dew on the grass should be brushed off the grass with a light bamboo.
- Top dressing of the lawn at least twice a year with a mixture of finely sifted leaf mould 6 part, 12 parts of fine sand, 1 part of bone-meal is essential.
- Liquid manure can also be sprayed to stimulate growth.
- During rainy season exercise caution that no stagnant water remains on the lawns.
- Wherever the lawn appears to be golden and green slums line substance is formed at the roots of the grass crushed lime stone should be sprinkled on the affected areas.
- If there are patches where surface crust is formed due to insufficient water, a light top dressing of coarse sand helps the growth of the grass.
- White ants can be controlled by sprinkling Gammaxene, BHC or DDT.
- Regular weeding and watering is a must. Care should be taken to remove all traces of motha (Cypress) which is the greater enemy of lawns.
- Wherever possible surface soil should be raked up, levelled and rolled.
- To increase the resilience of your lawn apply superphosphate 10 metric per 100 sq feet annually.

Fruit Garden

Planting

- Soil preparation is a must and must be done in advance to allow the soil to settle down.
- Nearly all fruits need deep cultivation.
- Mix annual manure in the soil and then green coarse bonemeal (150 gm) and

sulphate of potash (25 gm) as top dressing (per square metre).
- The soil should be crumbly and moist at the time of planting.
- Holes for trees should not be too deep. There should be enough room for the roots to spread out fully.
- Stakes are driven in position in the centre of the holes before planting the tree to avoid injuring the roots.
- Sever any damaged on decaying root before planting.
- Ensure that the soil around the roots is firm so that no air pockets are left.
- Trees brought in their containers can be planted at any time of the year provided the soil ball is kept intact and the roots undisturbed.
- Annual top dressing with well rotted manure and 20 gms of potash per square metre is beneficial.

Propagation

All fruits can be propagated by seeds, cuttings, grafting and layering.

Pruning of fruit trees is done to allow fruits and leaves to get plenty of light and air. However, during the first 3-4 years, pruning is done to form the frame of the tree according to the space available. Pruning could also be done to encourage the formation of several fruit buds on one young shoot. 2 shoots out of every 6 are cut back by one inch. The uncut branches from fruit buds more freely for nearly two years after which they are secured from the tree. In the meanwhile the pruned shoots will develop stronger fruit buds. Fruit trees should be pruned immediately after planting. Pruning is never done during winter.

Ringing: The back of a tree is removed in the shape of a ring. This method forces the tree to be less vigorous and to produce more fruits. Ringing is also done on individual branches to encourage growth of fruit buds.

Root pruning: is done to check the vigorous growth of roots.

Spraying fruit trees

- Lime sulphur, tar oil and derris powder are used.
- Tar oil application is done every 2nd and 3rd year to get rid of the moss, lichen or green scum on the bark.
- Spraying should be done during the dormant period or till just before the buds begin to grow. Remember to rub your hands and face with lanolin before spraying.
- Lime sulphur controls apple scab and red spider but should be applied on apple trees before they have blossomed.
- Blossom wilt diseases - make blossoms wilt suddenly. All wilted portions and branches should be removed.
- Brown rot attacks trees during the blossoming period. The fruit becomes brown and rotted. All infected spur bark should be removed and burnt.
- Caterpillars should be destroyed quickly by spraying with derris.

EXAMPLES:

Banana Trees: are propagated by suckers growing out of underground stem. Well dug ground, manured with ammonium sulphate is ideal for banana trees. Annual green manuring is a must.

Guava: requires a dry hot climate and is planted in sandy loan. It is propagated by seeds, layering and suckers. It is planted in July-August. Annual manuring is required and rotted animal manure is dug in around the tree. Guava trees require only light pruning.

Growing Vegetables

Method

- Select crops and varieties suitable to the climate and attitude of locality.
- Select suitable garden location near the house.
- Place rows three feet apart.
- Fertilize with animal manure. Apply fertilizer before the ground is plowed.
- Crop rotation should be done to maintain the balance of soil fertility. This implies that the same types of vegetables should not be sown at the same spot every year. This method discourages pests and diseases.
- Inter cropping - implies that two or more varieties of vegetables are grown on the same plot.
- Successional cropping helps to have a continuous supply of any one variety of vegetable. Seeds of different vegetables are sown at an interval to lengthen the time of harvesting.
- Catch cropping - under this no part of the garden is left idle quick growing vegetables e.g. spinach are sown in a bed for slow growing vegetables e.g. potatoes.
- Seeds should be bought from reliable resources and should not be stored for the following year.
- Potash, nitrogen and phosphates in equal quantities make a well blended fertiliser.
- Regular hoeing allows moisture and air to reach the roots and helps keep weeds away.
- Nursery beds should be raised slightly for better drainage.
- The soil for raising seeds is - 2 parts garden soil i.e. 1 part sand and 1 part leaf mould.
- Seed beds need regular and gentle watching.
- In summer seedlings should be protected against sunlight.

Flowers

To prepare a bed for growing flowers, dig well. Leave it exposed to the sun and rain for a few days. Now mix the following

For a '8×8' bed

Cow dung manure - 2 buckets full

Neem Cake - 220-250 gms

Bone-meal - 200 gms

Muriate of potash - 50 gms (Potassium Chloride)

N.P.K. 200 gms

If there is a zinc deficiency in the soil add 1 tsp of zinc sulphate.

After mixing the above with the soil. water it well. This should be done at least a few days before sowing.

Perennial flowers - lend permanence to a garden

- Soil preparation – The soil should be rich with a good drainage system.
- The trench for perennial is dug deep. The bottom of the trench is then filled with well rotted compost.
- Planting of perennials can be done either when they have just started to grow or when they have stopped growing in the winters.
- Space them 6-8 inches apart if they are edging plants and 12-18 inch for mid-

borders, 2-3 feet for the back of the borders.

Propagation of perennials can be done by discussion of roots. The original roots are divided and each discussion should have one shoot and some roots.

- Propagation is sometimes done by cuttings e.g. lupins. About 4 inch long shoots are severed from the plant and cut out just below the joints. These cuttings are inserted in about 2 inch deep holes made in sandy soil. The whole bed is then soaked in water.
- Seeds—this is a slow method. Usually plants raised from seeds are different from their parent plants but are vigorous and healthy.

AFTER CARE

- Soot can be spread around the plants to act as a deterrent to pests and diseases.
- Remove faded flowers. Except evergreen plants all the rest should be cut off upto an inch above ground level in autumn. This helps keep the bed clean and clear for long.
- After the first flowering season, plants should be provided with mulch (i.e. wet leaves and straw in autumn) which should then be dug into the roots in spring.
- Staking of perennials is important but should be kept as in conspicuous as possible.

Annual flowers

The time for seed sowing for annual flowers is the beginning of spring. The soil for annuals should be well drained and manured. The flower bed should be dug a week in advance, so that the soil soaks in sunlight and air. Sow seeds of annuals in pots first. Try and arrange annuals according to their height and colour.

Annuals for winter

Annuals sown is September-October on the plains bloom in winter. In hill stations annuals are sown in March-April and they bloom in summer.

EXAMPLES

Carnations—are propagated by seeds sown in shallow boxes. They are finally transplanted outdoors. They are sown in September-October and bloom in January-February. They can also be grown in pots.

Salvia—are propagated by cuttings. They can also be grown from seeds sown in nursery boxes. The seedlings are potted singly in small pots and are later transplanted to 4 inch pots and usually into flower beds. Ordinary soil and a warm sunny position is conducive to growing salvia.

Zinnia—flourish in rich and porous soil. It requires plenty of water and sun. They can be grown in summer and in the monsoon if sown twice.

Chrysanthemum

Chrysanthemums are grown from cuttings or suckers formed at the base of the plant after it has finished flowering or even while it is growing or flowering. Chrysanthemums grown from seeds are much inferior in size and quality.

Chrysanthemums can be grown both in pots and in the beds. The size of the pot depends, upon the variety you wish to grow - 8 inches or 10 inches or 12 inches.

The ideal pot to use is an earthenware pot of 10" size. Newly purchased pots are to be preferred over the old ones as they are free from insects and pests and viruses.

Potting mixture

The potting mixture should consist of the following:

Two Parts   Loamy soil

Two Parts   Cow dung/horse dung well rotted manure

One part Okhla Sludge (for residents of Delhi only)

One part Leaf mould

1 Tablespoon Bonemeal/Rallimeal/ Sterameal of Superphosphate

1 Teaspoon N.P.K. (Ammonium phosphate+Urea+Pot. Sulphate)

1 Teaspoon B.H.C. 5%

Handful of charcoal dust or charcoal broken into gram/pea size pieces.

Mix all these ingredients thoroughly and fill the pot tightly leaving 1.5" space from above.

For chrysanthemums slow release fertilizers are normally recommended. Cover the hole of the pots with concave crocks. The hole must not get clogged at any time. Water must drain out. The biggest enemy of Chrysanthemums is water-logging.

How to plant

When your plants are ready make a hole with a pencil in the centre of the pot and place the plant in the hole and firm it with fingers on all sides. The hole should not be very deep-1" depth will be enough. The roots should touch the bottom of the hole and there should be no air pockets between the plant roots and the pencil hole. After firming it, water the plant and place it in the shade for at least three days bringing it to sunlight gradually. In one week's time it should be able to withstand full sun. During this one week the pot should not get dry, it should remain moist all the time and during the next 10 or 15 days your job will be to see that the soil remains moist. No further care is needed till the plant has attained a height of six inches or so.

The plant should be watered once a day in hot weather and on alternate days in rainy season and may be after 2 days in winter. The important test is to pinch the soil and see if it forms a shape. If it is dry and the plant has started drooping and flagging, water it immediately.

Staking

When the plant is about 6" high insert a stake a little away from the plant so that the roots are not damaged and tie it loosely with a twine. At this very stage you may spray it with a systematic insecticide like Methasystox (Bayer) one ml. to one litre of water. When the plant is about a month old you may start giving it a top feed. One teaspoon of N.P.K. in 5 litres of water and half a litre of this solution to each plant. They must be watered before and after the application of this solution. Avoid spraying with Rogor, you may use Malathion.

De-shooting

As the plant grows it will start throwing lateral branches and at the base of the stem. If you are aiming at one flower only keep only the main stem and the crown bud. All other branches and buds (except the mainstem and the crown bud) should be periodically and systematically removed. If you are aiming at two flowers, cut the mainstem when it is 9" high and let two branches grows opposite to each other and if you want three flowers let these branches grow at an angle of 120 to each other.)

As the plant grows: spraying

At an interval of 15 days keep spraying the plant with "METASYSTOX" insecticide make 2 ml. to one litre of water. Drench the plant thoroughly, do not forget the undersides of the leaves.

Chrysanthemums must be given only balanced nutrients.

Potassium Nitrate	1 teaspoonful
Magnesium Sulphate	1 teaspoonful
Potassium Sulphate	1 teaspoonful
Ferrous sulphate	1 teaspoonful
Di-ammonium Phosphate	1 teaspoonful
Potassium Permanganate	1/2 teaspoonful
Tracel (trace elements)	1 teaspoonful

Mix all these in 30 litres of water. Give half litre of this feed every 10 or 15 days to the plant. Do not forget to water the plant before and after the application of these chemicals. Otherwise the plant might get burnt up.

Liquid manure

The above chemicals can also be added to the liquid manure instead of plain water. Liquid manure is prepared in the following way.

Take a basket full of fresh cowdung and dissolve it in plain water in a drum or in a pitcher or a plastic bucket. Cover it with lid and allow it to rot for 15 days. Keep stirring this solution from time to time. After 2 weeks decant the solution, mix it with more water till it gives you the colour of tea leaves boiled in water. In this weak solution dissolve the above ingredients. Give half litre of this solution to every plant after 10 or 15 days.

When the leaves become dark green and break into two on folding them, stop further feeding. The plant does not need any further dose of fertilizers. Leaves should be sprayed or washed with plain water. Dust on the leaves clogs their breathing.

As soon as the bud appears give it only bud feed, stop all other fertilizers.

10 teaspoonfuls or Rallimeal or Sterameal.

1 teaspoonful of Ferrous sulphate

1 teaspoonful of Magnesium sulphate

1 teaspoonful of Tracel

1/2 teaspoonful of Potassium Permanganate

Dissolve it in 10 litres of water. Give half a litre of this liquid to each plant. Do not forget to water the plant before and after the application of the above. Keep retying the plant to the stake. See that the plant is firmly supported by the stake and bloom should ultimately be fitting out of the stake clearly. It should be properly tied and supported.

When the plant has come to bloom, you can bring the pot to a shady place and even to the drawing room. The bloom will last for 3 weeks and seeing it fresh and shining you will feel amply rewarded for your whole year's labour.

After the flower has faded, cut the stem to six inches above the pot. Keep watering as you did before—no water logging—no over watering. It will start growing vegetatively again, it will throw suckers (rooted branches) at the base of the stem and start growing more branches. Take cuttings from the plant in February to form more plants from which final cuttings will be taken in July, August.

Potted plants/terrace gardening—As a result of urbanisation, shrinking land resources and the emergence of multi-storeyed buildings have necessitated terrace gardening or pot culture.

Different Types of Pots

Earthern pots are the best as they retain moisture and are easy to repot and shift.

Ceramic pots should be washed and soaked in water before use.

Cement pots are heavy and have a low water retention capacity.

Wooden Basket or Boxes – Before using wooden baskets its inner sides should be coated with a mixture of kerosene and charcoal, and the outside with green paint. Wood baskets should be of good quality.

Hanging Wire Baskets – are good for flowers, vegetables and green plants which have a tendency to drop (fall down).

Drums - are good for fruits and citrus fruit trees.

Soil mixture

The mixture should not only be meticulous but porous as well so as to avoid stagnation of water and allow free circulation of sunlight and air. An ideal mixture for pots can be:

1 part garden soil

1 part cow dung manure

1 part leaf mould manure

A handful of sand or Badarpur

Mix all of the above ingredients. Fill up the pots keeping a 1" space on the top to hold water. Now spreaded:

2 tbsp Neem khali

1 tbsp Sterameal

handful of river sand or Badarpur

1 tsp N.P.K.

Handy hints

Use clean pots. Old pots should be scrubbed both inside and out with coconut fibre and even washed in hot water to remove all dust and moss.

Use suitable soil

Use clean crocks

Pot firmly

Do not use over-sized pots

Do not plant too deep

Remove to shade after potting

Provision of drainage

The water supplied to the plant should pass out of the pot after wetting the soil. It should not be allowed to stagnate in the pot around the roots.

Hedges

Many dwarf shrubs and trees are used for making hedges. Grown next to barbed wire fencing, hedges provide privacy and protection. Ornamental hedges are grown in large gardens to mark off a drive way or one portion of the garden from another. For hedges, 60 cm deep and 60 cm wide trench is dug, all rubbles and stones are removed. Well rotten cow dung is added to the trench, next a hedge is during the rainy season e.g. Lantana, Camera, Doodnaea, Bougainvillea, Barleria, Prionites, Duranta ripens, Inga dulcis.

Manures

Manures are substances which are added to the soil to encourage plant growth and development. They increase fertility of soil directly by supplying the nutrients and indirectly by helping the soil in assimilating the nutrients received through other sources and by improving its water retention capacity. Manures should be given in, right season and in the right manner, otherwise they may even be harmful to the plant. Manures are of two kinds – Organic and Inorganic.

Organic manures

Organic manures are natural substances made of decomposed vegetation and animal matter such as animal waste, blood, bones etc. They are slow in action and increase the porosity and water retention capacity of soil. They also help in assimilation of inorganic manure and check the deficiency of micronutrients caused by excessive use of inorganic manures. Generally, they are not harmful to the plant; even if given in an overdose. The following are some of the important organic manures:

Farmyard manure

Farmyard manure is animal waste or dung of cattle, horse, sheep, goat, pigs etc. Generally cattle dung manure is commercially available in the market. It is complete food for soil sun as sun rays would deplete it of nutrients. The heap of manure should be covered by 2 cms. layer of soil or Shirki to give shade. It should never be used if it is not decomposed fully, as it would harm the plant by inviting insects and fungus diseases. It is advised that farmyard manure should be procured well in advance and stored in a pit covered by a layer of soil or any material which provides shade and should be used when it is fully decomposed.

It contains 0.7, 0.51 and 0.29 percent of nitrogen, phosphoric acid and potash respectively.

Sludge

Sludge is treated night soil and is inferior to farmyard manure but it is a powerful manure. In case farmyard manure is not available, Sludge can be used as a substitute. However, in lawns and in Bonsai soil mixture, it is preferred to farmyard manure. It is rich in nitrogen.

Bio-gas

Bio-gas is also used these days to substitute Farmyard manure. It is better to use Bio-gas after keeping it in a covered pit for 15 days along with some Neemkhali and wood-ash.

Fowl or poultry manure

It contains 1.46% of nitrogen, 1.17% of phosphorous and 0.62% potassium. It is richer than cattle or horse manure.

Leafmould

Leafmould is decomposed mixture of dry leaves, lawn mowings, softwood or any other plant material. (Tamarind and casurina leaves are best avoided.) It contains humus and is very light, so it is used to improve the texture of heavy soil. It can be applied to both clayey and sandy soil. It improves water retention capacity of soil and helps in assimilation of other plant nutrients. It is a must in pot mixture and also in soil mixture of seed beds or pans. It is very good for orchids, ferns, palms, bulbous plants and delicate annuals and foliage plants.

Compost

Compost consists of leaves, lawn mowing, kitchen refuse like vegetable peels and fruit peels, wood-ash and other natural ingredients which can be decomposed properly. It should not be in liquid form. This can be applied in combination with farmyard manure, leafmould or both. It gives nutrients and humus to the soil.

Oil cakes

Oil cakes are residue left after extracting oils from neem, groundnut, mustard etc. Oil cakes are used in powder form and also in liquid manures. For pots, oil cakes provide good food. Neem cake is good for warding off the attacks of insects. It contains 3 to 5% of nitrogen and 1.5 to 2% of phosphorous. Oil cakes are stimulating manures being rich in nitrogen.

Bone meal

Bone meal is powder of bones of animals. It is rich in phosphorous and contais about 30% of phosphoric acid. It is also slow acting by nature and is used for growing flowers, fruits and vegetables. It may be spread on flowers, fruits and vegetables. It may be spread on the surface of the soil at the rate of 120 gms, per square metre and forked in.

Sterameal

This also is made of pulverized bones like bonemeal but is sterilized and some micronutrients are added to this. In action, it is similar to bonemeal.

Hoof and hornmeal

This is also made of animal matter and is rich in nitrogen. It is good for soil as nitrogen from other sources is exhausted quickly, but this being slow acting in nature, releases nigrogen after sometime.

Blood meal

This is also nitrogenous manure and contains traces of calcium, sodium, potassium and phosphorous. This is dried blood of animals collected from slaughter houses.

Fish manure

Fish manure contains 8 to 10% of nitrogen and 6 to 9% of phosphorus and is advantageously used for fruit trees.

Woodash

Woodash is ash of charcoal and wood and contains 5 to 15% Potash. It is used for improving colour and flavour of flowering and fruiting plants and trees. It can be used as a top dressing at the rate of 250 gms per square metre. Root vegetables require liberal manuring with potash.

Charcoal dust

It is the powder of Charcoal. It improves the texture of soil, absorbs harmful gases and prevents snails and slugs from multiplying and harming the plants. It absorbs ammonia and has some manurial value. It is very good for ferns and orchids.

Soot

Though not available in the plains now-a-days, it is good for improving the colour of flowers. This is the powder scraped and collected from the Chimneys and given to plants by diluting in water.

Liquid manure

It is not commercially available. A manure applied to a plant in the form of liquid instead of powder is called liquid manure. It is given to accelerate growth at a time when the plant is well established. For flowering plants, it is given when flower buds are forming. For evergreens, it is given during their most active growth period, to fruit trees when fruits are setting till they change colour, and to vegetables during the period of active growth.

The advantage of liquid manure is that it gives nutrition which is immediately assimilated at a time when the plant needs it most. An organic liquid manure also improves water retention capacity of the plant. Liquid manure should not be applied when the plant is small or is in a dormant condition. A plant must not be dry when liquid manure is given. It is advisable to water it an hour or so before giving liquid manure. The principle is to give liquid manure less and often, rather than much and seldom. For trees and shrubs whose feedings roots are away from the stem, it is wrong to apply it very near the stem. It should be applied 15 cm-1.2m. (1/2-metre.) away from the stem upto the extent of the entire spread of the branches.

Liquid manure may be organic or inorganic. The most common organic liquid manure is of cow-dung or neem cake. Organic liquid manure is safest and very effective.

Green manure

Green manure is obtained from growing up crop in the soil and digging it into the soil while it is green; Dhania Soyabean or Cowpea is grown directly on the plot of land to be cultivated. This enhances the nitrogen content of the soil and improves the texture. It can also be used if compost, leaf mould or farmyard manure is not available.

Vermicompost

Organic farming is a sustainable farming system that seeks to maintain and improve productivity of soil by encouraging and enhancing biological process and minimising the use of chemical fertilizers and pesticides.

In this approach soil is treated like a bridge connecting living and non-living entities on this earth. Although it appears dead there is a living component present in it—the micro-organisms (bacteria, fungi and termites and earthworms), which are responsible in part for health of the soil. Soil organisms play an integral role in the breakdown and decomposition of organic matter and recycling of plant nutrients. They substantially rearrange soil and affect its physical process; the earthworms have capacity to influence these properties. They are called 'intestine of soil'.

Biology of earthworms

Earthworms are segmented animals, without bones. They have mouth but no teeth. Earthworms are hermaphrodites (bisexual) and under ideal conditions of temperature, moisture and food can double their population in a month.

What is vermiculture and vermicompost

Vermiculture means rearing of earthworms for production of Vermicompost, a mixture of excrements or castings of earthworms consisting of digested soil and particles of organic matter alongwith aerobically composted organic matter. It also contains live cocoons which on hatching produce 2-10 worms.

Making vermicompost at home

Vermicompost can be prepared at home by making use of kitchen waste and garden cuttings available in your backyard. The compost can be prepared either in earthern pots, plastic trays, cement tanks or in a pit under a shade or even by making a heap above ground.

Benefits of earthworms/vermicompost

The population of earthworms increases in the soil where vermicompost and other organic manures are added. The benefits of this technology are as below:

1. The burrowing activity of worms improves soil porosity, structure, increases infiltration and water holding capacity of soil.
2. It increases aeration of root zones and provides channels for root growth.
3. Feeding organic matter earthworms increases organic matter turn over, breaks up root mat and leaf litter, increases microbial activity in soil, breaks up and mixes organic and inorganic materials.
4. The excrements of earthworms have high concentrations of available nitrogen, phosphorous and potassium. They have higher microbial activity and produce zones of nutrient enrichment for plant growth.
5. The castings of earthworms are stable aggregates, which reduce surface crusting, increase water infiltration, improve seedling emergence and increase resistance to erosion.

In addition to above mentioned benefits indirect advantages like increase in resistance to disease, better quality of the produce, high sugar content in fruits, longer shelf life etc. are seen in crops grown on vermicompost.

Inorganic manures

Inorganic manures are chemical substances which contain plant nutrients. They are quick in action and show the results very fast. They are soluble in water and act as stimulants. They have some disadvantages also. An overdose of chemical fertilizers may be fatal for the plant. Lots of controversy is going on about the harmful effects of chemical fertilizers used in vegetables and fruits. They deplete the soil of its micronutrients. If used with caution they give immediate spurt to plant growth. Inorganic manures should always be used alongwith organic manures. Care should be taken that they should not come in direct contact with roots or stem. The following are some of the important inorganic fertilizers.

Nitrogenous fertilizers

Nitrogen helps in vegetative growth, promotes green foliage and a sturdy bush. It gives vigour to the plant. Its deficiency can be noticed when the plant has lanky and stunted growth and leaves have pale or yellow colour, but do not fall off from the plant. It is present in Urea (40%). Ammonium Sulphate (20%), Nitrate of Soda (15%). Ammonium Nitrate (35%) etc.

Phosphatic fertilizers

Symptoms of deficiency are dropping of premature fruits and flowers. It is available in single super phosphate (16%), double super phosphate (40%). Rock Phosphate (24%) and basic Slag (15%). The last two have calcium also and are good for acidic soil. Phosphatic fertilizer helps in production of more and better flowers and fruits. It is helpful for those plants where the 'head' is taken like cabbages and cauliflowers.

Potassic fertilizers

Potassic fertilizers are used for improving colour and flavour of flowers and fruits. It is available in Muriate of Potash and Sulphate of Potash.

Mixed fertilizers

A mixture of the above mentioned fertilizers is available in the market, which is known as NPK. In this mixture N stands for nitrogen, P for phosphorus, and K for Potash. It is available in different proportions, such as 15:15:15, 17:17:17, 19:19:19, 14:28:14 and so on. Diammonium phosphate is available in the market in which Nitrogen and Phosphorous are present in the ratio 21:53.

Apart for these three major elements plants need some other elements also which are available in the market through the following sources.

Calcium

Lime Stone	40%
Magnesium Dolomite	21%
Quick Lime	71%
Epsom Salt	20%
Slaked Lime	54%
Sulphur	
Plaster of Paris	23%
Ammonium Sulphate	24%
Super phosphate	19%
Gypsum	18%
Dolomite	30%
Super phosphate	8-31%

Boron iron

Borax	11%
Iron Sulphate	20%
Boric Acid	14%
Copper sulphate	

Calendar for Monthwise Gardening

January

Vegetables and fruits: Musk-melon. Water-melon, Radish Pusa Himani can be sown.

Preparation of the beds for growing Ladies-Finger and other summer vegetables like Cucumber, Ghia, Kakri, Seetaphal for which you have already raised the seedlings in polythene bags. Even if you have not put the seed so far you may do so now. The seeds of these above vegetables should be sown in polythene bags and they should be kept in the sun but should be covered by Alkathene at night to save it from frost.

Flowers—Roses: The plants after the flush of flowers in December exhaust and require rest for a while. When the blooms are over, cut out the dead blooms and continue doing so throughout the year. Remove suckers regularly.

In the second week of this month feed your bushes with cowdung or farm yard manure at the rate of about 3 kgs. per plant. Spread the manure in the plant and mix it well. Spray monocrotophos and Calixin or karathene to control the aphids and powdery mildew.

Watering should be done 8 to 10 days in beds and alternate days in pots and hoeing should be done twice a month.

Summer season flowers: Make the preparation for growing the summer season flowers like Zinnia, Portulaca, Gomphrena, Gallardia, Kochia, Golden-rod. Prepare the beds for sowing Tub-roses and Day-Lily. Clear the beds of Canna plant from dry leaves etc. and manure it.

Grapes: Pusa Seedless, Pusa Beauty variety of grapes can be sown. Pruning of old grape wine should be done.

Mango: Those who have not done the treatment for mealy-bug they should put plastic or grease band with mobiloil on the trunk about two feet above the ground level and put B.H.C. 10% in the ground. Spray Devicol or Nuvan as soon as you see the mealy bug in the first stage like aphids near the slippery bands. Cut the twigs of the tree if these are touching the building. Get the treatment done from expert for the mal-formation in the mangoes. The All India Kitchen Garden Association will help you in getting the experts.

Indoor-plants: Expose to sun and manure them. Do not let the dew dry on any plant. Sprinkle the leaves lightly with water in the morning.

Shrubs: January is also the best time to plant the cuttings of the various shrubs like Chandni, Bougainvilla, Raat Ki Rani etc.

Lawn: First thing never let the frost or dew dry on the grass. Sprinkle water on the grass early in the morning. Then in the third week of January give Urea, or Ammonium sulphate to the grass, and flood it immediately. For a lawn of 12'x12' give 0.5 Kg. Urea or Ammonium Sulphate. It will give to the grass required nutrient of Nitrogen and give it a green look. Then in the last week of January start mowing the lawn every fortnight. From now onwards watering and mowing is to be the routine for the lawn. In between keep a lookout for any weeds. Pull out the weeds.

Chrysanthemum: Cut off the main stem after flowering is over. Set aside the pots and water sparingly while protecting them from winter frosts. If they are out-doors protect them with a plastic sheet at night.

For food-preservation: Peas, Orange Mausammi, Sarso, Amla, Orange and Guava are available and are cheapest in the month.

Pumpkin, Potatoes, Beans and Papayas can be preserved throughout the year.

February

Vegetables: Sowing of summer vegetables like Tori, Ghia, Karela, (Bitter gourd). Khira (Cucumber) already grown in the polythene bags or 4" earthen pots may be transplanted in the ground, Lettuce, Onion, Tomato, Brinjal, Chillies may be transplanted. Other vegetables like Clusterbean, Cowpea, Frenchbean, Okra (Bhindi), Pumpkin, Palak and Tinda may also be sown.

Vegetables already in the garden may be given proper attention regarding hoeing and irrigation.

Flowers: Amaranthus and other lily bulbs may be sown.

Foliage plants: There is little growth in the foliage plants. Watering should be done after 7 to 8 days and excess watering should be avoided. Varieties of foliage plants like Crotons, Money-plant, Philodendron should be protected from frost and cold winds.

Bougainvillaea and other hedge plants may be planted.

Chrysanthemum: Feed with a pinch of Urea or Organic Fertiliser to encourage vegetative growth, while watering adequately. In third or fourth week the suckers start appearing from the 'stool' at the base of the stem. When they are 10 cm tall and well developed, remove the entire stool and wash the roots in fresh water to mitigate risk of infection. Then plant about five suckers per pot in rich soil or in a raised and protected flower bed. Chrysanthemums hate wet feet.

Roses: This is the time when your rose bushes need more care and attention.

1. Due to rise in temperature, there is severe attack of powdery Mildew on the plants. The young shoots, leaves and buds are coated with a white powdery film. You have to spray your rose bushes again in the first and third week with an insecticide and a fungicide. In this month spraying should be done only in the early morning. You may add foliar feed with both the sprays. It augments the growth activity in the plant and leads to healthy foliage and bright brilliant hues.
2. Termites also attack the roots of the plants in this month. Give Aldrin alongwith water, watering once a week in beds and daily in the pots has to be done. Hoeing twice a month as usual is recommended. Suckers and dead blooms have to be cut out regularly.
3. The plants will require additional nutrition in this month to sustain the out-burst of vegetative growth. An application of a well balanced chemical fertilizer of well rotted cowdung manure will be highly welcome in the last week of this month. Grafting on roses can be done in this month.

Lawn: Since the nights are still cool, give another dose of Urea or Ammonium Sulphate to the lawn preferably in the first week of this month. Keep on mowing the lawn as soon as it is thick and tall enough.

Indoor plants: Transplanting can be done from fifteenth February. Liquid manure may be given to all the plants including palms.

For preservation: Amla, China orange, Cauliflower, Tomato, Turnip, Carrot, Pea, Raspberry, Orange, Mausammi, Guava, Lemon are available.

March

Vegetables: Bitter gourd, Bottle gourd, Cluster bean, Cowpea, Cucumber, French bean, Bhindi, Pumpkin, Radish and Water-melon may be sown.

Planting of new trees, climbers, shrubs and hedges may be completed in the first fortnight. Seeds of the hedges and trees can be sown. Seed collection of the flowering annuals may be done. Care should be taken that seeds collected are properly lablled and bloom of wrong colour should be removed. Seeds of the summer flowering annuals should be put in the nursery during first fortnight.

Indoor plants: Manure them and put them in a shady place. Give liquid manure in the first week of March.

Roses: Continue cutting dead flowers and wood, remove suckers. Watering after every 5 to 6 days and daily in pots and hoeing twice a month has to be done.

In the second week repeat the spray of a fungicide and an insecticide. During the last week flush of roses will appear.

Cereals: Moong can be grown from the third week of this month. It enriches the land.

Chrysanthemums: Keep the plants in the shade till they stand erect in about ten days. Water them lightly and rest the plants.

Lawn: Give Sterameal to the grass, 1 Kg. Sterameal for a lawn of 12'x12' size. Again be on the look out for any weeds.

Seed collection: The seeds have to be collected. Put a small plastic on the seed pots where the seeds are very small. Seeds like sweet-peas, Calendula, Nasturtium, Dahlia can easily be plucked. Keep them to dry for a week in Semi-shade and then store them.

Preservation: Cauliflower, Tomato, Turnips, Carrots, Peas, Orange, Guava, Ginger and lemon.

April

Vegetable: Clear the winter vegetable field and prepare it for the coming season vegetables.

Foliage Plants: In foliage plants the growth will be resumed. Therefore, these should be kept in the shade to avoid direct sun. Propagation by seed, division, cuttings can be done in the first fortnight.

Chrysanthemum suckers should be transplanted in the bigger pots. The pot should be kept in the sunlight.

Flowers: Winter season flowers which have ceased flowering should be cleared and the beds should be prepared for summer season flowers, proper care should be given to the seedlings in the nursery. This is the best time for flowering of cannas, selection for cannas can be made so that it could be propagated in the next month, seed collection from the late winter season flowers can be done, casualties in the shrubs can be filled up. Shrubs already having over growth can be pruned and manured and fertiliser should be given to the old shrubs.

Roses: Watering every two or three days and spraying of insecticide once a month should continue. It should be in the evening hours especially for the control of white grub, beetles and caterpillars.

A forceful and thorough water jet spray on both sides of leaves and stem will dislodge and wash away most of the red spider mites. This may be done once a week in the morning. This spray also washes the accumulated dust and makes bushes more vigorous and healthy.

Attend to the removal of dead flowers, suckers and any dead wood regularly.

Start preparing new rose beds in the month of May for planting in July. The ground intended for roses must be thoroughly dug preferably to a depth of two feet or more and good drainage must be ensured so that there is no water logging. Get the beds filled up about a week before the onset of the monsoon.

Cereals: Moong can be grown by the third week of this month.

Chrysanthemum: When they are 20 cm tall, pinch off 5 cm from the crown above the leaf node. This results in bifurcation of growth and you will have two crowns instead of one. These two when pinched again after a fortnight, will give you four, then eight and so on.

Continue pinching and feed the plant every ten or fifteen days with Urea, Potash, and bone-meal and water it well. A top dressing of well rotted cow dung manure is a good alternative. Watch out for insects like leaf miner, aphids, red spider mite, powdery mildew etc. and spray with fungicides.

Lawn: Give another dose of sterameal with neemkhali. For a 12'x12' lawn give one kg. sterameal and one kg Neemkhali. Neemkhali will act as a deterrent for the insects.

Seed-collection: Continue the seed collection as in March.

Indoor plants : Save them from direct sun.

Preservation: China-orange, Mangoes, Jack-fruit, and Pumpkin are available.

May

Vegetables: Seeds of Brinjal, Cauliflower and Chillies can be sown.

Decay plants and weeds should be cleared, cultivated should be manured so that summer plantation can be done.

Cannas can be planted in the new beds. Seeds of the rainy season flowers should be sown in the seed beds.

Tube rose: Bulbs and other Lily bulbs to be planted.

Rose: Same as suggested in the month of April.

Chrysanthemum: Keep the plants in the shade. You may need to water them twice a day in very hot weather. Keep pinching, weeding and protect the plants from pests.

Lawn: Nothing to add except watering and removing the weeds and motha if any. If you want to pave the new grass in your garden then start digging the lawn in the last week to a depth of a foot.

Indoor plants: Protect them from direct sun rays and water them so that the soil remains moist all the time. Mulching by grass or dry leaves or moss-grass can be done to retain the moisture.

June

Vegetables: Bitter gourd, Bottle gourd, Brinjal, Capsicum, Cauliflower, Chillies. Cluster bean, Cowpea, Cucmber, Sem, Bhindi and Pumpkin.

Maize is also planted in this month.

Foliage plants should be given protection from direct sun rays and hot winds. Pots should be kept 4-5 days inside the rooms and then should be taken out for 2 to 3 days where they should get morning sun.

Canna suckers can be taken out and may be kept for replanting. Required irrigation should be given to the shrubs so that it could be saved from hot weather.

This is the time when you do the pruning of Bougainvillea and propagate it.

Roses: Same as applicable for the months of April and May.

Chrysanthemum: Prepare a 10 cm deep tray with sterilised sharp sand or Badarpur for rooting the cuttings. To sterilize, heat the sand to a high temperature for half an hour in a metal container—an iron tasla will do fine over an open wood fire.

With a sharp pair of scissors remove three to five nodes at the crown of each stem. Remove the lower leaves from the cutting and gently rub off the roughness with your thumb. Wet the end of the stem and insert the cut end into rooting hormone powder. Shake off the excess and insert one or two nodes in sand. Keep the cuttings in partial shade, and water lightly morning and evening till they are erect.

Gradually expose them to sunlight as they get stronger and new growth occurs from food stored in the stems. They will strike roots in six to eight weeks.

Lawn: For already laid out lawn just give water so that it does not get dried.

For preservation: Mangoes, Lichi, Phalsa, Plum, Pineapple, Cherry, Karonda, Jackfruit and Petha.

For new lawn: Digging was started in the last week of May. Now turn the soil inside and outside and keep on doing it 2 to 3 times so that the roots of the weeds and any other ant-holes etc. are exposed to the hot sun and destroyed by the heat. Keep the earth exposed for about two to three weeks. Then sprinkle some sand on the top soil and along with sand put some slaked lime. Do not be over generous with slaked lime. About one handful for 2 square feet is a fairly good amount. Water is necessary for taking the heat out of the lime. You may also add some cow-dung manure and steramel. Flood it with water. Let the earth dry out and then level the ground for the planting of the grass.

July

Vegetables: Amaranthus, Bitter-gourd, Bottle gourd, Capsicum, Cauliflower (Early Kumari) Cluster bean, Cowpea, Cucumber, Sem, Bhindi, Pumpkin, Radish, Sponge gourd and Tomato can be sown. In northern hilly areas and J&K you may sow Carrots, Cabbage and cauliflower in July and August.

Seedlings of early cauliflower may be transplanted.

Cereals: Bajra irrigated to be sown in the first fortnight and Rain-fed or unirrigated at the set of monsoon.

Flowers: Monsoon flowers should be planted in the beds. Chrysanthemum cuttings may be put in the Badarpur to get rooted. The chrysanthemum grown by suckers may be shifted into the bigger pot.

Excess watering in chrysanthemum and other foliage plants should be avoided.

Shrubs: Extra growth of shrubs may be pruned. Plants can be propagated by cuttings in this month.

Roses: Ensure that there is no water logging in the rose beds, otherwise roots are likely to be damaged, systematic insecticide and fungicide sprays have to be continued once a month. Dry and dead flowers and wood has to be removed as usual and burnt. Hoeing has to be regular as weeds growth is maximum.

Planning your garden: You can plan or replan your garden this month and in August, if not done in July.

For preservation: Mangoes, Phalsa, Plum, Pineapple, Karonda, Lichi, Cherry, Peaches, Jack-Fruit and Bel are available.

August

Vegetables: Carrot, Cauliflower, Palak and Mooli can be sown early. Cauliflower seedlings may be transplanted.

Uncommon vegetables: Celery is sown by July and August, it is highly nutritive.

Flowers: Early sowing of flower seeds like Salvia, Aster, Phlox, Petunia and Marigold can be done.

Early variety of Gladioli may be put in beds.

Chrysanthemum: From late July onwards pot the rooted cuttings in rich soil to which has been added one table-spoon of bone-meal and one tea spoon of anti-termite powder per plant if required.

If you want more than one flower per plant cut off 2.5 cm from the crown to encourage lateral growth. Select three branches at three angles and allow them to grow into sub-branches.

Roses: Same as in the month of July.

Suculents and Cactus: Keep them away from rain.

House plants: Put out all the ever green indoor plants in the rain (water-logging should be avoided). Plant and transplant any plant and new trees, creepers, shrubs so that they get rooted during the rains.

Lawns: Nature will take-charge of the watering etc., only keep a sharp eye on any stray weeds and mothas and pull them out at once.

Preservation: Jamun, Plum, Karonda, Apple, Mangoes, Lemon, Grapes and Peaches are available.

September

Vegetables: Cabbage, Fenugreek (Methi), French Bean, Knol Khol, Lettuce, Peas, Potato, Radish, Palak, Parsley seeds should be sown.

Uncommon Vegetables: Sprouting broccoli is Rich in Vitamin-A, B1, B2 and C.

Brussels sports: have high protein value and rich in Vitamin A.

Parsley: sown from September to October rich in Vitamin C.

Leek: is also sown in September and October.

Celery in Northern Hill areas of J&K.

Flowers: Aster, Antirrihinum, Carnation, Clarkia, Dahlia, Gerbera, Hollyhock, Larkspur, Linaria, Lupins, Marigold, Pansy, Poppy, Salvia, Stock, Sweetpeas, Cosmos, Sweet Williams and Verbena.

Put in the bulbs of Gladiolus. Amaranthus and other Easter Lilies.

Roses: Same in July and August. By the end of September one feed of cow-dung manure and one spray of insecticide mixed with fungicide will be good.

Chrysanthemum: Continue watering, fertilising and protecting the plant from pests till the colour of the buds show, stop feeding at this point but continue watering. No amount of feeding after this will make up for inadequate nourishment from July to September. Buds should appear by the end of September, if the top most break bud is weak, remove it. The first or second crown buds will flower better.

Lawn: After the rains, first pull out the weeds and then mow the lawn. Soon after mowing, give the lawn first taste of organic manure i.e. sterameal.

Indoor plants: Transplanting may be done including Palms from 15th September onwards.

October

Vegetables: Beet root, Brinjal, Cabbage, Chinese Cabbage, Carrot, Cauliflower (snow-ball), Fenugreek (Methi) Knol Khol, Lettuce, Mustard (Sarson), Turnip and Potato.

Flowers: Transplant all the ready seedlings. For late flowering sow Aster, Antirrihinum, Calendula, Carnation, Clarkia, Dahlia, Gerbera, Hollyhock, Larkspur, Linaria, Lupins, Pansy, Poppy, Stock, Sweet-William, Verbena.

Put manure in the Hedges and the Evergreen Dahlia Cuttings, Multi-coloured Gladiolus must be sown, Narcissus and Iris bulbs can be sown.

Roses: It is the time for hard work in roses. However this is the time when good work done in roses will show results in coming season.

1. This is the month when the pruning is done. Second week is ideal for pruning.

A week before pruning withhold watering of the plants.

i) Cut out all dead and dry wood completely. Remove suckers (suckers in fact should be removed regularly).

ii) Cut out completely all very thin stems and any branch which rubs against another. An open centred bush is ideal.

iii) Cut out all unripe stems: Test-Try to snap off several thorns. If the thorns bend or tear off instead of breaking off cleanly the wood is too soft and has to be cut off.

iv) The cut should slope away from the bud.

v) Hard pruning, Moderate pruning and light pruning depends upon the classification.

2. After pruning spray the roses with a mixture of Insecticides and Fungicides.

3. Remove the excess soil from the bed, but ensure that roots are not damaged. Exposure of Roots is not necessary. All weeds have to be taken out completely. Then give to each plant, half basket (about 3-4 Kgs) of well rotten farmyard manure and hoe the bed properly. Watering should be done immediately after manuring.

4. If you have roses in pots, they should be repotted after pruning them in this month every second year.

5. Give Aldrin along with water to eradicate termite or white ants. Aldrex at the rate of 33 ml in 5 Litres of water is sufficient for 10 rose plants. First flood the bed with water and then sprinkle the solution all round the bed or the pots so that the solution percolates to the root zone along with the water.

6. Watering has to be done about once a week in rose beds and on alternate days in pots during this month. Hoeing should be continued every 15 days and the suckers removed as and when they appear.

Indoor plants: Same as in September.

Lawn: Give Urea or sulphate of Ammonia to the grass and immediately flood it.

Chrysanthemum: Remove all the other buds except the ones you want to retain. Continue disbudding till the flowers are half open and remove unwanted axial branches. One table spoon per plant of wood-ahs near the roots will enhance the colour of the flowers.

November

Vegetables: Beet-root, Brinjal, Chinese Cabbage, Capsicum, Chillies, Methi, Mustard, Onion, Peas, Potato, Palak, Tomato, Turnip may be grown, Transplanting of seedlings sown earlier can be done.

Flowers: Seedlings can be transplanted, Narcissus and Gladiolus bulbs can be grown in this month also.

Roses:

1. Ideal time for planting new rose bushes.

2. A good time to give the recommended quality of chemical fertilizers around the plants. Rose mix with different names are also available in the market.

3. The rose bushes should be sprayed with good insecticide and fungicide. Third week of this month is ideal for foliar feeding. Urea and Potassium acid Phosphate mixed in the ratio of 2:1 make an excellent supplement to root feeding. Use half an ounce of this mixture to a gallon of water and spray on the plants thoroughly wetting both

sides of leaves and stems. The foliar feed could be added to the insecticide and fungicide spray thus doing two jobs in one operation.

Hoeing twice a month and watering once a week should be continued. Watering in pots be reduced to alternate days.

Protect them from Frost.

Chrysanthemum: Now just wait for the blooms to burst into glory. Feed them with manure.

For preservation: Cauliflower, Tamato, Turnip, Carrots, Sarson, Amla, Guava, Ginger and Apple are available.

December
Vegetables: Transplant Onion. Lettuce and Tomato seedlings.

Roses: This is the month when roses are in full bloom and you may leisurely enjoy the beauty of your roses.

Watering may be done at 10 days interval. Spray your plants with insecticides and fungicide along with the foliar feed in the 3rd week of this month.

Chrysanthemum: Cut off the main stem after flowering and set aside the plants while watering and protecting them from frost.

Lawn: Give Urea mixed with Neem Cake and water it.

Indoor plants: No manuring and transplanting required.

For preservation: Peas, Orange, Mausammi, Sarson, Amla, Guava, and Ginger are available.

■■

CHAPTER-14

Home Crafts

Knitting

The cheapness of the tools and materials used and the ease with which knitwear can be churned out makes knitwear one of the most popular homecrafts.

Materials required
a) Ball of yarn
b) two knitting needles

Methods:

1. **Casting on or putting the first line of stitches on the needle:** Make a slip loop-approximately 16 inches from the end of the yarn for 20 stitches. Place the loop on the needle and holding the needle in the right hand gently pull the ends of the yarn. Keep the loop near the pointed end of the needle and with the point of the needle draw in the yarn, which has been made into a loop around the left thumb, through the under side of the loop and then through the loop on the needle. It is this loop which becomes the stitch. Repeat until you have the required number of stitches.

2. **Knit or garter stitch:** Hold the needle with the cast on stitches in the left hand-holding the first stitch lightly with the index finger. The other needle is held like a pencil in the right hand. Insert the point of the right hand needle through the first loop from left to right. Put the yarn under the around the point of the right hand needle and draw the loop thus made through the loop on the left needle forming a new loop on the right needle. This is the first stitch. Repeat until all the loops on the left needle have been used. This is the first row and should contain the same number of stitches that were cast on. Change needles into opposite hands and start the next row. Keep pushing your work so that the stitch you are working on is near the tip of the needle.

3. **Purl stitch:** Hold the needles exactly as for knitting but inset the needle from-right to left. Always keep your yarn in front of your needle. That is the essential difference between knitting and purling.

4. **Increasing and decreasing:** The simplest way to increase is to knit into the front of a stitch to make one stitch and then knit into the back of the same stitch thus making two stitches to transfer to the right needle. To decrease, merely knit two stitches together.

5. Stockinette stitch is made by knitting one row and purling the next. Garter stitch is made by knitting every row.

6. **Binding off:** When the desired number of rows have been worked you end by slipping the first stitch off the left needle onto the right needle. Knit the second

stitch very loosely thus leaving two stitches on the right needle. Insert the left needle through the left side of the first stitch bringing the first stitch forward over the second stitch and over the tip of the needle so that you have one stitch instead of two. Knit the next stitch loosely and keep repeating. At the last stitch cut the yarn and pull the loose end through the last stitch very tightly. The important thing to remember is to bind off loosely.

Crochet

The basis of crochet is a slip loop, which is tightened by a knot and forms the first stitch of any work. This loop must be loose enough to allow the hook to slip in easily.

The abbreviations commonly used are:

K - knit
P - purl
KB - knit into back of stitch
PB - purl into back of stitch
St - stitch
Sl - slip
Wf - wool forward
Yf - yarn forward
Wft - wool front, bring wool to front of needle
Wb - wool back, take wool to back of needle
Wrn - wool round needle
Won - wool on needle
Psso - pass slipped stitch over
Tog - together
Tbl - through back of loop
Inc - increase by working into front and back of stitch
Dec - decrease by working 2 stitches together
Beg - beginning
Alt - alternate
Rep - repeat
Patt - pattern
Incl - inclusive
Ins - inches
Dc - double crochet
O - no sts

MI - Make I, by picking up loop that lies between st just worked and following st, and working into back of it.

MIK - Make I knitwise by picking up loop that lies between st just worked and following st and knitting into back of it.

MB - Make Bobble by PI, KI, PI, KI, PI into next st thus making 5 sts out of next st, turn K5, turn P5, slip 2nd, 3rd, 4th, and 5th sts over first st.

C2F - Cable 2 Front by working across next 4 sts as follows: Slip next 2 sts on to cable needle and leave at front of work, knit next 2 sts, then knit 2 sts from cable needle.

C2B - Cable 2 Back as C2F, but leave sts at back of work in place of front.

C3F - Cable 3 Front by working across next 6 sts as follows: Slip next 3 sts on to cable needle and leave at front of work, knit across next 3 sts, then knit 3 sts from cable needle.

C3B - Cable 3 Back as C3F, but leave sts at back of work in place of front.

C4F - Cable 4 Front by working across next 8 sts as follows: Slip next 4 sts on to cable needle and leave at front of work, knit across next 4 sts and then knit 4 sts from cable needle.

TW2 - Twist 2 by knitting the next 2 sts together but do not slip off left hand needle, knit into the first 2 of these sts again, then slip both sts off needle.

TW2F - Twist 2 purlwise by purling the next 2 sts together but do not slip off left hand needle, purl into the first of these sts again, then slip both sts off needle.

TW3 - Twist 3 by inserting point of right hand needle knitwise into 3rd st keeping point of this needle at front of work, knit the st in the ordinary way; work at the 2nd st in the same manner, now knit into the 1st st, then slip all 3 sts off left hand needle together.

LP - Lace Panel
B - Blue
BG - Bottle Green
C - Contrast
D - Dark
G - Ground Shade
L - Light
LN - Light Natural
M - Medium
PY - Pale Yellow
S - Scarlet
Y - Yellow
W - White

Position of the hands

Hold the work in the left hand, between the thumb and forefinger, the thread is taken over the former finger and middle finger, under the third finger and round the little finger. The crochet hook is held in the right hand (as you hold a pencil) between the thumb and forefinger and pressing on the middle finger.

To make a chain

With the first loop on hook, pass the hook under the thread on left hand and pull through a loop (making another stitch). This operation is called wool round hook (wrh) and is repeated until the chain has the number of stitches required, with one loop on the hook.

Double chain

Make 2 ch, insert hook into first stitch, * wrh draw through a loop, wrh draw through both loops on hook*. To continue insert the hook into the left loop, then work from *to*.

Slip stitch

On a length of ch miss the first ch, insert hook into top loop of next ch, wrh draw through ch loop and st on hook. In this way a new chain is formed.

Double crochet

Miss 1 ch, *insert hook into next ch, wrh draw through loop, wrh draw through 2 loops*. Turn with 1ch.

Double treble

Miss 3 ch, *wrh twice, insert hook into next ch, with, draw through a loop (wrh draw through 2 loops), twice, wrh, draw through last 2 loops*. 3 ch, turn.

Trible treble

Work as a Double Treble taking thread 3 times round hook in the first instance and draw through 2 loops 3 times, wrh draw through last 2 loops, 4 ch, turn.

Treble in relief

Work a row of trebles, 2 ch, turn.

Row 2: *Wrh, insert hook between 1st and 2nd sts horizontally and bring it out between 2nd and 3rd sts, wrh draw through loop, wrh draw through 2 loops, wrh draw through last 2 loops*, 2 ch turn.

Ridge stitch

Work a row of double crochet on the foundation ch, 1 ch, turn.

Row 2: *Work 1 dc, inserting hook into back thread at the head of each st of previous row*, 1 ch, turn.

Albanian stitch

Work a row of double crochet on the foundation, ch, 1 ch, turn.

Row 1: *Work 1 dc into each st inserting hook through front horizontal thread at head of st of previous row*, 1 ch, turn.

Russian stitch

This stitch is worked like Rose Stitch, with this difference, it is worked on the right side on every row, the thread being cut at the end each row.

Rumanian stitch

This stitch is worked like Ridge Stitch with this difference, it is worked on the right side on every row, the thread being cut at the end of each row.

Twisted russian stitch

This stitch is worked on the right side on every row, the thread being cut at the end of each row. Work a row of twisted double crochet on the foundation chain, ch 1, turn.

Row 1 and following rows: *Work 1 twisted dc inserting hook under both horizontal loops of each it of previous row*.

Double stitches

Row 1: 2 ch, and for each double stitch insert hook into 1 ch, wrh, draw through a loop, insert hook in next st, wrh, draw through 3 loops on hook*. For next double stitch, insert hook first of 2nd wrh.

Row 2: and following rows: work double stitches inserting hook under both horizontal loops of each double stitch of previous row.

Crossed stitch

Row 1: 2 ch, * 1 dc, 1 ch, miss 1 st, 1 dc * to end of row.

Row 2 and following rows: 2 ch, insert hook in first ch space, wrh, draw through a loop, insert hook in 2nd ch space, wrh, draw through a loop, wrh, draw through 3 loops on hook, 1 ch. Repeat from inserting hook first in ch space which drew the 2nd wrh.

Crossed half treble

Row 1: 2 ch, wrh, insert hook in 1 st, wrh, draw through a loop, wrh, insert hook in next st, wrh, draw through a loop, wrh, draw through 5 loops on hook, 1 ch*.

Row 2 and following rows: 2 ch, wrh, insert hook in last ch space of previous row, wrh, draw through a loop, wrh, insert hook in next ch space, wrh, draw through 5 loops on hook, 1 ch, Repeat from * inserting hook first in space which drew the 2nd loop.

Crossed treble stitch

Row 1: 2 ch, insert hook in 1 ch, wrh, draw through a loop, insert hook in next ch, wrh, draw through a loop, wrh, draw through 2 loops, wrh, draw through the last 2 loops on hook, 1 ch*.

Row 2 and following rows: Work 2 ch to turn and for each crossed treble, insert hook in each side of thread between 2 crossed treble of previous row.

Diamond stitch

Row 1: dc to end of row. 2 ch, turn

Row 2: wrh, insert hook under born horizontal loops of dc of previous row, wrh, draw through a loop, wrh, insert hook under both horizontal loops of next dc, wrh, draw through a loop, wrh, draw through 5 loops on hook, 1 ch*. The number of stitches is doubled.

Row 3: dc to end of row, inserting hook in each 1 ch space of previous row.

Row 4: as row 2.

Daisy stitch

This stitch is worked in rounds or on the right side on every row, the thread being cut at the end of each row.

Row 1: 3 ch to turn, insert hook in 2nd ch, wrh draw through a loop, insert hook in first ch, wrh, draw through a loop, then draw through a loop in each of following 2 ch, wrh, draw through 5 loops on hook, 1 ch.

Then * insert hook in centre st of preceding daisy, wrh, draw through a loop, insert hook in ch of last daisy, wrh, draw through a loop, draw through a loop in each of following 2 ch, wrh, draw through 5 loops on hook, 1 ch*.

Half daisy stitch

This stitch is worked on 2 rows, back and forth.

Row 1: Work daisies same as for Daisy Stitch, 2 ch, turn.

Row 2: dc to end of row, 3 ch, turn.

Repeat these 2 rows alternating 1 row of Daisy Stitch and 1 row of double crochet.

Arch stitch

Row 1: 5 ch, 1 dc in 3rd st of foundation ch, * 5 ch, 1 dc miss 3 st3, * 5 ch, turn.

Row 2 and following rows: * dc inserting hook in centre ch of 5 ch of previous row, 5 ch*. Finish row with 1 dc in 3rd ch, 5 ch, turn.

Check stitch

Row 1: 2 ch, 1 tr in each of next 2 ch, * 3 ch, miss 3 ch, 1 tr in each of next 3 ch*. Finish row with 3 ch, 1 tr.

Row 2 and following rows: 2 ch, 2 tr inserting hook in 3 ch space of previous row, * 3 ch, 3 tr inserting hook in 3 ch space of previous row*. Finish row with 3 ch, 1 tr.

Work check

On a foundation ch.

Row 1: 3 ch, * 1 tr in each of next 4 ch, 1 ch, miss 1 ch*. Finish row with 4 tr.

Row 2: * 4 ch, 1 dc inserting hook in 1 ch space of previous row*.

Row 3: work groups of 4 tr, and between each group work 1 ch inserting hook in the 4 ch space of previous row.

Fancy grating

Row 1: 5 ch, * 1 tr in first ch, 3 ch, miss 3 ch *. Finish row with 1 tr.

Row 2: 2 ch, * 2ch, 1 dc in 2nd of 3 ch of previous row, 2 ch, 1 tr inserting hook under both horizontal loops of tr of previous row *. Finish row with 2 ch, 1 dc.

Row 3: 5 ch, * 1 r inserting hook under both horizontal loops of tr of previous row, 3 ch*, finish row with 1 tr in 3rd ch of previous row. Repeat Rows 2 and 3.

Fish scales

Row 1: 3 ch, 3 tr in 1 st of foundation ch, miss 2 sts, 1 dc, * miss 2 sts, 5 tr in 1 st of foundation ch, miss 1 st, 1 dc*.

Row 2 and following rows: 3 ch, 3 tr inserting hook into back thread at the head of last dc of previous row, * 1 dc inserting hook into back thread at the head of 3rd tr, 5 tr inserting hook into back thread at the head of dc *. Finish row with 1 dc.

Clusters

Row 1: 2 ch, and for each cluster * (wrh, insert hook in 1 st of foundation ch, wrh, draw through a loop, wrh, draw through 2 loops on hook) 3 times into same st, wrh, draw through 4 loops on hook, 1 ch, miss 1 st of foundation ch*.

Row 2 and following rows: 2 ch, and for each duster insert hook in each ch space of previous row.

Brick stitch

Work 2 rows of Ridge Stitch

Row 3: 2 ch, * 3 dc in next 3 ch, insert hook through work in the last but one row, wrh, draw through a loop, wrh, draw through the last 2 loops, miss 1 ch*.

Row 4: 2 ch, dc to end of row.

Repeat Rows 3 and 4 but on odd rows move the pattern 2 sts forward.

Woven stitch

Row 1: 3 ch, ch tr in first ch, * insert hook through lower thread of h tr, wrh, draw through a loop, insert hook in next ch, wrh, draw through a loop wrh, draw through the 3 loops on hook.

Bushy stitch

Row 1: 2 ch, * miss 1 ch, 2 dc in next ch*.

Row 2 and following rows: 2 ch, * miss 1 st, 2 dc inserting hook under both horizontal loops of next st*.

Fancy crochet stitch

Row 1: 3ch, * (wrh, insert hook in next ch, wrh, draw through a loop, wrh, draw through 2 loops) 2 times into same st, wrh, draw through 4 loops on hook, 1 ch, miss 1 ch *. Finish row with 1 tr.

Row 2: ch * 1 dc in each motif, 1 dc in each space *.

Granite stitch

Row 1: 2 ch, * 1 dc, 1 ch, miss 1 st, 1 dc * to end of row.

Row 2 and following rows: 2 ch, * insert hook into ch space of previous row, wrh, draw through loop, wrh, draw through 2 loops on hook, 1 ch*.

Crochet drops

Row 1: ch 3, * 3 tr in 1 st, miss 2 sts *. Finish row with 3 tr in 1 st.

Row 2: 3 ch, * wrh, insert hook into back thread at the head of tr, wrh, draw through a loop, wrh, draw through 2 loops, repeat from to in next 2 tr, wrh, draw through the 4 loops on hook, 1 ch*. Repeat from Row 1, working tr in each st closing tr in each st closing the tr of previous row.

Mural stitch

Row 1: 4 ch, * 3 ch miss 3 ch 1 dc *.

Row 2: 4 ch, * 1 tr into first arc, 1 ch, 4 tr in next arc, 1 ch*.

Row 3: 1 ch, 3 ch, 1 dc (working each dc in ch space of previous row).

Repeat from row alternating motifs.

Pineapple stitch

Row 1: ch 2, * (wrh, insert hook in 1 ch, wrh, draw through a loop) 4 times into same st, wrh, draw through 8 loops, wrh, draw through the last 2 loops on hook, 1 ch, miss 1 ch*.

Row 2 and following rows: insert hook into 1 ch space of previous row.

Crochet small checks

Row 1: 5 ch, * (1 tr, 2 ch, 1 tr) into 1 ch st, miss 2 ch*.

Row 2: 3 ch, then work groups of 4 tr in each 2 ch space of previous row.

Repeat from Row 1, working tr separated by 2 ch between the groups of 4 tr.

Acacia stitch

Row 1: 3 ch, 1 tr, * 1 dc lengthen loop on hook, miss 3 sts, work (1 tr, 1 ch, 1 tr) into next st *. Finish row with 1 dc.

Row 2 and following rows: 3 ch, 1 tr in dc, * 1 dc in 1 ch space, lengthen loop on hook, work (1 tr, 1 ch, 1 tr) in dc*. Finish row with 1 dc in 3 ch space.

Judith stitch
Multiple of 4 +2.

Row 1: 2 ch, dc to end of row.

Row 2: 2 ch, * miss 1st, 1 tr in each of next 3 sts, insert hook in front of last 3 tr in missed st, wrh, draw through an elongated loop, wrh, draw through 2 loops on hook *. Finish row with 1 tr in last st.

Perforated stitch
Multiple of 6 + 3.

Row 1: 1 ch, 1 dc, * 1 ch, 3 dc, 2 ch, 3 dc *. Finish row with 2 dc.

Row 2 and following rows: 3 ch, * (2tr, 1 ch, 2 tr) in 2 ch space, (1 tr, 2ch, 1 tr) in 1 ch space*. Finish row with 1 tr in last ch space.

Hazel-nut stitch
Row 1: dc to end of row.

Row 2: 1 ch, 1 dc, * (wrh, insert hook in next st, wrh, draw through a loop, wrh, draw through 2 loops) 5 times into same st, wrh, draw through the 6 loops on hook, 2 dc*.

Double sale stitch
Multiple of 7 + 4.

Row 1: 1 ch, 1 dc, miss 2 sts, 3 tr in next st, * 3 ch, miss 3 sts, 1 dc, miss 2 sts, 3 tr in next st*.

Row 2 and following rows: 1 ch, 1 dc in first tr, 3 tr in dc, 3 ch, 1 dc in 3 ch space, 3 tr in dc.

Openwork stitch
Multiple of 13 + 1.

Row 1: 3 ch, tr to end of row.

Row 2: 3 ch, 3 tr, * 3 ch, miss 3 tr, 1 dc, 3 ch, miss 3 tr, 6 tr *. Finish row with 4 tr in 3rd ch.

Row 3: 3 ch, 3 tr, * 1 ch, 1 dc in first space, 3 ch, 1 dc in 2nd ch space, 1 ch, 6 tr*. Finish row with 4 tr as Row 2.

Row 4: 3 ch 3 tr, * 7 tr in 3 ch space, 6 tr *. Finish row with 4 tr.

Repeat from Row 2.

Treble arch stitch
Multiple of 6 + 1.

Row 1: 1 ch, 2 dc, * 3 ch, miss 3 sts, 3dc *, miss 3 sts, 2 dc.

Row 2: 1 ch, 1 dc, * 5 tr in 3 ch space, 1 dc in 2nd dc*.

Row 3: * 3 ch, 1 dc in each of 3 central tr*, 2 ch, 1 dc.

Row 4: 3 ch, 2tr in 2 ch space, * 1 dc in 2nd dc, 5 tr in 3 ch space *, 1 dc in 2nd dc, 3 tr in 3 ch space.

Row 5: 1 ch, 1 dc in each of first 2 tr, * 3 ch, 1 dc in each of 3 central tr*, 3 ch, 1 dc in last tr, 1 dc in last ch. Repeat from Row 2.

Stitch
Row 1: 2 ch, 1 dc, miss 1 st, 3 tr in next miss 1 dc, miss 1 st, 3 tr in next st*.

Row 2: 2 ch, 1 dc in 2nd tr, 3 tr in dc*

Row 3: 2 ch, 1 tr in 2nd tr, * (tr, 1 ch, 1 tr) in dc*.

Row 4: 2 ch, (1tr, 1 ch, 1 tr) in 1 ch space, * (2 tr, 1 ch, 1 tr) in next 1 ch space*. Finish row with 2 tr in last 1 ch space.

Alternate stitch
Odd number of stitches.

Row 1: 2 ch, * (1 dc, 1 ch, 1 dc) in next st, miss 1 st *. Finish row with 1 dc in last st.

Row 2 and following rows: 2 ch, * (1 dc, 1 ch, 1 dc) every 1 ch space *. Finish row with 1 dc in last.

Lozenge stitch

Multiple of 6 + 4.

Row 1: 4 ch, 2 tr in first st, * 1 ch, miss 3 sts, 1 dc, 1 ch, miss 2 sts, (1 tr, 2 ch, 2 tr) in next st, * 1 ch, miss 2 sts, 1 dc.

Row 2 and following rows: 4 ch, 2 tr in dc, * 1 ch, 1 dc in 2 ch space, 1 ch, (1 tr, 2 ch, 2 tr) in dc, 1 ch, 1 dc in 1 ch space of previous row.

Treble stitch

Row 1: 3 ch, (2 tr, 1 ch, 1 tr) in first st of foundation sh, * miss 3 sts, (3 tr, 1 ch, 1 tr) in next st *. To finish row, miss 2 st and work 1 tr in last st.

Row 2 and following rows: 3 ch, (2 tr, 1 ch, 1 tr) in first 1 ch space. Finish row with 1 tr ind 3rd ch.

Openwork stitch

Multiple of 7 + 2.

Row 1: 2 ch, *2 h.tr, 3 ch, miss 2 sts, 1 dc, 3 ch, miss 2 sts *. Finish row with 2 h.tr.

Row 2: 2 ch, * 2 h.tr, 3 ch, 1 dc in dc, 3 ch, 1 dc in same dc, 3 ch *. Finish row with 2 h.tr.

Row 3: 1 ch, 1dc in each 2 h.tr of previous row, 1 dc in 3 ch, 1 dc in each 2 h.tr of previous row, 1 dc in 3 ch space, 5 ch, 1 dc in next ch space, 1 dc in each 2 h.tr.

Row 4: 1 ch, * 2 dc, miss 1 st, 7 dc in 5 ch space, miss 1 st*. finish row with 2 dc.

Row 4: 2 ch, * 2 h.tr, 3 ch, miss 3 sts, 1 dc, 3 ch, miss 3 sts *. Finish row with 2 h.tr.

Row 6: repeat from Row 2.

Relief treble

Worked over an odd number of attaches

Row 1: 3 ch, tr to end of row.

Row 2: 1 ch, dc to end of row.

Row 3: 2 ch, * wrh, insert hook from right to left in 1 tr of Row 1, wrh, draw through a long loop, wrh, draw through the 3 loops on hook. 1 tr in next dc*.

Row 4: 1 ch, * 1 dc in top st of relief tr, 1 dc between the relief tr and tr*.

Row 5: Repeat from Row 3.

Relief treble

This stitch is worked like Relief Treble I, but beginning on Row 5 work the tr and the relief tr alternately.

Relief checks

Multiple of 3.

Row 1: 3 ch, tr to end of row.

Row 2 : 1 ch, dc to end of row.

Row 3: 2 ch, * 3 tr, 3 lengthened tr inserting hook from right to left in tr of first row*.

Row 4: 1 ch, dc to end of row.

Row 5: Repeat from Row 3 working the tr and the lengthened tr alternately.

Granit stitch

On an even number of stitches on a foundation chain

Row 1 and following rows: 1 ch, *1 dc, 1 tr*.

Fancy stitch

Row 1: 2 ch, * wrh, insert hook in first st, wrh, draw through a loop, wrh, draw through 2 loops, wrh, miss 1 st, insert hook in next st, wrh, draw through a loop, wrh, draw through 2 loops, wrh, draw through the last 3 loops on hook, 1 ch. Repeat from * inserting hook the first time in the st where the 2nd loop was drawn.

Row 2 and following rows: Repeat Row 1 drawing the first loop through the last ch of previous row, and the next loops through the ch of previous row.

Triangle stitch

Row 1: 5 ch, * miss 2 sts, (1 tr, 2 ch, 1 tr) in next st*.

Row 2 and following rows: 5 ch, 1 tr in 2 ch space, (1 tr, 2 ch, 1 tr) in next 2 ch space *. Finish row with (1 tr, 2 ch, 1 tr) in ch space.

Mat stitch

Row 1: 1 ch, 1 h.tr, * miss 1 st, 1 h.tr in next st. 1h. tr inserting hook between 2 preceding h.tr*. To finish row, miss 1 st and work 1 h.tr in last st.

Row 2: 1 ch, dc to end of row, inserting hook through horizontal thread at head of each st of previous

Bodkin stitch

Multiple of 10 + 2.

Row 1: 2 ch, 2 tr, * miss 3 sts, (2 tr, 2 ch, 2 tr) in next st, miss 3 sts, 3 tr*.

Row 2 and following rows: 2 ch, 2 tr, * (2 tr, 2 ch, 2 tr) in 2 ch space, 1 tr, in each of the 3 tr*.

River stitch

This stitch is worked with a strip of cardboard on a row of dc.

Row 1: lengthen the loop on hook to the height of the cardboard placed between this loop and the thread, wrh, draw through the long loop, 1 ch, * insert hook into next stitch, wrh, draw through a loop and lengthen it to the height of the cardboard, wrh, draw through the long loop on hook, wrh, draw through the 2 loops on hook *.

When inserting the hook, be careful not to lengthen the loop that is there. For this, slip the hook to bring to the height of the next stitch, and lower the thread in order to catch it more easily behind the cardboard to make the wrh. Of course, the cardboard must be moved progressively as you work between the River Stitch pattern, work 1 or several rows of dc as needed.

Busy stitch

Worked over an even number of stitches.

Row 1: 1 ch, 1 dc, * 2 dc in next st, miss 1 st, finish row with 1 dc.

Row 2 and following rows: as Row 1, working the 2 dc under both horizontal loops of the last dc of each group of 2 dc. Finish row with 1 dc in ch at beg. Of previous row.

Fancy motifs

Multiple of 3 + 1.

Row 1: 1 ch, * 1 dc, 1 h.tr, 1 tr) in 1 st, miss 2 sts*.

Finish row with 1 dc in last st.

Row 2 and following rows: as Row 1 inserting hook in dc of previous row.

Monique stitch

Multiple of 3.

Row 1: 2 ch, 1 h.tr, miss 1 st, * (1 dc, 1 ch, 1 tr) in next st, miss 2 sts, *. Finish row with 1 dc.

Row 2 and following rows: as Rows: as Row 1 but working (1 dc, 1 ch, 1 tr) in every 1 ch space of previous row. Finish row with 1 dc in 2 ch space at beg. of previous row.

Striped curve

Multiple of 6 + 4.

Row 1: 2 ch, * 1 dc, 1 ch, miss 2 sts, (1 tr, 1 ch, 1 tr) in next st, 1 ch, miss 2 sts *, 1 dc, 1 ch, miss 2 sts, (1 tr, 1 ch, 1 tr) in last st.

Row 2 and following rows: 2 h, * 1 dc in 1 ch space between 2 tr, 1 ch, (1 tr, 1 ch, 1 tr) in dc. 1 ch*. Finish row 1 dc, 1 ch, 1 tr, 1 ch, 1 tr.

Fancy lozenge stitch

Multiple of 8 + 1.

Row 1: 1 ch, * 1 dc, 4 ch, miss 3 sts *, 1 dc.

Row 2: 3 ch, * 4 tr in first space, (2 ch, 1 dc) in next space, 2 ch . 4 tr in first space, (2 ch, 1 dc) in next space, 2 ch*. Finish row with 1 tr in dc.

Row 3: 5 ch, * 1 dc in space before the 4 tr, 4 ch, 1 dc after the 4 tr, 4 ch *. Finish row with 1 dc in 3 ch space

Row 4: 4 ch, * 1 dc first space, 2 ch, 4 tr in next space, 2 ch *. Finish row with 4 tr in last space. 2 ch *. Finish row with 4 tr in last space.

Row 5: 5 ch, * 1 dc after the 4 tr, 4 ch, 1 dc before the next 4 tr, 4 ch*. Finish row with 1 dc in 4 ch space.

Repeat from Row 2.

Multiple of 4 + 1.

Row 1: 3 ch, 1 dc * 3 ch (small arc), 1 dc, 3 ch (big arc), miss 2 sts 1 dc.

Row 2 and following rows: 3 ch, 1 dc in the big arc, 3 ch, 1 dc in the same arc, 3 ch, miss the small arc*. Finish row with 1 dc in 3 ch space at beg. of previous row.

The friezes

Multiple of 3 + 1.

Row 1: 1 ch, h.tr to end of row.

Row 2: 1 ch, * 1 dc, 3 ch, miss 2 sts *. Finish row with 1 dc.

Row 3: * 3 ch, 1 dc in space *, 2 ch, 1 dc.

Row 4: 2 ch. 2 h.tr in first space, 3 h.tr in following spaces. Finish row with 2 h.tr in last space.

Row 5: Repeat from Row 2.

Close scallops

Multiple of 6 + 4.

Row 1: 3 ch, 2 tr in same st, miss 2 sts, 1 dc, * miss 2 sts, 4 tr in next st, miss 2 sts, 1 dc*.

Row 2 and following rows: 3 ch, 2 tr in dc, * 1 dc between the 2nd and 3rd tr, 4 tr, in next dc*. Finish row with 1 dc in the 3 ch space at beg of previous row.

Marion stitch

Worked over an odd number of stitches.

Row 1: 2 ch, 1 tr, * 1 tr I same st as preceding tr, wrh, insert hook in same st, wrh, draw through a loop, wrh, draw through 2 loops, wrh, miss 1 st, insert hook in next st, wrh, draw through a loop, wrh, draw through 2 loops, wrh, draw through the last 3 lops on hook.

Row 2 and following rows: insert hook into back thread at the head of the central tr of each group of 3 tr.

Lunar stitch

Multiple of 3 + 1.

Row 1: 1 ch, dc to end of row.

Row 2: 1 ch, 1 dc, * 2 ch, miss 2 sts, 1 dc*.

Row 3: 1 ch, 1 dc, * 1 h.tr in first missed st of previous row, 1 dc in space, 1 dc in dc*.

Row 4: 3 ch, * 1 dc in h.tr, 2 ch *. Finish row with 1 ch, 1 dc.

Row 5: as Row 3, beginning row with 1 ch, 1 dc in space, 1 dc, and finishing row with 1 dc in space.

Row 6: as Row 4, beginning row with 2 ch, and finishing row with 1 dc in 1 ch space.

Row 7: as Row 3, beginning row with 1 ch, 1 h.tr.

Row 8: Repeat from Row 2.

Macrame

Macrame is the ancient art of knotting, derived from netting and sailors' knots, and the decoration of fringes left after weaving. The equipment needed is a piece of board, a few pins, a pair of scissors and some thread. The knotting is done with the fingers.

Knotting board

This is a piece of board, not less than 8 by 12 inches, on which the work is mounted. It should be rigid, but pliable enough to insert pins. The best kinds are balsa wood, cork, asbestos, wood composition or strong foam plastic.

The knotting board can be used on the knee, or propped against a table. Arrange it so that the knots can be pulled tight without upsetting the work.

Knotting material

In the past only strong, tightly twisted, smooth thread was used for macrame work but since the recent revival of the craft a great variety of materials has been used - nylon, string, wool, cotton, jute, knitted rayon, lengths of fabric, raffia and ribbon.

The braids and the sampler are made with macrame string, which is the easiest thread to manage.

Pins

These can be ordinary dressmakers' pins, but larger pins with bigger heads are better. A lot of macrame workers use T-pins.

To begin

Cut a piece of string about 8 inches long. Make an overhand knot at each hand and pin it to your working surface. This piece is now called a holding cord. Cut two lengths of string each 4 feet long and double them. Loop each end onto the holding cord as shown. This knot is a reversed double half stitch, also called a Larks Head Knot, and is always used for this purpose. This process of fastening threads onto the holding cord is called 'setting on thread'.

The flat knot

This is made in two halves, each called half knot. Start by making a braid of half knots. With two double lengths of string there will be four threads hanging down. Number these from 1 to 4.

1 and 4 will be the knotting threads and the two centre lengths, 2 and 3, are the core of the braid. These threads are not used for knotting but are knotted over. Tuck them into your belt, or clip them into a bulldog clip and tie this around your waist to keep them taut.

Keeping these core threads taut, pick up the first thread and lay it over the core from left to right. Lift the fourth thread over the tail of the first thread, under the core threads 2 and 3, and up through the loop formed by the threads. Pull the knot firm as you push it up to the heading.

You have now made a half knot. Continue to make these knots bringing the left hand thread over each time. You will find that the braid twists of its own accord.

When the braid is ready to twist, let it turn over the right. Lay No 1 thread to the right and bring No 4 underneath to work to the left. Continue knotting as before, but laying No 4 thread across the core threads to begin the knot. After a few more knots, the braid will begin to turn again. The number of knots before it turns depends on the thickness of the thread, but is usually between four and seven.

You have now made a spiral braid of half knots. Work a few inches of this knot, then learn the other half of the knot. Pick up the fourth thread and lay it towards the left over 2 and 3. Lift the first thread and lay it over the end of the fourth thread, under the two central threads, and up through the loop formed by threads 3 and 4. Work a few inches of this kind and see the cord spiral to the left.

These two half knots worked alternatively form the flat knot. A cord made of flat knots will be flat, whereas either of the half knots worked continually will make a spiral cord.

Flat knots can be varied by Picots. In a braid of flat knots, each alternate flat knot is made a little way down the core threads, and then pushed up to form loops on either side.

When working braids of half knots or flat knots, the knotting threads will need to be seven or eight times longer than the core threads.

Each flat knot comes out alternately, that is to say that the first one ties with its loop to the left and the second to the right. If you have to stop in the middle of a braid of flat knots, and wonder which half knot to begin with then you return to it, the thread coming out from under the loop is the one that goes over the core threads next.

Bundling threads

When threads are too long to manage easily, wind them into bundles on the first two fingers. Start from the end and wind the thread up to eight inches from the holding cord. Secure in the middle with a rubber band. Wound this way, the thread can be gently pulled out as the work proceeds. Keep the bundles near to the work and in the right order.

Overhand knot

This is the same knot used at either end of the holding cord. It is often used to finish work, over one thread or any number of threads.

You have now learned to make overhand knots, to fix a holding cord, to set double threads with reversed half hitches, to make a braid of half knots, to make a braid of flat knots and how to bundle threads. With the help of these stitches, you can make a number of articles, e.g. rayon cord necklace with beads. For this you need 14 yards of tubular rayon cord and 5 beads with a large enough hole to make two threads. Cut two threads, 16 feet long, and two threads 4 feet long. Lay threads level at the top of the knotting board and make an overhand knot 5 inches from the ends. Pin this knot on the board.

Keep the shorter threads taut. These are the core threads. Pull the longer threads into bundles and secure with rubber bands. Work 6 inches of half knots.

Pass core threads of half knots through a bead, let outer threads encircle bead, then continue working half knots. With two inches of half knots in between each, thread on remaining four beads. Work on six inches half knots.

Undo knot at top end of work. Make an overhand knot over all 8 threads. Leave 2 inches for a tassel, cut ends.

CHAPTER-15

Flowers in the Home

Man has always tried to search for beauty and perfection in different objects. As a matter of fact, fusion and art is essential for his living. The beauty, form, colour and scent of flowers are among the most transient of things, yet their influence on our lives is great. In this chapter we will show how flowers can be arranged effectively, efficiently and economically.

Vases

The suitability or otherwise of vases is a subjective matter. However, a few points should be kept in mind:

- One should ascertain whether the container will hold water and if not is it possible to make it watertight.
- The container should stand firmly when filled with water and holding flowers.
- The container should be in harmony with the flowers one uses.
- The vase and the flowers should be in harmony with the surroundings.

Vases thus hold support for plant material and water. These could be home made or bought.

Kinds of vases and their uses

- Crystal glass vases are suitable for delicate flowers.
- Wooden containers are suitable for fruit and vegetable arrangements.
- Moulded plastic containers are increasingly being used these days.
- Candleholders, conch, seashells, corals, wire, glass and natural wood also make beautiful vases.
- Baskets vary in design, shape, colour and size. Generally speaking the design pattern for flower arrangements in baskets is either horizontal or vertical and it is of utmost importance that balance should be kept in mind (particularly visual balance). Baskets that do hold water can be fitted with bowls or tins on the inside that would serve the purpose. If these are not available it can be lined with a plastic sheet, pleated neatly to the inside shape and then cut around to just below the edge of the basket. Cellotape can be used to preserve the desired shape.

Japanese Flower Arrangement and its Requirements

Ikebana or the art of Japanese flower arrangement began with the making of an arrangement worthy of temple offering. The poetic imagination and ardent love of nature would strive to create a composition that would be so beautiful so as to elevate the thoughts and emotions of the beholder. Their demand was simplicity and aesthetic beauty.

Points to be kept in mind

- Moribana - In this arrangement needle point holders are used in combination with comparatively low receptacles.
- Nageire - No needle point holders are used. This style takes advantage of high vases.
- There are four basic styles of moribana and nageire:
  a) Vertical style
  b) Oblique style
  c) Horizontal style
  d) Falling style
- There should always be three branch groups in both the moribana and the negeire. They are:
  a) The first branch group (high)
  b) The second branch group (medium)
  c) Third (low)

Besides these three main groups one can use any number of subsidiary branches which should be lower than the three cardinal branches.

- The general rule regulating the length of the highest branch is
  a) To make a spectacularly large arrangement 2 (A+B)
  b) Medium height arrangement (A+B) $\underline{A+B}$ 2
  c) Small arrangement (A+B)

Here
A = Width of the vase
B = Depth of the vase

Utensils

- **Pruning shears**: At the hardware shop ask for the 'warabite' type shears and select the one which you think is right for your hand.
- **Kenzan (needle point holders)**: Round shaped or crescent shaped kenzan are the commonest. If one wants to use 'big materials' one should use the rectangle shaped one. In case kenzan is not available, one could use several stones the size of ones fist or smaller.
- **Saws**: are useful in cutting hard branches.
- **Water spray (pump):** can make the Ikebana lively and vivid.
- **Needle repairer**: are useful to correct bent needles of the kenzan.
- **Wires**: are used to tie materials together.
- **Pebbles and sand**: if used to cover the kenzan help make the arrangemnt look more natural.
- **Water change pump** is used to change water in containers.
- **Scissors**
  a) Leaves – in the course of trimming leaves give varying accents to those that are to be kept.
  b) Branches – make enough room between branches for concentrated effect.

To bend
a) hard branches - make a few slits at the stem's end and bend the branch with gradual force until the desired effect is achieved.

b) Flowers - crush or twist the part that you want to bend with your fingers.

Thus, one should always remember that successful arrangements are the results of a harmonious marriage of the materials, containers and the mode of living in which one finds oneself.

Western flower arrangements

Nobody really knows when the idea of using flowers for indoor decoration, as against giving them in the garden, was first introduced into English homes. A Dutchman called Levinus Lemnius wrote in 1560 about the 'nosegays' that he found in English homes. Flower arrangement in the west can therefore be thought to be 400 years old. During the Victorian period, the making of posies - tight little bunches of small sweet-scented spring or summer flowers -was one of the accomplishments of fashionable young ladies who always attended social functions with one in there hand. This no doubt was the origin of the posy style of small flower arrangements, which has remained popular ever since. Around Victorian age fashion magazine adviced: 'There is no doubt that arranging flowers according to contrast, or their complimentary colours, is more pleasing to the eye than placing them according to their harmonies. Therefore a blue flower should be placed next to an orange one, whilst red or white flowers should have abundant foliage near them'.

During the renaissance flower arrangement closely followed the trend in art and other forms of design. Urns and beautifully shaped pitchers, vases made from pottery, venetian glass and gols and silver were used to display unclustered arrangements of fruits, berries, cones, leaves and flowers. The main characteristic differentiating the western style of flower arrangement from the Japanese style is that an abundance of flowers are used as against the economy of the Ikebana style.

Indian flower arrangements

Long before the western and Japanese styles came into prominence, Indians knew about the fragrance and beauty of flowers. Whether in garlands draped around the figure of a deity, a fragrant string of Jasmines in a lady's coiffure or in a colourful rangoli at the entrance of the house on festive occasions made of different coloured flower petals. Floral embellishments have been a part of the life style of the people. Baskets, small earthen pots in which Jasmines and lotus petals float in the water are some of the ways in which flowers form a part of the Indian milieu.

Rangoli a traditional Indian art is also used for flower arrangements. A floral rangoli as it is called fives a warm and welcoming look. The pattern that one decides depends on one's imagination and creativity. Usually the flowers used are of the same size. However, if different sizes are used then it should be used to create a pattern. The flowers used however should be fresh and clean.

Flower arrangement for the table

- **Buffet table**: an arrangement for the buffet table should not interfere with the pitching up or putting down of plates, dishes, glasses and cutlery. They should occupy as little base as possible. Tall arrangements particularly should have a good firm base so that there is no danger of it being knocked over. One very simple method of decorating a buffet table is to use wire or champagne bottles and coloured candles clustered with small flowers. Between these spaced at suitable intervals small arrangements in little bowls or oasis cups again with coloured candles are placed. The whole arrangement is then linked together with ivy or other creeper trails.

- **Sit down dinner:** the arrangement should not be too tall as this would obstruct the view of the guests. The flowers and foliage should be in perfect condition and clean. Perfumed flowers should not be used. Colour scheme and design of the flower arrangement should match the colour and design in the crockery and napkins.
- **Birthdays and anniversaries:** Lily, Amaryllis, Tuberose, Cainalion and roses are used.

Tips for keeping flowers fresh longer

Flowers tend to wilt because they are unable to obtain sufficient water through the stems to overcome the evaporation through the leaves and flowers. To keep flowers fresh for longer one should adopt the following methods:

- Multiplication of bacteria in the water clog and destroy the stem tubes. To overcome this one could add salt, charcoal or listerine in the water in small quantities. This would slow down bacterial growth.
- Flowers should be cut either early in the morning or after sun down.
- The stems should be cut at an angle to increase water intake.
- The stems should be cut and water changed daily.
- Squeeze jelly like sap from stems of flowers like Hyacinth to facilitate drawing water.
- Flowers like Gardenias should be wrapped in wet tissue before display and sprayed on while on display. This is because these flowers take water only through their petals.
- Cut flowers at proper stage of development, i.e. Dahlias when fully open.
- Scrub containers clean, and avoid aluminum containers.
- Flowers should be kept cool and moist before use. They should be kept away from sun light and drafts.
- Ferns should be kept under water for 3-12 hours before use.
- Flowers that absorb a lot of moisture should be kept in vases containing at least 6 inches of water.
- Collect flowers and plant materials from areas where the soil is moist and plants are growing under sun light.
- Leaves, buds, half open and full bloom flowers should be collected and foliage stripped of lower stem.
- Charring method – Carbonise the stem of the plant with the help of gas, alcohol lamp or candle flame. Wrap all the plant with paper except the stem. When the end part is sealed black, put in water.
- Hot water method – Wrap the whole plant except the stem with paper and put in hot water. This methods is the most suitable for stop stem materials.
- Dipping in water – Dip plants into water upside down. Wrap newspaper around the plants while taking out of the water. Wet the newspaper and keep in a place where it is not exposed to light or wind.
- Slitting method – Cut many slits or crush the end part of the plant stems with scissors after cutting them in water.

- Chemical applying method – Chemicals such as salt, baking powder, burnt alum are used. Dissolve these chemicals in the water of the flower vase used.
- Chemical method – materials are placed in chemicals for sterilization from 10-20 minutes after having been cut in water. Chemicals such as alcohol, acetic acid, peppermint oil are used.
- Salt sprinkling method – sprinkle salt around the stamens or stick toothpicks in the center of flowers liable to fall easily.
- Water pumping method – with plants such as lotuses, lilies, water, strong tea or other solution e.g. tobacco stock i.e. a liquid made by putting cigarette tobacco in a cloth or cotton in the water are forced into the stem with a water pump.
- Sprinkle water only on the leaves and not on flowers.
- Put ice cubes in water for hot summer months.
- In order to make your flower arrangement last longer, try to keep it away from windows or fire so that they will not suffer from sun, heat or blowing wind.
- Putting an aspirin tablet or a pinch of salt in the water keeps the flowers stay fresh for longer.
- Avoid giving flowers rude temperature shocks.
- While buying flowers take care to pick up flowers with green stem.
- Pick buds or flowers, which are not fully bloomed.

Indoor Plants

Lack of space and inaccessibility to land and soil has enthused many to keep indoor plants. However one should consider the conditions under which the plants would be kept and then select the varieties accordingly. The following factors play an important role: -

- Soil and containers: a good soil compost is essential for growing a house plant. This should consist of 2 parts garden soil, one part each of leaf mould or FYM and sand. Houseplants can be grown in a sterile medium if they are fed with a nutrient solution e.g. vermiculate. Some plants however can be grown even in water without any soil e.g. money plant. A wide variety of containers can be used for growing house plants e.g. clay, plastic pots and so on.
- Humidity: Many plants require high humidity. Misting the plants with water

can do this. Spraying the foliage with water and putting the pots in bigger containers filled with water. One could also use room humidifiers.

- Gas: The fumes from gas used for cooking make it difficult to grow pot plants. However, some plants are much more resistant than others. It is essential to have free movement of air where the plants are kept.
- Re-potting: when the roots of the plant start growing through the drainage holes (i.e pot bound) they have to be taken out, the longer roots trimmed, outer rtoots cut and re-potted in a bigger pot with fresh potting mixture.
- Prunning: emables to maintain the desirable shape by removing over grown shoots. Diseased and insect damaged branches should be removed.
- Window boxes: may be used outside the house for decorative accents. These can be made of wood or metal. Hanging baskets can be used as substitutes. Plants should be selected on the basis of shade or sun in the location chosen.
- Watering: careful watering is essential, as these plants are grown in the shade. The plants should be watered only when the soil is dry or once in 2-3 days depending on the weather and the variety of the plant grown. Lukewarm should be used. Newly potted plants need less water than the older ones. By tapping the upper rim with a knife handle helps to judge the moisture of the soil. If it gives a clear ring the soil is dry and needs water. If the ring is dull and heavy, the soil is moist.
- Light: The plants should not be exposed to direct sunlight as ot may result in scorched leaves. However, indirect sunlight is essential. Thus indoor plants can be placed in partial shade or under flourescent light. However, it is important to remember that too little light can bresult in light coloured leaves and spindly growth. Generally east windows that receive full sun until noon are best suited for pot plants.
- Temperature: On cold nights, plants should be moved away from windows. The temperature of plants is more variable than that of light. The ideal temperature range should be around 15-20 C during daytime and never below 20 C at night.
- Manuring: Potted plants that are planted in a good soil do not require further fertilizing for one or two months. Fresh manure can be soaked in water for a few days and then the liquid taken off to feed house plants. Plants should be fed with liquid fertilizer only during their growing season. It is most effective to add fertilizer whwn soil is mosit. Spraying the manure is also beneficial.
- Cleaning: Dust that settles on the plants must be cleaned with thin cloth and drooping branches should be staked. Rubbing mineral oil on leaves helps brighten them.

Insects that attack household plants

- Red spider mite: are small in size and difficult to dtect. However if a plant has been attacked by it the top of the leaves will be a molted grey and yellow. While the underside will have a crusty webby appearance. Spraying the leaves with a stream of water will help reduce the damage. Pesticides may also be used.
- Aphids (plant lice): are small green,

brown or black insects. They can be controlled by using nicotine sprays.
- Scale: attack woody plants. They are difficult to eradicate and one should use pesticides.
- Mealy bug: If a plant is badly infested with mealy bugs, it is best to discard them. Oil emulsion sprays and nicotine soap will help check this pest. If the infestation is light, one could use a camel hair brush dipped in alcohol and touch it to the backs of the insect. However if an oil emulsion or nicotine soap spray is used the plant should be taken out for spraying and washed thoroughly after an hour.

Plant use requirements
- Tub plants: Big plants are suitable for lobby decoration or should be placed on floor homes for interior decoration.
- Planters: Plants suitable for small containers, dish gardens, small pots or for edges of interior planting boxes or beds. Care should be taken in using these plants in combination so that all plants used have identical light and moisture requiremnts.
- Vines: Plants that require support e.g. totem poles. These could be used for ground covers in the interior of planter boxes or as trailing plants on the edge.They could also be used over the edges of interior planter boxes.

Given below is a list of plant groupings for indoors.

What Flowers Say...

Acacia: secret love
Alyssum Sweet: incomparable worth
Ambrosia: your love is reciprocated
Aster: symbol of love
Azalea: fragile passion, take care of yourself for me
Bridal Pink Rose: happy love
Camellia (Pink): longing for you
Camellia (Red): you're a flame in my heart
Camellia (White): exquisite loveliness
Carnation (Red): divine love
Carnation (Solid Colour): yes
Chinese Rose: ever new beauty
Chrysanthemum (Red): love
Convolvulus (Pink): tender affection
Daffodil: unrequited love
Fern-Maidenhair: secret bond of love
Everlasting Daisy: continuing pleasure
Forget-Me-Not: constant love
Gardenia: secret love
Heliotrope: faithful devotion
Hibiscus: rare beauty
Honeysuckle: generous and devoted affection
Hyacinth (Blue): constancy
Iris: you mean so much to me
Rose (Thornless): love at first sight
Lily (White): it's heavenly to be with you
Orchid: love, beauty and refinement
Pansy: dedicated to St. Valentine means consideration
Ivy: wedded love and fidelity
Primrose: I can't live without you
Ranunculus: radiant charm
Tuberoses: illicit pleasure
Tulip (Red): declaration of love

Tulip (General): perfect lover
Tulip (Varigated): beautiful eyes
Violet (Blue): faithful devotion
Violet (White): let's take a chance on happiness
Rose (Red): the symbol of love
Rose (White): I am worthy of you
Rose (Hibiscus): delicate beauty
Rose (Pink): perfect happiness believe me
Rosebud (Moss): confession of love
Snowdrop: hope
Spider Flower: elope with me
Sweet Pea: hints at delicious pleasure
Narcissus: stay as sweet as you are
Lilac (Purple): speaks the first emotions of love
Lily of the Valley: increased happiness
Jonquil: I seek your affection

■■

CHAPTER-16
Interpersonal Relationships

If a family is to be considered the most important and basic unit of society, then the husband-wife unit forms the mainstay of this unit. A happy union between a man and woman is the starting point for a happy family. While at one time marriage was treated as a lifelong partnership between a man, a woman and their families, today many splinters are wrecking this relationship. Gone are the days when marriage was almost a master-slave relationship. A woman's identity was not synonymous with that of her husband's.

In some communities in India, a girl was given a new name once she was married and in symbolically throwing rice behind her when she left her parental home, she was supposed to forget both her life and those she left behind in her parental home. In the early decades of 20th century Bengal, for instance, a wife was expected to eat the leftovers from her husband's plate! Today, times and concepts have changed both in India and particularly in the West.

With education and as a hangover from the women's liberation movement of the late 60s and early 70s in the West, many thoughts and ideas have changed and at the turn of the 21st century the man-woman relationship stands challenged on all sides. This is especially true of the West where with increasing economic freedom of women, the decrease in social prejudices, and the move to make procreation a scientific system whereby a baby can be selected from a sperm bank and fertilised in a test tube, the increase in hostility between the sexes, has resulted in men and women becoming alienated from each other. The western concept of marriage has also changed and with 50 per cent divorce rate and with divorce laws heavily in favour of women, men are wary of making a commitment.

While the birth control pill gave women a great deal of liberty, it did not give her either stability or security. Man had a good time in any case, as he was able to drift in and out of relationships without getting tied down. Another trend was an increase in gay and lesbian relationships. Perhaps having found that men and women are basically incompatible, they formed partnerships with others of the same sex as social taboos and restrictions have been breaking down in Europe and America, especially since the hippie movement in the sixties where a whole generation of young people opted out of the straight-laced, rigid and competitive success-oriented society of that time. Live-in relationships, children born out of wedlock and a complete absence of any sexual restraint seemed to be the order of the day. With the AIDS explosion of the mid-80s and 90s and faced with high divorce rates, disturbed children and rampant drug abuse in all sections of society, a new era of conservatism has begun in Europe and America. Those who smoke are regarded as *pariahs* and there is a social movement to curb teenage pregnancies and encourage monogamous relationships. At the same time, men and women have become virtually hostile towards each other, which is why the gay and lesbian movement has not died out.

Women no longer want to be treated as a sex object and hence they are striving hard towards gaining employment and economic freedom. The traditional role in which the man was the breadwinner and the woman was the homemaker became topsy-turvy in which many men becoming househusbands and women earned high salaries in the corporate world. The quality of relationships had also undergone a change. Women no longer had to be gentle and caring—they were to be aggressive and articulate.

Some of these changes and attitudes have also affected the man-woman relationship in India. While in some societies, such as amongst the tribals in the North-East and in the matriarchal system of Kerala, women always played a major role. Some of the younger generation in the cities aped the Western norms by living in and demanding complete equality in the man-woman relationship. Predictably, man of these relationships break up as there is no question of there being mathematical equality in a relationship. The relationship between a man and a woman is a delicate one requiring great love, adjustment and constant communication. It should also be based on reality and not on a mythical image or concept which one may have about one's spouse.

What does a husband mean to a woman? To answer the question she expects him to provide for her, give her a respectable place in society, be a help mate and companion as also be the father of her children. These are not temporary needs and must be met everyday throughout life. Marriage is a lifelong union between a man and a woman and while there may be a few sparks of friction from any such relationship, by and large, despite all odds, the path of married life has to be negotiated hand in hand with each partner understanding the needs of the other.

Marriages may be arranged in which case the parents select a life partner who is of the same caste, community and economic background. It was seen as a merger of two families. Today, unfortunately, dowry has started playing a very detrimental role in the selection of a life partner. A marriage which is based on such greed and demand begins on an inauspicious note resulting in friction and bad feeling from the very outset. The ultimate degradation of a dowry fuelled marriage is when the bride is burnt by her inlaws for failing to bring in an adequate dowry. The ever-increasing demands of those parents whose sons are doctors, govt. officers, engineers, etc., have resulted in many girls seeking the career option so that their parents are not forced to pawn everything to get them married.

In love marriages, where the couple meet each other either in college or at the work place also does not guarantee hundred per cent success. Many marriages fail due to high expectations, unrealistic standards, lack of tact and understanding, intolerance and selfishness. Many relationships falter due to undue parental interference. Hence, whatever may be said about the subject, success of every marriage still depends on each partners' attitude. If you are to make the best of it, you must resolve to give it all you can. One's personal life, of which marriage is the bedrock, is most important to one's happiness. Therefore, no effort should be spared by either party to make a success of the relationship. True love, affection, care and commitment is never a waste—it will always come back to you manifold.

Love is said to bind a couple in marriage; it means different things to different people. To be everlastingly satisfying, love can be defined as the emotion that encourages intelligent self-expression with a partner and creates a congenial atmosphere in which the couple find greater happiness together than what they could have found separately. This emotion grows gradually in intensity and is based on patience and mutual understanding. A fundamental difference between a Western marriage and Indian one is that in the former, wedding is the culmination of love and thereafter the road ahead is often rocky and fraught with discord. In the case of the latter, love happens gradually and often even after one is married. Thus, marriage is not the culmination, but the beginning of a supportive relationship.

In analysing why some of the briefest marriages are those that follow a long period of cohabitation, Germaine Greer one of the chief architects of the women's liberation movement says that the dynamic of mutual accommodation that propelled a couple's informal cohabitation is unnecessary once marriage has confined them. As both are bound, the power will come to be concentrated on that person less prepared to take advantage of the situation, and that is the male partner. Having been so lucky as to acquire a wife, he begins to take the liberties that husbands have traditionally taken, comes and goes as he pleases, spends more time outside the connubial home, spends more money on himself, leaves off the share of the housework that he may have formerly done.'

'She sees her job as making him happy; he feels that in marrying her he has done all that is necessary to make her happy. The less she expected it, the more generous he feels for having done it. To her anxious question, 'Do you love me?' he has an easy answer 'Of course, married you didn't I?'

For a partnership to be truly happy and successful there should be an effort to please each other. While traditionally women were brought up to believe that their salvation lay in a marriage, boys today should also be brought up to respect women and to realise that a happy union forms the basis for a balanced and secure future.

Pleasing One's Spouse

Husband

1. Since in most conventional marriages, a man is older than his wife and since men are traditionally believed to be more balanced and in control of their emotions, it should devolve on him to be mature and understanding.
2. He should have a respect for women their physiology, psychology and thinking patterns. Instead of making disparaging sexist comments, a man should attempt to understand his wife not only as a person but also as a woman.
3. Women expect a high degree of communication and love and will never be content with a spouse whose idea of love is a few indelicate grunts in bed. Women need to be wooed with loving words and loving gestures such as kisses and cuddles which give her reassurance that her husband loves her and is not treating her as an object to satiate his sexual appetites.
4. Be an effective communicator - the strong silent man image be macho on the screen but it leads to unnecessary misunder-standings in real life. If you do not like something express yourself

but do so calmly and without resorting to either harsh words or biting sarcasm.

5. A sense of humour is a great asset and it is often suggested that a man who can make a woman laugh wins her heart. Sometimes in the tedious routine of daily life, there is nothing like humour to defuse the tension.

6. Try to be helpful in domestic matters, without interferring unduly and making tactless remarks to your wife. Help in repairs, shopping whenever required.

7. Self-control and self-restraint are great assets. If one feels like making a nasty comment - don't. Nothing can hurt like unkind words, which, like the sped arrow can never be taken back.

8. Do not hesitate to apologise if the situation so demands. It cleanses the atmosphere and ennobles the person who can accept his mistake.

9. Be a sport, be active and lively. Don't always refuse to go out and meet friends, go to a party, family gathering or a restaurant. A common complaint of too many wives is that her husband just likes to spend his holiday eating and sleeping. While undoubtedly one may be tired of working, travelling and eating out while at work, surely, the family should get something more than barking orders, sarcastic comments and a snore. Time spent together outside the home is important.

10. The days of a man being the tyrannical head of the house are virtually over. One should command rather than demand respect. There should be no reason to adopt rigid stances on domestic matters. Rather there should be a consensual approach whereby problems are tackled by mutual discussion.

11. Utmost tact has to be exerted while being the man-in-middle of wife-mother conflict. While lots of men adopt an ostrich policy whereupon they ignore any conflict between wife and mother, there has to be some intervention when either of the ladies concerned becomes obnoxious. A word in time will save nine later on.

Wives

1. A lot of men perceive women to be nagging, suspicious, moody, unreasonable and unduly materialistic. Behave in a manner that changes this stereotype. Dignity, self-respect and self-control will earn you lifelong respect.

2. Never fight over money and avoid unnecessary extravagances if your husband has a fixed salaried income. Try to manage within the budget and put off purchasing what is beyond one's reach. Remember that material goods are not worth fighting over.

3. Try to understand the male psyche and read marriage manuals to gain a better understanding.

4. While women are good communicators, there is a time and place for everything. There is no sense in greeting your husband with a mouthful of endless chatter as soon as he returns home from the office. The problem and travails of the day can be discussed later over a cup of tea, when the man will be in a more responsive frame of mind.

5. Be obliging and gracious if your husband wants you to cook a special dish, accompany him to a social function or entertain guests or his family. Do not get carried away by feminist rhetoric and look for

mathematical equality at every juncture. By acquiescing gracefully one builds up a better bond than one based on bickering refusals.

6. For a man, the physical side of the relationship is the most important as it has been part of his fantasy for a long time. While women dream of romance, men are more excited at the prospect of sex. He is also most vulnerable on this score and easily hurt. A refusal on this point may give an impression of rejection which will be deep-seated.

7. Good looks, good grooming, a good voice and charming manners are a great asset and should be maintained.

8. Be pleasant company—the atmosphere in the house is largely created by the lady of the manor. Many wives complain that their husbands do not converse with them nor do they spend time at home. How can they, with every conversation an unpleasant or tirade of complaints? Be well read and aware of current happenings so that conversation with your spous can go beyond domestic frivolities.

9. Do not seek praise and compliments on a daily basis. While it is true that everyone seeks appreciation and would like to be praised undue vanity on this front would result in discord. One wife wanted to be praised for the dishes she made and thought that her husband should bring in flowers for her on a frequent basis. When it did not happen, she became disgruntled and dissatisfied. It was not enough for her that her husband appreciated her cooking and ate with relish whatever she had prepared. Think instead whether one is praising one's husband every day for the work he does in the office.

10. Avoid being over-possessive, unduly suspicious and overly resentful or any attention that he gives to anyone other than yourself. These traits become obsessive so much so that often mothers become upset with their husbands' lavish attention on the children, particularly the daughter. As an adult person have a cool confidence and do not seek constant reassurance in order to fortify your self-esteem.

11. Avoid being an 'I-told-you-so' type and also be sympathetic even after someone has fallen ill or suffered because they did not listen to your advice.

12. While endeavouring to keep a beautiful house do not make this or cleanliness into a fetish in which the family members cease to feel comfortable in the home environment. A house is beautiful only if those who are in it can live happily amidst congenial surroundings. If the people are always too worried about the carpet, the knick-knacks and the bed cover, when will they relax? Do the cleanliness routine and the beautification unobtrusively.

While I have touched upon only 12 major points which spouses could be aware of, I am sure there are many more but for that one would have to consult a marriage guidance book rather than one on home management!

Experts have also culled out a few points which are a source of friction in this best and worst of partnerships.

1. Avoid criticising each other's family.
2. Avoid telling each other that he doesn't love you /she doesn't love you.
3. Do not tell each other that she/he is not as bright as you.

4. Do not tell her/him that you can earn more than her/him.
5. Avoid criticising each other's clothes sense, appearance, figure.
6. Avoid making comparisons with other men/women.
7. Don't go on telling him/her that other men/women find you more attractive than he/she does.
8. Show your care by making birthdays and anniversaries special days.
9. While for men, the way to his heart may be through his stomach so do not hesitate to pamper him by cooking his favourite dish. If the way to a lady's heart is through buying her a sari, taking her out to dinner or giving her roses then do so.
10. Be unselfish and unconditional in your love for each other. Put the other person before your own needs and pave the way for a happier relationship.
11. Time plays a great role in bringing a couple closer together as going through the ups and downs of life strengthen bonds and couples become attuned to each other. Frequent changing of spouses do not necessarily result in a better marriage! At the same time it may be difficult to live with someone who is violent, abusive, a drug addict, habitually unfaithful etc.
12. Avoid discussing shortcomings of your spouse with friends or family as this will not motivate the person to change for the better. Rather he or she may feel offended at being discussed behind their back. The best way of bringing about change is by explaining the shortcomings patiently and calmly. Rough words will only result in the other person becoming more adamant and averse to improvement.
13. Both should not lose their temper simultaneously. If one partner is getting angry it is better for the other to remain quiet until tempers are under control and then resolve the issue.
14. Avoid all disagreements, arguments and fights in front of others that is children, family members or friends, as it causes a great deal of embarrassment to any one who is witness to a quarrel. At all times one should strive to maintain dignity and self-restraint.

Dealing with in-laws, especially mother-in-law

It is said that in India, one does not marry a man but his whole family as well. This is why utmost care and caution is exercised in selecting a daughter-in-law as it is well-known that her entry into the family can trigger off the disintegration of the family unit. Due to the existence of the joint family in earlier times, a girl was brought up very strictly so that she would not bring dishonour to her parents by creating discord in the family she marries into. Girls were exhorted to be patient, tolerant and silent even in the case of severe provocation. In the rural areas this still holds true but the educated girl is now taught not to stand for any kind of real or perceived injustice. Neither stance is acceptable if carried too far. It is a disgrace if a girl is tortured and thrown out of her in-law's home either because of insufficient dowry or because she has not produced sons.

While the new daughter-in-law should definitely try to adjust to her husband's relations, they also, should try to be loving and patient with the new entrant into the family. By making her feel welcome they will get a far better response than by carping criticism at every stage.

A mother-in-law should accept the fact that while a son may remain dutiful towards her, he may transfer a lot of loving attention to his new bride, which is as it should be. There is actually no clash in the roles of a mother and wife if only both would shed their petty egos and jealousies as no one can replace the mother or the wife since their roles are so different.

It is important for the daughter-in-law to understand that everyone in her new home may be different from her parents and siblings and she should accept this with good grace. Accept people as they are and through good behaviour they will be won over.

Avoid saying harsh words and speaking badly about relatives. It is better to keep quiet than speak badly about others.

Accept the foibles and idiosyncrasies of others, especially of elders, with good grace and humour. Do not be over-sensitive and over react to every comment and situation.

Try not to be overpossessive about your husband/ son. Remember that he still has some obligation towards his mother. While the mother should not feel enraged if he goes out with his wife or buys her gifts. As the elder person, the mother-in-law should be above all competition and petty jealousy.

Do not try to make your daughter-in-law feel inadequate by telling her that she does not know anything, cannot cook, etc. Rather, be sympathetic and helpful but neither should treat the other as a domestic servant. Too often mothers-in-law put the burden of all domestic chores on the daughter-in-law and sometimes the daughter-in-law looks upon an ageing mother-in-law as a beast of burden who copes with all the housework along with looking after the grand children.

In some households, the domestic situation becomes such that even the children resort to what is called 'granny bashing'. This is an abhorrent phenomena and not at all a part of our accepted social norms. It is absolutely essential that our tradition of extending a great deal of respect and courtesy to our elders be upheld.

In a situation in which one is living in a modern joint family, the elders should not be too rigid and should allow the younger generation to socialise and move about freely. Let them enjoy their independence and give them their privacy.

Working wives

Both on account of women's education and economic emancipation and the ever increasing cost of living, many husbands have working wives. In such a situation, a man will have to decide prior to marriage whether or not he wants a working or non-working wife. The girl also must ascertain the extent to which she is keen on her own career. The couple should jointly decide this issue so that there are no hard feelings later on.

While the extra pay packet is always welcome, certain compromises and adjustments must be made in those households where the lady of the house has a full-time career. She cannot completely disown her domestic responsibilities, at the same time she cannot let the team down at work. Many opt for teaching jobs, either in schools or at the college level as these allow domestic duties to be fitted in as well. In office jobs, particularly those that are transferable, a lot of compromises have to be made both by the couple and their children. Fortunately, reliable domestic help is still available in India so one should invest in good full-time servants. Alternately, one would have to depend on one's own mother or mother-in-law to extend a helping hand.

As part-time jobs are not so easily available in our country particularly since the employment market is already clogged, some ladies opt to work from the house so that they can supervise their homes while exercising their creativity at the same time. To this end, many ladies are taking up the following: creches or day-care centres, cooking lessons and part-time catering, home-tuitions, keeping sarees at home.

Ultimately, every person has to decide for herself about how best to combine one's domestic role with a career. Some men are willing to be househusbands but the social pressures on them, especially in our country where there are a plethora of friends and family who are always there with piercing comments that give a jolt to one's ego. The increasing rate of divorces as also delinquent children are often traced back to the neglectful wife or mother.

All that one can say is, that money, status and ambition should not come in the way of one's domestic happiness and family life. A job is not always a substitute for a fulfilling personal life. Suffice it to say that when both partners are working they must also work extra hard to keep their marriage from being buffeted by adverse forces.

While the days when women waited all dolled up with their attentions focused solely on their husbands and families this thought is anathema to many of the 90s women who are able and capable of managing their many roles with aplomb. There is also a desire to shun boring domestic chores and a servant is employed to do the needful. Psychiatrists and therapists report that there is a rising crisis in the incidence of platonic marriages in Indian metros. Youthful, urbane and successful, Indian guppies or globalising yuppies, have paid a huge emotional price for their seemingly enviable international and materialistically successful life styles. They may have two thriving careers but opt for one child, a reflection of the sort of readjustment in personal priorities in which the family is no longer the centre of one's life. While professional success and social standing is a big pay-off, this is often a curiously hollow achievement in terms of personal happiness.

While some partners seek solace in spirituality and abstinence, others are seeking thrills in either clinching deals or extramarital flings, which are more 'exciting' than mating with one's spouse. Others say that the change in the marital equation has led to psychologically castrated men. Therefore in a highly successful working wife, marriage tiredness, stress due to endless work pressures and lack of mutual patience, tact and tenderness can lead to a platonic marital relationship which is detrimental to both parties and must be guarded against.

The working mother

There is absolutely no substitute for the love and care a mother gives to her child. Breast feeding increases this bond between mother and child and bottles are no substitute for mother's milk. Since careers are often top priority for a working woman today she either delays having children or marries late all of which have an effect on both childbearing and childrearing. In the West, for example, the increasing rates of divorce, working women and low importance given to domestic life has resulted in a falling birth rate. To counter this, many countries are giving working mothers as much as a year of maternity leave so that she can care for the child in the crucial early months. The argument of quality time versus quantity time is just absurd jargon as far as babies are concerned, as a baby requires many hours of devoted care. It is only an older child who can be fobbed off with 'quality time'.

In India, there are neither enough creches at the workplace nor is the lady given more than three months maternity leave. Servants are often used as substitutes and sometimes a mother or mother-in-law has to pitch in and help. A mother's influence is crucial and it is not for nothing that the phrase 'the hand that rocks the cradle rules the world'.

In the West, there have been many mishaps due to baby bashing. Nannies have not always been a good substitute for the mother.

In India too, it is not advisable to leave a baby exclusively in the charge of a maidservant. At the same time, it may not always be possible for the relative to come and help out over a long period. The problem is especially acute in a nuclear family as the traditional joint family can absorb these problems.

Women can do it, but the question is that not everyone can and nor are they equipped to stand the strain of a baby and a professional commitment simultaneously as a new mother also requires rest to recuperate from childbirth.

In a nuclear family a reliable ayah is a must. Also if there is a girl child it is best not to expose her to male domestic help as instances of child abuse occur even in this country.

The *ayah* must be kept under close supervision and one should try to drop in for lunch or come in unexpectedly to make sure that everything is alright.

The health of the *ayah* should be good as small children are vulnerable to infections. A working mother who entrusted her son to an *ayah* found to her horror after a few months that the maid had contracted tuberculosis. A nightmarish round of doctors and tests followed for all members of the family.

Make sure that you are always in telephonic touch with the house in case of emergencies. Keep a doctor's number handy with the maid. The working mother comes back to the house tired and it is at this time the child, craving attention, is at his or her worst. She has to look after the child and see to whether or not she/he had been properly cared for during the day. She also has to take care of the household chores ranging from laundry to cooking. At this time if the husband and others are also demanding it adds to her woes and fatigue. Therefore the spouse of a working wife should be helpful in trying to lessen her burden.

Today the social and financial pressures necessitate that a woman take up a job. A frequent question today is 'Are you working'. A negative answer often draws a negative answer as many do not believe that homemaking and motherhood are full time responsibilities and that when the home flounders so does the society. Westerners have revised this but family bonds there have broken down to a large extent and it may be difficult to turn the clock back. A housewife or mother should not feel bored, frustrated or inadequate as she is doing something that no one can substitute for.

Early bonding with the mother is therefore of great importance in order to build up security and attachments. While for many in India a whole-time career is a necessity one must make certain concessions for the child:

1. Try to take leave after the baby for as long as feasible.
2. Take a part time job instead of a full time one, which will be less exhausting.
3. Choose something close to the house so that too much time is not spent in tiresome commuting.
4. Carefully choose the ayah and day care centre before entrusting your child to their care.
5. Be happy in whatever you are doing.
6. Do not overindulge a child in order to substitute for your absence.
7. Spend time with the child after your return.
8. Some children resent their mother's absence at work. Explain why you do so and do not get bulldozed into feeling guilty if it gives you intellectual and financial sustenance.
9. Make fool-proof arrangements before leaving your child.

Today women must think before they either give up their job or continue it for the sake of their child after carefully weighing the pros and cons of either decision.

Who will make the chappatis?

This kind of conflict in the working couple's household may sometimes be rampant.

Traditional wisdom worldwide has always held the household as the female domain and the world outside as that of a male. This is especially pronounced in the rural areas. However, the low prestige attached to homemaking and the sheer drudgery of housework in a servant-less western world triggered off the women's liberation movement in the late 60s and 70s. With increased education they also did not want to be either dominated or ill-treated by their husbands as economic emancipation was within their grasp.

In India too the tired working woman is faced with coping with the household chores after a long day at work. Women traditionally had to perform at only one level hence generations of men were used to being looked after by either their mothers, wives or their daughters. Nobody envisaged that one day men would be expected to cook, clean and care for themselves. Those who can afford to do, keep servants so that domestic chores are not a part of the conflict.

Problems arise in those families which are nuclear and servantless a la in the West. The wife also returns tired and sees red when her husband places leg upon leg in front of the television or with the newspaper and demands a cup of tea. Little wonder that when the village woman asked her husband if she could attend training camp on panchayats he in turn asked her, ' And who will make the chappatis?'

No set rules can be made regarding this question. There are many men who make the bed tea or wake their wives with a cup of coffee. Some men are better cooks than their wives, while others solve the problem by keeping domestic servants. Suffice it to say that the couple should work out their own strategy without resorting to harsh words, gender bias and a rigid stance. If the double pay-packet is welcomed at the end of the month then the couple must make the necessary compromises and adjustments so that the double income does not lead to double stress in marital relations!

Latch key children

This term originated in the west initially and referred to those children, particularly single parent ones, who returned home from school, let themselves into the house, ate, watched television and did their homework while their mothers returned from work. A similar situation is also creeping into many of our urban centres. While smaller children go off to creches after school, those who are slightly older return home and stay alone till their parents return home after work.

Psychiatrists say that 75 per cent of such children have no emotional or behavioural problems, but the emotional development of 25-30 per cent of the children is affected. In villages where most women go out to work, children are better adjusted than children of urban, working and professional parents. This is perhaps on account of the nuclear family.

The only child of a working couple says of his 'latch key' days now that he is in college: 'I learnt to warm food, do my homework, take down messages on the phone - I grew up fast but having no one to confide my thoughts to or talk about school often disturbed me.'

Children returning from school are at a highly vulnerable stage as the combination of study and peer pressure makes them want to come in and share their thoughts and frustrations with some one sympathetic. Most children resent their mother's absence even when they know and realise that she would feel resentful at home.

Children miss their mothers the most when they are sick or during holidays. Schools often complain how working parents pressurise them to keep the schools open for longer hours and to keep the holidays to a minimum as they find it inconvenient to keep away from work. An unscheduled holiday is virtually a calamity for such parents!

The pangs of loneliness, rejection, alienation, and isolation are often exhibited in an aggressive behaviour and poor performances in school.

While all working mothers cannot give up their jobs, they must be conscious about their parental responsibilities, spend adequate time with the child on their return and strive not to take on the frustrations of a bad day at work on an innocent child. Children must be given time and attention and one can keep in touch by phoning when the child returns from school.

Children and their schooling

The education of children is a major preoccupation for most parents. The difficulty is that with ever rising numbers, quality education is available only in a limited number of institutions. As they are in great demand, they are imbued with a considerable arrogance and demand exorbitant fees. Parents feel that once their child is put in an English medium school, he or she is made for life. Hence, the lives of three and four-year-olds are made miserable in the scramble to get into a good school.

In any case, the working mother marches her child off to play school as early as possible saying that the child will be able to 'mix' with other children. These playschools and nurseries are basically creches but the emphasis is on studies and there is very little play.

Today the alphabet, numbers, rhymes and general knowledge is stuffed into tender minds starting from the age of two years. Little wonder therefore that many children become wayward, resist going to school and suffer burn out in class X or even earlier. While the playschools claim that there are no formal studies but in truth a survey has shown that this is not so and moreover many parents want their child to study early as they believe that this would give them a headstart in life. This does not always happen. While in the West and even in Singapore the school bag is getting lighter, in India it is getting heavier as parents push their children into doing well so that they can get into good schools make it to the IITs and IIMs, get into the IAS, become an engineer or a doctor and earn megabucks.

Every school going child is taught early in life the need for success and the bigger the bag the better the chances of his success. In the process, idea of success seems to have been homogenised to the point where flashy materialism is equated with success.

Earlier nursery classes of the established schools had horrendously difficult entrance exams. Due to a lot of writing in the press and the better judgement of some enlightened teachers and parents, this trend has been rationalised somewhat. While one cannot step back from the rat race altogether and whereas it is necessary to remain within the system, do not stress your child in order to get him into a good school. Remember that a good student can never be kept down and the best result of those taking the board examinations are often of students from less touted government schools.

1. Put your child in a school close to your house so that he/she does not have to commute long distance.
2. Keep track of the advertisements that come out in the newspapers regarding school admissions especially at the nursery level so that one can apply at the right time.
3. Do not chastise your child for failing to secure admission.
4. Schools today want a balanced and emotionally secure child so do not build up tension in the child so that he or she cries during the admission formalities.
5. Do not link your child's success with your own and use their triumphs to boast on social occasions.
6. Do not bore others by constantly talking about your child and his/her exploits.

Is tuition necessary

Due to overloaded, lopsided curriculum no matter how good the school, many parents find it necessary to appoint private tutors to coach their children especially before the board examinations (Class X and XII) and for admission to the IITs and medical colleges. In fact, the overloaded curriculum has fuelled a parallel industry of guides, tutor bureaus, and coaching institutions. It is now felt that if the curriculum were rationalised, simplified or reduced then the needs for this 'ancillary industry' of guide books, tutors, and tutor bureaus would be removed and many would be rendered unemployed.

Presently the courses are so vast that teachers are forced to teach at a rapid pace. All students are not, and cannot be outstanding in every subject. Hence it sometimes becomes necessary to keep tutors so that the child can cope with troublesome subjects such as maths, physics, English and Hindi.

Students make up a small proportion of the home tutions market, while professionals and those teachers who had earlier taught in schools form this group of professional teachers. It is a constantly burgeoning market because of the symbiotic relationship between the taught and the tutor. While the teacher needs the income the enormous size of the classes makes extra help necessary for the students.

Some tips for dealing with tutors
1. Select the tutor carefully, either on the recommendation of friends, neighbours or from a reliable tutors bureau.
2. Decide the day, duration and time of the tutor and desist from breaking this routine.
3. If girls have to be coached it may be advisable to hire a lady teacher.
4. Keep a close watch on the tutor and monitor what your child is being taught.
5. Ensure that the tutor is a help and not a burden to your child. The tutor should explain those topics which the child is unable to understand in school. The tutor should not burden the child with practice sums and homework or tests in lieu of explaining and working out the problems.
6. Make sure that the tutor teaches your child for the agreed time period otherwise the monetary loss is yours.
7. Offer a refreshment to your tutor.

At one time only those children who were poor in studies required tuitions. Today, even those students who do well go for tuitions not only to improve their performance but because the large classes and shoddy teaching even in reputed schools have made it necessary.

Many working parents are relieving themselves of guilt and the daily botheration of children of packing them off to boarding schools. It appears to be a suitable arrangement. When children apparently grow up to be disciplined individuals, parents are spared the trouble of paying them attention after a gruelling day at work. When they come home during the holidays, they can make some adjustments to slot the child in.

Ironically in wanting their children to have the best, they put them away from themselves, till a stage is reached when the children are happy the day the holidays are over and they can go back to school. The earlier wails and tears, bouts of crying quietly under pillows give way to alienation and resentment against those who send them away. In fact, many of them later do not understand what the fuss and hype of parental love is all about.

Coping with examination fever
The life of our children is blighted by a constant stream of exams. Whether it is nursery school entry, or admission to a larger school, the board exams and the schools of engineering, medicine and management, life is punctuated by examinations. Ultimately one is only as good as the last examination result as that alone signifies entry or rejection in to schools of higher education. A child may secure 90 per cent in the 12th board exams but if he/she does badly in the IIT entrance test, then an engineering degree is out.

Relentless pressure by teachers and overambitious parents have reduced these exams to nightmare for students since success or failure in them determines the future. Overambitious parents drive their children too hard to become achievers and in the end the children and sometimes the parents pay a heavy price for this maniacal pressure. The seeds for heart trouble and diabetes are sown right at the school level by haranguing teachers so it is little wonder that India tops the world in both these diseases!

In order to make the children study, parents hold out all kinds of blandishments or else they are extremely harsh and strict until the desired results are achieved. How much of it is actually benefiting the child and how much of it is a parental ego trip is the real question.

Examinations play a crucial role in deciding the schools, colleges, and careers of the children hence great stress is placed in achieving success in them. Careers and lives remade on the basis of a fraction of a mark. Examination fever, anxiety, burnout and suicides due to failure are some of the problems resulting from an outdated and unrealistic education system. Dr Achel Bhagat, psychiatrist at the Apollo Hospital Delhi states, 'Contemporary Society maintains a very narrow definition of success. If one doesn't make it big at a young age, one is condemned as a failure'. Reena who scored 75 percent in her XII boards and not 90 percent and Anil who did not go to IIT but only to the Delhi College of Engineering (DCE) were branded as failures. Part of the alienation and depression amongst the youth is on account of the conditional love, of parents and the conditional friendship of peers. The teachers are reduced to being constant naggers who want to scare and browbeat children into studying for exams. They are playing a crucial role in making the base for diabetes, hypertension and nervous disorders in the next generation! Faced with these unbearable stresses and pressures from all sides children are either becoming violent, suicidal, indifferent or crammers so that they can cope with exams.

Had examinations been the real test of calibre then the people who top in the engineering and medical entrance tests would make the best professionals. This has not always been proved subsequently. Indians who migrate and now hold top jobs abroad are not necessarily toppers but persons whose talents have not been utilised in India. In fact, toppers may often be lacking when it comes to real life situations. While presently there seems to be no alternative to the ritual of examinations and entrance tests, with incompetent marking, lost answer sheets, lopsided setting of question papers and so on making a candidate's results, examination phobia has to be tackled in order to help youngsters to cope with the stress that results from this ordeal. Class X students fearing their first public exams are particularly prone to getting examination phobia hence the problem has to be understood and tackled to ensure that your child does not suffer a breakdown prior to a crucial test of this sort.

If one draws a chart, the problem of examination can be analysed clearly and visually.

With parental and societal pressure of high academic achievement with marks touching unrealistic level, examination phobia in students is a reality that manifests itself both in psychological and physiological symptoms. It is also important to differentiate between anticipatory anxiety which is common to a situation where this anxiety converts itself into a phobia. While anxiety to do well and achieve success is natural and can be managed by giving

Examination Phobia

Lack of Preparation	Lack of Concentration	Lack of Understanding
	RESULTS IN	

Physiological symptoms
a) Diarrhoea
b) Palpitation
c) Stomach cramps
d) Fever
e) Headache
f) Nausea

Psychological symptoms
a) Poor concentration
b) Poor retention
c) Restlessness
d) Inability to organise
e) Inability to write

social and emotional support, where it degenerates into a phobia, professional help is called for. It is necessary for parents and teachers to become conscious that their prodding should not drive a child towards examination phobia.

Most psychologists believe that the phobia is the result of an unrealistic perception of exams in the student's mind. The best way to overcome this is to densensitise the child which means helping the student to appreciate exams in a logical way. By setting unrealistic targets in which parents and teachers convey that getting below 90 percent would mean the end of the world, results in unnecessary stress and strain.

Fear can lead to physiological disturbances such as lack of sleep, loss of appetite, fever, breathlessness, irregular periods and so on. Phobia can also be related to certain subjects the most common one being mathematics. Poor teaching in the school, vast courses and lack of understanding of the subject leads to anxiety and phobias. Examinations are best handled by adopting a systematic and regular mode of study.

There is no need to cram. There should be an effort to understand the matter at hand so that unnecessary pressure is not put on the memory. When children learn by rose or 'mugs', there is unnecessary emphasis on memorisation. While memorising, if one point or a single sentence is forgotten, the association of ideas is broken and the student often blanks out. Another negative aspect of cramming is that often there is no understanding hence questions are answered according to what the student has memorised rather than what the question requires in terms of an answer. At the same time many students feel that since question papers are repetitive they can score well even in science and maths by 'mugging' things up.

Helpline for Students

1. Students create their own difficulties if they are not systematic and regular with their studies. Vast courses cannot be handled by trying to study at one go. Hence, they should break up their study time into shorter periods of concentrated study with a high degree of both assimilation and retention. There is no sense in sitting at a desk without motivation and concentration.
2. Study schedules should be planned in advance with long term and short term daily targets. The targets should be realistic and the effort should be to concentrate on the target at hand rather than on the results. Study at least two months before exams.
3. The number of hours put in are not as important as the output per hour. Instead of cramming one should rely more on understanding.
4. It has been found that the human mind can concentrate for only about thirty minutes at a time. Therefore, it is important not to go on studying a single subject for hours at a stretch. A good way to go about this is to study subjects that are not similar. If one studies science or maths for an hour, one should then revert to a language for one hour before going back to science or maths.
5. It is necessary to take a short break after concentrating for a few hours. One can go for a stroll, do some exercise, listen to music before going back to one's desk and study books.
6. Retention is helped by relating new information to that which one already knows. Don't just read and revise the work. Write it down as this helps to transfer knowledge to long term memory.
7. While studying one should break up topics into sub-topics. Which could further be subdivided so that learning becomes easier.
8. Breathing exercises such as pranayam are useful as they increase concentration by relaxing the body and increasing the quantum of oxygen inhaled.
9. Stick to the drawn up time table of revision so that one does not suffer from last minute panic attacks when faced with an unfinished syllabus.
10. Avoid burning the midnight oil. Wake up early instead and revise the old chapters before going on to new ones.

Since examinations are a necessary evil in our education system, it is best to tackle it in a positive and systematic manner so that students do not suffer from anxiety attacks and breakdowns and examinations phobia. Shyama Chona, Principal of Delhi Public School, R. K. Puram, 'The competition on the macro level is getting tougher by the day, since the number of seats in the colleges of choice are few. And since the students can do little to change the educational system, its best that they prepare themselves mentally for it'. While the nation and students in particular. pray for better sense to dawn on educational administrators and those who prepare the unwieldly syllabus for the present, children must be helped to cope with the system by all concerned.

For Parents

1. Regulate the number of hours your child watches television but do not put

a ban on it altogether as children need to unwind.

2. Avoid comparing your child's performance with that of other siblings or other children. It increases stress and may result in resistance towards studies.

3. Do not make exams into a do or die event as so many children are committing suicide when faced with poor results or failure. Parental pressure is one of the main causes of exam related suicides. Parents are increasingly not acting as the friends, mentors and supporters they are expected to be.

4. It is psychological stress, an inability to communicate their fears to parents, teachers and peers which accounts for this sad state of affairs. Parents are busy with their careers, teachers with their never-ending syllabus and friends can be impatient and insensitive to the call of desperation.

5. Ensure that your child gets adequate sleep, good food which is nourishing and to the child's liking. Vitamin supplements can also be given to boost the child's health and concentration.

6. Help your child to organise his or her work and offer assistance without being overbearing.

7. Refrain from organising elaborate family get-togethers during examination time.

8. Avoid eating out at least a month prior to examinations so that the child does not get jaundice or typhoid or upset stomach. Make interesting and palatable food at home instead.

9. Working mothers should ensure that they are relatively free to help the child during the period of the Board Examinations.

Handling Teenagers

Adolescence marks a period of rapid and profound change in body and mind. Coping with adolescence and its attendant physical and psychological changes the teenage years are a trying time for both parents and children. Children become more vocal about their opinions, their expectations and their desire for freedom. Often they seek to adopt a collision path with their elders, arguing and questioning until parents lose their patience. In fact teenagers have an inbuilt desire to rebel and rail against any authoritarian stance adopted by their parents. In many ways it is as if they are sporting of a fight. Parents, being older in age and hopefully wiser, having passed through a similar stage themselves, should, to use a popular phrase 'play it cool'. Try not to lay down the law at every junction. Avoid making too many rules and regulations. Above all, try to avoid rigid postures and unbending stances as these will only fuel rebellion. This does not mean that parents will not exercise their judgement or lay down certain parameters of behaviour. In fact, they want that certain norms and standards should be adhered to. Parents need to understand that growing children must be handled with care and respect. Parents should adopt a pleasant and consensual approach to all matters rather than one of confrontation and blind obedience from their children.

Times have changed and unquestioning obedience is a thing that went out with the Victorian era. Parents should lay down a few basic rules and ensure that these are adhered to, rather than make too many irritating regulations. Teenagers require support, love and guidance from their parents but not constant policing. One would get a far better response if one dealt with teenagers as if they were responsible adults rather than irresponsible unreliable juveniles, as one normally gets the behaviour that one expects to get. If one has built up a good bond of love and closeness during the childhood years, the teenage years may certainly pass off more smoothly.

While traditional psychologists and poets of the Romantic era such as Shelley and Goethe made out that the period of adolescence was one of 'Sturn and Drang' in which the period of angry, dark terminal marked the storm - crossed transition into adulthood.

While adolescents tend to see much of their behaviour as a 'personal' matter, affecting no one but themselves and therefore up to them entirely, their parents tend to stand for 'conventional thinking', which sees society's rules and expectations as primary. This dichotomy provides for common place clashes regarding dress, studies, cleanliness of the teenager's rooms and so on.

A child of 12 or 13 generally has little use for conventions when it comes to family issues. Between 14 and 16 the teenager realises that conventions are ways in which society regulates itself. Between 16 and 18 there is again a period of rejecting conventions but more thoughtfully. Between 18 and 25 conventions are once again seen as playing an admirable role in facilitating the business of society. This is usually why by the age of 15 or 16 quarreling subsides and is replaced by a period in which the family 'negotiates' issues such as staying out late, going out with the opposite sex and so on.

Parents who try to exert too much control over their children find it impossible to yield in a conflict in which their teenaged children are trying to establish their own identities. In this trying period in which teenagers are trying to express their individuality even as he or she wants to maintain a close and caring relationship with their parents, the parents have to be positive and loving in order to tide over this difficult period. In those cases where the parents adopt the stance of being the last bastions of conservatism or in those cases in which they are harsh and judgemental there is a great danger of alienation. When faced with a consistently negative and hostile environment at home, children will be driven towards their peer group. Peer pressure and camaraderie often lead towards anti-social behaviour, drug addiction, experimentation with cigarettes, alcohol and sex. It is only with sympathy, love, understanding and by keeping the channels of communication open at all times that parents can exert influence during this trying time of psychical and psychological changes in young adults.

By giving the teenager some measure of freedom, privacy and respect as a young adult parents may even avoid the hazard of teenage rebellion. Laying down the law and trying to exert authority and exhibiting one's ego is counter productive. It will only result in losing touch with the children at a time in which they require all the love and support they can get.

Handy Tips

1. Early bonding - the closer the relationship in the pre-teen years, the easier it is during the teenage years. Confidence and self esteem should be built up by listening to them, so that they do not have to do outstanding things to grab your attention.

2. Share decision making - parenting does not mean being a drill sergeant. By offering your child options, including them in decisions regarding the decoration and cleanliness of their

room enables them to full participation in household affairs.

3. Understand growing pains- don't exert your will over them for every trivial issue but keep a grip on the main ones. Do not shepherd them at every stage - give them space and privacy.

4. Share your world with your child and keep the lines of communication open on all topics including sex. Ask his or her opinion regarding your clothes, make-up etc. so that they are given a sense of being valued.

5. Make mealtimes a happy hour for family bonding and light conversation. Do not chastise them harshly during the period.

6. Know your children's friends and encourage them to come over for meals or to drop in. Avoid harsh criticism of their friends.

7. Set reasonable limits for going out, returning home after a party, going out for marries and studying. Adopt a balance between unrestrained license and a jail warden mindset. Share your worries with your teenaged child and convince him that your concern for her comes out of love and not distrust.

8. Remember your own teenaged years and understand that your child may take a bite of the forbidden fruit! See that accurate information about alcohol, drugs, sex and AIDS is given well before the teenage years, through appropriate reading material and frank discussion.

9. Patience, understanding, love and sympathy go a long way towards harmonious family relationships and your teenaged child rocked by internal psychological and physical changes needs this the most. Loving things should be liberally dispensed at the appropriate time.

Avoid being...

1. A control freak who monitors every minute of your child's day. I was recently shocked when a mother, who also happens to be a teacher in a top Delhi school, told me that she had come to my house for lunch after she had locked her teen aged daughter in the house! She had also taken the precaution of taking out the TV plug and disconnecting the internet! As it is, teenagers have little freedom. If they feel that their parent or parents are jail wardens they will be driven to escape this clastrophobic atmosphere. Children on whom unreasonable grubs and discipline is imposed thrive on rebelling against authority.

2. Avoid harsh criticism and a judgmental attitude. Teenagers are just learning how to joy - assist them, rather than damage their self-confidence with your carping and critical attitude.

3. Do not try to compete with them. The fact that one has a teenage child means that one has grown older. Don't try to fight the years by dressing in tank tops and having a perm so that people ask you which college do you study in?' While today's society demands that everyone look young and fit, in trying to look and behave like a teenager one will have conflict with one's teenage children who see a father or mother's attempt to dress and behave like them as a matter of competition.

Dr. Ashima Puri a clinical psychologist asserts: 'Shaving and caring with authority is what the child's usual expectation from a parent child relationship is. Even though parents would like to act young. Some discrimination should be exercised. They should realise that their role involves a lot of maturity and understanding. They are seen as 'guides' and not as 'peers' to the child. Also, there is the danger of an unconscious, underlying competition developing between parent and child'.

This is especially true when the mother is slim, good looking and sophisticated and her daughter is a plump, gauche and acne-skinned 14 year old.

Adolescence is the time when children require the maximum guidance but in a subtle manner. A boy would hate to be hugged in front of his friends for fear of being labelled 'Mama's boy'. When a father dyes his hair and goes to the disco to share his son's girl friends and when mama wears a tank top to match her daughter it reflects low self-esteem in which parents play the 'child's role'. At this time adults must behave like adults so that they can guide their teenaged children into adulthood since most teenagers disapprove and are embarassed by frustrated dads and mini-skirted moms who shriek and giggle and act as teenie boppers.

In conclusion, young adolescents of South Asia had a conference in 1998 during which they took out a document that cooked their opinions and their feelings about world around them.

Coping with Mother-in-Law

In the Western world, the mother of the girl is traditionally viewed with apprehension by her son-in-law and the relationship between a man and his wife's mother is the subject of many jokes. In India however, it is the mother-in-law daughter-in-law equation which is the subject of so many films, stories, television serials such as 'Tu tu, Main Main' and the centre of family harmony or discord, as the case may be. The dominance of the man's mother is the natural offshoot of the dominance of the male in a traditional society. Girls were thought to be 'paraya dhan' menat to be in her parents' house for just a brief period, before she commenced her real life at her in-laws house. Since girls were married off at a tender age, she grew up and was moulded to blend in with her in-laws. She was taught to cope with any slights, insults and scoldings given to her as there was no greater disgrace than a marriage that did not work. All insults, taunts and barbs were expected to be swallowed and a woman got her chance when she too became a mother-in-law. To a large extent this scenario still prevails in our society and unfortunately a mother-in-law is viewed with great apprehension by a new bride. However, with the changes in education, economic status and the consequent emancipation of women, not everyone is willing to tolerate injustice at the hands of one's mother-in-law.

It is a sad reality that irrespective of whether it is a love or an arranged marriage, the bickering and the fault finding begins early. Mothers-in-law invariably find fault with the bride's appearance - her height or the lack of it, her complexion, her dress sense and her hairstyle. If the criticism is not overt, it is covert and mother-in-law may well say, 'Your hair is too curly. My son likes straight hair. Why don't you get yours straightened?', an example of literally getting into daughter-in-law's hair! Next, there are the acid comments regarding the daughter-in-law's lack of domestic skills, her failure to produce the son and heir, and in those instances where there have been dowry demands, a campaign to extract more is launched at the earliest opportunity. Neither education nor media attacks on this drawback in our social system has helped appreciably, as can be seen from the number of dowry deaths, suicides and divorces.

Why does a perfectly normal human being change as soon as she becomes a mother-in-law? What demons drive her to behave with her daughter-in-law as she never would with her own daughter? Why is the rest of the family a mute spectator to these vicious assaults on a new member of the family? Most importantly, why is the husband who has taken a vow to protect his spouse struck dumb by his mother? Finally, what is the social fall-out of this domestic situation?

Perhaps more than any other society, family relationships occupy a paramount position in our country, which, in itself, is a very good thing. The western experience where the individual has tried to break all norms and tries to live his or her own life has proved to be a disaster, which is why leaders in the West are repeatedly harping on the necessity of family values. Some of the individualism, lack of tolerance and economic independence have also crept into our society as a result of industrialisation. Therefore, since there is financial independence from the paterfamilias, there is also resentment at having to put up with unreasonable demands from elders. How far Indian society has descended can be gauged from the fact that during the Rig Vedic Age a girl could choose her life partner at a 'Swayamvara', whereas today, even as we enter the new millennium, quite a good number of girls are virtually sold off to the highest bidders. Money, rather than the traditional requisites of family compatability and a common culture have made a mockery of the innate stability of the system of arranged marriages. Parents today are careful to see that their daughters are well educated and qualified so that they have a 'fall back position' in case they face humiliation at the hands of their in laws. No girl and no section of society is immune from this menace, regardless of whether they are from the village, NRI's living abroad or officers and engineers living in cities and towns within the country. The unfortunate reality is that every groom has his price, depending on his professional qualification. The highest dowry is given to IAS officers and engineers and doctors are next on the list. To a large extent some of the corruption in society stems from the dowry system. Parents feel they are justified in extracting the price of their son's education from his bride. Little wonder that relationships which are based on a system of barter, flounder during the years ahead.

It has been said that the hand that rocks the cradle, rules the world. It is sad that the high ideals of Indian womanhood have degenerated to the extent that mothers are at the very forefront during dowry negotiations. Instead of imbuing her son with a sense of high morals and self-respect, he is indeed taught arrogance and is convinced by his mother that there is no wrong in extracting the maximum from his future life partner. Whereas we may smugly point out that life in the West is highly materialistic and consumerist, are we any better when we harass a bride because she failed to bring in a colour television or a fridge? Education has not brought in its wake an enlightened attitude in either mothers or their sons.

Handy Tips

1. The first step in re-establishing decency in society is by deciding neither to give nor take dowry at the time of marriage. If parents broke off negotiations where

there was a compulsion to give money, land or a car, then there would be no question of facing harassment at the hands of an avaricious mother-in-law.
2. A mother should select her daughter-in-law carefully or give in gracefully should her son present her with his own choice.
3. As the elder person, the mother-in-law should tackle her daughter-in-law with love, kindness and patience. Utmost self-control and restraint should be exercised over one's tongue so that hurtful remarks do not scar the young bride.
4. The mother-in-law should also not try to control the newlyweds, particularly if all are staying together.
5. An attitude of sympathy and tolerance would be far healthier than one of disapproval.

Coping with Daughters-in-Law

While mothers-in-law have been seen as dictators, awesome figures who dominate the household and terrorise their hapless daughters-in-law, this is not increase in all households. In fact with the, in case in love marriages more and more young women being financially independent and interaction between family members decreasing due to constraints of time and distance, it is the mother-in-law who has to be wary of her daughter-in-law.

A daughter-in-law was traditionally thought of as the Lakshmi of the household and was accorded love and respect as the mother of the future generation. When this concept became on account of the introduction of dowry and the desire of the mother-in-law to dominate her son and extract both material and emotional sustenance from him, family discord and unhappiness ensued. In many families and communities however the daughter-in-law continues to occupy a paramount position and this is essential for the well-being of all concerned. For example, Sonia Gandhi, although foreign-born had been an ideal daughter-in-law to Indira Gandhi and today it is she who has done her utmost to keep up the traditions of the family.

Where every mother-in-law is not an ogre, every daughter-in-law is not an angel either. Often the mother-in-law takes lots of trouble to select a suitable wife for her son so it is in the interest of all to maintain a cordial relationship. The institution of marriage has a solid foundation in our country and our culture has been widely praised for this. If there are any minor clashes or differences of opinion these should be taken in one's stride as they could happen in one's parental home also.

A college educated or working girl may not find it important to maintain good relations with her in-laws but this is not a correct attitude. By adjusting with one's in-laws and tactfully handling any criticism or unpleasant situation one will also have a better relationship with one's husband rather than by creating a rift in the family by continuously harping on the shortcomings of his family.

Handy Tips
1. Do not enter marriage with the idea of opposing the in-laws. Take the situation as it comes and try to steer clear of conflict.
2. Tolerance and accommodation help in the long run. One should try to create harmony in the household rather then discord.

3. The daughter-in-law should adopt a respectful and helpful attitude towards her mother-in-law. If she does not like something it is best to voice her feelings pleasantly.
4. Mother-in-law and daughter-in-law should iron out their differences on a one-to-one basis, rather than by involving others. It is particularly difficult for a man to choose between his wife and his mother but at some point of time it may become essential for him to intervene depending on the situation.
5. The daughter-in-law must try to adjust to her new environment without expecting everything to be as it was in her parental home. She should try to understand and even imbibe the customs and traditions of her new family.
6. If the Indian family is to remain united and retain its position as the most important and primary unit of society, it is essential that mothers-in-law and daughters-in-law strive to maintain family harmony through a combination of self-restraint, love, tolerance and patience, attributes which have always been valued in our culture but which are today being devalued in an increasingly individualistic and selfish trend coming in from the west.

Coping with Sons-in-Law

The Indian son-in-law is a VIP in the family tradition of this country. While only some tribal societies and the matriarchal system in Kerala required that a bride price be paid, in all other communities parents run through their life time's savings to acquire a good husband for their daughter. However society has degenerated a great deal today from the Rig Vedic Swayamvara to the present day dowry demands. Despite modernisation and education the problem of dowry remains a scourge in our society. Young men whether they are in the All India Services, doctors, engineers or lawyers stand by idly and watch as they are bartered away to the highest bidder by their parents. Why do they remain silent spectators to this disgraceful conduct when surely their education should have taught them better? Family obligations such as sisters who have to be married off also with huge dowries make dowry taking and giving a never ending vicious cycle that has now percolated even to those communities where dowry was traditionally never asked or given. In an increasingly materialistic society, a son's marriage is seen as an occasion to acquire status symbols such as cars, TVs, flats, land, gold and so on. Marriages made in the basis of such demands begin on an unhappy note and often end in discord.

Young men should therefore have the moral courage and self-respect not to demand and not to allow their parents to demand dowry from bride's family. In this connection, love marriages have not solved the problem as much is asked and given even in these alliances and if not given, the relationship is broken off.

Son-in-law should...

1. Not ask, demand or expect dowry to be given at the time of marriage. They should look at the girl and her family in terms of compatibility as a life partner rather than as a goose that will lay the golden egg.

2. He may accept gifts for himself and his family that are socially acceptable and are part of our culture such as a diamond ring, a watch and clothes.

3. He should not be arrogant and make derogatory comments about his wife's family and other relations. He must show respect to the family elders.

4. He should consider himself a part of his wife's family also and participate in weddings, birthdays and even funerals. This example will also encourage his wife to be more dutiful towards her in-laws.

Respect and appreciate the love and honour given to the son-in-law and be gracious rather than arrogant about it.

Parents-in-law

1. The relationship with one's son-in-law must always have an element of formality and the in-laws must at all times be cordial and pleasant.

2. The girls' parents must avoid interfering in her household. They should also not attempt to flood their daughter and son-in-law make the son-in-law with expensive gifts etc. and feel that he is being undermined. The film 'Kora Kagaz' is an ideal example of interference by the gir'ls parents which ultimately brought about discord in the marital life of the young couple.

3. Do not intervene and take sides in petty quarrels.

4. Do not try to monopolise the grand children and make them a bone of contention between the other set of grand parents.

5. Do not repeatedly insist your daughter and stay in her house for months on end as this will cause conflict and a tug-of-war with her in-laws.

Bonding with Grandchildren

The love and affection showered by grand parents on grand children has long been the stuff of our folklore. Grandmothers told exciting stories and cooked one's favourite foods. She offered unconditional love and offered a refuge from the scolding of one's parents. Grandparental love is, infact, a part of one's growing up years and as essential a part of it as food and learning.

Today on account of nuclear family patterns, particularly in urban areas, grandparents are not so closely involved in the upbringing of the next generation. However, working mothers the world over have realised the value of having their parents around so that they can keep a benevolent eye even if servants are present.

As with everything else, the industrialised modern society has devalued human relationships so that ties are not what they used to be. Many independent minded and slightly selfish grandparents do not want to be 'dumped' with their grandchildren. They cite ill-health, age, lack of space and so on for their inability to help out, but the underlying sentiment is more selfish. Having brought up their own children and sacrificed for them they do not want to be tied down to fresh commitments. Some working parents are also too demanding and expect their parents or in-laws to take charge of the children while they immerse themselves in their careers. At the same time they are dismissive of the help given by the elders and ungrateful for it. No parent wants to be taken to task by his son or daughter-in-law for real and imagined neglect of their child.

The Pitfalls of Being Grandparents

Even as one forges a bond with the next generation and increases one's closeness to one's children by being in close touch with them one should guard against certain pitfalls while being grandparents.

1. Grandparents are not substitutes for parents hence they should appreciate their position and not seek to undermine that of the mother and father as an ego trip by saying 'my grandparents are fonder of me than of his/her father/mother'.

2. Do not interfere when the parents are disciplining the child. Any opinions that one has regarding the parents behaviour should either not be voiced, or if it is, should not be done in front of the children. Children are natural born politicians and it does not take them long to sense discord and capitalise on it by playing one against the other.

3. Avoid rivalry by refraining from comparing your grand children either to their own brothers and sisters or to the children of your other children. At one time it was felt that by encouraging rivalry and competition one could spur a child on to greater heights and greater achievement. Today psychologists have disproved these methods and have shown how badly childhood rivalries can affect one's personality.

Grandparents need to be loving, non-judgmental and uncritical of their grandchildren. Harshness and disciplining should be left to the parents. Moreover, since many grandparents do not stay with their grandchildren, their arrival with a bagful of admonitions only causes a rift between the elders and the youngsters. What has traditionally been a beautiful relationship between grandchildren and their grandparents is unnecessarily strained by unwarranted carping and criticism.

Grandchildren—do's and don'ts

1. Grandchildren must at all times be respectful to their elders, even in the face of their scoldings and criticism. Any resentment that one may feel can be conveyed subtly and not by being rude. Accepting criticism is part of the growing up process.

2. Try to be understanding and helpful. Frequently elders are crotchety on account of their ill-health hence one must make allowances for them.

3. Try to include the grandparents in your activities and keep them abreast of what you are doing in school.

4. Grandparents are a fund of knowledge and experience hence one should spend

time with them while they relate anecdotes about their lives and those of your parents.

5. 'Granny bashing' is a popular activity in England and perhaps even in the US where grandchildren make fun of their infirm and sometimes incontinent grandparents. Whatever their infirmities, these should NEVER be made fun of, as just one illness or a few decades can reduce today's youngster to the same condition.

6. One can offer to give them their medicines and put in their eardrops. Old people also require a visible show of love and care so that they feel important and wanted. It is reported that about four million children in the United States live in households headed by grandparents due to child abuse, child neglect and divorce. Grandparents may suffer from problems like high blood pressure, anxiety, strokes and stress, part of which doctors link to the stress that they face on being forced to play a parental role at an elderly age.

Relations with Neighbours

The Biblical dictum enjoins us to love our neighbour as we would ourselves. However a glance at the newspapers would reveal that this is rarely the case in real life. Reports of feuds, fights flirtations and even fisticuffs seem to have become routine as people live cheek-by-jowl in crowded neighbourhoods. In the more affluent neighbourhoods, on the other hand, people do not even bother to know who lives next door. This kind of indifference too, brings in its wake new and fresh difficulties.

In choosing our neighbours, we have little or no choice, hence it is best to adopt a policy of friendly non-interference. While one should know one's neighbour and at least have a nodding acquaintance with them, barging into their homes without regard for their convenience or privacy is unwarranted. Too close an interaction may result in the classic case of familiarity breeding contempt. At the same time there has to be some contact with them, both for reasons of politeness as well as convenience and mutual security.

If there are any problems that sometimes arise, as for example in the parking of cars, placing of potted plants, playing of loud music and so on, these should be tackled very politely and with restraint. There should be a positive effort to accommodate rather than to confront. An aggressive stance only vitiates the atmosphere and creates discord. If one is unfortunate enough to have unpleasant neighbours, one should nevertheless strive to adopt an attitude of adjustment, since two wrongs never make a right.

One should also be careful not to intrude on one's neighbour by indulging in undue curiosity, needless gossip and unnecessary borrowing of daily necessities such as milk and sugar. Also, one should never try to lure the neighbour's servant by offering him or her a few more rupees to work in your house, as this would invariably and inevitably lead to bad feelings.

When one moves to a new neighbourhood, it is prudent to make the acquaintance of those who live nearby. After that, one can decide with whom one can have a closer friendship and those from whom we would rather keep our distance.

If there is an illness or bereavement in the neighbour's family, one should make the effort to pay a call and offer help. On joyous occasions such as births, birthdays or marriages, one could pay a visit and offer one's good wishes. Where this is not possible, one could send across a note or a card, along with some flowers or sweets.

Hence, whereas we may not always be able to follow the Biblical dictat of loving our neighbours as we would ourselves, one can atleast make an attempt to maintain cordial ties with them so that there are no unpleasant confrontations.

■ ■